THIS MOTH SAW BRIGHTNESS

THIS MOTH SAW BRIGHTNESS

A. A. VACHARAT

DUTTON BOOKS

DUTTON BOOKS
An imprint of Penguin Random House LLC
1745 Broadway, New York, New York 10019

First published in the United States of America by Dutton Books,
an imprint of Penguin Random House LLC, 2025

Copyright © 2025 by A. A. Vacharat

Penguin Random House values and supports copyright. Copyright fuels creativity, encourages diverse voices, promotes free speech, and creates a vibrant culture. Thank you for buying an authorized edition of this book and for complying with copyright laws by not reproducing, scanning, or distributing any part of it in any form without permission. You are supporting writers and allowing Penguin Random House to continue to publish books for every reader. Please note that no part of this book may be used or reproduced in any manner for the purpose of training artificial intelligence technologies or systems.

Dutton is a registered trademark of Penguin Random House LLC.
The Penguin colophon is a registered trademark of Penguin Books Limited.

Visit us online at PenguinRandomHouse.com.

Library of Congress Cataloging-in-Publication Data is available.

ISBN 9780593698600
1 3 5 7 9 10 8 6 4 2

Printed in the United States of America

BVG

Design by Anna Booth
Text set in Sabon LT Pro

This book is a work of fiction. Any references to historical events, real people, or real places are used fictitiously. Other names, characters, places, and events are products of the author's imagination, and any resemblance to actual events or places or persons, living or dead, is entirely coincidental.

The publisher does not have any control over and does not assume any responsibility for author or third-party websites or their content.

The authorized representative in the EU for product safety and compliance is Penguin Random House Ireland, Morrison Chambers, 32 Nassau Street, Dublin D02 YH68, Ireland, https://eu-contact.penguin.ie.

*If you notice anything,
it leads you to notice
more
and more.*

*And anyway
I was so full of energy.
I was always running around, looking
at this and that.*

*If I stopped
the pain
was unbearable.*

*If I stopped and thought, maybe
the world
can't be saved,
the pain
was unbearable.*

—MARY OLIVER, "The Moths"

"I am not angry with anybody, for how can you be mad with somebody when the evil has no name— when the evil is just part of life."

—LEOPOLDINE MAIER,
survivor of child experimentation at Am Spiegelgrund

THIS MOTH SAW BRIGHTNESS

MEMORANDUM FOR THE RECORD

Draft ▮▮▮▮▮
SUBJECT: Project ▮▮▮▮▮, Subproject 6

1. Subproject 6 is being set up as a means to continue the present work in the general field of ▮▮▮▮▮ at ▮▮▮▮▮ until March 28, 20▮▮.

2. This project will include a continuation of a study of the biochemical, neurophysiological, sociological, and clinical psychiatric aspects of ▮▮▮▮▮ antagonists and drugs related to ▮▮▮▮▮. A detailed proposal is attached. The principal investigators will continue to be ▮▮▮▮▮.

3. The estimated budget of the project at ▮▮▮▮▮ is $11,405,500. ▮▮▮▮▮ will serve as a cover for this project and will furnish the above funds to the ▮▮▮▮▮ as a philanthropic grant for medical research. A service charge of $228,110 (2% of the estimated budget) is to be paid to ▮▮▮▮▮ for this service.

4. Thus the total charges for this project will not exceed $11,633,610 for a period ending March 28, 20██.

5. ██████████████████████ (Director of the hospital) are cleared through TOP SECRET and are aware of the true purpose of the project.

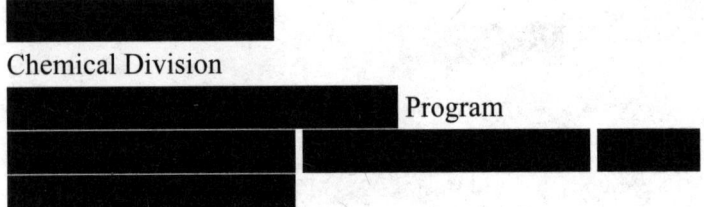

Chemical Division

Program

SECRET AGENT MISSION: 4:37 P.M.

The mail *fwumps* through the brass door flap. It falls directly into my lap.

The mail that I *absolutely am not* stealing consists of the following:

On top: Two promotional postcards. The first is the weekly "20% off any drink!" coupon from the Tiki Bar (actually a café), inside the recently de-and-re-malled Marley Station Shopping & Experience Center.[1]

The second has a coupon code for the selfie "theme park and experience simulator" that recently opened outside downtown Baltimore. I pocket the code. You never know when you're going to need Salvation of Your Future Self Through the Now™.

Below that: A "certified" letter with a holographic seal of Johns Hopkins University in the return address corner.

It's addressed to me. Sort of.

"ATTN: Mr. Dwayne Le," it says. The invisible *D* in 'Wayne is not only visible on the envelope but also slightly out of line, as though someone intentionally added it after the fact.

"URGENT" is stamped diagonally down the right side. "OPEN IMMEDIATELY" is stamped down the left.

---

1. Kermit says the coupons are part of a marketing push targeted at high school students to persuade us to spend our free time inside "their rectangular corporate utopia."

Spam, clearly. Or part of one of Kermit's elaborate pranks.

A cardboard box meant for recycling lives by the front door. My father is of the convenience-equals-art mindset, as far as interior design goes.

I use the box.

On the bottom: What I've been sitting by the door waiting for. The reason I've been tiptoeing around the house in my spy socks[2] for the last hour.

The envelope is from Glenville High School. It is addressed to my father.

I open it immediately.

---

2. . . . which are the same as my regular socks but pink. Sent due to company error. I kept them because Olive begged me to, and now I like them. They remind me of the soft pads on a big cat's toes, what Olive calls "squinkleberries." Pink socks—> panther squinkleberries—> maximum stealth.

NUMERICAL PRECISION

My father works from home. His schedule is precise and—mostly—unwavering.

As of the last day of summer vacation, which was the last day I was home to witness his entire weekday structure, his schedule was the following:

At 8:58 a.m., he slips off his home shoes and slips on his work shoes, which he ordered custom-made from England for their "quality leather exterior" and comfortable-yet-functional, sweat-wicking "Harris Tweed" interiors.

Then, he "goes to work" (i.e., goes into his office, which is next to the living room) at exactly nine. He turns on his solar-powered mirror that keeps sunlight optimally directed at his walls, stashes his bento box (prepared the night before) in the "office kitchen" (mini fridge with microwave on top), and then works until twelve, doing something involving numbers, a spreadsheet, and "quantifying risk." He microwaves and eats lunch before going for his speed walk until exactly one, when his electric kettle (on a timer) prepares him a cup of genmaicha. Then he puts on a fresh shirt and resumes working at his desk, or, maybe once a week, goes somewhere to meet with clients.

Finally, he "comes home," slipping on his home shoes, at exactly, precisely, five.[3]

---

3. His schedule changes only when he has new ideas to shave off time between tasks. For example, the day he realized that slicing his chicken thinner would reduce three whole seconds from reheating time. A landmark day.

I bring the envelope into the kitchen, which also serves as our dining room (efficiency, again).

The clock on the kitchen wall says 4:42, meaning I have eighteen minutes before Dad "comes home."

Dad leaves his tablet on the counter while he's "at the office," to minimize the time between "getting home" and starting to make dinner.

I swipe past Olive's artwork that serves as the lock screen, open a new tab behind today's recipe. Then I dump out the contents of the Glenville High School envelope onto the table: a short note and a cardstock square.

It's the cardstock square I care about. It's printed with the six-digit two-factor auth code that ensures that my father is the only one who can log in and confirm my mid-trimester grades.

"Ensures."

On the Glenville High homepage, the familiar image of a former student dunking a basketball welcomes me. I log in using Dad's password, generously provided to me by Kermit for a mere one hundred dollars (his "best friend discount"), and type in the code.

I check the box to confirm that "I, Peter Le, parent/guardian of 'Wayne Le, have seen and acknowledged my student's mid-trimester interim progress."

I log out. I return the recipe tab to the front.

4:48. Master Spy Am I.

DNS FACE

Yes, I know, Dad is going to see my grades eventually.
The thing is, though, Dad makes faces.

An introductory glossary:

ODC: Olive Did Cute. Dad ODCs whenever Olive is around. Can't blame him. Everything she does is unnervingly likable. Everything. Like doing math homework. When she figures out an answer, she pops up her index finger an inch like she's raising her hand for herself before writing the answer down.

IKB: I Know Better. Inevitably followed by a lengthy explanation of exactly what he knows better, how, and why.

DNS: Disappointed, Not Surprised. The worst of all faces.

Dad DNSes every time he looks at anything related to my school records. Also in regard to many other things I do. And all the things I don't do.
Every school report Dad doesn't have to look at is another day he can thrive in his carefully crafted paradise of maximized, risk-averse numbers.

THE SLIPPERY SLOPE OF DIRTY PANTS

A door clicks shut somewhere in the house. The clock reads 4:49.

Tiny arms drape around me and squeeze.

Olive, home early from Art Club, gently rests her bag on the floor before taking the chair across from me. It squeaks and rolls backward slightly. We've had office chairs in the kitchen since Dad closed his non-quotation-marks office downtown.

Olive scoots herself back toward the table. "Whatcha doing on Dad's tablet?"

"Homework."

She eyes the envelope on the table. "You opened Dad's mail again." The envelope is crumpled, but *Peter Le* is clearly visible in the address field. "You need to stop doing that."

"I didn't do anything."

"Yes, you did."

"I didn't!"

She puts her head below the table edge. "You're wearing your spy socks."

"I need to do laundry."

"You do this every time."

"There's no evidence." I crumple the envelope further and toss it into the kitchen recycling box.[4] "See? Absolutely zero evidence."

---

4. This box lives in the doorway of a glass tile wall that separates our kitchen-slash-dining room from the actual intended dining room, which is now a guest room that we never use.

Her eyes narrow.

"No one has caught me so far."

"Um. Except *me*. Your eleven-year-old sister, emphasis on *eleven*. No PhD, no FBI training, merely a modest eye for detail." She adjusts invisible glasses on her nose and glares at me.

I glare back.

Finally, she sighs. She squeezes down onto the floor, picks up the envelope from where I tossed it. "You would make an absolutely terrible secret agent." She buries the envelope under other papers. "Good thing you have me as your sister."

Olive isn't technically my sister, and Olive isn't really her name. She's a removed cousin, or something like that. Her parents, my first cousin and her husband, are Vietnamese. They sent Olive to live with us so she could go to American schools.

She's been here since she was four, minus a month each summer when she has to go back to renew her visa. Dad tried to officially adopt her, but he couldn't get it approved. Still, she thinks of me as her brother. I think of her as my sister.

I get the better end of the deal.

I roll my chair to the fridge and pull out the bagels. "Your usual?"

"Mm." She stacks more envelopes on top of my guilty one in the recycling box. "You know, hiding your grades is a waste of time."

"Untrue. I'm reducing the number of bad days by half." The toaster hums as it heats up. I pull Olive's special blue plate out of the dirty dishwasher and run it under hot water.

"Huh." She joins me at the counter, leans over the sink as if she's very interested in what's happening to her plate. "Well, I'm about to do my homework." She watches my hands pick a dried rice grain free. "You could join me."

"Oh, I could, could I?"

"If you're ready to admit your career as a secret agent is a total failure and that you need to take the same drudging path as the rest of us civilians."

I don't know where she gets this stuff. "Oh, yeah?" I turn off the water and face her.

"Yeah." She puffs out her lower cheeks. She's wearing a bright green T-shirt with a large white chicken printed in the middle. The chicken is labeled "Dinosaur." "Well?" she says.

"Well."

I take the dish towel from the oven handle and wipe her plate dry, lay it on the counter. Next to it, Dad's tablet lights up with a news notification.

Here is something that is hard to describe: how knowing you've already screwed up makes it infinitely harder to keep trying. It's like forgetting to put your dirty pants in a hamper one time. There's no hope for any future pants, because why bother? Your room is already a mess. From that day on, all your pants will end up on the floor.

The toaster dings. "I'm planning to do my homework. Later."

Olive puffs her cheeks again, then blows the air out. "Okay."

I plop the bagel onto the plate, then cut a cube of cream cheese next to it, far enough away that they aren't touching. She told me a couple months ago that she's fine with them touching now, but I'm pretty sure she still prefers it this way.

"Homework or not, you're my favorite." She takes the plate, and her bag, and heads into the living room to work.

The warm bagel smell fades quickly. The sink drips. The clock on the kitchen wall ticks loudly.

WHATEVER I MAY NOT BECOME

March (Seven months ago)

Setting: My Room, or rather, The Hallway Outside My Room

Background: I was already three minutes late for a PvP *Drone Wars IV: Hellfire* game against Kermit. Dad had followed me upstairs on the pretense of "needing the upstairs nail clippers."[5]

Dad:	So. Your last trimester of junior year.
Me:	*(Pauses with one foot in doorway.)* . . . Yes?
Dad:	It starts tomorrow.
Me:	That's true.
Dad:	After that comes senior year.
Me:	I remember.
Dad:	Glad to hear it.
Me:	

---

5. My father has been on a lifelong hunt for the grail of nail clippers like other dads might hunt for, I don't know, the best-weighted golf clubs. Nail clipping, like any other repetitive life chore, is a prime candidate for optimization.
   The upstairs clippers were crafted by ex–sword makers in Japan. Dad bought them because he saw a doctor's review saying they were sharper than her best surgical tools.

Me:
Me: Okay. (*Puts other foot through doorway.*)
Dad: I've been doing some thinking. About your
           future.
Me: (*Takes foot out of doorway.*)
Dad: Do you remember how you used to be on the
           honor roll?
Me: Ah. I actually have a meeting right
           now . . .
Dad: You remember that bridge you made? The one
           with marshmallows. It won a prize? The
           strongest bridge.
Me: Right.
Dad's Face: Flash of DNS.
My Stomach: Dropping into my feet.
Dad: I've been doing some thinking.
Dad: About your future.
Me: You mentioned.
Dad: . . . and about what happened.
Me: What happened?
Dad: I've been thinking about what I've . . .
           what *I* could have done . . . might have
           done . . .
Me:
Dad: It's just so hard to know the reason for
           your change . . . without your mother
           here . . .
Dad: I'm thinking maybe it could have been
           different if I had . . . *I* had . . .
Dad:

Dad:	It's too late now.
Me:	What's too late?
Dad:	Your high school average, that's what colleges will see. What is there left, now, that we can do?
Me:	. . . Are you saying that there's nothing left I can do? That nothing I do matters anymore?
Dad:	No.
Dad:	No, that's not what I mean.
Me:	What *do* you mean?
Dad:	
Dad:	
Me:	
Dad:	What did I come upstairs for?
Dad:	Oh, right. *(Pokes head into the upstairs bathroom, opens and shuts medicine cabinet.)*
Me:	
Dad:	Actually, I think the downstairs nail clippers will be fine. *(Goes back downstairs.)*
Truth:	The downstairs clippers are never fine.

    I lost the PvP against Kermit.

BURNT VANILLA

My headphones are pressing on my head, comforting as a mother's hands checking for fever.

At least, I imagine that's what a mother's hands would feel like.

Through the headphones, Clarissa Patel is singing to me. Soothing my soul with the wise, wise words of her third album, *Allegorist*.

I'm sitting on my bed, which was maybe not the best choice, given it keeps tempting me with more horizontal positions.

Next to me, spilling off the pillow, is a pile of failed attempts at origami animals. I hate origami. The paper gets soggy and wrinkled, and the only animals I can successfully make are roadkill.

But it's mind consuming. You can't think about your future when you are trying to coerce paper into a mountain-valley fold. Can't think about the bright orange tags in your school progress report, how they are tags on your life, how your entire existence is labeled with glowing flags that say "Warning: Action Needed," like you're an airplane that's about to go down.

No, you can't think of any of that when you are busy trying to understand what "mountain-valley fold" even means.

I turn Clarissa up.

Suddenly, there's a faint smell of . . . cookies? No. The smell intensifies. It's like vanilla but burning.

I toss my headphones into the pile of paper monsters. "Kermit! Stop lurking!"

My door swings open. It reveals Kermit, one hand on the doorknob, the other holding his phone, a teal sneaker toe impatiently tapping on the rug. He's shaking his head and waving the phone at me. "A hundred and forty-six seconds. That's a record. An incorrigible record, D. Despicable. Over two minutes to notice I was here."

"How about you leave, and time how long it takes me to notice *that*," I say, but I'm smiling.

"How'd you not hear me come up the stairs?"

I wave a hand at the headphones. "Clarissa."

"Clarissa?!" He shakes his fists at the imaginary gods of my ceiling. "How am I friends with someone with such poor taste?" His gaze moves down to the paper pile. His god-shaking hands land on his head. "Oh *no*. D. D, D, Invisible D 'Wayne. Not *this* again. Talk about poor taste."

"There's nothing wrong with origami."

"You and I both know this isn't about origami."

"Transitively."

"She's not going to be impressed. This is not impressive. Look at this. Just *look* at this. What is this? An elephant . . ." He turns the paper over. ". . . seal . . . hybrid?"

"That's a tulip."

"This is not the right way to go about it. A basketball star wouldn't be impressed with you for being able to recognize a basketball. Jane the origami champion—well, *almost* champion—isn't going to be impressed with you for being able to fold paper in half." He picks up a failed frog. "An approximation of half."

"She'll appreciate the effort."

"Effort put toward talking to her might be more efficient."

I flop back onto my bed. The pile of paper animals spills off the pillow and onto the floor. "Eh."

"'Eh' is right." He takes my chair and throws his legs over my desk, then leans forward and adjusts the tongue on a sneaker. "So.

It's mid-trimester. You do the deed?" He mimes me typing my father's authentication code.

"The deed is done."

"The. Deed. Is. Done." He nods with each word. "Mmmhmm, mmhmm." Then he leans toward me. His gaze darts to my forehead, then to my cheeks.

"What? What is it?" He's looking at me like I have something Sharpie'd onto my face.

He leans closer. Closer. The burnt vanilla smell of his cologne—The Domestic Hunter—is overpowering.

"*What?*" I shove him away.

His mouth twitches. "A slight furrowing of your brow. An almost imperceptible pursing of your lips."

"Kermit."

"Also, your pulse is elevated."

Instinctively, I glance under my desk.

Kermit wired up his own house, and probably half the school, with Raspberry Pis and Arduinos. He can build anything. This (or more specifically, the information he gets from his contraptions) provides him with bottomless sneaker funds.

Once, I found a black box with a blinking light stuck under my desk.

"We agreed no more hidden sensors."

"I don't *need* hidden sensors." He points at his eyeballs, then at my throat. "Your pulse is so strong I can count the beats. One-two-three-fo—"

I push his hand down. "*Why* am I friends with you?" This is not entirely a rhetorical question.

He ignores me. Raises his eyebrows twice in quick succession, and grins. "So."

"So . . . *what?*"

He points his finger at me again, then slowly brings it back to point at himself. "You . . . tell me."

"I have no idea what you're trying to get at."

"*Allegorist*! One hundred forty-six seconds! One hundred. Forty-six. Seconds! Twice your average!"

"Your point?"

"Beep beep beep, my sensors detect . . . rumination."

"Huh?"

"You, Mr. 'Wayne Le, are ruminating. Something is on your mind. What happened, *hmm*? Go ahead, Kermit is listening."

Kermit's definition of *listening* is him accumulating data to blackmail you with later.

He leans back in my desk chair and peers at my face so intently, it starts to itch. His gaze moves down my neck.

"*What?*" I pull my shirt collar up.

"I don't believe it. You got one of those letters, didn't you? Is *that* what you're ruminating about?"

I feel confused about 86 percent of the time I am around Kermit. "I already told you I got the letter? The one from our school? 'The deed is done'?"

He slaps me on the side of the head with a paper kangaroo. "Not *that* letter."

"Kermit. Please. What are you talking about?"

He takes his shoes off my desk. They clunk as they hit the side of it. He types something on my laptop.

"*This* letter."

He tilts the screen down so I can see it, today's *New York Times*. There's a photo of a white envelope with a shining hologram. "URGENT" is stamped on the right. "OPEN IMMEDIATELY" slides down the left.

OUTSMARTING THE DOMESTIC HUNTER

"I didn't get that letter," I say.

As I had originally suspected, the letter is part of an elaborate Kermit prank.

Evidence: The *New York Times* (fake websites are one of his oldest tricks), the use of snail mail (he says this makes things feel legit), his conveniently timed visit.

It's been about four months since his last prank, wherein he convinced me that an artist in my class, Miranda, was paying for opinions on their new line of hand-painted leggings.[6] Little did I know, as I observed Miranda's leggings from afar, that at a recent soccer game Miranda's mother had spotted Lydia Tillman looking at Miranda's legs in a "predatory manner" and consequently inflicted great destruction on Lydia's life.[7]

Fortunately for me, neither Miranda nor their mother noticed my extensive legging ogling. Unfortunately for me, that left Kermit's prank tank unfilled.

---

6. Our freshman year, the school hired Miranda to paint a mural in the school's lobby. Well, not exactly paint. More like edit the one that was already there, from when the school building was city hall. Miranda's job was to edit the mural to make it more "representative of our ideal society." Now, in the painting, the original horse tackle shop sits next to a PacSun, and a woman in a bustle is also sporting Yeezys, and two people in grizzly bear onesies are trading beaver pelts for colorful cloth.

7. Lydia did not get any part in the Glenville High musical, which she was counting on for her résumé, even though she has an agent and is on track to be a Broadway star. Apparently, Mrs. Richards runs the summer musical, and the musical gets funded by Mrs. Richards' cousin, who goes to the same church as Miranda's mother. You can't *prove* that Miranda's mother is to blame for Lydia's exclusion, but the evidence speaks for itself.

"Only mail today was the mid-trimester code." I pick a piece of lint off my knee. "Oh, and a coupon for Selfation. I saved it. We should go."

He says, "It would've been fun if you'd been a candidate."

I don't bite.

"I didn't get one either." He slumps into the chair. "People are talking about this. They want information. I think they'll pay." Kermit's always looking for "valuable information" to support his sneaker habit. "They're saying how it might be more than it seems—that it might even be dangerous."

"You're disappointed because I'm not a candidate for something dangerous?"

He nods.

I point at his teal sneaker and attempt to change the topic. "New SG Highs?"

He looks down. "AJKO. Ankle flaps, remember?"

"New or restored?"

"Restored 'em last night. Meet Albert, Lu." He points to his left foot, then his right, before turning back to my laptop. "Can I check your email, just in case they sent some of the invitations by email?"

"There's nothing in my email. And no, you can't check it. Thanks for asking, though." The *New York Times* photo glows on my laptop screen. "Wait. How'd you log in to my computer?"

He slaps my desk and stands. "Welp, I gotta get out of here. Family dinner."

"Bye, then."

From the hallway he turns back. "Throw away that coupon. I am not going to that selfie theme park." He points a finger. "And you are not going either."

"*Bye*, then."

His cologne wafts toward me in a solid wave as he pulls the door shut.

I lift my laptop closer and change my password, even though I know that Kermit will have it again within a week. I close out the fake *NYTimes* website.

For about ten seconds I feel the warm hum of outsmarting Kermit. Then the hum fades. I put Clarissa back on at full volume.

HOW TO FOLD AN ORIGAMI DRAGON

1. Fold paper in half. The fold should be a mountain fold.
   1a. "A mountain out of a molehill." Dad used to say that to Mom a lot. Surely, thinking and thinking about some comment Dad made seven months ago is me making a mountain out of a molehill.
2. Fold paper along its diagonals. These should be valley folds.
   2a. Valleys. Don't think about valleys, ditches, pools, things people can fall into and die in. Don't think about how you're in a bottomless pit, falling and falling, the handholds covered in slime.
3. Unfold everything.
   3a. Don't think about how the rest of your life will be spent undoing the consequences of mistakes you've made.
4. Along your folds, the paper should collapse naturally into a square.
4. Paper should *collapse* naturally into a square.
4. Paper *should* collapse naturally into a square.
4. Paper should collapse *naturally* into a square.
4. Naturally, naturally, naturally. Force the paper naturally into a square.
   4a. "You can't force yourself to be natural." One of the last things Mom said to us before she left. Don't think about that.

4b. Don't think about how your natural self is always unsurprisingly disappointing.
5–97. Don't think about steps 5–97.
98. Fold paper corners down into a head, tail, and feet. Use a pencil to curl the wings for a realistic touch. Ta-da!

TASTE BUDS OF MY HEART

Dad is in his pajamas, making tomorrow's boxed lunch and his midnight snack—chicken soup with yesterday's rice. He's shredding ginger. The smell of ginger always makes me a little nauseous.

"Want some?" he says.

I shake my head. He turns back to the stove.

I don't know why I came down here.

Sometimes I get this urge to be around my dad. This optimism that our relationship is going to be better if I give it a chance. Like if I come and sit here, we will talk things through, and all that stuff with grades and my future will disappear.

He clears his throat.

I clear mine.

Plop, plop, plop: him dropping chunks of ginger into the boiling water.

He clears his throat again.

My optimism about my relationship with Dad is like Olive's relationship to water chestnuts. Every time they're on the table, Olive eats them. "Eventually my taste buds will change," she explains. "It might be today!"

In coming to sit with my father, I'm testing to see if our taste buds have changed. Only, the taste buds of our hearts.

I get the pickled peppers from the fridge, find a slotted spoon in a drawer. I place them next to the paper towel Dad already folded and centered in front of his seat, like he's about to entertain guests, and not eating alone, in his pajamas, at midnight.

"Actually, I'll have some soup."

Dad nods and clanks a second bowl down from the cabinet.

He clears his throat again. His spoon scrapes against the side of his pot with every third tick of the second hand.

I fidget with the corner of an old paper towel, then fold it into a triangle to match Dad's. Then I fold it some more, to make a wilted origami crane. I place it next to Dad's pickles. It makes his perfectly set place look messy. I stuff it into my sweatpants pocket. The wheels on my chair squeak.

"There wasn't any mail today? Any letters?"

"No," I say, too quickly.

He stirs his soup.

"Any reason you're interested in the mail today?" I keep my words slow.

"No reason."

He pours the broth into the bowls and clicks off the stove. Then he sits in his chair, the one that backs up to the glass tile wall. He rolls two feet to my side of the table. He puts my bowl in front of me. He rolls two feet back to his side.

His spoon dings on the bowl. He slurps his broth. I count the slurps. The hot steam licks at my face.

Paper mail, as far as Dad is concerned, is an unreliable and inefficient way to communicate. As such, Dad doesn't care about mail unless he's expecting a package, in which case he knows exactly what time it will arrive. Usually, days' worth of envelopes and catalogs will accumulate on the vestibule floor before someone, meaning Olive, moves them into the recycling box.

Four slurps.

"Eat," he says.

I pick up my spoon.

He gets to slurp seven. "There's a thing on the news."

"Oh?"

Slurp eight. "About a special letter."

My breath of relief blows the steam from my bowl across the table. It's not beyond Kermit to include my father in his schemes.

Dad takes off his glasses and defogs them on his pajamas. "You know what I'm talking about? A letter. It got sent to high school students near Baltimore and DC."

"I saw a picture."

"Not all the students got the letter. It's an *invitation*. From Johns Hopkins. You know Johns Hopkins? A very good university. They are starting a project, for health research. They need young people to do it. They have selected certain, special people to get the invitation to participate. You earn money and get a commendation—a great thing for a résumé, for college applications. It's a good opportunity. The letter. If you qualify."

His head is bent over his bowl. All I can see is his forehead, and it's smooth, furrow-free. The forehead of someone daring to be optimistic that his son might qualify.

"You're sure the letter is real? You didn't . . . get a suspicious email about it? Or see it on an open tab on your computer? The *New York Times*, maybe?"

He peers at me over his glasses. "What do you mean, 'real'? It's on *all* the channels. Every news website. *Every*body is talking about it."

He spins his chair to grab the tablet from the counter. "Look." He clicks on the tabs as they load. "Look."

"Hopkins Requesting Minors for Health Research," says the *Washington Post*.

"New Study Aims to Improve the Health of Our Youth." That's the *New York Times*, with the now-familiar photograph.

"JHU May Increase Average Life Span to 150 Years," printed in the *Baltimore Sun*.

"Hopkins' Nefarious History of Unethical Research: The Cold War, and Maybe Now," from the *Atlantic*.

Dad flaps the tablet cover shut, and there it is, the DNS. "Everywhere. Every website. Every channel. It is an important thing." He pats a drop of spilled broth from his sleeve. "Some of your friends might have been chosen. Kermit? Was Kermit chosen? He must have been."

I shake my head.

"They must be looking for something *very* special." Another flash of DNS, around his mouth. He points his spoon at my soup bowl. "Eat. It's getting cold."

His bowl is empty. His face has returned to a neutral blank. He stands, runs the tap water into his dishes, and then he's headed toward the stairs. "Read some news," he calls back. And then, five seconds later, "Don't stay up too late."

I want to open my letter, but I force myself to swallow a spoonful of the soup first.

Today was not the day for taste buds to change.

THE LETTER

Mr. Dwayne Le:

Your Social Security number has been selected by our random integer generator. Johns Hopkins University is extending you an opportunity to participate in a consensual health and nutrition study.

This research is being conducted to evaluate the effects of diet during a person's developmental years on heart health and lifespan. This study is *entirely optional* and there will be no penalty for not participating. You will be informed of potential risks and may leave the study at any time. Your health and well-being during this experiment are, and will remain, our priority.

The first phase of the study is expected to last approximately two (2) months, with optional check-ins over the next 10–120 years to monitor long-term effects. For the most part, you will be able to complete this study from your home. It should not have any major effects on your daily schedule. Accommodations can be provided for participants who face difficulties in transportation to any required in-person events.

If you are interested in this opportunity, please scan the QR code below and sign the Article of Interest to be assigned a screening appointment time. Participants under the age of 18 will need a parent/guardian signature. Screenings will be held this coming weekend, October 15–16, at the Johns Hopkins Bayview Medical Center.

Participants who successfully complete the first phase of the study will receive: a stipend of $200, medical coverage from Hopkins University Hospital lasting for the entirety of the participant's term of cooperation, and a signed letter commending the participant for their responsibleness, dedication, and valuable contributions to society.

Thank you for your consideration.

M. Mikulski

M. Mikulski, MD
Research Director

THE WHOLE THING

I sit on the vestibule floor. The cold seeps through my sweatpants. I read and reread the letter.

Dad moved to the US when he was eight, older than Olive when she first came, which is young enough to not have a strong accent but too old to not feel like a foreigner.

At least, this is how I explain his obsession with the United States: the bookshelf filled with biographies of American presidents, the Westerns I hear playing from the living room late at night, the movie quotes he'll drop in a conversation when he's meeting with his clients.

" 'Sure is a hard town for a fella to have a quiet game o' poker in,' " he'll say, and then he'll laugh and make eye contact with the client like this quote is their inside joke, *the* inside joke for the All-American Anyone.

In the moments when I'm not too annoyed with him to see him as a real person—which is, to be honest, not very many of the moments—it makes me sad. How some part of him believes the key to being an All-American Anyone is knowing details about the childhoods of Lincoln, Polk, and Bush. The key to being an All-American Anyone is wearing a cowboy hat.

I was born here and couldn't name a single thing Polk did. It's almost more American to *not* know. I would never wear a cowboy hat.

Anyway. One of the quotes he uses the most is from *High Noon*, which is maybe his second-favorite movie after *The Magnificent Seven*, which means I've seen it at least once a year on his birthday or Father's Day and maybe five times in the months after my mother left.

At the beginning of the movie, the main guy, Kane, is riding out of town with his new wife, planning to get as far as possible before some bad guy rolls in to kill him. Suddenly, he turns the wagon around and his wife says why would he go back, she doesn't understand, and Kane says, "I've got to. That's the whole thing."

That's the line, the moment, that keeps playing in my head now.

The Hopkins seal is textured under my thumb. There's a hologram on the letter itself, too. I tilt the paper back and forth in the dim hallway light.

My instinct is to put the envelope back in the recycling box—or maybe a less accessible box, like the laundry room box or the den box—and go on pretending I didn't receive it.

Something about the word *consensual* feels off.

It'd be like if Kellogg started putting *edible* on Pop-Tart boxes. I wouldn't have worried until someone felt the need to clarify.

Then I remember Dad describing the letter over his bowl of soup. His smooth forehead as he imagined the *honor* of me participating. He called it *an invitation*.

My gaze lands back on the logo for Hopkins. An esteemed United States institution. A *university*.

I skip down to the bottom of the letter, where they mention the reward for completion: a letter of commendation. Signed, with real ink, by a real person, by a reputable someone, vowing that I am a worthwhile human being.

It's a reset button.

This is everything my father could want from me rolled up in one. It's a burrito made of all the things that I am missing.

A non-failure burrito.

A burrito that matters.

SWEATY TUSKS

"Internal temperatures reaching one hundred degrees," Tusks warns me. "Shall I activate climate control?"

Tusks is Dad's car and has many gadgets. She was named and pronoun-ed by Olive, of course, in honor of a tool-using fish.

Dad purchased Tusks after giving up his office space downtown, ironically when he would no longer need to drive every day.

"A business expense," Dad said as we parked Tusks in our driveway for the first time. "A practical purchase. Without an office, we need this to impress clients." Even though he had told us only that morning that the most practical car purchase was always, always, always a used Japanese car.

He usually doesn't let me touch Tusks' door handles without him wiping them off after. The fact that he let me take her indicates how much this study means to him.

Which is perhaps why instead of going inside, I am sitting in the parking lot at Hopkins Bayview, baking myself into a cornbread cake. A very sweaty cornbread cake.

My sweat is dripping onto Tusks' pristine seats, the thought of which makes me sweat even more.

The lot is surrounded by large brick buildings. They're unimpressive, except in how ubiquitous they are. I'm supposed to go into one of them, one called the Justin James Research Center.

"Tusks, take me home."

"Excuse me," Tusks replies. "Did you just ask to leave? Don't you have an appointment?"

My finger hovers by Tusks' Start button. "Kermit."

Tusks coughs, which I assume is her software trying to transmit Kermit's laughing.

Kermit was very excited when I told him that I had indeed received a letter. In fact, *excited* is perhaps not an adequate word. It rarely is, when it comes to Kermit.

When I told him, he jumped up and slapped the side of one of the empty vending machines in our school's hallway, making a crashing sound that brought four teachers into their doorways to glare at us. Or to glare at *me*, rather. Teachers love Kermit.

Then he went on some long rant about opportunities to sell "the inside scoop" to conspiracy theorists, and made me chant—yes, chant—"In-for-ma-tion" all the way to the lower cafeteria.

Now, in Tusks, I address the radio. "This counts as an invasion of privacy. FYI."

"Putting a smart car in your driveway knowing Kermit will be around is like putting a marshmallow on a plate in front of a five-year-old. You're lucky I didn't do this sooner."

"Am I?"

"You're right. I did this a while ago." Tusks coughs again.

My finger moves back toward the Start button.

Tusks' stereo turns on. It shuffles itself to the Easy Listening station. "Tick tock. Time to go inside. Before you are drowned in Smooth Jazz." The volume counter creeps up.

"No." I hit the power on the stereo. Then, "Oh, no," because a familiar maroon blur has darted into the building closest to me: Jane Gallagher, second runner-up for national origami champion, wearing her oversize maroon sweater.

Kermit doesn't say anything about her, which means he must not have access to Tusks' cameras. The stereo turns on again, to the country station this time.

"Fine! I'm going!" I get out and slam Tusks' door.

Sort of. Her hydraulic closing mechanism catches and shuts the door gently. It sighs an extremely unsatisfying, almost inaudible hiss.

AP CHEMISTRY

I sit on a bench to calm myself before going inside. On my phone, I bring up a folder named "Chemistry." It's not a folder about chemistry. Not school chemistry, anyway. This folder contains things I've found on the internet about Jane. Everything I've put in this folder I could easily find again by Googling her name. Making a folder was simply efficient in a way that might make my father proud, if it had any sort of quantifiable endgame.

Inside the folder are:

1. An assortment of my favorite photos from Jane's various social media accounts.
2. A picture of Jane and her mother and father all pretending to be presidents next to the heads of Mount Rushmore. Jane's mom died three years ago. This was the photo they used for her obituary.
3. News articles from Jane's origami competitions. Last year, Jane came in third place for the national origami championship.
4. The video of the competition finals is my favorite thing in my folder. I save it for my most stressful days.

Now I press Play.

A commentator narrates as the red numbers on a large digital clock count down. His voice is animated, almost wild with excitement as the ten semifinalists hunch over their squares of paper. At t=4:34 the camera zooms in on Jane, her cropped hair pulled behind a headband, the arms of her sweater pushed back over her elbows, silver tweezers tucked behind her left ear.

The two people on either side of her have their lips pressed together, pink splotches rising on their necks. A bell dings to signal that there are only twenty seconds left. One contestant knocks his cup of finger-dipping water to the floor. The commentator says, "Oh no!"

Jane flips her paper over and slowly runs her bone folder down a new crease. It's like she doesn't even know there's a clock. That she doesn't know the contestant next to her has burst into loud, messy tears. It's like she doesn't know that the fate of her origami-folding career rests on every fold she makes. No. Nothing matters but this paper swan, no, not even the swan, only this crease, one crease in this, this singular moment.

Maybe one day I'll talk to her.

But what do you say to someone who is beyond time?

SQUICKLE

The door squeals when I pull it open, the sound echoing down the long, dark hallway to my right. It takes three seconds for my eyes to adjust.

There's a bucket underneath a leaking, whining air conditioner. Brown tile floors, the grout even browner, many tiles broken and missing pieces that leave dirty, uneven triangles pointing in all directions. PSYCH SCREENING, printed on recycled computer paper like a sign for a last-minute yard sale. The faint smell of mold.

A knot forms in my chest.

Squickle-squickle-squicklesquicklesquickle. Rusty metal moving rhythmically somewhere in the building.

The word *consensual* pops into my mind.

Around the corner, down another hall, there's an unmanned metal desk by a door. Light from behind the frosted glass window beams over the folding chairs along the walls, filling the floor with long-legged shadows. Three people have spread themselves out in the chairs. One person's leg is bouncing.

Squicklesquicklesquickle.

Jane hunches over her phone in the seat closest to the desk. Her short hair covers her face, but there's no mistaking that too-big sweater, the wrinkle over its right shoulder where a hole has been hastily stitched back together. She wears that sweater every day.

A paper taped to the front of the desk says, "Sign in here." A notebook is filled with names and appointment times. I have to shake the pen to get it to work, bang it on the metal desk. Jane doesn't look up.

I take the seat farthest away.

TEXTS

KERMIT
So?

ME
I'm here. In the waiting hall.

How many people?

Three.

Anyone you recognize?

No.

Well...?

It's very unimpressive. Un-glamorous.

🍇🔺🍓

^ Your fruit platter, sir.

?

Some glamour for you.

...

Any more info?

Not really.

Ugh.

THIS MOTH SAW BRIGHTNESS • 39

News is covering tornadoes in Tennessee, the new Clarissa Patel album, which does *not* deserve coverage, and, for some reason, a video of a puppy riding a rooster. The only people talking about this study are the folks in the conspiracy forums. It's like, now that this is actually happening, no one's interested in it anymore.

> That's because it's not interesting.

> Unlike the new Clarissa Patel album.

I really wanted this to be exciting!

> Wanting something to be more exciting than it actually is is how those conspiracy theories get started, isn't it?

Can you please send a picture?

> No.

Please.

> *[Uploads crooked picture of broken tile floor, chair feet, people's feet.]*

...

I acknowledge your effort.

> 👍

You're right. Not as impressive as the letter led me to believe.

> Not impressive at all. Not interesting. Not exciting in any way. I think you're going to need to find another avenue for your next business venture.

Wait, that red in the corner of your picture.

Someone is wearing a sweater.

It looks familiar.

YOU ARE HIDING THINGS FROM CAPTAIN KERMIT

Never.

I'm getting called in, I gotta go.

HONOR

I'm not getting called in. Nothing has changed.

I turn the phone in my hands. One two three four. The corners. One two three four. In time with the person's leg, bouncing. Squickle two three four.

The person directly across from me yawns loudly. They stretch their legs into the hallway. "What are y'all here for?"

I double-check the paper above my head. It still says PSYCH SCREENING. I point to it. "Is there something else going on?"

They stretch their arms above their head, then collapse back like a rubber band. "No, no. I mean, why are you trying to do it? What do you want out of it?"

"Like the two hundred dollars?"

"For me, it's the health coverage. My parents' insurance is total ass. It won't cover the monthly blood transfusions I need to, like, stay alive? RIP me and my parents' ability to afford life. So yeah, I get into this thing, and as long as I live near good ole Charm City, that saves us, like, five K a month. Huge."

"Insurance can do that? Choose to not cover what you need to live?"

"They do whatever they want. Because my getting bit by the mosquito was avoidable, apparently. Fuck them. Fuck mosquitos." They flip off the imaginary mosquitos flying down the hallway.

"Wait." I lean forward. "*If* you get into this? Aren't we all already in?"

They point at the paper sign. "*Screening.*"

I fall back against the wall. I understand, now, Dad lending me Tusks. Tusks is for impressing others. He thought of this like an interview.

The mosquito person flings their arm toward the rest of us. "So, I shared. Your turn. What's in it for y'all? Gotta be something."

The metal chair stops squeaking as the person's leg stops bouncing. "*I'm* not doing it to get something out of it. I'm doing it for the love of my country." He sits up so we can see his shirt, a faded American flag behind three wolves, howling. "It's my duty as an American to assist with research that may improve our future well-being. It's all of our duties. Our *honors.*"

Jane looks up for the first time. "Is that right?" Her expression is unreadable.

The door clangs open. Someone comes out, someone about my age. They push their glasses higher on the bridge of their nose and sniff, like they're about to sneeze.

A woman in a white lab coat follows them into the hall. She leans over the desk and checks something off the list. I relax, some. Her white coat is clean, but not too clean. Her shoes are white, too, slip-on, professional. You can imagine her at home, drinking coffee in fraying pajamas before driving here in a Subaru.

"Thanks again, Mia," she says. "See you in a few weeks. I'll take the three thirty appointment now. Chester Jackson?"

The chair squickler patriot stands. "Ready, ma'am."

"Come inside, please."

"Good luck, everyone." Chester salutes us before walking into the room. The woman trails directly behind him, blocking our view of anything inside. The window rattles as the door shuts and locks.

The mosquito person cracks their neck, then smirks at me. "So. You also here for 'the *honor*'?"

I shake my head. "I'm here because . . ." I imagine Jane giving me the same response she gave Chester Jackson. "Is that right?" she'd say, her lips turned up, the angle of them the precise and slanted blade of an assassin.

So instead I put my arms above my head like I'm stretching and force myself to yawn. "Wanted something to do on weekends, I guess."

UNCANNY VALLEY OF SMILES

Five minutes pass. A silhouette centers itself in the door's window. The door unlocks and opens a crack.

From inside the room, Chester Jackson's voice. "What do you mean?"

"I'm sorry." The silhouette shakes her head. "You don't meet the qualifications."

"Like hell I don't, lady."

"Thank you for your time."

"Let me talk to someone higher up."

"I'm sorry."

A scraping squeal, metal on tile.

Chester's voice, again. "I know this is more than a health study. I love my country, and I want to contribute. I'm *going* to contribute."

The silhouette moves away from the doorway, and there's the sound of things falling, crashing. Something glass breaks.

The door opens. A man in jeans and a too-tight black T-shirt is gripping the wrists of a squirming Chester Jackson. From the man's belt dangle various weapon-shaped holders.

As Chester thrashes, his shirt rises up in the back, revealing a gun handle protruding over the waist of his jeans.

Every muscle in my body prepares to dive under the metal desk.

"Let me go!" The soles of Chester's shoes squeak against the tile, and his pant leg shifts, exposing a second gun strapped to his inner ankle. "Is this a test to prove my dedication? I'll show you. I'll show you *exactly* how dedicated I am."

"We're just going to take a walk, Mr. Jackson." The black-T-shirted man gives Chester's torso a tug.

Then he looks at the three of us, each of us in turn, and smiles. He *smiles*.

"Sorry about the disturbance, folks." Then the sound of his belt, his weapon-laden belt, clinking down the hall in time with his footsteps.

I risk a look at Jane. Her face tells me nothing, but her fingers on her phone are white.

The mosquito kid springs out of their chair. "I'm out of here." They scratch a name off the paper on the desk.

Jane's white-fingered hands have returned to typing on her phone.

"You're staying?" Mosquito kid seems to be waiting for us to stand up, too. "*This* is what you had in mind? For filling your weekends?"

I move my shoulders up and down in a shrug.

They scoff audibly. Then they're gone, and the hallway is weirdly quiet.

Jane's head rests against the wall now, her eyes closed.

The black-shirted man clinks back around the corner, stops at the desk, and checks the list. "Gallagher?"

Jane opens her eyes.

"Looks like you're up—come on in." And then that smile again. The smile like he wants us to think of all of this as normal.

TEXTS

ME
You won't believe what happened

KERMIT
You passed the screening?

I haven't gone in yet

I knew it. I KNEW IT

You talked to her?!?!

A kid just got taken out of here

By force

He had a gun

The kid, I mean. The guy who took him out also had a gun. And a taser.

. . . really?

No, only trying to get you worked up

Oh

Yes for real!!!!!

Whoa

Whoa whoa whoa

Holy shibas

Why?

Why'd they remove him?

> He went on some tirade about how he thought this study wasn't really about health.

> And how he wanted to pledge his life for the good of the American people

Holy shiba inus

Was it the police? That removed him

> Some guy in a black T-shirt

> Big biceps

Whoa

. . . you didn't get a pic did you?

> Kinda feeling like I should leave right now

And miss the excitement?

> Not helpful

Please stay to see what happens

Respond to me!

D!!

TEXTS

DAD
Any news?

ME
No.

Tusks okay?

Yes.

Keep me updated.

👍

MICROWAVED LASAGNA MIRAGE

"Thank you, Ms. Gallagher. See you in a month."

Jane zips around the hallway corner before I can even think about talking to her.

"'Wayne Le. Last one for today." The white-coated woman crosses my name off the list.

I hover awkwardly between the chairs and the door. She writes something at the bottom of the paper, then signs it. The silence presses on me. "Your day is almost done," I say.

"Yes. I'm excited to be home." She smiles. It's different from the black-shirted man's smile. It's a smile like Kermit gets in last period, when he's thinking about his after-school PB&J.[8] A normal, end-of-the-day smile. "You ready?"

I try to imagine this woman as I did when I first saw her, driving here in her Subaru. I force myself to imagine her at home, later tonight, drinking a glass of red wine, eating microwaved lasagna from a plastic tray, putting her feet up and watching *American Idol* reruns while wishing tomorrow was her day off.

---

8. Kermit's "PB&J" does not involve jelly—Kermit does not believe in mixing sweets with savories. He won't even try one of my favorite—the best—peanut butter cookies from the Marley Station Tiki Bar. PB&J stands for "peanut butter and Jordans;" Kermit eats a peanut butter sandwich while checking in on the day's sneaker announcements* and value developments "before the market closes."

---

* To say "checking in on" is inaccurate; it implies he was not already aware of all of them. To spend a day with Kermit is to spend a day with a constantly dinging, buzzing, honking, and mooing phone—each sound carefully keyed to some change in sneaker values.

As she's shutting the door behind me, though, I realize: She correctly pronounced the *D* at the beginning of my name, despite looking at the *D*-less name I'd written on the sign-in sheet.

Everything is suddenly feeling big again, bigger than the clip-art signs and broken tile floor.

I do know this: This woman doesn't eat microwaved lasagna unless that's exactly what she wants.

LITTER-BOX ROOM

The room smells like chalk dust. There's a chalkboard on one wall, with faint letter-like marks that could have been written yesterday or forty years ago.

The man in black is in the corner at a little desk, his biceps looking large, actually all of him looking large, with his knees coming out way past the desk edge and his gun dangling halfway down to the floor. He's scribbling on a yellow legal pad.

There's a large sink in one corner. A broken Erlenmeyer flask sparkles on the floor under the window, presumably the handiwork of Chester Jackson. A dusty set of test tubes sits on the sill.

In the center of the room there's a chair with one of those desks that swing up over the arm. The chair is brown, like the floor. It is the blandest chair I've ever seen. It's as though someone had a straw and sucked all the personality up and this chair was what was left at the bottom of the cup.

Overall, this room—it's a forgotten room.

Dad's voice plays in my head. "We don't have any rooms we don't use," he said to Olive once, when she again asked for a cat. "Where are you going to put the litter box? Logically, practically, we can't get a cat."

This room is where you'd stick a cat's litter box.

In my head, my father's litter-box protests morph into all the advice he's felt necessary to drop on me over the past week.

Research requirements are very strict.

Make sure you follow all instructions.

Make sure you listen to directions.

Keep good, steady eye contact.

Give a firm handshake.

Do only what they say.

Have good posture.

Pay attention.

Speak clearly.

Focus.

I focus. On the center of the desk, in contrast with the crumbled beige and tan of the rest of the room, sits a shiny tablet. Its screen is turned on and bright. I'm immediately tempted to walk toward it.

Do only what they say.

The white-coated woman has crossed the room to stand by the windows. "You look so nervous. Don't worry. There isn't any right or wrong today."

I shift my weight, resist the urge to adjust my T-shirt.

She picks up a legal pad from the windowsill. "I'm Dr. Richmond. You can call me Charlotte. You've already met Abrams." Abrams gives me a two-fingered wave.

"Hello."

Charlotte points to the chair. "Please take a seat."

I make sure to do absolutely nothing else until she tells me to, especially not touch the screen glowing in front of me.

JUST

Charlotte moves in front of the old chalkboard, next to Abrams' desk. She refolds her white coat's cuffs. "We're just going to have you take a test."

The words *just* and *test* in the same sentence should be illegal.

"Whenever you're ready, go ahead and look at the screen in front of you. Tap anywhere on the screen to begin. The test is five questions and should go quickly. Don't think too much about the answers. What's most important is that you're honest. Just be yourself."

Just just just.

You can't force yourself to be natural. My mother's voice joins my father's in my head.

Charlotte removes a pen from her lower pocket, adjusts the cap, and clips it into her chest pocket. "I want you to remember, there is no right or wrong. Just answer the questions."

Just.

Sometimes, in the middle of lunch, Kermit will spring out of his chair, trash a perfectly good tray of cheese fries, and storm outside. "I can't hear someone say the word *literally* one more time. It doesn't mean anything anymore. At this point, it should be removed from the dictionary, don't you think?"

And I'll nod, because he isn't really wanting an answer, though *literally* doesn't bother me.

If I could remove any word from the dictionary, it would be *just*. Now, that's a word with no real meaning.

TEST

Please click anywhere to start. You will see one question per page. Please answer all questions with T/F.

1. I like poetry.

2. The person who leaves property unprotected is more to blame than the person who steals it.

3. I don't know why, but people I work with sometimes seem a little uncomfortable around me.

4. If I were an artist, I would like to draw butterflies.

5. I know who is responsible for most of my troubles.

FINE PRINT

When I click Submit, the tablet vibrates. The test resets to the glowing white start screen.

"Excellent." Charlotte nods at Abrams, and he marks something on his legal pad. "You've passed. I'll now give you a little more information about what you can expect, and we'll officially welcome you to the program."

"That's it?"

"That's it."

"I'm in?"

"You're in! Great job!"

The screen, where the questions were a minute ago, has returned to white. Charlotte's papers rustle as she pulls out a sheet from the back of the legal pad. "I'm now going to read you the more detailed description and disclosure. You will have an opportunity to ask questions before giving your final consent.

"Feel free to interrupt me or ask me to read slower. I've read this a lot of times this week, so I might go too fast." She lifts the papers closer to her face.

"'This experiment will require you to complete daily tasks and questions via web application. The application may be accessed on any phone, tablet, laptop, or desktop computer. It may include a variety of question types or activities. All must be completed. Signing the consent form also indicates your agreement to answer all questions honestly and to the best of your ability.' Sound good so far?"

"Sounds good. Sounds great."

"'You will be required to wear a bracelet on your right wrist for the duration of the experiment. The bracelet tracks some basic information about your body such as your heart rate and blood pressure. The bracelet will serve as an identifier, allowing you access to the application for your daily reports.' Got that? All good?"

"Good. Great. Easy."

"'In addition, you may be required to attend several appointments at the research facility . . .'" She looks up from the papers. ". . . In other words, come here . . . 'at specific dates and times required by the research director. These dates and times are not reschedulable, and tardiness or failure to appear will be considered resignation from the study.'" She looks up at me again. "We can help you with transportation arrangements, if needed."

My whole body is smiling. "Won't be necessary. I'm sure my father, my dad, will let me use his car."

"Great. Only one more item!" She pulls out a paper from near the back of her pile and moves it to the front. She squints, as if what's written on it is very small.

"'This study will require you to take a pill once every several weeks. You will be required to take this pill on our premises at an assigned date and time while being monitored by security. We may also choose to administer the contents of these pills via other methods, such as aerosol dispersal, injection, or dermal patch, at the discretion of the research director. You may experience side effects from these pills, including but not limited to nausea, vomiting, shortness of breath, fatigue, headaches, or other mild symptoms. These symptoms, if present, should be short-lived. However, you will have access to medical treatment as needed during the course of this experiment, and for as long as you remain cooperative after the initial phase is concluded and the long-term monitoring phase begins.' All good?"

The straw that sucked all the personality out of the chair now sucks all the moisture out of the room. My mouth feels as dusty as the chalkboard in front of me.

"'Wayne?"

"The letter didn't mention pills."

"They're very small."

"Can you tell me what's in them?"

Charlotte and Abrams share a look. "It would invalidate the whole study if you knew what we were testing for. I am actually not even *capable* of telling you. It's a double-blind study, which means that most of us who interact with the participants don't know what we're testing either. That way we can't bias what we observe. All I'm allowed to do is reread the list of known possible side effects. Shall I?"

I shake my head.

"Then, if you'd still like to participate, we need you to sign the tablet in front of you."

The muscles in my leg twitch.

The tablet in front of me glows, white, still blank. Charlotte watches me. Abrams' pen has stopped moving, poised half an inch above his yellow paper.

I put my finger to the screen and swoosh the letter *D*.

As soon as my finger stops moving, Charlotte takes a plastic package out of her pocket. She scans it with her phone, then opens it and hands me what's inside. It's an elastic band, similar to something

Olive would use to tie up her hair, but much wider and with significant heft. On one side there's a circular piece of black plastic.

"Just go ahead and slip that on. That's for monitoring your pulse. Two finger lengths beyond your wrist, that's where it's best." She taps her own wrist. "That black part should be on the inside of your wrist, here."

I pull it on. It fits snugly, almost as though it was crafted to be exactly the minimum size for my wrist.

"You'll also use that wristband to log in to the application, starting tonight." She pulls a slip of paper and a dongle[9] out of the package and hands me those as well. The paper shows a URL and a QR code. "Use that to set up your account as soon as you can. After going through the initial identity setup, you'll scan your wristband to log in. All the instructions will be within the app."

Charlotte puts a pill on the desk. It spins three times. Its white stands out against the cracked brown wood, a miniature echo of Charlotte's white shoes against the brown tile floor.

There's the sound of running water as Charlotte turns on the sink. The rising pitch of the water filling a cup.

She places the cup next to the pill.

Even with the water, the pill sticks as it goes down. The bitter spreads over the back of my throat and crawls its way up my tongue into my mouth.

---

9. In ninth grade, Kermit and I competed in using the word *dongle* in as many assignments as we could. We got bonus points if we used it on a quiz or test, especially in one of those state standards tests. Kermit won, of course.

POLKA DOTS

My mother had pills that were small and white and perfectly round.

She never liked to take them. "They make me feel like not myself," she said.

Dad would encourage her. "Dr. Albert instructed that . . ."

"They don't listen, the doctors. Especially not Dr. Know-It-All Albert. This is not what I need."

One of the few things I remember doing with her is baking. She loved to bake, though she was self-conscious about loving to bake.

Once we made sugar cookies. Well, a lot of times we made sugar cookies, the recipe passed down through nine generations of proud New Yorkers. But one time in particular, the last time, she went all out with the decorations. Sparkles, sprinkles, a rainbow of frosting. There were too many decorations. She'd bought four bags full, and they overflowed off the counter and into the sink. There was hardly room to do the decorating.

She spent an hour making a bear. She used frosting to give the bear a suit jacket and a long tie. "I'm making it for my doctor," she said. "I want to make it special." She gave the bear's tie polka dots.

I was making a snake. I wanted to give my snake polka dots, too. I couldn't figure out where she got them from, the polka dot decorations. In all these four bags, there weren't dots like hers.

"We're all out of those. Sorry, sweetie."

The dots were small, white, and perfectly round.

EOFF

When Tusks turns onto our block, our front yard looks empty.

As soon as I park, though, Dad materializes out of the shrubs clutching a pair of yellow gardening shears. Even from here I can see that the shears' safety is still on. In fact, those shears might be from Olive's old play set.

He approaches the car and leans down to inspect the bumper. Then he leans close to the hood and flicks something off. I take a deep breath and open the door.

"Car looks okay," he says.

"That's good."

"Why didn't you send me a message when you were on your way?"

I pull out my backpack and water bottle from the passenger seat. "Can't you track the car?"

"You should have said something."

"Okay." I climb out and shut the door. "I'm sorry."

Then he stands there, clearly wanting me to tell him what happened. His face is a blank slate, waiting for my words to transform it into Disappointed Not Surprised. He's wearing his slip-on "around-the-house" sandals (different from his "home shoes"), the ones he got from the kitchen goods section at H-Mart, which are printed with tiny green frogs. Those silly yellow shears are still dangling from his hand. He looks almost vulnerable. I almost want to hug him and tell him to relax, everything went fine.

The problem, however, is that what's underneath DNS, lying in wait, is EoFF:

EoFF: Expectation of Future Failure. Involves one or more eyebrows being raised. Often accompanied by a verbal utterance such as "I guess we'll see how it goes." Morphs seamlessly into DNS after expected failure is realized.

Behind him, the screen door squeaks. It opens slowly, and only wide enough for Olive to slip out. She shuts it carefully behind her. She always opens doors like that, like she's afraid of losing the cat we don't have. Then she sprints across the lawn in her bare feet.

"You're back!"

"I'm in! I've already started." It's easy to tell Olive.

"Well done, my good sir." She holds her hand out for a shake. "I commend you."

"I appreciate your acknowledgment and support."

"Hear, hear." She nods with faux seriousness and moves my hand up and down twice.

My father's expression is still unformed. "What will you need to do?"

"Not much." I gesture at the band on my arm. "I have to wear this." It doesn't feel snug anymore. It's comforting, even, like having a little scarf on my wrist. "It monitors my pulse."

"Very fashionable," says Olive.

I strike a pose.

Olive rolls her eyes.

"That's all?" Dad says.

I fish the slip of paper out of my jeans pocket. "I have to make an account on this app and do . . . something."

"Something?"

"I'll get the instructions once I log in. I'm supposed to do something every day."

"Every day! That's a lot." Dad sounds either appalled or pleased at how much work this is turning out to be. "Anything else?"

"I have to take some pills."

"Oh!" Dad's eyebrows triangle up. "This is even more involved than I thought."

He holds out his hands and gestures at me to give him my arm. He turns my hand over and touches the black plastic circle on the inside of the wristband. Then he takes the gray wool and rubs it between his forefinger and thumb. "It's good material. Quality."

He lets my hand fall.

Then, it happens: His face moves. It moves again.

When it settles, it's a face I've never seen before. I'm not sure if it's positive or negative. It's blanker than his neutral face.

He lifts his right hand. At first, I think he's going to hug me. That's how he used to hug me when I was small, one hand up, one down, a diagonal sweep. But his hand falls lower, so it's clear it's not going to be a hug.

And then I think he's going to pat me on the shoulder, friend-like. Instead, here's what he does: He waves at me.

A single hard wave. Like I'm a neighbor who lives down the block and we've finished exchanging knowledge on ideal tomato growing conditions, good talkin', gotta get back to it.

He waves, turns up the driveway, and goes up the porch steps. The screen door slams behind him.

D+ MOVIE SCRIPTS

Kermit is a terrible person to watch movies with. He analyzes everything, from the originality of the camera angles to the quality of the dialogue. One of the things he loves the most is when characters don't respond to what another character says.

For example, if Character A says, "Dusk makes me sad. The sounds the birds make as they go to sleep, the way the wind seems louder because your vision has been dulled by impending darkness . . . At dusk, I always end up questioning whether my life has any purpose at all."

And Character B says, "Should we get tacos for dinner?"

. . . that's what Kermit thinks is capital-*A* Art.

When this happens, Kermit will clap once, point at the screen, and yell, "Now, *that's* how real life works. This writer, *yes*, this writer knows how to *write*."

Most of my conversations with Dad feel like they are one of these brilliantly written movie scripts.

If I said, "I feel like I'm drowning under the weight of your expectations and floundering in the quagmire of my own self-loathing and I feel like there is no way out, no way up, no way to escape the tendrils of the mistakes I've made, no way back to the perfect son I apparently once was; I am a vase that has been dropped and glued back together, and I will never again hold water; I will forever and evermore leak" . . .

He would say, "You finished your math homework, right?"

Palme d'Or award for the household of 'Wayne Le.

I wish my life with Dad was instead a D+ Hallmark Channel holiday special. In the capital-*A* Art films, everyone dies at the end.

HOPKINS STUDY APP

Welcome! Thank you for agreeing to participate in our health study.

Please hold still for thirty seconds as we match your wristband's ID to our records.

S C A N N I N G

Scanning complete! Your identity has been verified and your participation confirmed. Please return tomorrow for the first of your daily activities.

See you soon!

RADIOACTIVE HALF-LIFE OF PERFECTION (!)

The light above Mr. Houston's door is taking forever to turn green.

Mr. Houston is the school counselor. I know him well. I get the privilege of spending my study hall talking to Mr. Houston every other week, which seems counterproductive to me, but what do I know about getting work done?

That's not why I'm here today, though. This is an extra, bonus meeting. The school was sent a document containing a list of students participating in the Hopkins study. That way, we can get permission, if needed, to leave school for appointments. In homeroom this morning, I got a note from Mr. Houston that said, "Re: Hopkins Study... We need to discuss your workload, come today."

This means, I think, that he is worried I won't be able to handle both the requirements of the study and the requirements of my schoolwork.

I'm casually browsing upcoming Jordan 1 special releases, something I try to do while I'm waiting.

From the wall, an oil portrait of a white guy with white hair leers down at me with his white-haired lapdog. Our school is filled with things like this. This building, what is now Glenville High, was originally the city hall and courthouse. Several years ago, when we started getting more tropical storms in the area and the rivers and creeks kept flooding, the parents lobbied to move us into this building, which was farther inland. The city's government officials now work in the more-likely-to-be-destroyed-in-a-natural-disaster high school building.

This decision was sudden and low budget, so a lot of stuff that wasn't high priority didn't get moved. Like random white guy portraits, or the now-empty vending machines, or the long wooden benches that line many of our hallways.

Mr. Houston's office was originally a room where jurors were held. It has two doors. One, on the side where I'm sitting, leads into a vestibule-like entry room where people might have left their bags and coats. Mr. Houston has furnished this room with a plaid love seat and a small bookshelf of self-help books that has been hand-decorated—presumably by students waiting on the love seat—with inappropriate quotes.

Above the bookshelf, there's a large poster advertising an upcoming school event—Dave Appleright, the school's basketball MVP two years ago, will be coming home on leave from the army. He's decided to grace the school with his presence at a brunch fundraiser for something called Good People Do Good.[10] Despite Dave graduating two years ago, Glenville is still obsessed. He's constantly featured on the school's home page with the banner "Glenville High Strives to Care About Stuff Like Dave Cares About Stuff." The poster on Mr. Houston's wall uses one of the most popular Dave pictures, the one where he's ripped off his jersey after winning States.

Next to the bookshelf, there's a cylindrical fish tank repetitively looping through bubbling sounds and in which I have never once seen a single fish.

The fish tank's glass reflects the light above the door. The light changes from red to green. This means I should open it.

---

10. Tickets: $150 for brunch, $300 for brunch plus signed basketball, $500 for brunch, signed basketball, and selfie with Dave Appleright himself.

"'Wayne!" Mr. Houston stands up from his desk chair. Behind him, the exit door is closing after the previous student. That door leads into what was once a courtroom but has been converted to a small gym.

Mr. Houston sweeps me into his room. "Welcome back, welcome back. Congratulations on getting into the Hopkins study."

There's a file open on his computer with my eighth-grade school picture, and in big black letters: HEALTH STUDY PARTICIPANT.

"Thanks." I sit down, expecting him to do the same; instead, he lifts his arms above his head like he's won an Olympic medal. His tie, which is decorated with a purple unicorn, does its own little leap. "I'm so proud of you!"

"For—the study?"

"No! I mean, yes. That is why I called you here. We'll get to that. But first, I am proud of you for something else!"

His arms linger above his head. He's waiting for me to ask him why he's proud of me. Mr. Houston is like a grown-up version of Kermit.

I hold in my sigh. "What are you proud of me for, Mr. Houston?"

"Check *this* out." He sits, using one hand to hold his unicorn tie close to his chest. Three of his fingers brush across his computer screen so my picture slides left and a window with our school website appears.

It's logged in to the teacher interface and displays a spreadsheet. He tilts the monitor toward me. The spreadsheet is a list of all my classes, with columns for grades and teacher comments.

"Do you know what this is, 'Wayne? Do you see what I am seeing?"

"A blank spreadsheet?"

"No! I mean *yes*, but what *else*?" His fingers do the *come on* gesture in fast-forward.

"A computer? Your unicorn tie?"

He looks down, holds up his tie. "Do you like it? I wear it once a week. It means my daughter and I are going to get something special for dessert." He drops the tie. "But seriously. Look at the spreadsheet and you'll see it is not really empty."

I squint. It contains my class names, but I know Mr. Houston well enough to know that's not what he's referring to. I hold in my sigh. This room is bursting at its seams with all the sighs I haven't sighed. "I don't know, Mr. Houston, but I sure am excited for you to tell me."

He raises his arms again. "*Possibility!* That table is filled with *possibility*, 'Wayne, with *potential*. That's what I see. That spreadsheet is a clean slate." He points at it. "A clean slate! There is not a single mark of imperfection on the record for the second half of this trimester. Your attendance—flawless. Your assignments—one hundred percent turned in."

"There haven't been any assignments."

Mr. Houston pauses. "My records indicate perfection. Are you arguing with my records? This record of perfection?"

"It's the first week of the second half of the trimester."

"The first week of your perfection."

My gaze wanders to the top of his screen, where he has twenty other tabs with names of other students who will be coming in here sometime after I leave.

"I don't say this to everyone who comes in here, 'Wayne. Even though everyone obviously does, of course, start each period with a perfect record. It's meaningful to *you* in particular. I want to show you something else." His voice has lost some of its enthusiastic edge. This makes me nervous.

With a few swipes and clicks, he's brought up a graph. The vertical axis is labeled "Performance" and the horizontal axis has dates.

"This is an AI metric added to our system—a new way to analyze student performance. It averages everything—your grades, your behavior, your attendance, I'm not even sure what else—and allows us to see how your performance changes over time. It allows us to see trends.

"This is your performance from last year. As you can see"—he points at the left side of the graph—"you start out every term with perfect performance. As does everyone. But what's interesting is that your performance is excellent for the first two weeks or so." He draws his finger along the nearly straight line. He keeps moving his finger along the line to where it starts to dip down. "And then—it's just a steady decline for the rest of the trimester. It doesn't go up and down, it's this . . . *linear*, consistent decline.

"Now I want to show you something else." Mr. Houston swipes right, and another copy of the same graph slides in. "What do you see?"

Another one of Mr. Houston's trick questions.

"I'm guessing it's *not* merely another copy of last trimester's wasted possibility?"

Mr. Houston grins. "And your guess would be absolutely correct. You are on *fire*, Mr. Le. Perfection upon perfection. Yes, this is not a copy of the same trimester, this graph is *two* trimesters ago." He jabs his finger at the screen, indicating the date.

"Now watch." He swipes right again, scrolls back another trimester. Keeps scrolling, slowly. Every trimester, there's more time at the start of the graph before my performance starts dropping off. Until finally, he gets to a graph where my performance is a straight line across the top for the whole period.

"Fifth grade," he says. "Look at that."

I do look. MRS. ROTH is printed at the top. Her face floods into my memory. Her curly hair, her large white teeth, the room down the hall with posters of cats wearing glasses where I'd get sent once a week with other "gifted" children for "extra challenge" under the tutelage of Mr. Layer. Kermit was in that class. We partnered together to build a bridge with toothpicks and marshmallows for a strength competition. I desperately wanted to win.

Mr. Houston touches a finger to a lip as if he once had a mustache to stroke. "I see your face falling, 'Wayne. But this is a *good* thing. The AI system flagged this, and I'm showing this to you not because I want you to see how much you haven't accomplished but to prove to you how much you can be. The potential is there. The ability is there. It's always been there.

"I don't know what happens to you every time. Those are things you should think about, and we could maybe talk about. But what I'm trying to show you here, in this session, is that you have the capability to succeed, if you want to. Do you want to?"

The unicorn on Mr. Houston's tie gives me the evil eye.

Mr. Houston clears his throat. "Seriously, 'Wayne. I'm asking you. Do you want to succeed? Do *you* actually *want* to succeed?"

When I continue to not respond, he holds up his hand.

"I'd really like you to think about that question. There are a lot of people who have reasons they don't want to succeed. Secondary gains, or sometimes fear; with success comes responsibility. Expectation."

I want to bring this conversation around to its purpose, so then it can be over, and I can leave. "Wasn't this meeting supposed to be about the Hopkins thing and my workload? Are you saying the Hopkins study will get in the way of me reaching my potential?"

"Absolutely the opposite! I wanted to tell you that I'm glad you're doing it. That in fact, I think you should prioritize your focus on the Hopkins study at the same level as, if not more than, your schoolwork. Sometimes having something else to focus on, something else to try and succeed at—a hobby, a sport, in this case a research study—which isn't exactly a hobby, but close enough—can make it easier to reach your potential elsewhere. The added challenge, the added motivation, it carries over. Plus, the commendation letter will do a lot to open up your options for colleges."

He flips back to a more recent chart, one with a line that falls off a cliff.

"If I know you, or if our statistics know you, you'll start off strong in the study. How are you doing so far?"

"It's been a day."

"A day of perfection?"

"Well..."

Mr. Houston's eyes are large. He's nodding at me.

"...Yes."

"Excellent. So let's break the pattern of these charts and *stay* strong."

He stands up. I stand up.

He holds his unicorn tie to his chest as he leans forward to shake my hand.

"You're free to go! I hope you feel uplifted. I hope you feel inspired. All you have to do is keep doing what you've done the past two days. *Inspiring*, yes?"

"Well..."

"And maybe give that question a thought, hmm? Whether you actually want to succeed?"

"Okay."

"And remember that anything is possible."

"I'll remember that."

"Now go! Go continue that perfection you have begun."

He gestures toward the exit. The word *EXIT* is printed in green—the same green as the light at the entrance, like the exit is itself an entrance into a brave new world of possibility.

HAMSTER

Olive, for a few months, had a pet hamster, a silvery gray one. Dad got it for her on one of the days he got bad news about officially adopting her. He said a hamster was the same as a cat—"it has stick-up ears and lives in a litter box"—but was more conveniently sized.

Olive named him Maxwell after the Beatles song, which she thought—and still thinks—was about Maxwell the Silver (and vicious) Hamster. Maxwell, the actual hamster, had a tendency to bite.

Which is how he escaped during a cage cleaning and disappeared into the walls of our house. We—meaning me and Olive—hunted for days. Olive spent hours calling his name. I bought special hamster treats and made trails that led to his cage. I even tried playing his theme song loudly on our living room speakers.

We never saw him again.

Every so often, though, we would hear him in the walls or find a half-chewed cracker in the center of the living room rug.

That's what I think of after talking to Mr. Houston. Lost hamsters. That's what "potential" is like after you waste it.

Others may stumble upon remnants of your potential scattered in unswept corners—your occasional original idea or clever phrase. But really, it's gone. Reduced to hard, black droppings behind the microwave.

HOPKINS STUDY APP

Today's assignment is a game. Please try to relax and *Have Fun*.

You will see words falling from the top of the screen toward the swamp at the bottom.

Type the first word you think of when you see the falling word (other than the word itself) before it reaches the swamp. Don't let the alligators eat your words!

You will get 10 points for each word you respond to. The words will fall faster and faster as you progress. You must score at least 1,000 points to pass today's exercise; you have unlimited tries, so as long as you want to succeed, you *will*.

Have Fun!

PERMANENT STRANGER

The Marley Station Shopping & Experience Center is busy for the lunch hour. Not with students—the weekly 20-percent-off coupons and the truly stellar peanut butter cookies have not convinced my classmates that the Tiki Bar is better than the Wawa, despite—or perhaps because of—it being walking distance from the school.

No, the center is filled with elderly couples, some in walking shoes who have finished their slow mile circuit, and others in crisp jackets, carrying beaded handbags like coming to the mall for lunch is a fancy date.

I did spend the first three minutes of my lunch period in the school's lower cafeteria,[11] which, out of the two cafeterias, is better for disappearing in.

But the talk there centered on the study—how Abby Wong got an assignment in the app conveniently during a pop math test, for example. Bryce Orr, his hair even more gelled than usual, was talking loudly about how he'd been *selected*. And Kermit had, over the course of the morning, sent me at least four texts with links to obscure articles that he "planned to discuss over lunch."

On days like this, when the conversations circle topics I'd rather not think about, I come here.

---

11. Because our school is in the converted city hall, we have two cafeterias—the upper cafeteria being the smaller one the judges and government officials used, and the lower one, which is larger and louder and originally meant for the plebeians.

The Experience Center—"The First of Its Kind!"—used to be the mall. Last year, as the sign near the entrance explains, the mall was "de-malled and redeveloped" into, as far as I can tell, another mall. The hallways still stretch long with storefronts. The same names brand the entranceways. The floors still reflect too much noise, too much light—more so now that they've been "modernized" with white tiles instead of gray.

The main difference is that the "stores" don't carry inventory anymore. Instead, they host "experiences" that let you try the products in designated ways. After you try the products, you can order them from a row of tablet kiosks. Usually you get something like 10 percent off for ordering "In-Experience" and free one-day shipping.

Real estate is cheap near Baltimore. I guess that makes us good fodder for experiments like this and a selfie theme park.

The Tiki Bar café, where I've been sitting for the last five minutes, faces the vacuum store, and is connected to the Welcome Center, where there's a booth where you can pick up today's Experience Schedule & Map. Fabric flame torches line the bar's perimeter. "All Life's a Party, so Experience It!" is scribbled on a chalkboard by the entranceway. Clarissa Patel's second album fills the space with positive energy, the delightful taste of the peanut butter cookies lingers on my tongue, and the plastic grass crunching under the feet of people coming and going all provide a soothing backdrop to *Drone Wars Mobile: Double Tap*, where I've got only thirty seconds left to clear out the enemy drones from a building's heating vents.

Twenty seconds left in my mission. My drone enters the final stretch of vents. I take out an enemy stealth drone that swings in from the right.

"Hey," someone says, near my ear. "Mind if I sit with you?"

My drone nicks a wall and spins out of control.

I throw the phone into my backpack on the floor.

"So sorry to interrupt." The voice is finely edged, like an assassin's sword. In a familiar way.

I scramble to push my cup and cookie crumbs into a tidier pile. "You're not."

"Mm." Jane sits in the chair across from me. " 'Wayne, right? The one with the invisible *D*?"

"Yes," I say, a little shakily.

"You go by *D*?"

I nod, my face stoic and peaceful because I don't at all care that she knows this.

She pauses. "Why? Your name *doesn't* have a *D*."

"That's the point."

"What's the point?"

"I want the *D* to be *not* secret. As visible as invisibly possible."

"Why?"

"Well . . ." Suddenly the plastic of the chair seat feels very hot.

"Actually, don't tell me. I shouldn't have asked. I don't want to know. I'm Jane, by the way."

"Jane." I nod, as if I am committing an unfamiliar name to memory.

Jane's backpack thunks on the floor. "First things first. I think it's ideal to start any new relationship with establishment of expectations and communication preferences. Do you agree?"

"I . . ."

"I'll go first. As far as communication goes, I prefer direct, blunt conversation. No white lies. No dancing around truths even if you think the truth would be rude or hurtful.

"Another note: If I'm tired or thinking hard, it may take me a very long time to get the words to my mouth, so you need to be comfortable waiting in what people tell me is an"—she makes air quotes—"'awkward silence.' And, if I'm not responding to you, I'm not being"—more air quotes—"'difficult.' It's only because I didn't realize you expected me to talk—so you might need to ask a direct question. I'm autistic, if that box is helpful to you. Okay?"

"Okay."

"Do you actually mean 'okay'? Because I don't feel like you gave that much thought."

"Yes. I can be honest."

"And?"

"Wait for your words to form."

"Great. Now. Do *you* have communication preferences I should know about?"

"I—I've never thought about it."

"Most people haven't. They don't need to. That's fine. If you ever realize your preferences, and I do recommend that you give it some thought, let me know. Will you?"

I nod.

"Perfect. On to business." She motions toward my wrist, where a hint of gray is poking out from under my sleeve. "I see you got through the screening. Glad it went well for you. I was hoping you'd get through."

"You . . . were?"

"Yes."

I arrange my features in what I hope looks like a thoughtfully interested but not overly excited mask.

"You're probably thinking, *Oh my, this is strange, some random person rooting for my success in a health study, now interrupting my private lunchtime . . . or cookie time, as it was.* So, let me tell you why I followed you here, to this corner table, warmed by the fluttering flames of fabric tiki torches." She rests her arms on the table, which wobbles toward her. The remnants of my coffee slosh against the sides of the paper cup.

"Participating in something like this, a university-led study, one that you may or may not want to participate in, one where you're ingesting pills and such? It's a lot. You're going to have a lot of feelings. *Feels*, if you prefer. It's probably healthy to have someone you can talk to. Someone also going through the same things. Someone you feel safe around. You agree?"

"You feel safe around me?"

"Not exactly." She picks up one of the scattered Experience Center flyers on the table and folds it as she talks. "I've been thinking about situations where people feel most comfortable talking about how they feel. Like therapy. Suicide hotlines. Stuff like that. Those things *work* in essence because, why?"

"Um..."

"I'll tell you. It's because, at least in part, it's an anonymous person. Someone who isn't going to judge you. Someone who isn't going to make you feel guilty or anxious or like you're burdening them with your existence. You can just *talk*."

"Uh."

"Just *think* about it."

"I am!"

"I mean of course those people are trained and everything. But I'm pretty sure the anonymity is a contributing factor. Imagine your best friend, for example. Do you particularly want to tell them your most intimate thoughts? Or someone in your family? Do you want to talk to them? And even if you did, are they interested in what you have to say?"

Her expression darkens. Then she puts her newly folded whale on the table between us and pats its head cheerily. "It's the hardest to talk to people closest to you."

An elderly couple moves into the table next to us, each holding a coffee with a pink umbrella blooming from the ice. They look at each other quickly, shyly, like it's a first or second date.

"So, you're saying you wanted me to make it into the study because . . . you want to talk to me about the study because . . ." I reach my finger out to touch her whale, then put it back in my lap. ". . . Because you don't know me."

"Exactly!" Jane throws her arms in the air. The table wobbles back toward me. The couple next to us looks up. "You're the person in our class I maybe know the least about. The person I'm least interested in getting to know. The only thing I know about you is that you're 'that guy with the invisible name.' I didn't even know your last name. I had to look it up."

"Oh." I resist the urge to drown her whale in my coffee remnants.

She clasps her hands. "Now I want to do an exercise. Close your eyes."

"What?"

"Would you please close your eyes?"

She is definitely not the Zen-like, origami almost-champion I'd thought she was. She *is* precise, though. It's hard to imagine her having trouble with talking, because currently her words, her *ideas*, feel as crisp as her paper folds. I close my eyes.

"Now, try to picture the person you know the least. Out of all your classmates."

"If I don't know them, how can I . . ."

"*Shh-tch-tch*. You're overthinking it. Just let their face float into your vision. *Flo-o-o-at*. Are you doing it?"

I'm definitely not doing it. I nod.

"Well? Whose face do you see?"

I scrunch my nose, hoping it makes me look like I'm concentrating. I *do* see a face. Her face. But I often seen her face when my eyes are closed. Even when she's not directly in front of me I can picture the rounded shape of her eyebrows and the shadow of her sharp, but not too sharp, chin. ". . . I see . . . your face."

The table clunks again; she must have leaned back down. "I *knew* it! We are both the people we know the least about! Okay, open your eyes. So what do you think? Will you be my partner? Will you talk with me about this study?"

The couple next to us is now giggling and tucking sugar packets into their pockets.

I nod.

"Yay!" She sits up straight again. My coffee sloshes some more.

With two fingers, Jane picks up a remaining cookie crumb from the center of the table and drops it into my pile. Then she places a folder on the table between us, right by her whale.

"So. Here's my plan. We don't talk to each other at all, outside of very designated times and places. And we don't say anything outside of the designated topics, or topic, rather, because the study is the *only* acceptable topic."

"It is?"

"Otherwise we'll learn too much about each other, and then we won't be helpful to each other anymore! Now. In this folder, you will find the information you'll need to contact me. You'll also find the list of hours at which it's appropriate to do so, as well as some other rules I thought might be helpful to structure our conversations."

I lift up a flap of the folder. I see some cardstock with instructions on it. It looks like an official legal document. "You made this?"

"Yep."

I let the flap fall. "But . . ."

Her eyes narrow. "But what?"

"Don't you do . . . origami?" I point to the whale she's left between us.

She blinks at me, before narrowing her eyes further. "Oh. My. God." The table clunks as she leans back again. Her mouth twitches two times to the left. "You manic-pixie-dream-girled me."

"Huh?"

"You did. You did! You thought that because I do origami—What, I'm some whimsical magical being from the fifteenth century? I go home and have tea ceremonies and practice my lettering and polish my fairy wings that I'll sew to my Renaissance ball gown in a charmingly incompetent way that speaks of my refreshingly restless, untameably free spirit? You thought I can't be organized, or handle real-life tasks, or accomplish real things!"

"I did not!" But my palms are starting to sweat.

"No? Well, then, was it because I have *breasts*? My mammary glands get in the way of me handling responsibility?"

"No!" I say, much too loudly to sound believable. The couple next to us looks up again, and one of them gives me a wink. "I don't have any problems with breasts. I mean, with them being in charge. I mean! Not problems. I mean . . . my sister is very organized! Not really my sister, and she doesn't have breasts yet, that I know of, anyway, I support her getting things done . . ."

Jane holds up a hand. "You need to stop talking, because now I know you have a sister. Or a not-sister? Which I'd love to ask about, but I won't. I'm learning too much about you. On that note, I should probably skedaddle." She leans back onto the table. "How about Saturday at eight a.m.? Right here. This table if possible. That'll be a full week after we started the study. By then we'll have accumulated some experiences to talk about. Work for you?"

"Eight a.m. The eight a.m. that's in the morning?"

"Yep. Now. Remember: In school, I don't know you. You don't know me. We pretend the other person doesn't exist. Sound good?"

That sounds like exactly the opposite of good. I'm not sure if I should be bluntly honest.

She points one finger at me. "I see what you're doing here, by not responding. Wow. Yes, exactly. Don't say anything. I love it. You're already in character. Goodbye, Permanent Stranger! Don't say goodbye back. I shouldn't even say goodbye myself. Goodbye!"

She takes off from the table. It rocks back toward me, hard. Cold coffee spills all over the front of my shirt.

MY NAME

The invisible *D* in my name is my mother's second-most-lasting contribution to my life.

When I was a kid, before she ran away from us, literally screaming—which is, by the way, the winner for *first*-most-lasting contribution to my life—she used to tell me that she'd given me an invisible letter in my name because it felt intimate and special.

"Sometimes things are so precious, you don't want to put them into words," she said. "That's what you are to me. Too special to express. My special secret."

I will not point out here that this name, her second-greatest contribution to my life, is in fact very similar to her first-greatest contribution to my life:

a kind of absence.

this contract was entered into in Maryland and any dispute will be litigated or arbitrated in Maryland.

3. Termination

This Agreement may be terminated at any time prior to the Project's completion, by either party on seven (7) days' notice for any reason. This contract shall be terminated should either Participant cease involvement with the Study. Also, as already noted above, but definitely worth noting again, should either Participant show too much interest in either (a) revealing personal information or (b) obtaining personal information about the other, the Project will be ended immediately (!).

'Wayne Le   **Jane Gallagher**

_____   _____
Signature   *Signature*

_____   _____
Name   *Name*

_____   _____
Title   *Title*

_____   _____
Date   *Date*

HOPKINS STUDY APP

Make sure the plastic surface of your wristband is correctly positioned on your wrist.

Please rest your hands lightly on a flat surface. Spread your fingers. Make sure you are truly feeling the surface.

Close your eyes.

Wait until you feel calm, calm enough to have fun!

At this time, say, "Go!" A soothing voice will read you a random array of words over the course of five minutes.

Attempt to keep your breathing as regular and even as possible, until the words come to an end.

- Armadillos
- Jelly
- Texas
- Pickles
- Toaster
- Strangers
- Immigrants
- Pixie
- Sleeping
- Origami
- Rice
- ...

THE MARLEY STATION SHOPPING & EXPERIENCE CENTER, 7:44 A.M.

The Experience Center is somehow even more busy at this ungodly hour, overflowing with jumpsuited joggers and walkers. There's also a number of single parents with small kids, who actually seem to be shopping, or experiencing, or whatever it is you are supposed to do here. All of the Tiki Bar's neon signs are on, announcing "Good Morning, Sunshine" and "Hot Donuts" and "Fresh Coffee and Vibes."

It is absolutely an excellent place to have an impersonal conversation with someone. There is no risk of intimacy here. I barely recognize the sound of my own thoughts in my head.[12]

I pass the Sony store, where a poster invites me in to watch full-immersion VR movies. I pass a few clothing stores where you can make hologram projections of yourself wearing different outfits. There's the lotion store, where you can, this week only, experience a blindfolded trip around the world via smells. And PetSmart's roped-off area with fake grass where you can "lie down and quietly meditate on the joys of life amidst a field of rabbits," which unfortunately is not open yet.

The line at the Tiki Bar spills out of the flame-lined archway of the door, and I think there's no way I will be able to get a table, let alone the same table as last time. Fortunately, someone has abandoned a

---

12. "That's because you don't have any thoughts in your head," Kermit would say.

half-eaten croissant and a spilled latte, which is dripping onto a chair, deterring anyone from sitting there.

As I clean up the table, the Experience Schedule in the plastic stand informs me that this morning the vacuum store is hosting competitions in fifteen-minute intervals. Contestants using the store's vacuum brand compete against contestants using "another leading manufacturer's similar model." They started at six a.m. (!) for "the working parents."

There's a lot of commotion in there. They have squares of rug laid out, and a trash can pushed into the corner from which a man is scooping cups of rice to dump on each square. The Halloween decorations dangling from the store's ceiling bobble and wave.

It's 7:58. Two minutes left until the meeting with Jane.

The vacuum competition starts. Even with the store's doors closed, the sounds of the vacuums' howls and the clapping and screaming of the crowd inside stream over the Tiki Bar's peppy nineties rock music.

Watching the pursed lips of the vacuum contestants as they hurry the vacuums over the carpets as if that is the most important thing in the world, as if winning the vacuum competition *matters*—it makes everything feel smaller, manageable.

Then, "Hello," Jane says, and she pulls out the chair across from me.

THE KEY TO SELLING A CAR

As Jane gets settled, as she cycles through the range of expressions I've watched and wondered about so many times, I want to convince her that we don't need to limit our conversation to the study. We don't need the signed contract.

She doesn't want to be my Permanent Stranger. She wants to be my Non-Permanent Stranger.

Or my Permanent Non-Stranger.

I feel the need to present myself as a product. Something as useful as a vacuum. Something Jane would want to buy.

For example: Dad wasn't originally going to buy Tusks. Originally, he was going to buy a used Honda.

But the saleswoman was good at her job.

"You're very good at your job," Dad said to her as she helped him through the signing of an endless stack of papers. "You know all the tricks."

She laughed. "There are no tricks. Not good ones, anyway." She turned a paper over and pointed to the next X. "Selling something isn't really about the way you stand, or about making bad jokes, or whether you open with a low offer or high. It's about truly believing that what you're selling is worthwhile. *That's* the key."

And then she'd handed Dad Tusks' fob. "And here's *your* key."

Dad liked that.

I think about Dad when I got home from the screening.

I think about his hand, giving me the short, tomato-convo wave.

I think about myself as a product, and whether I believe what I'm selling is worthwhile.

I think that if getting someone to like you is anything like selling a car, I don't have a chance.

A WEIRD AGENDA

"Phew." Jane tucks her bangs behind her ears. "Sorry I'm late."

"You're not late."

"I am"—she taps her phone so the time lights up—"exactly two minutes late. I'm sorry to have kept you waiting. Should we get down to business? We should. Let's get down to business."

Jane looks out of place here. The backdrop of this neon-lit Tiki Bar makes her sweater look more faded and torn than ever. Her hair has slid out from behind her ears and is going every which way.

It makes her seem more real. Hyperreal. Like, if she wanted, she could take this escape from reality and crush it with two fingers.

"Thanks for signing my contract." She settles her bag on the floor next to her chair. "Rules are good, I think. They can be comforting." She removes some paper rectangles from her pocket. "On that note. I, uh, I made us an agenda."

"A what?"

"I wasn't going to give it to you, because I thought maybe you'd think it was . . . overkill? Some people tell me it's overkill. 'Just too much.'" She makes air quotes. "'Is an agenda really necessary for a conversation?'" More air quotes. "But, this isn't just *any* sort of conversation, right? Also, I like agendas. I think they're helpful in lots of situations, even normal conversations. It's like a map, because it's like, you don't *have* to use it, you can wander around and get lost in conversation if you're feeling up for being lost, but when you're ready to know where you're going again, you can look at your agenda!

"As you'll see, we're right on schedule, in the middle of the first item." She thrusts one of the rectangular papers at me. It has a triangular tab that says "Pull." I do. The paper accordions out, revealing the print inside.

First Conversation Agenda

1. Awkward hellos (5–10 min)
2. Discuss how Wayne is feeling. (5–10 min)
3. Discuss how Jane is feeling. (5–10 min)
    *Items 2 and 3 may be reversed in order.
4. Arrangement of next meeting or decision to arrange later via text/email. (3 min)
5. Awkward goodbyes. (5 min)

"Uh."

"You don't like it. You think it's too much."

"It's not that. It's . . ."

She tugs at the top of my paper. "It's okay, you know what? Here, just give it here. I'll put it back in my pocket. Oh, look, there's a trash can shaped like a giant coconut. I'll put the agenda in the giant coconut. Okay? We'll forget I did this. Please? It was silly."

"It wasn't silly." I snatch the paper away.

"I can tell you don't like it."

"I *do* like it. I think it is very . . . organized. Like the contract. I appreciate that. It. You."

"I can tell there's something wrong."

"There's not."

She crosses her arms. "This isn't going to work if we aren't honest with each other."

"Ah."

"Well?"

"It's . . . it's . . ."

"What are you *feeling*?"

I take a deep breath. "Really nervous." It feels strange to say that out loud.

But Jane nods. "Thank you for telling me. That makes perfect sense. It's also a great lead-in to agenda item two. What you're feeling. Want to move to item two and expand upon your nervous feelings?"

One of the vacuum contestants is jumping up and down and waving their arms. Their rug square is rice-free. The store employee high-fives him.

Does Jane actually want to hear about my father, how everything feels pointless, how my future is resting on getting that signed letter at the end of this study? Is all of that too personal and against the rules? And if it's not against Jane's rules, is it against the secret social rules—as in, does *anyone* want to hear that stuff, ever?

The couple at the table next to us begins discussing whether they should catch the scent-guided meditation at the candle store or participate in the New-New Gothcore Fashion Soiree.

"Would you mind going first?" I say.

"Of course! By which I mean, not at all. I prepared a list of some of my feelings ahead of time, so I can be concise." She unfolds another paper. "The first thing I wrote down—okay, hear me out—is that I feel *weird*. Which I know isn't a *feeling* word, like, no psych textbook is going to have a chapter or diagnoses related to feeling weird, but, it kind of is a feeling. Right? Don't you think?" She tucks her bangs behind her ears again and stares at me, like she cares what I think, whether she's allowed to feel "weird."

"Of course it is. Weird is definitely a feeling."

"Right?" She flaps her hands down, palms up, onto the table. "*Weird* captures so much. It's a negative feeling, or at least not positive, and it's something you experience physically, like for me it's in my chest—my low chest, like between my sternum and my stomach. How about you?"

I think about it. "I feel weird higher, I think. In my throat."

"That's so interesting!" She touches her throat, as if imagining what it must be like to get your Weird Feels there. "I think weirdness is the feeling that comes before you have *other* feelings. It's the tunnel feelings go in to get sorted into their final place. It's a pre-feeling kind of feeling. Weirdness is how you feel, for example, in that short second after you drink a sip of milk and something's wrong but before you realize it's gone bad. You don't feel disgusted yet, you feel *weird*. Or, for example, when you're in chemistry class, and you take off your sweater because all the Bunsen burners are making it hot, and your old man chemistry teacher immediately comes over and points at the design on your T-shirt, the words that go right across your boobs, and says, 'I love this.' *Weird*. You feel weird and then you feel gross and it can take a whole week or even a month before you feel angry. You know?"

"I know," I say, because I know what she's talking about, even though I'd never thought about it that way or had a chemistry teacher stare at my boobs.

She smiles at me. "Thanks for understanding."

I smile back.

"Anyway. Weird. That's how I feel about doing the study. I know health studies are going on all the time, and most of them aren't exceptional in any way, well, at least not *these* days—but doesn't it seem like the incentives are a lot? Why is our participation worth so much? And the way that man was just *there* at the screening to deal with the wolf-shirt kid, like they *expected* that to happen, and then the questions that weren't even questions, and these assignments we have to do every day.

"And yet here I am, being so much like the wolf-shirt person myself—that's what you're thinking, right? And probably you are judging me, because that's how things are now—if you mention 'conspiracies,' you're 'crazy,' even though that's kind of the ironic beauty of the whole thing: It's easier for real conspiracy plots to exist because reasonable people refuse to see them because of the political 'team' it associates them with or whatever.

"But still. I can't help but think there's something strange about the study. I can't help feeling like a lot is at stake. My hackles are up. By which I mean what it *actually* means when hackles are up, not that terrible, misleading idiom that frames poor dogs as being aggressive. No. I'm feeling a little curious, alert, and maybe, mostly, a little afraid. And that's silly, right? Am I being paranoid? Not understanding stuff isn't a good reason to think something is *malicious*.

"Talking out loud like this to you, I'm answering my own questions. It's becoming clear to me that I've been reading too much history. It all probably feels weird simply because I'm doing something different. Doing anything out of the norm can feel weird. When they change the aisles at the grocery store—weird. When there's an assembly and the periods are seven minutes shorter—weird.

"Probably I'm doing what I always do, which is become so

obsessed with something that I overthink it, and then I get overwhelmed by it, and then I can't do it anymore. Which is why I'm doing this study in the first place."

She leans back. Her hair falls in front of her cheeks, and she crosses her arms. The fingers of her left hand twist the skin by her right elbow, release it, then twist it again until her skin turns white.

"You're doing the study because you overthink things?"

Her fingers release and grab at her elbow one more time before she slides both of her hands underneath her thighs. "Eh!" Her voice is suddenly cheery. "That's a long story. It will put us off our schedule. It's your turn! Thank you for listening and it's your turn, please. Please. Tell me what you're feeling."

I let my agenda refold along its creases. "Well, I think what you're feeling makes a lot of sense. Not that it needs to make sense. But I feel all of those things, too, to some degree."

She's nodding. "Thank you for saying that. Can I just say, you're better at this than I expected you to be. You're, I don't know, nice? Not that I expected you to be mean! You listen. You let me talk, and it worked! I feel better. I know that's what the plan was and the whole point of meeting here, but still, it's rare. It's rare to have someone listen and care about what you say. Not that you *do* care. No pressure to care! But you make me feel like I can be myself, like I don't have to try to act like some expectation you have of who I'm supposed to be, which is how most people make me feel, like last time with you thinking I would be a certain way because of origami. Anyway. I probably shouldn't have said that, too personal, right? But, it's also good to express gratitude for things, people. Because you never know . . ." Her lips twitch twice to the left. "There I go again! Back to you. What are you feeling?"

What am I feeling?

Mostly I am feeling things about Jane.

I love watching her talk, the way she turns her head back and forth, excited about everything. I love *how* she talks, with the words that spill out like there's an unlimited supply of thoughts in her brain. I love what she talks about, how it's all interesting, it's *ideas* and *feelings* and not play-by-plays of stuff that happened earlier today.

I love how her worn, loved sweater, its ripped shoulder, and her messy hair stand out against the background of this pristine, too-perfect mall.

I love how easily she talks about her feelings, mentions things like boobs, like everything is fair game, nothing is off-limits despite us having a literal set of rules that says almost everything is off-limits.

In a way, the real Jane is everything I had thought she would be, and also none of it, and also more of it—she's beyond time, beyond awkwardness, beyond the expectations I had for her and anyone could have for her, beyond rules despite her love of creating them.

Beyond. Jane is beyond.

So, I guess that's what I'm feeling.

"Um," I say.

"Close your eyes if it helps. Think about the pills. Think about the wolf-shirt kid."

I try. I try to take all the weirdness I've been feeling and boil it down to something small enough to put into words. "I feel fear, too. I don't like the pills. But mostly I feel like I'm going to do something wrong." I open my eyes.

Jane doesn't laugh or make any faces. "Something wrong like what?"

"I don't know. Which makes it worse. The fact that there isn't much to do wrong but I'll find a way."

"Mmm." She's leaning forward, her hands clasped on the table between us, the textbook pose of demonstrating full attention. She's probably sitting like that on purpose to make me feel listened to, and that makes me like her even more. "Mmm," she says again, "go on."

"Well . . ." My phone buzzes.

I've gotten an email. And everything I was feeling disappears: Jane, the study, gone. I feel nothing. I feel absolutely nothing.

THE EMAIL

The email address: naomi.le1124@gmail.com.
    My mother's name.
    And birthday.
    And in case I still had doubts about who this was, the subject: "Hello 'Wayne, this is from Your Mother."

LOOKING TIRED MEANS I LIKE YOU

"What is it?" Jane sits up straight. "What's wrong?"

Some of my ability to feel is coming back. It's painful, like after you lose blood flow in your foot.

The people at the table next to us leave. They've dropped bread crust under the table, and two birds, escaped from the PetSmart rabbit field, have swooped down and are fighting over it, tearing it apart. I feel like that. The bread crust.

"Hey." Jane scoots her chair an inch closer. " 'Wayne?"

I want to slide off my chair and join the actual bread crust on the floor.

I lock my phone so the screen goes dark. "Personal. Breaks rules."

Probably I should leave, because I can't stick to the agenda when I am a bread crust, but I'm not able to leave. Bread crusts don't have legs.

Jane is watching me. Her mouth keeps twitching to the left. "Okay, screw it. Screw it. Yes, the rules are important and I think they were working, but I can't just sit here while you're obviously in pain and not act like a real person about it. What's wrong? Or no pressure to tell me that, but, if you want to, forget the rules and go right ahead, okay? Whatever this is, this is more important than the rules."

Something about her saying that, backing off from her official-looking contract and official-looking agenda, her saying I am more important than her rules, her saying that I am important at all, it's too much. My eyes start to burn.

"Hey. Hey. Oh, 'Wayne. Oh, hey."

The sound of her chair legs, scooting even closer.

"It's okay. I'm okay. It's only an email.[13] I haven't even opened it yet. It surprised me."

Jane is much closer than before. I can see the pores of her nose and her freckles. My fingers are shaking, and I watch her observing that. She opens her mouth to say something, then shuts it. "All right."

My phone screen lights up with a text from Olive, and I see the email notification again.

"It's from my mother." I don't know why I say it. Jane doesn't know why an email from my mother would matter, that this is the first time I've heard from my mother in eight years, since the day she ran from our house, from me, screaming.

Jane gently puts a finger on the table next to my phone. "Do you want to open the email while I'm here?"

"I think I should go home," I say, even though the last place I want to go is home. Sometimes wanting to go home is an optimistic impulse.

"Oh." She pulls her finger back into a fist. "Okay."

---

13. A memory, freshly peeled: My mother and father, sitting next to me at the kitchen table, peanut butter hot chocolate in front of all of us.* Small plates, pushed to the side—crusty cake frosting on the edges and fork. A birthday. My seventh. "We debated this a lot," she's saying. "Whether it's too early. But I want you to have independence. Figure out who you are." My father hands me a wrapped box. "And we trust you," he says. It's a cell phone. "We set up your email account, too," she tells me, and shows me how to look at my email settings. "The only thing I don't want you to change is—we set ourselves up as starred contacts. That way, if you ever hear from us, you'll get an alert immediately." She takes out her own phone, types something, and my own phone buzzes. "See?"

* *Spoon with peanut butter dunked in cup of hot chocolate. The peanut butter does not come off the spoon, and if it does, it sits unmoving like a blobfish on the ocean floor. But we all liked it anyway.*

I flip the phone over so only the anglerfish, Olive's sticker choice,[14] is staring up at me, its giant teeth ready to gnash at my throat. An improvement. "I haven't heard from my mother since she left. I was eight."

"Do you know why she's . . . ?" Jane's finger points at the phone again, then retreats.

I shake my head.

We sit there, side by side, staring at the anglerfish sticker. Across the corridor, another vacuum competition has started. The crowd cheers with the rise and fall of the machines.

Jane's hand disappears into her lap. "My mom died three years ago."

She turns toward the PetSmart enclosure, which is in the process of opening. An employee is setting up ropes, letting the rabbits out of their hutches.

"She had OCD. It took her a long time to figure that out because her symptoms were mostly thought-related, rather than physical compulsions. And then when she did figure it out, she didn't want to take meds because she believed her thoughts were rational, like, it was *helpful* for her to be constantly visualizing the worst things that might happen to me and Dad." Jane sticks her hands under her hips. She closes her eyes, and at first it seems like she's done talking, but her lips are twitching, like they are working on what to say next. I wait.

She opens her eyes. "Then Dad found out he'd be losing his

---

[14]. Olive wants to be a marine biologist. What that meant for a couple of years was that we watched *Blue Planet* on repeat, and she decorated everything with deep-sea-themed stickers. She said giving me the anglerfish sticker—the ugliest sticker I have ever seen in my life—was a great honor, since it is one of her favorite fish. There's also a blobfish sticker on my bedroom door, right by the doorknob. Olive says this is not because I am a profoundly ugly gelatinous mass good for nothing but wallowing around on the ocean floor, though I do have a "tendency to wallow." She says it's because blobfish are super cool—blobfish evolved to survive under immense amounts of pressure. In fact, they collapse outside of it.

job at the end of the school year. The added stress, worrying about money—all of it made Mom's thoughts way worse. We'd be standing in line at a food truck and she would start crying. She said she couldn't help thinking about the people around her in the moment of their death, imagining, like, heart attacks or cancer in vivid detail. She finally agreed, Dad and I convinced her, to try the meds, and that first week . . . apparently there's a potential side effect where, when you first start taking them, antidepressants make you *more* suicidal."

A sound escapes me.

"Yeah." Jane pushes her bangs behind her ears. "Sorry. I didn't mean to make this about me . . ."

"It was similar with my mom. Kind of. She had problems with her medications, too."

Jane bites her lip and looks away.

In the vacuum store, a new winner is announced. Cheers erupt. People place orders for vacuums at the kiosks.

"I really, really don't like that aspect of the study," she says. "The random pills."

Jane looks back at me, and it's different. Steady and open and unselfconscious like we've known each other for years. She also looks tired, twenty times more tired than she did fifteen minutes ago, and I think, *When people trust you, that's the only time their eyes show you how tired they are inside.*

The Experience Center is crowded, sure, but it makes this table with her, at the Tiki Bar, an island of familiarity in an ocean of strangeness.

She reaches for the loop on the top of her backpack. "I should leave you alone so you can open that email. Listen, though. If you want to call or text me about it, you can. Then we can resume our nonpersonal agenda and rules next time?"

I don't want her to leave me alone. "That sounds good. Thanks."

"No, thank *you*. You did most of the listening. That's the hard part."

She stands and picks up her bag. I stand too.

"Okay." She shifts her weight. "I've got this weird urge to hug you goodbye. Even though I barely know you. And I don't like hugs."

Her mouth goes to the right. Her mouth goes left. My heartbeat speeds up.

She puts three fingers onto the edge of her lip, then moves them to her chin, then to her other wrist. She pinches her skin there. "I guess I want to say, again, thank you for listening. Good luck with your email. Even though luck is somewhat irrelevant. So." She waves her hand in a circle. "Talk to you soon."

Then she spins on her heel and marches past the vacuums, past the fake grass field of rabbits, and out of sight.

Even without her hug, I feel softer, calmer than I did before, as if the whole conversation had been an embrace.

LATER, MUCH LATER, FROM THE SAFETY OF MY BED, I OPEN THE EMAIL

My dearest special secret:

I am writing you from a train. We are somewhere in Arizona. The rocks loom around us like towering red saints. It's beautiful, and I'd love to spend hours describing it for you, but I know you weren't much of a reader (I wonder if you like reading now? So much I don't know), so I'm making you a video instead. Attached below.

With as much love as it is possible to love:

Mama

The thumbnail for the video is at the bottom of the email. There is her face.

There it is.

She's in a yellow dress, looking at the camera, holding a paper cup with a tea bag string draped over the side.

Seeing her face.

It's like stumbling across a movie that you loved as a kid. The one that you watched over and over. The one that your parents "accidentally deleted from Netflix."

You see it again ten years later and you can still say all the lines, predict the jokes.

You can't say whether you still like it or not, this movie. You *know* this movie, that's all you can say.

DOING NOTHING IS THE MOST YOU CAN DO

She's nervous. The angle of her head, the way she's rubbing her index finger against her middle finger on the side of the cup. Her gaze keeps flicking away from the camera.

"Hello, 'Wayne."

Her voice. It's more intense than seeing her face. Like a favorite song, it conjures smells, a place, a sense of time that has been lost.

She swallows. I swallow.

"First, I want to thank you for watching this video. I know we've been through a lot, by which I mean, I know I've put our family through a lot. Put *you* through a lot. You are probably very angry at me. Watching this video is probably very stressful for you. So, thank you."

She runs a hand across the top of her hair. Arizona's red rocks speed by in the window behind her head.

"Last week I emailed your father. I started a conversation about coming to visit. Visit *you*, that is. It's been a while since we've seen each other." She bites her lip. "Since . . . I . . . left . . . you. Since I left you. I've been working on taking responsibility for my actions.

"Your father told me that I needed to ask you about visiting. He's right. I should have contacted you also. Or *first*, even. I didn't want to talk to you, because—

"I love you so much. It would kill me—no, it wouldn't kill me—I'm also working on being careful about what I say . . ." She looks out the window. "It would be very, very hard for me to hear that you do not want to see me." She looks back again.

"It's also hard for me to acknowledge the things I did—it feels like those things were not me, that they were a different person. In some ways, that's what having a mental illness feels like. Like there's a separate person that comes in and takes over. And when you're back to yourself again, it doesn't feel like you have to take responsibility for what that other person did, because it wasn't you.

"But of course, it *wa*s you, *me*, hurting people I love. Even the person I love more than anything."

Her eyes fill. Her cheeks turn pink. She looks up at the ceiling. The train lists to the left and a tear leaks down her cheek. She swipes it away.

"These last eight years, I've done a lot of work. On myself. I'm on medication, or a cocktail of various medications, that work. They finally, actually work—I feel like I'm my real self, finally, most of the time. I do yoga. I am renting an apartment on my own. I have a job again—I'm not writing for *The Atlantic* anymore, just . . . writing reviews of computers for some affiliate marketing site."

She looks to the side. "I'm a little embarrassed about my job. But it's a job, and I've kept it. Plus, can you believe I'm writing reviews of computers? Me! The person who needed to take her laptop into a computer store for help with software updates. But probably you wouldn't remember that." Her eyes start filling with tears again.

"Anyway, I've been there almost a whole year. I know a lot about computers now. And they are sending me on this cross-country trip, to write articles about the rural communities' perspectives on computers. So that's nice." She smiles, sniffles. Swipes at her eyes with the back of her arm. Takes a long sip of tea.

"Look. What I guess I'm trying to say is that you have every right to be angry. To feel like you were abandoned. I . . . did . . . I did . . .

ab . . . abandon you." Tears escape this time and collect in a wrinkle next to her lip. She didn't have that wrinkle the last time I saw her.

"I'm sorry, and I want a chance to make it right. I think seeing you—getting to know you again, becoming a part of your life as best I can—is the way to do that. The way to start making things right.

"But I don't want to hurt you more than I have already. And if you're not ready to see me, then it won't do either of us any good." She nods once, as if making a decision, like Dad does. I wonder whether they got that from each other. The blanket I have on my lap suddenly doesn't seem warm enough.

"So, I want to leave this up to you. If you don't want me to come, I . . . I won't. Just respond to this email telling me 'No, don't come.'

"Though I guess probably that's a tough thing to write—it's asking a lot of you. Better idea: The default will be I'm coming, and any response from you is like a code for 'Don't come!' Like if you reply with a random word, *Porcupines!*, or anything, I'll know what you really mean.

"Oh gosh. Do you remember your porcupine Halloween costume? In second grade? You went into the backyard and found all those twigs, and we painted them black, and I spent hours gluing them to a sweatshirt. You looked . . ." She chokes back a sob. "So cute.[15]

"Anyway. I'm going to stop this video now. The conductor keeps glancing at me: I'm making him concerned. I—I think about you every day. And I love you as much as I've always loved you. I hope you know that. Though I know you probably *don't* know that. Which is my fault. I really hope that I will have a chance to help you know that in a couple weeks."

---

15. I do remember. We emerged from my room and Dad said I looked like a bush killed by wildfire or plague. "Very creative subject," he said, before kissing my mother on the cheek.

Then her body leans toward the camera. The video ends.

The water from Olive's shower is gurgling down the drain behind my wall. I feel like *I* need a shower now. Or a walk. Or a one-way ticket to, I don't know, Peru.

I sit there on my bed, staring at the last image of her, my mom, blurry as she leans to turn off the recording, her cheeks stained with tears, that wrinkle tucked into her cheek.

My finger hovers over the Reply button. I could send a blank email. Then she wouldn't come, and my life, my relationship with Dad, this whole health study thing, could go on as it was going on.

A strange feeling tugs at the bottom of my stomach.

I archive the email and open *Drone Wars Mobile* instead.

AWARD FOR BEST SCREENPLAY

Setting: Dinner table

Me: I got an email today.
Dad: Okay.
Me:
Me:
Olive: From who?
Me: My mother.
Olive: Really?
Dad: She contacted you, then.
Me: . . . That's what I sa . . .
Dad's Face:
Me: Yes, yes, she did.
Olive: What did she say?
Me: She wants to come and visit.
Dad: Good.
Me: Good?
Olive: What did you say?
Me: Nothing.
Dad's Face: DNS.
Me: Which means she's going to come.
Dad: Oh.
Dad's Face: EoFF.

Dad: Good.
Me: Why do you keep saying "good"? Why is that *good*?
Dad:
Dad:
Olive: I wish my mother could come and visit.
Me: You can have mine.
Dad: Eat before your food gets cold.

SEE YOU LATERGRAM

From *Allegorist*
Lyrics by Clarissa Patel

> *Lying on my couch alone*
> *Three weeks since your last DM*
> *The constant buzzing of my phone*
> *Is all your posts with the nouvelle femme.*
>
> *That's how I find out after the fact*
> *Your portrait of us as perfection*
> *Was elaborate fiction, an act,*
> *Each kiss a step toward rejection*
>
> *Whispered: You're an artist.*

The last memory I have of my mother. From the living room window seat. I'd been coloring, maybe. Harvey my stuffed hippo on my lap.

She is standing in the hallway with my father. Her pale face is blotchy and wet. I don't know why she's crying. She was crying a lot in those days.

"Naomi," Dad said. "Nay." He tried to hold her arms.

"Don't touch me." She pushes him.

"It's *me*, Naomi."

"What does that even mean?"

>Chorus:
>
>So I'm sending out the LaterGrams.
>I'll see you later, fam.
>The outtakes that were really the intakes
>Let the world see the source of my heartbreak.
>
>By posting up the LaterGrams
>Show you as traitor, fam,
>See you later means never-never
>Ever come back, goodbye.

Then somehow she had raw meat in her hands. She must have been making dinner. She threw one handful at my dad's chest. She threw the other at the wall. It stuck for a second. Then it slurped off.

I wanted to hide behind the couch. I was afraid to move. I slid closer to the curtains and tucked my feet behind them.

The meat blood oozed down the wall in thick droplets.

>In the selfies we passed over
>The ones we chose not to post
>Your closed-off look betrays
>You were always a ghost.
>
>Whoops, my fingers slipped
>I'm spilling the dirty tea
>And posting the more honest pics
>That show our true reality

> *. . . and filling up your feeeeeed.*
> *(Key change, bridge)*

She had a suitcase. It must have already been packed and stashed in the hall closet. A red one. It matched the red still staining her palms. It had a little yellow scarf tied around the handle.

"I can't do this anymore." She turned to me, looked right at me. "Remember this, 'Wayne. You can't force yourself to be natural."

She's sobbing now. She says something else. I can't understand. The door slams.

I try to run after her. Dad blocks the door.

"Let her go."

I run back to the window seat.

She gets smaller and smaller. The yellow scarf blows off her suitcase and into a bush.

My fingers run over and over the soft inside of my hippo's ears.

> *I know I should drink less rosé,*
> *I know I should turn off alerts.*
> *But I've got a lot to say*
> *In my portrait of the artist as a huge young jerk.*
> *Whispered: That's you.*

A while later, days, maybe, or months, I don't know, Dad said he didn't think she was coming back.

"It's scary to not understand something," he said. "It's worse when that something is yourself."

I didn't understand what he meant. I still don't.

> *(Chorus)*

Dad couldn't get the stains off the wall. He repainted the walls white. Not only that wall. All the walls in the house. The house smelled like paint for months.

> *See you later means never-never*
> *Ever come back.*
> *(Whispered:) Goodbye.*

HOPKINS STUDY APP

You are a lost child in a large store.

As you watch the screen, obstacles will come toward you—strangers, shopping carts, and more. Press the arrow key that would move you in the opposite direction from these hazards.

The goal is to find your parent or guardian! They will keep you safe from the dangers of the Walmart.

Your final score will be tallied based on your accuracy and speed.

Remember to *Have Fun!*

BINARY REALITY:

How Small-Town Communities Think & Feel About Digital Technology

An Oral History, by Naomi Le

I still remember the day our town got broadband. That's not uncommon, I think most of us remember, it was a big occasion. At that time most of us had computers, but no internet, and those of us that did have internet, it wasn't fast enough to load half the websites.

Angel Desoto: Needles, California

REMINDER: HOPKINS STUDY APP

Please complete today's assignment by 11:59 p.m. EST.

REMINDER: HOPKINS STUDY APP

You have 1 hour left to submit today's assignment. Please complete the assignment now by <u>clicking here</u>.

REMINDER: HOPKINS STUDY APP

You have 10 minutes remaining to submit today's assignment. Please complete the assignment now by <u>clicking here</u>. This is your final reminder.

THE MORNING AFTER

I wake up the next morning sprawled across my bed horizontally, still dressed.

From my pillow, my phone buzzes. A text from Kermit, wanting to know if I want to come over for a 2v2 this afternoon.

"Yep," I reply. If Kermit is good for anything, it's a distraction.

Then, from somewhere downstairs, a voice that sounds vaguely familiar.

DISRUPTIONS

Parked outside my house, a blue Subaru hunches in the shade of our oak tree. The bumper sticker is visible from my upstairs window: "I work in a MIND field."

The voice downstairs speaks again. Dr. Charlotte.

My phone buzzes with another text from Kermit, and I now see the four missed alerts for my study assignment.

In the app, the assignment is grayed out. There's a red padlock icon next to it and the text "MISSED," which looks very permanent and very bad.

I move my legs out of my bed, but the upper half of my body remains immobile. My internal organs have morphed into a concrete-like sludge.

A pattern on my ceiling makes the down-sloping shape of one of Mr. Houston's graphs.

Charlotte's voice again. An unintelligible mumble from Dad in response.

She'll have already told him, of course. His face will be in polite guest mode, waiting to explode into DNS later when he's alone with me, when he'll say, "I'm not feeling like cooking for some reason. Leftovers tonight."

I heave my concrete-filled torso to the door. All I can catch is an occasional word, and trumpety music from Olive's TV show. I creep down to the landing. The stair creaks.

"That you, kiddo?" Dad says. " 'Wayne?"

Kiddo?

"Come down here. You have a visitor."

On the mat by the door sits an extra pair of shoes—high-heeled blue ones.

I go down the stairs as slowly as I can, but the staircase has gotten much shorter since yesterday.

There, sitting on my living room sofa in stockinged feet, in a crisp blue suit, is Dr. Charlotte.

"'Wayne," she says, emphasizing the invisible *D*, exactly like she did last time.

Dad guides me into the room, his face—as expected—arranged into his *we have guests* façade. "This is Dr. Charlotte from the Hopkins health study."

"We've already met." Charlotte stretches out her hand for me to shake.

"Oh?" says Dad.

"Hi, Dr. Charlotte." The words are sandpaper in my throat.

"Come, sit with us." She pats the open couch cushion next to her. I sit.

Dad is dressed in his Sunday attire, which is the same as his workday attire—crisply ironed slacks and button-down, argyle socks—but without a tie. He looks underdressed next to Charlotte. I'm extremely conscious of my dirty, slept-in T-shirt and jeans.

They both have empty coffee mugs next to their chairs.

"Now that 'Wayne is here, I can speak to why I'm here, if that's all right with you?"

"Absolutely!" Dad brushes invisible dust off his knees.

Charlotte angles toward me. "As I've already said to your dad, sorry to surprise you with a visit. I know Sunday morning is a hard time for handling impromptu drop-ins."

"No," Dad says. "It's an honor to have you. Any day, anytime. It is nothing compared with all the hard work you are doing."

"Thank you, Peter."

No one calls my father Peter. He is always Mr. Le. He makes sure of it.

Charlotte turns her empty coffee mug so the handle is facing away and parallel to the edge of the table. "Unfortunately, something has happened that has made an in-person visit necessary. Something unexpected and, well, frankly, negative. Something that needed to be handled face-to-face. So, 'Wayne . . ."

"I'm sorry." I jump to my feet. "I promise I won't do it again. Please, let me keep going. Please."

Charlotte blinks. The muffled trumpet music from Olive's *Fuzzy Cats Pow Pow Pow* show fills the space.

"What are you talking about?"

I hesitate.

"Did you forget to do your assignment?"

"Well . . ."

"You forgot your assignment?" Dad says, and there it is, the fully formed DNS, earlier than expected.

But Charlotte smiles. "Oh, honey. We're working with teenagers. Of course we've accounted for people missing an assignment or two. It's not the biggest deal in the world."

"Oh." I sit back down, even though I'm highly aware that "not biggest" doesn't mean "not big."

"Don't worry." She's looking directly at my eyes, unblinking. The concrete sludge inside my stomach stirs.

"As I was saying, there has been some negative news, so I needed to ask you questions in person."

She leans down to where, by the side of the couch, she's stashed a leather bag. From the bag, she pulls a bundle of black and red cords. She finds a connector and plugs it into her phone. She points at my right hand, where it's currently gripping my right knee.

I give it to her. Her fingers are cool and dry. The edges of her nails nick my finger pads, and it's very difficult to leave my hand in hers when every instinct in my body is telling me to rip it away, even if I lose some fingers in the process.

In one swift motion, she's affixed the alligator clips to two of my fingers. Then she returns my hand to my knee.

Dad leans forward. "A lie detector?"

"We prefer to call it a 'truth encourager.'" She opens something on her phone that fills its screen with colorful shapes. "Less intimidating."

"This is amazing," Dad says. "Amazing."

Charlotte clicks a yellow hexagon, which transforms into a dozen dancing lines. Then she angles her screen away from me. "'Wayne, just like at the screening, first I'll remind you that there's no right or wrong, all I want is the truth." She waits, in case I want to respond to that. I don't. "I want to talk to you about mistakes. Admitting to your mistakes can help us rectify any issues as soon as possible and limit all possible consequences."

"Consequences?"

"First, some calibration. Name?"

It's amazing how having someone analyzing what you're saying makes you forget the most basic things.

"'Wayne!" my father says.

"'Wayne. 'Wayne Le."

"High school name?"

"Glenville High."

She keeps looking between my eyes and her phone. Dad is nodding with each question, enjoying this whole experience, which makes me feel *weird*.

Charlotte says, "Did you or did you not fail to complete the Hopkins assignment last night?"

The clips on my fingers dig in. "But I thought you said this *wasn't* about me missing the assignment last night."

Dad says, "Just answer the question."

"But I already admitted to it!"

Charlotte smiles without looking away from her phone. "Would you like me to ask the question again?"

A truck rattles down our street, moving too fast. A cat yowls cartoonishly on Olive's show.

"I did. I did fail to complete the assignment last night. I promise I won't do it again. I promise I'm not hiding anything!"

"Have you ever before failed to complete the assignment?"

"No!"

"*Why* did you fail to complete the assignment?"

"I fell asleep. I told you this already. You said not to worry about it!"

"Have you ever, for any reason, removed the wristband after starting the study?"

"Only to shower."

Charlotte looks up at me. "You're supposed to leave it on while you shower." She looks back at her screen. "Have you ever been confronted by anyone, known or stranger, requesting information about the study you are participating in?"

"I mean . . ."

Charlotte affixes her shark stare back on my eyes.

". . . My father?" Dad's chair groans, but I don't look. "And my friend Kermit."

Charlotte's gaze does not waver, not even to check those wavy lines on her screen.

"You're sure there's been no one else?"

"Uh..."

"Remember: The faster we figure out your mistakes, the faster we can remedy them."

I look away and focus on a dark spot on the wall, where Dad's paint didn't quite cover up my mother's meat stains. "Olive. And a girl in my class, Jane?"

"Hm."

Above the stain, there's another stain—that one from a water leak.

"Was I not supposed to talk to people? I'm really sorry. I thought it was okay; the other participants at school are all talking about it way more than I am. I'll stop."

Charlotte wiggles the wire that goes into her phone. "This has nothing to do with whether you've talked to people. It's whether anyone has *solicited* the information. Anyone who has seemed *overly* interested in the study. *Think*, 'Wayne."

The clips on my fingers feel like they're getting warm.

There is no right or wrong.

"I can't think of anyone overly interested. Well, Kermit is overly interested, but that's how Kermit is, I promise, he's interested in everything, it's kind of annoying actually, but..."

"That's fine. That's enough." Charlotte unclips the sensors from my fingertips. "Thank you."

"Yes?" Dad leans forward in his chair.

"All is well."

Dad runs a hand through what little hair he has.

Charlotte wraps her cords into a tidy bundle and drops it into her bag. She checks a notification on her phone, then puts that into her bag, too. "I don't want to scare you. But we are getting word that there are some people out there"—she waves her hand at the windows—"who are being . . . let's call it 'disruptive.' They're trying to convince people to sabotage the study—give false answers, do the assignments incorrectly, and so on. They are not dangerous in an immediate sense—they aren't going to, you know, *stab* you"—she chuckles—"so like I said, I don't want you to be *scared*, but messing with a scientific procedure is always dangerous, perhaps more so than things like bullets and knives. So if anyone should seem overly interested, or otherwise disruptive, I need you to contact us immediately. We've added a contact form to the app. Any questions?"

"What about— Am I not supposed to talk about the study anymore? Or about this visit?"

"We are happy to sign an NDA," Dad says.

"Oh, no," she says, her demeanor suddenly cool and light, like a gust tossing flurries onto a wide, snowy plain. "You're welcome to. What we are doing, it isn't a secret at all. Just a health study. Important, of course, meaningful, but nothing to hide. We just want it to not get . . . disrupted." She picks something invisible off the edge of a fingernail, flicks it onto the floor. "That's all for today. Thank you, Peter, for the coffee. Thank you, 'Wayne, for your cooperation and time."

"It's been an honor." Dad leans across the table to shake her hand with both of his. "Thank you for forgiving my son. He will not miss an assignment again. 'If there were a season for gratitude, they'd show it more,' right?" He meets her unrelenting gaze.

I brace myself for the wrinkled forehead, the fake smile. But she tips an imaginary hat before standing. " 'Only the farmers have won.' *The Magnificent Seven*. An American classic."

Dad grins, delighted. He signals that I should walk her to the door.

"Thanks for coming," I say.

"My pleasure." She slides her feet into her shoes and steps onto the porch.

As she takes the single step down, I think of something. "But why?"

She turns back.

"Why would anyone want to disrupt the study?"

"Oh." Her mouth purses for a second before relaxing back into that placid snowfield smile. "Just for fun. You know. Some people just have strange ideas of fun."

Her smile, it is so still, the snow that the breeze has tossed, and that now has drifted, and fallen, and sits quietly in perfect puffs, as perfect as her unwavering, unblinking gaze.

SOMETHING FISHY & AN AFICIONADO

When I'm done talking, Kermit stands up from where he was sitting, cross-legged on his messy floor, and flops into his oversize throne of a desk chair.[16]

"Hmm." He lets himself slowly twirl. "Hmm."

"So?" I say, trying not to sound desperate. "Do you think it's possible? That the study is bigger than we thought? That it's like the ideas from the conspiracy theorists you were hoping to sell info to? That it's like that wolf-shirt kid said, and about more than teen heart health?"

"Hm."

"And like what Jane said, about how the high value of the incentives shows that the study means a lot to someone?"

Kermit pushes off his desk and twirls in his chair some more. "Hmmm."

"That's all you're going to say?"

"No." He spins again. "But this situation requires careful thought. Hmm."

I try to make myself comfortable on the tiny patch of carpet I've claimed amidst the piles of screws and wires.

Kermit has been uncharacteristically calm, almost disinterested.

---

16. Kermit's house is two blocks from my house and was built around the same time using identical prefab units. The units were configured as a ranch instead of a Cape Cod, but the rooms are the same as the rooms in my house, just put together in a different layout.

The scent of The Domestic Hunter hangs heavy over the room, mixing unpleasantly with the delightful smell coming from the kitchen.

To make matters worse, on the music-making table by Kermit's door, giant speakers are playing a DJ Kismet original—as in, Kermit wrote the song.[17]

The DJ Kismet song goes through four identical loops before Kermit's chair slows to a stop. "First of all, yes, it's possible that the study is about more than your heart health. *Most* things in the world are *possible*."

I glare at him.

"The question we want to ask, what we *should* be asking, is, is it *likely*." He nods conclusively.

"Well?"

He lifts the lever on the side of his chair so air puffs out and he comes down to my level. "This is where we have to be careful, my disciple. We must not jump to conclusions. Especially in situations like the current one, where we both have something to gain if it is true. That is how wolf-shirted tyrants are born. So, no. Overall, I would say it is *un*likely."

"So you don't think a person spontaneously showing up at my house to give me a polygraph test was at least a little bit, a tiny teensy-weensy bit, weird?"

"Using sensors doth not maketh a person weirdith, my friend." Kermit slowly rotates his hand until his finger is pointing at the corner of his wall of sneaker boxes, where a small blue light is blinking. His hand rotates some more, until it's pointing to a green light glowing from under his bed. Then his hand opens wide and makes a sweeping gesture at his whole floor, which, as already mentioned,

---

17. "Classical-EDM-Fusion" is how Kermit self-defines his genre. "Better-Turned-Off" is how I do.

is covered in electronic parts, minus the six-inch-wide pathway from his door to his desk, and the small square that I've made for myself to sit in.

I flick a screw at his feet, which are cloaked in yellow low OGs, despite his house being, like mine, a no-shoes household.

"The thing that I'm confused about, though, as a self-proclaimed *aficionado*—I will modestly refrain from using the word *expert*—of sensors myself, is why they needed to come to your house to use their lie detector on you . . ."

"So you *do* agree! It's a least a *little* . . ."

Kermit raises his hand. "It's weird because they already have that gray band. Which should be able to monitor everything they need." His hand, still raised, turns back into a pointer finger that angles toward my wrist. "With no need for in-person equipment."

He smiles as he watches my understanding solidify. "Correct, Disciple. Something doesn't add up. The math ain't mathing. As Kermit sees it, there are two possible explanations:

"The first is that this Dr. Charlotte wasn't honest about why she was there. It wasn't to administer you a lie detector test. She was there for some other reason—the lie detector thing being a flashy coverup—and if that's the case, we must wonder . . . what was the real reason?

"The second option is that the reason for her visit *was* the polygraph, but if that's true, then that tharr wristband ain't monitoring your pulse. Which means we have to ask, what does the wristband *actually* do?" He taps a fingertip on his chair arm. "It could also be both."

"All of that still sounds suspicious to me."

"It is, at least, *intriguing*."

A wave of energy tingles down my arms. "So how do we figure out which *intriguing* option it is?"

"That"—Kermit pulls his chair lever and puffs back to desk height—"I'm not sure of yet."

On his stereo, a new DJ Kismet song starts playing.

I pick up random parts from the floor and shove screws into holes, stick electrodes into boards, while trying to focus on helpful ideas. Instead, my mind keeps going to Jane, and whether Charlotte met with her, too, and whether I'm allowed to tell Jane about it despite Charlotte saying I could tell people, in which case do I trust her to not tell others that I told her, and whether I *should* tell Jane about it or if it will simply scare her when she's already nervous about exactly this, and Kermit is saying it's not a big deal anyways.

I swipe the pile of parts off my knee. "Either way, they lied about something."

Kermit frowns at me. He doesn't like it when I interrupt his thinking.

"Isn't that inherently bad?"

"Ah, ah, ah. Lies, in this instance, are like secrets. And secrets, like sensors, are not inherently bad. Sometimes, secrets are necessary to accomplish great things. Look at birthday gifts. Surprise parties. Nondisclosure agreements on brilliant new AI advancements.

"A scientific study with humans? I'd guess they need to have lots of secrets to make it work. Even subconscious desire for certain results can change the outcome."

I remember, then, how Charlotte said even *she* didn't know what the study was about. "Right."

"So, no, the study is not inherently bad, just because something is secret. Just more *intriguing*."

"Are you saying you're 'overly interested'?"

He rolls his eyes. "Let me focus. And don't break my diodes."

Then he pushes off one more time. His chair makes soft squeaking sounds as he revolves.

One of his diodes pokes me through my jeans. "Well..."

Kermit throws eye daggers at my head.

"It's going to be pretty difficult to figure out alternative reasons for Charlotte coming to my house. But this wristband is right here. And..." I pretend to study the offending diode. "... also right here, conveniently in the same room as the wristband, is a self-proclaimed *aficionado* of sensors. One who might have the tools and knowledge to figure out what this wristband actually does."

Kermit's daggers soften into surprise, which widens into an uncontrolled, maximally excited grin.

BLIPPITY BLAH

A few hours later, and no progress has been made.

Kermit has slid off his chair and onto the floor, where he's arranging wires in a breadboard to spell out BLAH.

My gray wristband has been poked, prodded, waved in circles around the open Hopkins app, scanned with blue light, and bombarded with magnets, all while still attached to my wrist. Everything had zero effect, aside from making my forearm sore. Kermit has also spent at least an hour scouring forums, looking for anyone reporting a similar truth-encouragement session, with no luck.

The delicious smell of whatever Mrs. Shah is baking in the kitchen is getting stronger. I realize I haven't eaten anything today.

"Should we stop?"

Kermit sighs. "Maybe it's a camera?"

"Because my leg is so very worth studying."

Kermit looks at the wristband resting on top of my thigh. "Right." He picks up a tiny metal bit from the pile next to me and holds it to the light before tossing it into a different pile.

A pan clangs in the kitchen. Whatever has been baking is complete.

"It must be the other answer, right? The wristband tracks my pulse, but the polygraph test was a fake. Which means they had another reason for visiting. Because if this band did anything else, you'd have figured it out by now."

Kermit falls backward onto his piles of parts. Something crunches. He moans. Then, suddenly he pops back up to sitting. He grabs at his phone.

"What is it? You figured it out?"

He types something frantically. "Almost forgot to set my alarm for a Jordans drop."

It's my turn to moan. "Maybe we should talk to other kids in the study? Compare experiences?"

"I guess. I can reach out to Bryce or something, I need to connect with him anyway. He owes me for some Airs. Though knowing Bryce, if this happened to him, we will all know too much about it by lunch tomorrow. The fact that no one has posted about it online—I don't know. Makes it seem like it wasn't widespread."

"Or the researchers are removing posts from the internet?"

"Hopkins employees are not going to have that much power." He tosses his phone away and falls back into his crunchy parts.

DJ Kismet originals continue to thump at us.

"Can we turn this off?" I gesture at his turntables. "Not that I don't love it"—even though Kermit knows how I feel about DJ Kismet.

Without looking, Kermit grabs a terminal block from one of the piles near his hand. He throws it toward his speakers. It hits the wall, then clanks down onto the table of music equipment. The music keeps playing.

"Remarkably," I say, "that had zero effect on the—"

"Shh!" Kermit's up on his elbows. He's staring at where the terminal block fell, his throwing arm still half raised.

Suddenly, he jumps toward his table of audio equipment. He lands on one of his floor piles. Metal bits fly every which way. He grabs a cord from a giant microphone and jams its plug into his laptop. The laptop screen displays a green line that bounces in time with the noise of his clearing space on the table. "Come here!" He grabs my arm and pulls me toward him.

"Ow! Please remember I'm not wearing shoes because *I actually follow your house rules.*"

"SHHH." He thrusts my wrist, the one with the gray band, right in front of the microphone.

"Wha—"

"SHHHH." Kermit uses his free hand to turn audio knobs. Then he stands completely still. The green line goes flat, flat, flat.

Until.

Blip.

It spikes. Barely there, only a millimeter or two high, but it's clear: a tiny spike, a sharp, short peak.

Three seconds later:

Blip.

And three seconds later, again:

Blip.

Kermit slams the laptop shut, springs over to the light switch, and plunges the whole room into darkness.

CALM BEFORE THE STORM

Kermit waves me through his doorway and down the hallway.

"What was—"

Kermit looks back at me and shakes his head once.

He gestures me toward the kitchen, where Mrs. Shah is leaning on the counter, her back to us.

The Shah family kitchen, like Kermit's room, is "decorated" with sensors.[18] Monitors hung around the cooking area report on the oven's temperature (358 degrees F) as well as the humidity and amount of light. There's also one dedicated to playing an endless stream of Ghibli movies, Mrs. Shah's guilty pleasure.[19]

The kitchen is warm. The plate cooling on the counter is filled with uneven yellow clumps—muthiya, my favorite.

But my stomach can no longer process food when it's busy processing whether my wristband *has a pulse*.

Kermit takes his phone out of his pocket and places it on the table. He indicates that I should do the same.

---

18. While the rooms in this house are the same as in mine, the interior decorating more closely resembles a spaceship. Or, perhaps more accurately, a pastel linoleum relic that has been hooked up to life support. Seemingly arbitrary screens and blinking lights accessorize the sparse, simple furniture. Through the kitchen window, you can see their orange tree. There is a blinking light nestled between the roots. I don't question Kermit about how or why this tree not only survives in our climate but also produces bountiful, juice-filled fruits. I also do not eat said fruits.

19. Kermit set up the monitors a few years ago for Mother's Day, though he confided to me that it was really for himself. "Food comes out better when she's thinking about, and controlling, the environmental variables. And I'm the one who has to eat her cooking." To me, though, her food has always been perfect. When you eat it, you feel like you belong.

Act normal, he mouths at me.

Then he reaches an arm past his mother to grab a piece of muthiya. Mrs. Shah slaps Kermit's hand. "It's not dinner yet."

"You know 'Wayne loves these. This is for 'Wayne." He pops it into his mouth.

Mrs. Shah spins around. " 'Wayne! I didn't know you were here. You want to sit? Eat?" She grabs a plate from a cabinet and stacks it full. The steam dances above her hands. "How lucky that I am making muthiya today, and you are here. I haven't seen you in weeks. How's school? How's Olive?"

I look at Kermit, unsure if I'm allowed to respond.

"Mama," he says, in the special voice he uses only with his mother, "if my phone dings, will you come get me?"

"Take your phone with you."

"Mama, please?" Kermit reaches for the plate, which Mrs. Shah deftly moves away. "We're very busy and trying to limit our distractions."

Mrs. Shah shakes her head. "Always so busy, you boys, running around, looking at this and that. Fine. Here." She shoves the plate into my chest. "These are for *'Wayne.* Keshav, you can have yours at dinner. Okay? Hey. Hey! Look at me, Keshav. You hear me? Okay?"

"Okay, Mama. But you won't forget to get me, right? If my phone dings? Especially if you see it's a notification from GOAT."

Mrs. Shah presses her hand to my arm. "Always good to see you. Keep staying around my Keshav, please. You keep him good. Unless he eats your muthiya, in which case, please kick him out of my house."

"Mama?"

"Yes, I *know*, Keshav. I won't forget. Not like you need more shoes."

Kermit waves me toward the opposite doorway.

Mrs. Shah gasps. "Keshav, what is this I see? Sneakers inside?"

"They are *new*, Mama. Never worn them outside."

She swats at him with the hand towel.

"D, let's go!"

"Always good to see you, too, Mrs. Shah." I give her a quick hug, and she squeezes me tight, and it gives me a momentary break from thinking about how the wristband, too, squeezes.

"D!" Kermit scurries down the hallway. He leads me to a part of the house, to a doorway, where I've never been.

In front of the door, in the doorframe, a pink gauze curtain waves lightly. Kermit pushes it aside, puts his ear to the door, turns the knob, and peeks through the crack.

"All clear." He takes the plate out of my hands. Then he steps inside.

THE SECRET LANGUAGE OF TECHNOLOGIES

The room is nearly empty, but it's not a litter-box room. It's not abandoned. The room feels loved.

The floor is wood, shiny and light, reflecting the sun from the large, high windows. There are many purple pillows pressed against a wall made of square glass tiles, identifying this build-a-house box as the equivalent of my house's kitchen. Another wall has been covered in mirrors, and the last two are painted purple, a shade lighter than the pillows.

"Not supposed to eat in here." Kermit grabs a pillow and sinks onto it, positions the plate between us on the floor. "But we need to be in here to talk, and our talk requires brains, and our brains require food, so . . . law of requirement." He picks up a piece of muthiya and bites. Crumbs fall onto the perfectly clean floor.

I point to my mouth, requesting permission to speak.

He nods.

"Why do we have to be in here to talk?"

He holds up a finger as he takes another bite. "Mmm. These came out good this time."

"And what was that back there? Why'd you turn off your lights? Does my wristband have a heartbeat? Is it . . ." I roll one of the pillow's tassels between my fingers. ". . . is it alive?"

Kermit does not laugh. I swallow.

He points at the plate. "Aren't you going to eat? My mom would not be happy if you didn't eat any of these." He waggles a lump of muthiya in front of my face.

I slap his hand away.

He sighs and explains that in an empty room, there is no technology. No smart devices. No cameras or mics. And that matters because my wristband, while it is not going to eat my arm, is a technological beacon.

I run my finger through my pillow tassel, only to realize that I've tied it into knots. "So, my wristband is not alive?"

"Technically that depends on how loose your definition of *sentience* goes." Kermit's sneaker toes bounce three times. "But, eh, most people would say no. Not alive."

"That's good."

"Depends on the looseness of your definition of *good*."

"It's not good because the wristband isn't monitoring my pulse and blood pressure? And that's a lie?"

Kermit tilts his head back and forth. "I meeeean . . . the wristband *might* be monitoring those things, too. Even if not directly, it's probably able to get that data from other tech that it's talking to. But I would say it's a more generalized monitoring of"—he swings his whole arm in a circle—"all of you and your life." Kermit looks pleased by this turn of events, not unlike my dad watching me go through the polygraph test.

"They're spying on me?" Something inside me twists, like a sharp turn on the left joystick before your drone crashes into a wall.

Kermit shrugs. "Eh." He picks at a bead that's loose on one of the pillow's tassels. "Your whole life is being spied on anyway. Mostly for targeted advertising, but"—he shrugs again—"same-same." He jingles the bead up and down the tassel. "Speaking of marketing, you haven't heard any dinging from the kitchen, have you?" He stands up, opens the door, sticks his head out into the hallway.

Our earlier conversation trickles back to me. Secrets aren't inherently bad. Lots of things need to be kept secret to work. Sometimes those things are good things. Impressive things. "So I . . . do you think I should quit?"

"On the contrary." Kermit taps me on my wristband as he sits back down. "That technology is costly to develop. I hate to admit this, but you were right. Something important is going on here. Something big. That's why I brought us in here to talk—I don't want them to know that we know. Secrets that mean that much to someone?" He lifts his eyebrows twice in a row. "They are worth a lot. You know what I always say. *Value* is spelled I-N-F-O-R . . ."

"You do always say."

"Annnd if they *do* turn out to be bad secrets—which doesn't mean *dangerous* secrets, mind you—revealing those secrets is worth even more." He does not entirely conceal what sounds very much like a maniacal giggle.

"So you're saying . . ."

He taps his fingertips together. "That's right, my apprentice. Valuable, showstopping, sneaker-funding secrets. And you and me? We're gonna figure them out."

A scene floats into my imagination. I'm standing on a stage. People are cheering. *Thousands* of people are cheering.

Wait. No, it's not a stage. It's my front lawn, and I am walking toward my house. Only two people are there, and neither one is cheering. My father turns to Olive. His lips form the words "There he is. My son." Then they turn up into a smile.

HOPKINS STUDY APP

Today is a writing exercise. Sorry! No one likes those. Don't worry, though, it will be quick.

Imagine a friend of yours has an idea. It is a bad idea. You know it is bad.

Now for the fun part!

Please list three ways you would tell your friend that they are wrong.

BINARY REALITY:

How Small-Town Communities Think & Feel About Digital Technology

An Oral History, by Naomi Le

The government has been a real help to us. The recent focus on closing the "digital divide," they call it. They make sure all our kids have laptops, have started initiatives in our schools to get our youth up to speed, make sure they know how to AI.

    We're starting to see the results. My grandkids, they have friends they've never met, through those games they play. They like that one with the little airplanes. *Drones*. I hear them having real conversations over their headsets with people in New York! Tokyo! I wish I had had that as a kid. It's going to make life so much easier for them when they grow up. They'll have connections. And me, I'm going to benefit, too. I've put all of our savings into The Bitcash.

Sakari Collins: Skull Valley, Arizona

A PLAN TO PLAN THE PLAN

Jane's head is bent over the papers I handed her five minutes ago. Around us, the Experience Center swirls with activity. This afternoon the mall is running a trick-or-treat experience, where kids can rent costumes and visit participating stores for promotional giveaways.

There's also a coffee company doing a Halloween-themed promotion at the Tiki Bar. People chatter as they wait for drinks like chocolate-peanut-butter lattes and nougat-bar cappuccinos. The espresso machine whirs constantly, and occasionally a barista screams out a name.

Jane seems oblivious to it all. Every so often, she squints as she puzzles over my handwriting.

On those papers I wrote down everything I could remember about last weekend's visit from Dr. Charlotte and her truth encourager and everything Kermit and I concluded about the wristband being a beacon.

I wrote it by hand, with a pen, while sitting in the back of my closet. It took three sessions over the week. My whole arm cramped.

I've also been placing myself in unusually public places around school, hoping to hear Bryce's loud voice announcing how his "*selection*" for the study had become even more personalized with a visit to his house. But all I've ended up hearing are Bryce's detailed play-by-plays of basketball practices, spiced with complaints about the team missing Dave Appleright, all punctuated with the acrid scent of Bryce's styling gel.

Behind Jane's hair, I can see enough of her mouth to know that she's started chewing on her bottom lip.

She turns to the last page, on which I'd written the plan Kermit and I came up with—how I would stay in the study to figure out what was going on and potentially gain information even more valuable than the incentives.

Jane finally looks up. "Well. That was interesting."

"'Interesting'?"

Her gaze is resting on something over my left shoulder. Her right forefinger taps the top of the papers. Her lips twitch to the left.

I fidget with the edge of my sleeve. "Should we go talk outside? Where there's not . . ." I indicate my wristband.

Jane folds the papers in half. "Too many smart cars and video cameras and phones. No. No good. Follow me." She springs from her chair, loops her little satchel over her wrist, and marches toward the department store at one of the mall's ends. In the wall, there's a green metal door. It looks like a staff-only exit. Jane pulls it open.

Cold moisture seeps up the dark, concrete stairwell.

"Are we allowed to . . ."

She thumps down the stairs, letting the door slam. The darkness consumes us, except for a soft green glow emanating from somewhere distant.

"Where are . . ."

"The basement."

The green light glows stronger at the bottom of the stairs, and it leads us down the hallway, if *hallway* is the appropriate term for the rubble-esque jumble of concrete pillars and walls.

It's like a ghost mall. A mall that someone forgot to finish. It's space that was forgotten, and then forgotten again, and then maybe remembered, but incorrectly. And then forgotten again. A litter-box room on steroids.

There are store-like spaces, sort of, their edges demarcated by the lightly green-glowing concrete walls. Crumbling plaster columns outline squares where storefront windows might have been. Some rooms are stuffed with old shelving units and posters and mannequins.

Or bodies?

"Come on." Jane turns on her phone flashlight and leads us toward the source of the light. It gets colder, and damper, but then the mold smell gives way to the scent of something artificially sweet, and we turn the corner and see the neon green sign:

"Mirona's Five Dollar Miracles: The Classy Mega-Discount Non-Experience-Store Store"

Smaller, cursive magenta neon directly underneath says

"Buy things like you used to, the simple way."

There's storefront glass, new and shiny. Taped to it, a large piece of hand-painted poster board announces, "Absolutely NO modern technology in this store whatsoever! Touch things! Hold things! Shopping here is the antidote to the digital devolution!"

A battery-operated parrot squawks "Welcome" as Jane walks inside. The sound echoes down the concrete hallway.

Another poster board sign stands on a tripod right inside the doorway: "Gloriously DEAD zone! Proudly NOT connected!" with a Wi-Fi symbol covered by a large red X.

"I read about this store on the neighborhood listserv. Apparently Mirona"—Jane points to some coffee tumblers on a nearby shelf branded with "Mirona's Miracles" in magenta letters—"organized protests against the de-malling and creation of what is now the Experience Center. Stuff about how Experience Centers will make it easier for AI to take over the world, how the death of the American mall is two steps away from the death of humanity. Which is, actually, pretty ironic, considering the 'American mall' is already representative of humanity's death, in a way. Did you know that? How malls were invented out of fear of nuclear war? Safe facilities 'coincidentally' just outside of the fatal bomb radius of notable cities that could double as fallout shelters where we could also live out our post-apocalyptic days in climate-controlled utopias." She waves behind us at the hallway of concrete. "Welcome to Glenville's nuclear haven, tribute to 'humanity.'"

"I had no idea."

"Most people don't have ideas about most things." Her voice has taken on that assassin's-blade edge. "Sorry. I shouldn't have talked about that. It's not related to the study. What I was trying to get to is that Mirona managed to drum up a lot of public support for her Death of Humanity protests. So she opened this store, Mirona's Miracles, where people can shop 'without it being an Experience.'" Jane shakes her head at the shelf of scented markers we are passing. "So, we should be safe. Mirona chose this location because you literally cannot get Wi-Fi or cell service down here. Even if your life, for whatever reason, depended on it."

Jane rounds the corner and peers down the next aisle over. "The location can't be good for foot traffic, though." She looks down several more aisles. The store is completely devoid of people. Even the checkout counter lacks a checkout person. "Oh, dear. I wonder how long this store will last. But wow, look at this place. Just look at it!"

At first glance, if you ignore the fact that it's in an unlit, unfinished nuclear bomb shelter of a basement, Mirona's Miracles could pass as a regular store—the kind of store you'd stop at to pick up an inflated birthday balloon or a glue stick. But then you'd realize that the shelves are filled with vintage stuff. And then you'd realize none of it is *actually* vintage, it's just made to look that way.

It's like one of those souvenir shops on a beach boardwalk, filled with plastic seashells instead of real ones. Except Mirona's Miracles is a beach-walk souvenir store for the 1990s.

"'Wayne, are you seeing this?"

"I am."

"Look at it!"

"I am!"

The sweet smell in the hallway has grown in intensity as we've moved down the aisle of round magenta containers claiming to contain six feet of bubble-gum tape.

I pick up a brown, lumpy stuffed animal out of a bin. The tag says "Baby BeanBean: My name is Grizzle!" It's reminiscent of my origami roadkill. "Wow."

Jane touches a plastic yellow egg labeled "Tommy's Gotchu." It buzzes. "Feed me!" lights up on the screen. "This is incredible! Don't you think so?"

"Well . . ."

She rests her hand on top of a shelf of Goosepimples books, runs her finger over the raised title. "Don't answer that. Unfortunately, or maybe fortunately, we aren't here to shop. And we are on the verge of, or perhaps we've already dipped our toe into, non-study-related topics. Let's go to the back."

She leads me down an aisle of butterfly hair clips and a full row of "snapping bracelets," to the very back corner of the store, where she leans against a wall full of vintage anti-internet swag. "So. This." She waves the stack of papers at me. "This is not good news."

"I know."

Her gaze catches on something on the page. For the first time today, her expression reveals concern. "It's exactly what I was afraid of. This study means a lot to someone."

"You didn't know any of this? Dr. Charlotte didn't visit you?"

"Nope. And though it could be explained by our being in different test groups or something, I still . . ." She gently pushes a dangling stack of "Stop AOL!" stickers. They sway on their hook.

"Do you think you'll quit?" I swallow.

"I can't."

"The letter said we can."

"I mean, *I* can't quit."

She pushes the sticker stack harder this time. One spins off and falls to the floor.

"Do you . . ."

"Don't ask."

"Because it's personal?"

She looks at me sharply, like even that question was too personal. But the look quickly softens. "It is personal. But mostly, it's not interesting and it's not logical. Don't look at me like that. I'm not being coy. It's really not interesting. And we have more important things to talk about, and ultimately we are nowhere close to the point where I would consider quitting. In fact, we may be even further away from it than we were before. The end."

She picks up the fallen sticker and hangs it back on its hook. "So! Let's come up with an initial plan."

"We did that already." I point at the papers. "On the last page?"

"You mean the part where you say you're going to stay in the experiment and figure out what's going on?"

". . . Yes?"

"That's not a plan."

"It's not?"

"If planning to plan was a plan, where would it end? Could you plan to plan to plan to plan and that would count as a purposeful agenda? Could your whole life be counted as productive if you have plans to later plan to plan out your goals?"

"Uh . . ."

"Did Kermit make this 'plan' with you?" She puts *plan* in air quotes this time.

"You know I'm friends with Kermit?"

"No."

"But how . . . ?"

"This is the problem with Kermit. He's so much talk. Let's do this, let's do that, big idea big idea big idea, grand scheme grand scheme grand scheme. Let's make this *plan*, oh, I'm so brilliant, I will present you with this *plan*—when actually he's just setting you up to do all the hard stuff yourself."

I stare at her. "I didn't even realize you knew each other."

Her mouth goes left. "I don't. We don't. He's in most of my classes, that's all. Anyway, it's not my business who you're friends with. I'm sorry I even know that you're friends. I will do my best to forget that! My point is that whatever this is, whoever you made it with, this is not a plan."

"So what should—"

"We should make a list!" She springs off the wall and wiggles her shoulders. Then she explains, her shoulders wiggling every time she pauses, how since the wristband is tracking our behaviors, we should *also* focus on our behaviors. If we keep a list about changes in our behaviors since starting the experiment, then that could lead us to what the pill does to us. Then, if we know what the pill does, we might be able to figure out the purpose of the study.

"We should also keep a list of the assignments we get in the apps.

So we can compare and see if those mean anything, too. Yes! Two lists!" She's bouncing up and down on her toes. "Hopefully, we won't discover any changes in our personalities. Because when you put it like that, it sounds quite creepy, doesn't it? Like crossing through the thin tape between maybe-not-okay and clearly-not-okay." Her mouth goes right. "Let's not think about that part. No point in thinking about that. Not yet. Yes, the lists are correct. Lists are the thing to do. You agree, right? Yes, this is great. We're off to a fantastic start, really making progress already. Isn't it nice, how a plan can take fear and fold it up into a tiny square so you can put it right into the fear disposal slot?"

"I feel better," I say, willing myself to mean it.

She smiles up at me. And then I actually do feel better.

Her bouncing subsides. "I wanted to ask you, how was the email?"

"Email?"

She becomes very focused on a "No Connection Means Real Connections" key chain. "From your mother."

"Ah." I swallow as my study fears get engulfed by a larger, person-shaped fear. "She's coming to visit."

"Wow."

"Yeah." I take one of the anti-AOL stickers off the rack near Jane. Tilt it. The iridescence catches the fluorescent lights, makes a rainbow on Jane's cheek.

"I know I shouldn't have asked. I'm breaking my own rules again, kind of. But I had to ask. It would have been wrong not to ask, right? But I didn't ask just because it would have been wrong not to. I asked because I cared."

"Thank you."

"Not in a personal way, though."

"Good."

"We should go." She doesn't move.

She's close to me, so close that if I extended my fingers, bent my wrist, I would be touching her.

I hold my breath, hoping that if I don't exhale, time won't pass, and we can stay exactly like this. If we stayed like this, right in this moment, we wouldn't have to worry about mothers visiting or maybe-bad-maybe-not-studies with maybe-lie-detectors. If we stayed like this, here in this basement, we wouldn't even have to worry about nuclear war.

A door right next to me slams open.

INDUSTRIAL-STRENGTH CROWBARS

A cart wheels through the swinging door. A pile of candy balances precariously on top.

"Hey, y'all! Sorry I wasn't out here to greet you! I was in the back prepping for the trick-or-treat event. Which—I know what you're going to say—*technically* it's an 'Experience, T dot M dot,' so shouldn't Mirona's Miracles be protesting it? But trick-or-treating for candy is also retro, good grass-touching vibes, so . . . Oh, hey!"

A body appears to accompany the voice, a body topped with a volcano spewing bright red, slightly wavy hair. A beautiful, hand-embroidered dragon wraps around the body of their shirt and up onto the collar of their blouse, its mouth open, holding the wearer's throat in its jaws.

"Miranda." All of Jane's list-related exuberance has evaporated. Her voice is flatter than a week-old soda.

Miranda, the painter of the PacSun-horse-and-tackle-shop school lobby mural, the subject of Kermit's look-at-my-legs-I-dare-you prank, descendant of the well-connected, my-child-is-an-innocent-and-godly-pearl mother, adjusts their name tag. "Oh my god. Oh my god! Li'l Janey! Hey, you! It's so good to see you!"

"I didn't know you worked here."

"Nah. I actually work at Selfation, the new theme park. This week I'm just helping out Aunt Mirona. You've met her, yeah?"

"Maybe." Jane crosses her arms, crumpling my handwritten notes.

"I'm store manager while she's on her annual volunteer trip. I'm missing classes, but the school is giving me credit for the leadership experience."

Jane picks at a thread on her sweater.

"How've you been? How's, what are you into these days . . . origami, yeah? So cute."

I expect Jane to launch into a speech about how origami doesn't make her fairy winged and magical, and especially not *cute*, but her lips are clamped tight. She's plucking at the sweater threads on her arm like they're guitar strings. "Fine. I'm fine. Good. Origami's good."

Miranda snatches a lollipop from their candy cart and unwraps it. "I love that for you. Really matches your vibe." Their embroidered dragon breathes as they turn their head toward me. "And if it isn't 'Wayne Le, yeah? Don't see you out much. Aren't you going to say hi, 'Wayne? Or should I call you D?"

I grunt. Memories of my near-fatal leggings-ogling have glued my tongue to my teeth.

"That's not quite a 'hi,' but it'll do." They pull a strand of their hair, then let it spring back into place, their dragon's flickering flame. "Well, don't just stand there. Speak to me! What has led you to the anti-AOL corner of our universe, hmm?" They're looking directly at me. "You look like you're up to something secret. You planning an anti-Wi-Fi riot? I didn't expect you to be a rebel." They lick their lips and cock their head, as if to look at me from this new, apparently delicious angle. Then they stick their lollipop in their mouth.

The shelves of the store are closing in. I redirect my eyes from Miranda's lips to their boots to the safety of a still-wrapped Tootsie Roll. "No. No rebellions planned. Not up to anything secret."

"Mmm. Exactly what you'd say if you *were* planning a rebellion, yeah? No problem. I'm not going to pry." They laugh. "That's absolutely not true. Janey knows that's not true. Of course I'm going to pry. I'm a fucking industrial-strength crowbar. Tell me, then, how do you two know each other?"

"We don't," says Jane sharply.

"Ohhh. I see. Wow, Janey. I'm kind of impressed. And surprised?"

"It's not like that."

"Finally growing up."

"I said, it's not like that."

"Okay, okay. You don't know each other. I get it. Keeping your sitch on the DL. Don't worry, you were never here. D, Janey can tell you, I'm a nosy bitch of a crowbar, but my secret-keeping safe is made of that same industrial-quality steel." They're still looking right at me. Their neck dragon seems to be eyeing my neck, too. "And I've still gotta get my costume on, so I'll return to the stockroom so y'all can have your privacy. Janey? We should totally hang out sometime, yeah?"

"Mm."

"'Wayne is invited, too, of course. Or especially? Lydia and I don't mind, well, sharing." They pick a lollipop out of the cart and toss it to me. "In the meantime, enjoy yourselves. You've got an hour before the trick-or-treating kids arrive, yeah? Wrap it up before then. They aren't prepared for *that* kind of scary. Ghostly moans only, if you get what I mean." They park the cart against the wall and pat Jane's shoulder once before returning to the stockroom.

Beside me, Jane makes a quiet, high-pitched sound. Something between a hiccough and a wail and a sound effect for one of the Ninninedo GameFolk games stacked on the aisle endcap. She looks like she's been hit by a tornado.

"Do you . . ." I fuss with the lollipop stick. The orange wrapper crinkles. "Do you want to tell me what that was about?"

Jane's focus stays glued to the doorway Miranda left through. Her fingers have progressed from plucking to twisting at her sweater threads.

I say, "I'm guessing it's personal. But, like you said when I got my email from my mom, you couldn't watch me not be okay and not be a real person about it. You can tell me what's wrong, if you want to."

Jane is frozen except her fingers, twisting, twisting. The walls of the store are opening back up now, expanding, until it feels like we are in too big of a space, too far apart, in an endlessly growing universe of a store, cold and vulnerable and each of us about to be totally alone.

I step toward her.

She jumps away. "I want to go now." Her voice is not an assassin's blade, it's a guillotine's—large and efficient and on a single, deadly track. She speeds out of the store. The lollipop wrapper crinkles in my fist.

STEREOTYPICAL ARCHETYPES

I loop around the mall twice, looking for Jane.

On my second loop, a burgundy sweater is curled up into a tight ball at our table in the Tiki Bar. The bar has quieted down since earlier today. Most parents seem to be getting their kids ready for the main "experience."

The sweater ball doesn't acknowledge me when I join it, and neither does the person inside it. She's sitting sideways, her knees pulled under the fabric. She seems to be entirely entranced by the PetSmart enclosure, where kids in pirate costumes are playing with the rabbits.

Currently, a man is trying to coax his tiny pirated kid to relinquish an even tinier black-and-white bunny.

"Pirates did not have rabbits," the man says. "It doesn't make any sense for you to have a rabbit."

The kid holds the squirming rabbit even tighter. "I'm a modern pirate! Why are you trying to make me fit into your outdated pirate stereotype?"[20]

The father shakes his head.

Jane sighs and looks down at her knees. Her mouth goes left, then she sighs again. "I'm sorry for leaving like that."

---

20. Over the past year, a Japanese anime show has exploded in popularity. The show is about pirates, sort of, but they don't act at all like pirates. This has resulted in a swarm of children talking about "outdated stereotypes" (a tagline repeated every episode by the main character). Olive has watched this show but prefers the "understated humor" (her words) and "cat inclusivity" (my words) of *Fuzzy Cats Pow Pow Pow*.

"It's okay."

"No, it's not. It's not okay."

She puts her head onto her knees and shakes it.

"Are *you* okay?"

She emits that noise, the one that's somewhere between a wail and a beep. The sweater ball moves up and down with Jane's breathing. Finally, Jane lifts her face out of her knees and rests her chin on them instead.

"Miranda was my best friend. They moved here in first grade. So, yeah. I *have* met Aunt Mirona. Twice, actually." She rubs her nose. "But in seventh grade, Miranda . . . changed. In class they would kind of, I don't know, brush me off. Or not be around. It's hard to describe. They were still *there*, in all the same places, but they weren't *there* anymore.

"And before you say something about it being in my imagination, I *know* it wasn't because I confronted them about it. They said they still 'really liked me,' I was still their 'best friend,' but they didn't want people to see us together anymore because it was embarrassing."

"What?"

Jane picks at some loose sweater threads by her knee. "Specifically, they said it was embarrassing because I don't 'wear fitted shirts.'" She makes the smallest air quotes ever to exist.

"What?"

"I know. *I know.* Bad. Sad. All of it. I don't know what the most sad part of it is. That it happened? Or that I took what they said about my shirts literally? That day, I begged my mom to order me some of those trendy cut-off jacket shirt things—do you remember those?—and she did, even though she didn't agree with the reason. And let me tell you, those shirts were really uncomfortable, they had these super-tight cuffs that rub around on your wristbones, but I wore them anyway, and of course that didn't change anything, because of *course* it didn't, because what it was really about wasn't literally my clothing, it's what my clothing says about *me*.

"And the fact that I missed understanding that kind of, like, proves their point? I'm embarrassing. It's embarrassing to be friends with someone like me." She rests her chin back on top of her sweater-covered knees.

"I . . ."

She waves her hand at me. "Don't. I don't need to hear that I'm fine how I am, blah blah blah, it'll get better after high school, blah blah blah. It's not that I wish I was someone else. Not exactly. Actually, I prefer how I am to how most people are. Sort of. It's complicated."

Everything about her curled-up posture and the straight, hard set of her mouth reminds me of Olive when she gets upset. When Olive gets like that and you talk to her, the ball of Olive flattens into a face-down, over-spread cookie.

So I leave Jane and get in line for a Halloween-themed latte, with extra whipped cream. I pair the latte with one of their special peanut butter cookies.

I put the latte and cookie on the table near Jane.

She turns her head so it's her cheek on her knees, and not her chin. I can see her face now, though she's staring at the floor. "No. That's not the saddest part. This is the saddest part: I always thought, I still do think, they are so amazing. Miranda. They're friendly and funny and comfortable in any situation. They are truly themselves, despite their family and the world. They've got rizz, if you like. Like, even the fact that they told me they didn't want to be around me anymore—that's kind of cool, right?

"And, yeah, yeah, I like who I am and all of that, I *do*, but at the same time Miranda is exactly like what I wish I *could* be."

Jane picks up the latte, cradles it between her palms. Takes a long, deep breath, and I see her body relax a little bit.

In the PetSmart enclosure, the pirate kid has tucked the rabbit inside his vest. The dad, shaking his head, takes out his phone and tries to pay.

The blue-shirted PetSmart employee looks annoyed. "These rabbits aren't for sale. They are only for *experiencing*. If you want to buy a rabbit, please visit PetSmart dot com or use one of our In-Experience sales kiosks."

Jane holds her nose over the cup's lid, breathes in. "That doesn't make sense, does it? How can I like who I am and also want to be someone else? Maybe they're just the person I feel like I *should* be.

"Anyway. I can't seem to let go of the hope that the friendship is still there. They always say things like, 'We should hang out, Janey,' and I keep thinking they mean it, and we are friends again, and then I nudge them about it, trying to get an actual plan into place, and then I end up feeling like an obsessive fan girl, creepy and lurkery and a lot like a dog you fed once and now won't leave you alone, except that's a bad example because I really like dogs. But, yeah."

She takes a tiny sip of the latte, rubs her nose, and turns back toward the rabbits.

The pirate kid is leaving, closing the gate to the enclosure. He isn't screaming or crying. Instead, he looks like a plant that hasn't been watered for a week. The dad bends down to take the kid's hand, and the kid lets him, his arm a limp leaf. The black-and-white rabbit has been picked up by another pirate kid now. It has resumed squirming.

"Like I said, it's complicated. I like who I am. Really. It's just, I also wish the rest of the world liked who I am, too."

I can't help myself. "I like who you are."

She finally looks at me.

"You don't know who I am. That's the whole point of this."

Before I can respond, she unfurls from her sweater. "Gosh. What am I doing? If I'm not careful, that won't be the case anymore. We'll just be two more people that know each other, which, what good is that? What use will we have for each other?"

"People who know you can be useful, too."

She bows her head over her latte, inhales deeply. "Thank you for this. Nuts and sugar and coffee. They help everything." Then she hands me three origami animals from her sweater pocket—a bat, an elephant, a bear. I recognize my own handwriting on the paper, the fragments of sentences describing my session with Charlotte.

"Thanks for this information, too. Remember our plan, yeah? The lists." She stands up and adjusts her sweater sleeves so she can hold them in her fists. "And thanks for listening. Really." Her mouth twitches to the left. She picks up the latte in one of her sweater mitts. She pushes the cookie toward me. "I like who you are, too. Though, of course, I also don't know who you are."

A crowd of little pirates walks by, and she disappears into the midst of it.

LEVEL UP

When my Lyft drops me back at home, Dad is standing by Tusks with a hose in one hand and a pink washcloth in the other. The hose is not turned on. The washcloth is clean. There are no puddles.

Dad: Oh, 'Wayne, it's a surprise to run into you. I was just out here washing Tusks.
Me: So I see.
Dad: Lucky thing, because I wanted to let you know the mail came.
Me: Lucky indeed.
Dad: It came early today, because it's Saturday. It comes early on the weekends. Different mailman, too, on the weekend. Greg instead of Charles.
Me:
Dad: (Pulls a letter from his back pocket.) This came for you.
Letter's Return Address: Johns Hopkins University
The Hologram: *sparkle*
Me: Oh.
Dad: I thought you might want to open it.
Me: I'll take it inside.
Dad: What if it's urgent? What if you need to respond?

Me: They wouldn't send urgent things by snail m—
Dad: Might as well do it now. What if you forget? It would be bad to forget. Best to do important things right now. While it's on your mind.
Me:
Dad:
Me:
Dad:
Dad's Face: EoFF.
Me: Fine. *(Opens envelope.)*
Dad: Well?
Dad: What is it?
Dad: Is something wrong?
Me: Let me at least *read* it.
Me: Please.
Letter: Dear Dwayne Le: #33923810, Thank you for your continued participation in our study. We are returning to paper mailings for important communications for security reasons. Your attendance is required at an in-person appointment on November 12 at 11:30 a.m. Your school has been notified of your expected absence. It is your responsibility to make arrangements for makeup schoolwork ahead of time. We look forward to seeing you then. Thank you again for your contributions to our project.

>   This letter, with your participation
>   ID, serves as official confirmation of
>   your appointment. Please do not attend
>   any appointments sent to you via email,
>   that lack the official Hopkins seal and
>   signature, or that lack the correct
>   participation ID, which may be confirmed at
>   any time in the Official Hopkins Study App.

Me: It's scheduling my next in-person
           appointment. It's November twelfth.
Dad: You made it to the next level?
Me: I guess?
Dad:
Dad's Face:
Dad: Tusks is clean now. Time to go inside.

My Darling Secret,

Hello from New Mexico! Slowly making my way toward Baltimore. Toward you.

It is beautiful here, like it was in Arizona. The red rocks, the desert landscape. I took a short break for meditative hiking at Ghost Ranch—and learned that parts of the newer *Magnificent Seven* movie were filmed there. I never saw it; a remake of a remake of what was ultimately a Japanese film is, well, it's not for me. I did think fondly of your father, though. Wondered if he saw the new one or, more likely, is clinging stubbornly to what he already knows and loves.

I haven't heard back from you, and by now I'm assuming that even if you deleted my email without reading it, your father has told you about my intent to visit.

This means, I like to believe, that you decided not to respond, and that means you would like me to come see you. Or you don't mind it enough to stop me.

Imagining this—the potential that you might talk to me, let me back into your life after what I did to you—it makes me very happy. It fills me with hope for the future. It makes me believe that kindness, forgiveness, exist. It makes me proud that those things exist in *you*.

I thought I should take a short moment to reassure you about how I'm doing now. I know I mentioned it in the video, but you deserve to have it in writing:

I'm doing okay. No fake promises—sometimes my mind still gets trapped in negative cycles, and sometimes I have trouble sleeping because I get an idea and my mind can't put it down. The bad things are still there, but it's like their sharp edges have been polished off. I have a better understanding of myself. I haven't lost total control for a long time. Haven't thrown any meat on the walls.

I'm a vegetarian now, anyway.

That's my sad attempt at a joke.

More soon,

I love you,

Mama

SELF-ERASURE

Olive hunches at the kitchen table, moose-slippered feet tucked up under her skirt, head bent over her book of math problems. Every few minutes, her eyebrows shoot up, she raises one or two fingers, and then she scribbles something frantically onto her paper.

I finish off the last sip of my orange juice and wait until she's between problems. "Do you think you know who I am?"

She doesn't look up. "Uh-oh."

"Why 'uh-oh'?"

"That sounds like a question someone would ask when they are in the middle of a profound session of wallowing."

I smile, pick up her special blue plate from the table and put it in the dishwasher, wipe her bagel crumbs off the counter and into the sink.

She puts her pencil down and adjusts her legs so they're crossed the other way. "Are you?"

"Am I what?"

"Wallowing!"

"Nah."

Her cheeks puff.

I roll into the chair next to her. "Can you answer me, though?"

"Of course I know who you are."

"Would you notice if I changed?"

"This seems like a trick question."

"Would you?"

"Are you planning to get a nose ring or something?"

"No."

"I would notice. And so would Dad. And then he would kill you."

"I'm not."

She strokes an antler of one of her moose slippers.

I boop her moose's nose. "I mean more like a personality change. Like if I was acting differently."

"Like if you suddenly were the type of person that *wanted* to get a nose ring?"

I shrug. "Okay."

She picks up her pencil and rolls it between her fingers. Her special eraser, one shaped like a cat, smiles at me from the top of it. "It's hard to answer. You need to say what kind of change and how much. Like, my brain is growing every day, and you probably don't notice."

"But I'd notice after a month or two."

"I guess."

"And I'd notice if you were a totally different person."

Her forehead creases. Her fingers stop swirling her pencil. "Like if I turned into Kermit? Or transformed into a cat?"

I shake my head.

She adjusts her legs again and bends back over her paper. "You're being weird."

"Weird how? Like different? Like *changed*?"

"Just regular-you weird. Regular distracting-me-from-doing-my-homework-because-you-don't-want-to-do-yours kind of weird."

"Would you tell me if I changed?"

"I don't know."

"I mean, I'm asking you to do that. To tell me if you think I've changed."

She sighs. "Sure. I'll tell you." Her cheeks puff again. I love how she's resisting telling me to leave her alone, even though she wants me to leave her alone, because she would never tell someone that, probably ever, and a hard lump crawls down my esophagus, a worry that what she said is true, how she is changing every day, and I won't notice until who she is today is gone.

She erases something on her paper. Not using her special cat eraser, but a regular rectangle one from her pencil pouch.

I roll back to the other side of the table, pull out my computer from my bag, close the email from my mother, and settle in to work with her.

THE LIST

How I've changed:

1.

UPGRADES

When Tusks pulls into the Hopkins parking lot, I'm prepared to look at everything in a new light—the light of This Could Be More Than We Thought.

But this is not the light that shines down upon the squat brick building.

The light that shines down is a weak, late morning sun. A regular sun. An Everything Is Exactly How It Appears sun. It highlights the mold growing along the bottom of the walls and emphasizes how badly the windows need to be cleaned.

I half jog toward the Justin James Research Center, very ready to get this appointment over with.

I grab the door handle and pull.

It doesn't budge.

I pull again. The lock catches against the doorframe.

A small, red button next to the door glows. A paper note is taped to the bottom, unevenly cut:

"Study participants: Please buzz for entry."

I push the button, but the door still won't open.

A voice speaks from above the doorframe. "Please put your face up to the camera."

I see, then, a small lens next to the red button, the oh-so-regular sun glinting off the glass. The ghosts of metal sensors from Dr. Charlotte's truth encourager press down on my fingertips.

But then another car pulls into the parking lot, its turned-up stereo vibrating its windows and my feet.

I step toward the lens.

"State your name," the voice says.

I do.

There's a long, long pause. I try the door again. Still locked.

"Hello?"

"Your ID has been confirmed. Please come inside."

There's a click, and this time when I pull, the door swings out and open.

I WAS HERE

"Welcome back, 'Wayne." Charlotte stands in the classroom doorway.

Like the sun on the mold and the clip-art signs still lining the Hopkins hallways, Charlotte projects normalcy. It's wafting off her shoulders in great steamy streams of status quo. It's rolling off her wrinkled lab coat lapels and onto her plain white shoes.

"Come on inside."

Yesterday, Kermit instructed me to look for "anything that has changed, and also anything that is the same." Helpful.

But still, I try.

An obvious difference: Black T-shirted Abrams is absent. His desk has been pulled forward so it's directly facing the desk where I sat last time.

Charlotte takes this desk and gestures me toward the other. I sit.

She clasps her hands on top of her desk, where a hand-carved heart mars the wood.

I mirror her posture. My desk has the tablet, shut off this time, and "Harry was here" grooved deeply in a bottom corner.

Charlotte puts a pocket-size notepad on her desk, followed by a capped black pen, which she delicately aligns exactly parallel to the edge of the pad. "First, let's talk about how you're doing."

I press my heels into the floor. Kermit predicted this would be part of the session. His instructions were "Avoid giving answers, and when possible, make your answers questions."

"How have you been feeling?"

"What kind of feeling do you mean?"

"Have you noticed any side effects?"

"What kinds of side effects should I be trying to notice?"

Charlotte crosses her ankles. "Yes or no: Have you noticed any side effects?"

I push my feet down again. My socks feel too tight for my toes. In my head, Jane's voice is telling me that my plan wasn't much of a plan. "No. I haven't felt any side effects."

"Have you had any problems with the web application?"

"What kinds of problems with the web application?"

"Yes or no."

I fight my desire to sigh. "No, no problems."

"Last question." Charlotte adjusts the still-capped pen so it's, if possible, even more parallel with the edge of the still-blank notepad. "Have you noticed any suspicious activity related to the study?"

My socks keep shrinking. I move my hands under my desk and pinch the web of skin between my thumb and forefinger. "What kind of suspicious activity?"

"*Any* suspicious activity." She looks me straight in the eyes.

My legs twitch, and my knees whack against the metal chair. Pain travels down my shins, and I look away.

It's then that I notice the broken glass from the flask the wolf-shirt kid smashed. It's gone—which isn't what's notable. Directly above its absence, atop the lab bench, gleams an unbroken flask, coated in a film of dust that perfectly matches the rest of the room.

"'Wayne?"

I swallow. "No. No suspicious activity."

"Perfect." She drops a hand into the pocket of her white coat. The pill bottle rattles. "I'm going to give you your second dose, and then we'll be done for this session." She pushes down on the lid of the pill bottle and turns. She bites her bottom lip. Her nose wrinkles. "No matter how many times I do this . . ."

She pushes up her sleeves, then presses down on the cap again.

I glance from her nose wrinkles to the perfectly dusted flask and back again. "Do you . . . Am I supposed to . . . Do you want help?"

"Thank you. I'll get it. You'd think with all the advancements they've made in science . . ." It pops open. "Phew. There we go."

From the hallway, there's a crash.

INSTABILITY OF FOLDING CHAIRS & FEELINGS

The sound of folding chairs collapsing into each other reverberates through me. There's the hollow bang of something heavy hitting the metal desk in the hallway.

My mind is still on the flask, on the wolf-shirt patriot getting escorted out. I jump up, map the shortest path to the shelter provided by the lab table.

Charlotte yanks open the door. "Michael." Her shoulders lift closer to her ears.

"Tripped," a tinny voice responds. Presumably-Michael crouches on the floor. The light from our room illuminates his plaid shirt, the white whiskers of his trim beard, his copper eyeglass frames, and the silver clasp of the now-empty clipboard in his hand. Papers flutter around the hallway.

Two of these papers slide inside the room. They skate across the floor like water bugs.

"I've got it." Charlotte swoops under me to grab them. She flips them so they are upside down and hands them to Michael like a teacher handing back tests, hiding our grades.

I've already seen, though.

At the top of the papers was stamped:

OWNING FUTURES

"We're just wrapping up." Charlotte holds out a hand to pull Michael up. "I'll be ready for our meeting soon."

Michael grunts as he stumbles to his feet. He flaps his handful of papers at her before clipping them back to his board. "No rush, no rush. I'm early." He leans past her and sticks the top half of himself into the room. "Are you one of our participants?"

I blink at him. Letters are scrolling across my brain, repeating and bright, like a giant marquee.

CIA CIA CIA CIA CIA.

Big is not bad, I tell myself. *Secrets are not bad*, I tell myself.

Secrets can even be good, my imaginary version of Kermit tells me.

CIA!

"He is a participant." Charlotte follows Michael back into the room.

Michael's brown loafers shush against the tile. He's not a tall man, but he's slender and spry.

He extends his hand, the one not holding the clipboard, and shakes my hand vigorously. "I don't get to interact with participants much, not in my role. Which is a real shame, a real, real shame. Because you people, you *kids*, are the real heroes of this little operation we've got going on. You don't even know. You do not even know." He runs his fingers along his chin. His beard hairs bristle. "In fact, can we talk for a bit? Yes, let's do that. It would be nice, I think. Let's just have a little chat. I'd like that."

My stomach is churning, like if I open my mouth, something will spill out, all the butterflies, all the

Moths.

Charlotte hesitates, her hand on the door handle. "I don't think chatting with participants is in the protocol."

Michael folds into the desk facing me. He waves me to sit back in mine. "It's not *not* in the protocol, is it?"

"It clearly . . ."

"The protocol is a written document. And when we have a written document, it would be in our best interest to imagine what the author intended when he *originally* wrote it. I feel certain that the author—such a careful, brilliant author as the man who wrote this document—would have included a specific rule against it, should he have intended it. Don't you agree, my dear?" He picks up Charlotte's perfectly aligned pen and stacks it on top of her notepad at an irregular angle.

My quads tense, ready to run. That unbroken flask is looking like a promising weapon.

Charlotte's chin is jutting out like she's pressing her bottom teeth into her top. Taut muscles rope down her neck.

"Don't you agree?" Michael prompts again.

"Yes." Charlotte shuts the door, picks up her pen and notepad, and positions herself in the corner by the window, where she looks, suddenly, small. Small and person-like. Not like a simulacrum of someone who drives a Subaru, but like someone who actually does.

Which, I realize, she is. She does. I saw it. It has a silly bumper sticker. She probably puts groceries in the back.

Michael taps a finger on my desk, next to the "Harry was here" engraving. "So, tell me, my good fellow, what's your name? How have things been going for you so far?"

"'Wayne. With a *D*. Not a visible *D*. An auditory one." My voice comes out scratchy and hoarse. "The study has been fine."

"'Fine,' eh? No problems?"

"No." My imaginary Kermit is still trying to get me to ask questions, but I can't.

CIA CIA CIA CIA.

"The wristband working for you okay, Dwayne? It's not itchy, is it? We were worried it would be uncomfortable."

"It's not itchy."

"Any problems logging in to the website? We had reports of some issues the first couple days."

"No."

"What do you think of your assignments? Too many? Too hard?"

"The assignments are fine."

"Notice any side effects from . . ."

Charlotte places her notepad on the heater. "We already talked about all of this."

Michael runs his index finger through the small mustache on his upper lip. "Notice any side effects from the pills?"

"No."

"Good. Good." Michael looks down at the desk. He tilts his head, like a bird listening for worms.[21] "Any idea," he says, still looking at

---

21. My mother loved* birds. My father, too. It was one of the activities we'd all do together—walk through a nature preserve. No one needed to talk. Dad liked the birds for the colors, the flashy feathers, and the efficiency of flight. My mother loved them because, she said, she trusted them. She trusted that after humans destroyed themselves, the birds would make the world right again.

* *Loves?*

the desk, and beginning to trace the heart carving with a forefinger, "what we're researching?"

My leg kicks out into the desk leg, again sending pain down my shin. "No."

He cocks his head to the other side. "You've thought about it." He flicks his gaze up at me, then back to the desk.

"It's heart health. It said that in the letter."

"No need to be shy about it. It would be unnatural for you not to wonder if that was the whole truth. So, have you? Wondered?"

I force myself to breathe slowly. The cold air burns my throat. "A little bit."

"Of course. Of course you have. I'm *glad* you have. Yes, humans are naturally curious. Not all animals are, but humans, that is something that sets us apart. Don't you think?"

"I . . ."

"Goats are like that. Curious. Do you like goats?"

"Goats?"

"Yes. You know." He holds his fingers up on his head, making little horns.

"I . . . I, uh, haven't considered much how I feel about goats."

Two lines wrinkle his forehead.

My quad muscles jump. "I love goats!" I say.

He nods. His forehead wrinkles disappear. "Yes. A fine specimen of a creature. There's something delightful about them, isn't there? So playful. So smart and so *useful*. Milk, cashmere, the ability to clear land. And what's best is, goats are naturally curious. They want knowledge. Creatures that want knowledge are easy to make useful, because you know just what carrot to dangle."

I swallow.

"They have goats at that new theme park, have you been? The selfie park. It's an interesting concept, that park—the current, intense obsession with the image of the self. The definition of self is itself an interesting question, don't you think, Dwayne?"

"Well..." My wrists have gone cold. My thoughts are still stuck on Michael's comments about carrots, and what carrots could theoretically be dangled in front of *me*. Value *is spelled I-N-F-O-R-M-A-T-I-O-N*.

"Excuse me." Charlotte takes two steps away from the windows. "We still need to finish up 'Wayne's appointment and I have to..."

"Your next meeting is with me. I will forgive you if you're late." Michael puts one forefinger on his desk, next to his clipboard. He puts it right in the center of the little carved heart. "I wonder what this carving was about. Probably it's not about much. Even unextraordinary people want to leave their unextraordinary marks." He taps the heart. "Have you been in love yet, Dwayne?"

"Excuse me?"

"Not necessarily romantic love. Have you ever loved someone so much that you would carve their name on something? Felt that their name is more important than your own? Like this person who carved this heart loved..." He adjusts his glasses. "Josie. Have you ever felt like you would do *anything* for someone?"

"I..."

"Let me give you a word of advice. I know you aren't here for advice; you probably want to get home. But humor me. After a man reaches a certain age, it is his right to bestow advice upon others. Hopefully, you will get there someday." He runs his finger through his mustache again, slowly, thoroughly, like he's wiping off foam left from sipping a whipped mocha. The word *hopefully* joins the CIA CIA CIA marquee in my brain.

"I've learned some things in my life. And one of those things is that doing something for someone you love . . . it's a mistake. That person needs to do it, whatever it is they are trying to do, on their own. They have to stand up for themselves. If you do it, it does them more harm than good." He looks up at me, over the top of his copper-framed glasses. The rims of his irises are very clear. The whites of his eyes are very white. "I know this personally. It is the reason I am involved in this project, this research." He puts his hand right at the edge of his desk so that his fingers cross over—barely, but clearly—into the territory of mine. His nails have been bitten back so far that his fingertips are scab-lined, swollen pillows; these he rests lightly on my desk.

Charlotte runs a hand over her tied-back hair. "You shouldn't be giving him this information."

"Oh?" Michael's fingers retreat. "Charlotte doesn't think I should be talking about this." He winks and pushes himself out of the desk. "Again, nice to meet you, Dwayne. You really are a hero." He shakes my hand. His brown loafers shush. The glass in the door rattles as it shuts behind him.

D WAS HERE, TOO

Charlotte takes the seat across from me. Her eyes are focused on the blackboard behind my head. Her cheeks are splotchy. "Okay." She rubs her face, once. "We were just wrapping up. So." The pill bottle reemerges from her pocket.

"That guy is an asshole."

Charlotte's cheeks get splotchier. The pill bottle is frozen in her hands, midair.

Then, all at once, her expression completely changes. She looks at me strangely. Like I'm an injured horse that needs to be put down.

She wipes at her face again. She opens her mouth. Her lips hint at a consonant, but then she blows out air in a long stream, and I understand it, now, the carving on my desk—"Harry was here"—the need to establish your existence, to convince yourself that you will continue to exist.

"Let's get this wrapped up." She places a pill next to my hand on my desk. Her fingertips stay on the pill for a long time, like she's trying to balance it there.

Then she stands up, fast. Her desk's legs bump into mine. The pill rolls. I catch it.

She turns her back to me and walks to the windows, kneels to rummage through a bag that's on the floor. "That's it. We're done for this session. You'll get a letter regarding your next appointment. Until then, keep on in the same way. Great work so far."

The pill is still in my hand. "I can go?"

"Yes, you should go now. Your appointment is done."

Her head is bent deeply over her bag. The light from the window makes purple shadows on the edges of her white coat. She is entirely turned away from me.

The sun moves out from behind a cloud. It catches the flask sitting on the lab bench and makes a bright rainbow on the wall by Charlotte's head.

I roll the pill in the crevices of my palm.

In my pocket, my phone vibrates, rattles against the wood of the chair.

I know, without checking it, that it's my father. I know, without reading it, that he's making sure everything went okay today.

Secrets are not necessarily bad, I tell myself.

I shove the pill into my mouth.

WHAT IS THE QUESTION

From *Allegorist*
Lyrics by Clarissa Patel

> *Wake up, black hole's still there*
> *Infinite gravity*
> *Pulling me toward it*
> *Something I don't know*
> *I need to know*
> *If I could know*
> *I would stop falling*

The pill sticks its sharp edges into my esophagus as it walks its way down, while Tusks drives me home in the bright crisp light of autumn, away from the red-stamped confidential papers.

> *Eggs for breakfast,*
> *Pajama pants,*
> *It's way too easy to*
> *Climb back into bed.*
> *The answer could be there*
> *It's not out here*
> *When can I stop trying to find it*

CIA CIA CIA CIA CIA

> *You say if I work harder*
> *You say if I try harder*
> *Or smarter or longer*
> *Or faster or brighter or*
> *Anything Other*
> *You say I will find it*
> *You're so full of lies*

Goats, carrots, the definition of self.
The pill that's currently breaking apart inside my chest.

> *You've sent me searching for that one magic answer*
> *Tell me*
> *Tell me*
> *Tell me*
> *What is the question?*

Even Clarissa at max volume can't drown out the question that keeps looping:

Does my future still matter if my future is no longer mine?

HOW I'VE CHANGED:

1. Stood up for Charlotte
2.

A NEW EXPERIENCE™

Setting: The front entryway, next to the front door recycling box.

Me: *(Opens door and sees Dad standing in vestibule, stack of papers in hand, as if he's come here solely to use the recycling box.)*

Dad: So much junk mail.

Me: Uh-huh.

Dad: Why do they send this? *(Holds up an envelope.)* Waste of paper, waste of time. *(Leans past me to drop it into recycling box.)*

Me: *(Heads toward staircase.)*

Dad: Actually, 'Wayne, while you're here . . .

Me:

Dad: I got an email from Mr. Houston today.

Me: Mr. Houston?

Dad: Your guidance couns—

Me: I know.

Dad: I think we should talk.

Me: Oh.

Dad: It's about your grades.

Self-Pity: Rises to unsurvivable levels.
Me: I'm actually busy right now.
Dad's Face: Flash of DNS.
Dad: You are? You don't look . . . (*Glances down at the remaining pile of mail in his hands.*) . . . I mean, okay. That's okay.
Me: . . . That's . . . "okay"?
Dad: Maybe later tonight? Or tomorrow. Or this week? How about you text me a time that's good for you.
Me:
Me:
Dad: Your appointment?
Me: It was fine.
Dad:
Dad: You're still doing the study?
Me: As far as I know.
Dad:
Dad: Okay. Have a good night. Don't stay up too late. Unless you need to. Okay. Have a good night. (*Dumps rest of junk mail into recycling box.*)

HOPKINS STUDY APP

Ready, set, *FUN*! You will have three minutes to find as many words as you can using the following letters:

G O O D E N O U G H

BINARY REALITY:

How Small-Town Communities Think & Feel About Digital Technology

An Oral History, by Naomi Le

They've started giving our kids laptops. I won't let mine use them. What's so important on the internet that the government is giving us thousands of dollars' worth of equipment to access it?

My kids tell me I sound crazy. They say they need the laptops for school. But to me, it seems too easy. Who's going to say no to a free computer? Then they're in our homes, all these computers, loaded up with secret software that can control the microchips that they injected with the vaccines and, yeah, I don't know. Does that sound crazy? Maybe I am crazy. I don't know.

The tricky thing is, some of it is real. I'm old enough to remember MK-ULTRA, and the UFOs—not aliens, those classified military tests. I've also been around enough to know that conspiracy theories, being suspicious that the government has secret agendas, that's the stuff of those neo-nazis. It's dangerous. It's anti-democracy. And I'm not saying anything anti-democracy. I'm not, right? I don't know.

All I know is that if you're going to give us thousands of dollars' worth of stuff, know what could do more good than laptops? Food. Clothes. A place to live where I can feel safe, where my kids can feel safe walking home at night.

Ianna Knox: Truth or Consequences, New Mexico

SMART PEOPLE BALLET

The Glenville High library is devoid of people, save for the librarian typing furiously near the door on his vintage mechanical keyboard.

The library was previously the Public Information room of city hall, the room where you could pick up transit maps or use information kiosks. It's got impressively high ceilings and sits close to the entrance of the building, which means you must pass by it to get most anywhere else.

Kermit asked me to meet him here. The most modern tech is computers so old they're on the verge of being fashionable, and despite the prime location, hardly anyone comes in.

I pick a study table and carefully arrange a notebook on top of it. I'm hoping that over the course of the next forty-five minutes, Kermit's going to enlighten me on what I should think and feel about what happened yesterday.

After my appointment, I told Kermit about Michael, the CIA papers, and Charlotte leaving me with the pill, hoping he'd offer me reassurance. Instead, he said, "Well, shit." Then he shooed me from his house, saying he had to "get to work."

Several hours later, I got a text message telling me to meet him here tomorrow, which is now today. After a few minutes of hesitation, I also sent Jane a text, inviting her.

The second bell rings. The library door whacks against the wall.

The sound ricochets around the whole space. The high-ceilinged room carries noise extremely well.

"Rodge, my man!" Kermit's voice breaks the librarian's stream of typing. Then there's the slapping and snapping of an elaborate handshake.

"The usual?" the librarian, presumably Rodge, says.

"Please. But also an extra with cane."

"On it."

Kermit slides into the chair across from me. He nods briskly and arranges his own notebook on the table. The burnt vanilla scent hangs heavy—heavier than normal.

I employ Jane's air quotes. "'The usual'?"

"Mmm. I've fixed the library espresso machine at least twice. Rodge is a writer. Working on a fantasy set in outer space. Writers love their coffee. They *need* their coffee. Thus . . . I'm kind of a hero."

On cue, Rodge appears by our table with two tiny, steaming cups.

Kermit takes them and sets one in front of himself and one in front of the empty seat to his right. "My brother."

"Call if you need."

"Same-same." They slap hands again, and Rodge leaves.

Spiders of irritation crawl up my spine. "Well? What's your news?"

Kermit holds up one hand and, with the other, takes the tiniest of sips from his minuscule mug. "Twenty more seconds, because she'd have been coming from the east wing . . ." He looks at the face of his phone. "Five, four, three, two . . ."

The library door smacks the wall again.

"Rodge! Hi! How're the dragons?" Jane's voice filters sweetly over the room.

"Roaring silently into the great, soundless void. So—good."

"Glad to hear it."

My mood improves slightly, simply hearing her.

"Hey." Jane rounds the nearest bookshelf. She smiles at me, and my mood improves a whole lot. Her smile falters. "Hello, Kermit."

"Hello, Jane. Nice to see you."

They watch each other.

Kermit nudges the extra cup delicately. "I got you your favorite drink."

"I thought you two didn't know each other," I say.

Jane eyes the tiny cup. "He does not know me. We do not know each other. Kermit likes to establish dominance in the intellectual hierarchy early in the conversation through intimidation tactics."

One of Kermit's eyebrows creeps upward.

Jane rests her hands on the back of the chair. "A dominance dance is not something I'd normally engage in because I think intimidation tactics are *not* healthy, and the way he does it as a surprise is unfair because it catches people who might otherwise outmaneuver him. And, frankly, it's annoying. But since you invited me here, 'Wayne, and you presumably would not have broken our contract if this was not of utmost importance, it seems I have no choice but to converse with Kermit.

"As you can see, Kermit has attempted to throw me off guard by surprising me with a Cubano, which is, in fact, my favorite café order. He wants to disarm me, send me off into spinning circles of *But how could he know? What else might he know?*"

Jane takes a tiny spoon out of the front pocket of her backpack and lays it on the table between them. "Fortunately, I knew that Kermit would be here, with my favorite drink, wanting to gloat about how he figured out what that drink was."

I feel like I'm at a party I wasn't invited to. A party that is delaying a very important meeting.

Kermit gives a small bow. "Touché. I'm impressed. You're impressive."

Jane rolls her eyes. "Thanks." Her voice is flat, but she takes a seat, clicks her tiny cup against Kermit's, stirs it with her tiny spoon, and they both take tiny sips. Then they give each other tiny, synchronized nods.

"Are we . . . okay to start things now?"

Jane eyes me. "Things *are* started. But it's time to get down to business. I assume there is business."

Kermit wiggles his fingers. "There's more business than D even knows."

Jane stabs her finger onto Kermit's notebook. "Kermit. Let's get something straight right now. Your gloating? It takes up time. And do you know what is equally, if not more, valuable than information?"

Kermit sits back in his chair, like the truth of Jane's observation has pushed him upright. "Well, then." He makes his hand into the universal signal for phone.

Jane and I both hand our phones over, and Kermit disappears into one of the library stacks.

ULTRA BOOM

Kermit reappears from between the library shelves, phone-free. "Stuck them in a back corner, underneath *History of Vacumatic Fountain Pens*, which no one will ever read. We *should* be safe, but I've also got a new way to confirm that."

From his backpack, he pulls out an old purple Xbox controller. He presses the A button. Nothing happens. Kermit looks pleased.

"I've modified this controller to do two things. First, to detect smart devices, at least the most popular types, so we can be at least eighty-two percent confident of privacy whenever we want to have a conversation. Secondly, I've enabled it to detect the sound coming from a wristband, so we can detect who is, or who is not, participating in the study."

He presses the B button while pointing the controller at me. It vibrates twice.

Jane's index finger is tapping the top of her other hand. "I'm actually a little impressed."

I shake my head. "Don't be. There's always an ulterior motive."

Kermit grins and flops into his chair. "What?! Never! It's useful! You can tell when you're safe! We can compile a list of participants for our own education! If someone offered to buy that list for an exorbitant fee . . . well now, that's just a bonus." He lowers his voice. "But it might be likely. Especially after I tell you what I'm about to tell you." He wiggles his fingers.

Jane's hand slams onto the table. "Kermit!"

Rodge, from the front of the library, shouts, "Space dragons cannot come into being when voices of Earthlings distract!"

"The gloating, Kermit."

"Okay, okay." Kermit leans toward me conspiratorially. "We'll get the tea from the D on the C."

"What?" Jane says.

"Ignore him." I push his forehead to sit him back up and out of my space.

He crosses his arms. "Fine, *fine*. Go ahead, D, share your news."

I do, watching Jane's face the whole time, trying to gauge whether anything I'm saying is making her upset or anxious. But her face has become that blank mask she's so good at. In fact, if anything at all, she looks borderline pleased. Overly interested, even, one might say.

"Well," she says when I'm done. "That is fascinating."

"It is?"

"Well, of course it's worrying, too. But it's also fascinating. Especially the end, where Charlotte turns away. Maybe she did that because she knows that something about those pills is dangerous, or . . ."

"Or maybe the whole thing was an act. A test," Kermit adds.

Jane nods. "Exactly. Interesting. *Interesting.*"

Kermit points a finger at her. "That's why I needed to investigate immediately, starting with the low-hanging fruit."

Jane points her finger back at Kermit. "As Robert Lang likes to say, you let the dead people do the work for you."

"Boom." Their two pointed fingers turn into fists that then bump together.

I clear my throat.

"History." Kermit turns to me. "I researched the history of times the CIA has done studies on humans. And then I expanded from there to all of the US government."

"There's a history?"

He squints at me. "MK-ULTRA?"

"A . . . type of gun?"

Jane's fingers are tapping the table next to her tiny cup. "It's the project where the CIA was secretly drugging civilians with LSD." Her voice has changed, gone softer, like her assassin's blade has transformed into one of those pirate kids' plastic swords.

Kermit points at her, but this time she doesn't point back.

My calf muscle twitches. "They did that?"

"Mmm."

"You think we're being given LSD?"

Kermit snorts. "No." He gives me a look, face squinched up, like he's checking to see if I'm joking.

Jane's tapping finger has sped up, and her lips have tightened.

"No!" Kermit says again, when he realizes I'm serious. "Come on, D, don't you think you'd have noticed . . . ? Never mind. No, it's not LSD. That's just an example. They've tried all sorts of stuff. MK-ULTRA isn't even the worst of it. They did some other pretty nasty sheeeeba inus."

"*Worse* than secretly drugging people?"

Jane's index finger is tapping so quickly, it's a blur. "Governments have done a lot of things to their own people."

Kermit tips back the rest of what's in his cup and pushes it to the side. He opens his notebook. "There really is *a lot*. Even I, Captain Kermit, had no idea."

ONLY MEGORTHEROX SURVIVES

Kermit is excited about his research. He doesn't make us wait. He doesn't make us ask. He simply spins his notebook toward us so we can read his scrawled chart.

The first column is headed *Name*, and it lists words like MK-ULTRA, *Artichoke*, *Bluebird*, *Midnight Climax*. At the bottom of the list is *Mothlight*.

He points to this column. "I made a list of various human research projects that have been declassified." He points to a column farther to the right. "This column summarizes what the agency did for each project. LSD, for lots, but they've given people other drugs, too. Also poisons. They've purposely made people sick—or tried to, anyway. Dropped little bomblets of anthrax over unsuspecting Ohioans . . . not that Ohioans would have been a real loss."

I blink.

"I'm kidding! About Ohioans being a real loss. Not kidding that they did it. What's *worse* are the experiments the US has run outside of the United States—on Canadians, even, which just seems unfair, like picking on a baby donkey. It's like they thought if the people dying weren't US citizens, it was even more okay."

Jane isn't looking at the notebook. Instead, she's looking between her hands, which are no longer tapping but instead are pressed onto the tabletop. Her gray wristband pokes out from under her sweater sleeve. Only her jaw muscle is moving, like in Mirona's, when Miranda appeared with their candy cart.

Kermit continues to jam his finger into his notebook. "Look at this one. Here the US encouraged *other* countries to run the studies so we didn't personally get our hands dirty. Then we traded stuff for the data. The studies involved, like, shaving skin off people, or freezing them, or sewing arms where legs go."

"But," I say, "this doesn't mean that *this* study is like that, right? These are historical examples. The country surely has made advances with our understanding of, like, ethics . . . ?"

Kermit snorts. He looks to Jane, but she doesn't echo his scoff. She still has both hands pressed flat on the tabletop. She opens her mouth, then shuts it. "It's not that they thought Canadians were less valuable." She's so quiet that Kermit leans forward. "It's that it was technically illegal to do things like vivisection. So, it was *easier* to run those experiments outside of this country. Legal technicalities aside, pretty sure they would have had zero qualms about running those studies on Americans." She swallows. It looks as though every word hurts to speak. Her fingers are spread wide, like she's trying to push her whole arm through the table.

Her lips twitch. Kermit, for once, is sitting still, even though there's a long silent space for him to fill, like he understands Jane already, that she has more she wants to say.

We listen to Rodge's frantic keyboard clacking.

One of Jane's fingers begins to tap. When she speaks again, she directs her words to the table. "A lot of countries were running those studies without US encouragement, and the US simply bought or traded for the results after the fact. It's not just the US to blame. So many governments have done it, decided which citizens are more useful as test subjects. Because in the grand scheme of things, there are lots of people on earth, right? The world is swarming with us. Why not trade a few measly lives to get knowledge that improves the well-being of the more desirable people? Especially when you're only giving up the lives of people that 'can't contribute enough to society to offset their cost to it.'" Her finger stops tapping and does mini air quotes from the tabletop. "When the behavior is so pervasive, it makes you wonder, doesn't it, if it's just built into who humans are? Like how separate groups of people independently figured out fire or developed similar ways to express laughter or grief."

She takes her hands off the table and puts them inside her bag. They emerge holding a single square sheet of red paper, which she begins to fold. "Don't mind me. It helps me stay calm. Continue on."

Kermit studies his notebook like he's going to continue, but then he looks back at Jane. He watches her hands moving over the paper as she makes one crease, unfolds it, then folds somewhere else.

"Why do you know so much about this?"

Jane creases another fold. "You didn't figure that out when you were getting my coffee order?" A hint of playfulness has returned to her voice.

"I know your father is a historian."

"And you know how to amputate a toe because your mom is a dermatologist?"

"Touché."

Jane nimbly tucks a triangle of paper inside another fold. She looks up at Kermit. "You're going to be disappointed in my reason."

"You've uncovered secret data that you plan to sell?"

"Oh, come on. You wouldn't be disappointed in that." Her voice has returned to normal volume and regained a slight edge, more like a butter knife than a plastic dagger. "I know because I'm interested. That's it. Basic. Simple. That's all."

Kermit crosses his arms and rests them on the table. He watches Jane.

Jane's fingers move swiftly, deftly, unfalteringly. There's no trace of the twitchy, involuntary tapping.

I rub my knees. "So this whole time we've been talking and not-talking, you've known about this?"

"Correct."

"You didn't think to mention it? Even after I wrote you that long letter about the truth encourager and the stalker-y wristband?"

"Correct. Well, I thought about it. And decided not to."

"But why?"

"It's . . . personal."

"It's not."

"It is. It's a personal interest of mine. A hobby. It would be like, like, you talking about that flying game you play on your phone."

"Which would have been an important thing to bring up if there was a chance, for example, that this study was part of a coordinated drone insurgency!"

A loud smack resounds between the shelves. "Vacuum! Space is a vacuum! That means *soundless*!"

Kermit gives me a stern look. "You need to chill your chinchillas. You're going to do something you regret. And you"—Kermit squints at Jane and waggles his finger—"I don't believe you."

Jane's fingers momentarily pause mid-crease. "Well, it's true."

"Mmm."

"It *is*. It *is* personal. I am interested because it relates to me, personally. Did you see in your Wikipedia wanderings that Hans Asperger, the 'hero' who recognized autism, was recognizing it and then sending those 'recognized' kids away to be used as test subjects? That some of those kids' brains were kept in jars and studied for over fifty years?"

"No. I didn't know that. But that's not what I'm referring to. I believe that you are personally interested. But I sense there is something else. *More.*"

Jane folds four more folds. "Fine. Yes. You're right."

"Ha!" Kermit raises his hands as if he's going to slap the table, then, glancing toward Rodge, thinks better of it. "I knew it. That's all I wanted to hear. That I am right. We don't have to talk about it."

"That's very generous of you." Jane rolls her eyes.

"Excuse me," I say, "I hate to interrupt this meeting of minds with my plebeian brain, but I still have no idea what's going on. All I'm getting out of this is that the CIA may be trying to kill us?"

Kermit shrugs. "That's the gist."

"No, it's not." Jane takes tweezers from somewhere in her sweater sleeve and crimps some folds. "It's more nuanced. Walk him through the rest of your list."

"It sounds like you might know more than I do. What did you call my research? My 'Wikipedia wanderings'?"

She waves her tweezers in his general direction. "You'll get more enjoyment out of sharing."

"Truth." Kermit turns to me. "Okay. So. Look at this one, Operation Paperclip. After World War II, the United States straight up hired the lead Nazi scientists . . ."

"Himmler, Göring, Strughold, von Braun, von Ohain . . ."

"Excuse me?"

"Names."

"Are you sure you don't want to do the talking?"

Jane waves her tweezers.

"Right. So. D. The point is, they gave the highest-up, most Nazi-est of the Nazis, safe, happy jobs in the United States! Totally erased their history, gave them fake backgrounds, gave them powerful positions leading other powerful people. All the bad things they had done? Poof, forgiven, in exchange for the data the scientists had accumulated from murdering so many people." He waves his hands over his head, like brain waves are exploding through his finger tentacles. "Like, sure, let's purposely put the Nazis in charge! It's just— WAHH!"

Another slam from the front of the library. "How will you defeat the Megortherox, Drago?" Then, in a high-pitched voice, "Why, I won't *ever* defeat Megortherox because I cannot *focus* on the Megortherox."[22]

Kermit whispers, "There's a lot. A whole lot. Just, just . . . look at all of this!"

I try to look at the notebook. I do. But the words keep going fuzzy, in and out. I see *poison*, I see *death count*, I see *anthrax*.

"This one! And this!" Kermit's jabbing his finger at the paper, harder and harder the worse the experiments are, as if the worse they are, the more interesting or exciting or important they are, the ones we need to remember for a pop quiz later.

---

22. In Rodge's book, during the "final" battle with Megortherox (*final* in quotes because Megortherox will continue to act as the main antagonist for sixteen of the remaining seventeen books in the series), our hero Drago lets Megortherox escape when Drago is distracted by a "colony" of teen humans who are tossing fast food wrappers out of their spaceship's waste vent.

In the last book (#spoileralert), Drago realizes the real enemy is the teen humans. Drago teams up with Megortherox, defeats the humans, and then gets eaten by the space equivalent of a giant raven.

"Absurd, horrifying, yet somehow comfortingly predictable," one reviewer would write. "Like a cheese and chicken taco that's been served like salad in a bowl."

POP QUIZ

1. **What was the Nazi Party's original inspiration?**

   a) Hitler himself. He was a man of many original ideas.

   b) Russia. Russia is never up to any good.

   c) The United States. A young Hitler, in fact, sent fan mail to an American named Madison Grant, thanking him for writing *The Passing of the Great Race*, a eugenics manifesto that Hitler was using as "his bible." In later years, the majority of Nazi legislation was explicitly based on America's race laws, such as those enforcing segregation, banning interracial marriages, and stripping unwanted people of citizenship—American eugenicists, in fact, assisted with crafting these laws to help Germany follow the path blazed by the magnificent US of A. In addition, the United States' ongoing experimentation on "expendable populations" showed how sacrificing some of "lesser" society could be used for the common good. For example, infecting these lesser folk (such as those pesky Black people) with illnesses, and intentionally keeping them sick, led to the cure for syphilis. Brilliant! Perhaps the single most notable thing the Nazis did *not* find inspiring in the United States is that its policies were a bit too harsh. The Nazis weren't trying to be monsters, after all!

2. **What happened to the Japanese scientists responsible for murdering and torturing thousands of Chinese and Koreans—freezing them to death, flaying them, rearranging their limbs, trying to erase their minds?**

   a) They were imprisoned. Obviously.

   b) They were given immunity in exchange for sharing their research results with the United States.

3. **What happened to the Nazi scientists after World War II ended?**

   a) They were imprisoned. Obviously.

   b) Right? . . . Right?

   c) The United States secretly arranged to bring almost eight hundred of these clearly brilliant, fearless, groundbreaking folk to this country to work for US government agencies. Their backgrounds were erased and rewritten or simply ignored. Yes, the people who designed the gas chambers, who led mass murders, who delighted in recording details about the lengths of time it took people to die under various poisons, were awarded, by the United States, bonus stipends and large salaries and control of some of the most powerful organizations on US soil.

CONVENIENT RAT

"It's incredible, right?!" Kermit picks up his notebook and flaps it in the air.

"Is it?" I say. Which is an honest question. Is the fact that these pills might be poison actually, somehow, a good thing?

Jane takes a metal bottle from her bag and fills her empty Cubano mug with water. "It's not that incredible. All of these are public knowledge. Anyone can read about them on Wikipedia. Kermit's experience being our case in point, here."

Kermit frowns, but he quickly recovers. He thwacks the notebook down onto the table. "It *is* incredible. It's *incredible* that despite these being public knowledge, *despite* them being on Wikipedia, they aren't *general* knowledge. How is this stuff not part of our history classes?"

Jane dips her fingertips into her water. "For me, what's most incredible is how pervasive it is. Kermit's list doesn't include all the other studies that probably exist but haven't been declassified. Or all the ones that didn't involve the US at all. Meaning that this impulse to treat bodies and minds and people like they are the property of whoever's in power . . ." Her voice goes quiet again. "It's a part of humanity. The desire to decide who gets to live *is* humanity. Because why else would it happen again, and again, and again, across societies and cultures." She presses her dampened fingertips to a crease, then turns the paper inside out. Her fingers shake. The paper tears.

I lean back and stare out of one of the distant library windows.

There's not much to see at this hour, only a couple seniors on their free period loading into their car, probably heading to WaWa. It looks like they're arguing over who gets to sit shotgun.

"So I'm what? A . . . a convenient rat?"

Jane's fingers shake, but she smiles. "Good band name." She takes a deep breath, reaches into her bag for a fresh sheet of paper, and starts folding again.

Kermit pats my arm three times. "Also, it's not necessarily 'poison,' per se."

"Oh?"

"It might not even be harmful. But whatever it is, it's probably for, what's the word . . . ?"

Jane finishes a crease with an only-slightly-shaky flourish that turns into pointing at Kermit. "Biowarfare."

Kermit points back. Their fingers turn into exploding fist bumps again.

"Warfare?" I say. "Who are we warring with?"

"It's weapons development."

Kermit claps. "A superstar. What she said. It's a weapon for *future* wars. Well, our government would probably say it's to *avoid* future wars, though other countries probably wouldn't frame it that way."

Jane adds, "If it was successfully developed, it would be used as a contact-free weapon."

"Yep! Think *Drone Wars*, but even more hands-free. If we, meaning this country's military, could make other people sick, or have them lose their minds, or make them spill all their secrets, we'd win without risking the lives of our own people."

"Minus the people in the study, that is." Jane bends back over her paper.

"True. True." Kermit turns to me. "Isn't this like a video game? Covert stealth teams! Assassination missions! Races to develop new formulas first!"

I stare at him. "Video games are fun because they aren't real. This is real."

"Incorrect. Video games are fun because they are *safe*."

"So you think this is safe, then? Is that what you're saying?"

"Well . . ." Kermit becomes very focused on closing his notebook and zipping it into his bag. ". . . it's safe for me."

The stream of typing from Rodge's computer doesn't stop. All of us in here are, in some way, dealing with dragons.

THE PROS AND CONS OF QUITTING

Pro: No more wondering, no more ambiguity.

Con: "No more wondering! No more ambiguity! No more *fun*! All this information was meant to get you *interested*, not *panicked*!" — Kermit

Con: "Think of all the money you could make if you don't quit! Figure this out, sell the info . . . or don't sell it, just give it to people and become renowned for your big exposé!"—Kermit

Con: "Maybe you could finally get some decent shoes!"—Kermit

Con: "Plus it'll be fun!"—Kermit

Pro: "What's fun is no more dealing with *you*, Kermit."—Jane

Pro: Jane will no longer need rules in place to manage your conversations.

Con: Jane will have no reason to talk to you at all.

Pro: The CIA CIA CIA marquee in your head will slow down, fade away.

Con: A new marquee: DNS DNS DNS.

Con: No one likes being called a quitter.

Con: "You can't quit! You're finally getting to the interesting stuff! It's probably not even dangerous! Quitter!"—Kermit

Pro: What people call you is irrelevant if you are dead.

ROARING INTO THE VOID

The Hopkins Study App instructs me that to quit, we need to submit an actual paper form by mail, with an actual pen signature.

I'm almost giddy—for once, I know exactly what I need to do. I stand up, ready for our joint crusade to the ancient library computers. The fact that I have lunch period next, meaning ample time to deposit the form in the mail, is extra evidence that it's meant to be.

Kermit's frown is deep. "This is *not* the effect I wanted to have by sharing my research."

I point to Kermit's notebook. "You know we don't really have a choice."

"You always have a choice." He sighs. "Meet you at the printers." He packs his notebook into his bag, picks up his tiny coffee cup, and shuffles down the aisle toward the front.

Jane, though, has semi-raisined. She has tucked her feet up onto the chair and is sitting on them, like she plans to stay in the library for the next hour or maybe she lives here now.

"Are you coming?"

Jane bends closer to her piece of paper, her nose almost touching her tweezers.

"Jane?"

"Oh, me?"

"Yes," I say. "You."

Jane dips her fingertips into her tiny cup of water. "I think I'll stay here."

"What do you mean you'll stay here?"

She folds another fold.

"Jane?"

"Oh, was that an actual question? Sorry, I thought my answer was unmistakably clear. I mean, I will stay here, literally. At this table, in this library, exactly where I am now."

I rest my hands on top of my chair. "Aren't you going to quit?"

"Nah."

"What?"

"Sorry. I mean, 'No.'"

"But . . ."

"But what?"

"But . . ."

"Listen. I understand why you're quitting. But all of what we discussed today isn't news to me. I mean, having it confirmed that it *is* the CIA is news, but the history? The studies? That was all information I knew, suspected, considered even before I signed up. I signed up anyway. So, why would I quit just because now I know that it's true?" Her paper tears. She tosses it into the center of the table. She puts her head in her hands. "It's just . . . Give me a minute to find my words."

Her fingers twist at her sweater threads, and her forehead occasionally creases, then relaxes, then creases again. A series of Dave Appleright motivational "care about stuff" posters taped to the wall behind her—Dave ripping his shirt off, Dave flying toward a net, an aerial shot of Dave reaching out a hand to help a player from the other team get up off the ground—frames her shoulders.

"It's probably a bad choice, not to quit." Her lips form the words haltingly, yet precisely, as if she's reading a complicated script for the first time. "Especially given how much I know. But that's also the reason I can't quit. I know the extremes that this study could be. I know how often this has happened before. I know how far stuff like this has gotten. As someone with knowledge—because like Kermit said, this isn't general knowledge, even though it should be—it's my responsibility to do something about it. And how can I do the most? Stay in it, be in it, watch."

Her hand lets go of her sweater, gestures in the air. "It's not that I'm hoping this is a corrupt human study. But I'd be lying if I didn't say I am a little bit excited that it *is* the CIA. I mean, what are the chances? I've spent years reading about this stuff, and then I get this letter and I sign up thinking, *Something about this letter feels off, but am I just paranoid from all of my research?* And of course they still might not be doing anything wrong.

"But, *if* they are doing something wrong—not that I'm *hoping* they are—but if they *are*, if I could stop it or help stop it or totally fail but at least have tried . . . well, it feels to me like I'm honoring those people. Those people who were told they were less than, who 'weren't worthy of a life.'

"I think of it like this." She scoots her folded paper on the table so it's right next to her cup. "Let's say this cup is mass murder. Where does responsibility end? Here?" She moves the paper so it's an inch away. "Where I'm someone like Charlotte, involved but merely enacting the demands of someone else?" She moves the paper four inches away. "Or here? Where I'm a participant who knew and chose to simply walk away?" She slides her paper back and forth, closer and farther from the cup. "Is there a line you can draw where blame falls away? Who draws that line? And also—is this distance really two or three dimensions?" She unfolds the paper so one corner of it touches the cup, and then she gently curves the opposite corner over to meet it. "Or is the distance of blame more like space-time?"

Her lips twitch as she lets the paper go. "Does that make any sense? Am I being completely ridiculous? It's okay if I am. I often am. You can say so. It won't change my mind."

"You're not being ridiculous." I run a finger under my wristband, which suddenly feels scratchy. "I don't think anyone would blame you, though."

"Well, my decision is made. Like Kermit pointed out, there's another reason I'm not going to quit, but it's personal, so I can't share it with you. Though I'm not sure what will happen to our rules now, since you're quitting. Which is fine, by the way. I'm not going to hold you accountable if people die."

I scratch under my wristband again.

She goes back to folding her paper, her knees now entirely pulled up into her sweater. She is so tiny and so purposeful and determined and precise and also enormous, filling up this whole room.

I shift my weight. "Are we still going to talk? Or not-talk? You still need someone to talk to, right?"

There's a break in her flow of folding, dipping her fingers, folding.

I hold my breath.

"Okay. Yes. I would appreciate that. Though it's certainly not as good as if we were both doing the study, it would still be helpful to me. You don't mind? And we can keep our rules in place? I'll have to get you an updated contract."

I nod.

"Okay, great. Thank you. That's very generous of you. Which does, of course, make me question your motives, but I won't literally question you, and I'll stop mentally questioning now because we have to resume as much anonymity as possible. On that note, we should stop talking." She stands her paper up on the table. It's a dragon wearing a space helmet, very clearly roaring into the soundless void.

GLOAT IN DISGUISE

Kermit is leaning on the printer with a paper in his hand. "Figured I'd be productive while you two had some alone time."

"You printed the form?"

"Ready for you to sign."

"How'd you log in to my Hopkins account?"

"Why do you even bother to ask?"

I snatch the paper from him. "Back to gloating, I see."

He grins sheepishly before bending down to unnecessarily untie and then retie his left Phat.

The quitting form takes up half the paper. Name, date, my ID number pre-filled, a checkbox confirming the decision, a line for a signature. I fish a pen out of my bag and sign it on the printer. "We can go. Jane isn't coming."

"Cool." Kermit stands up, starts walking toward the door. "I'll come with you to the post office."

"Jane is not quitting, and you say 'cool'?" I realize his hands are empty. He only printed one paper. "You knew?"

He shrugs a lopsided, robotic dance move of a shrug, like he took his gloat and stuffed it into a Halloween costume three sizes too small.

BECOMING UNGELLED

The hallways are empty as Kermit and I walk toward the parking lot exit. My step is loose, light. My shoes make happy squeaking sounds on the tile.

"Someone's in a good mood. You sure you don't want to change your mind? Keep on with it?"

"Absolutely sure."

"Can we at least fix your shoes? They shouldn't be squeaking like that."

"I like it." My legs skip. My sneakers squeal.

Kermit frowns, making my skips even sprightlier as we round the corner. A pair of students is approaching, and the sour smell of hair gel prickles my nose.

"Bryce! Hope you're doing well!" My voice is uncharacteristically exuberant and friendly.

"Oh, hi." Bryce, on the other hand, sounds less exuberant than usual.

In fact, he looks scared to see me.

And then I notice his usually perfectly gelled hair is slightly less perfectly gelled.

And the person he's with isn't a student.

Her makeup is carefully, extensively done; pink outlines her lips and eyes, like she's a coloring book that someone's hastily filled in. She's wearing a long black sweater and bright blue shoes.

My sneakers stop bouncing.

"Hi, 'Wayne." She emphasizes the *D*, as she always does.

"Dr. Charlotte."

"Good to see you." She smiles at me. The hallway walls narrow.

One of her hands is resting on Bryce's forearm. It is not resting lightly. Her grip is making a cratered terrain of his skin.

Bryce's pupils are darting all over like he's tracking invisible flies. It makes my arms itch. He's totally terrified.

Or drugged.

A sour taste spreads across the back of my tongue.

Kermit has turned back to make faces like *let's go already*, and I lower my chin half an inch, hoping that this is enough to communicate that this is serious and stay over there and don't get involved and maybe you should leave the building alone or create some sort of explosion or other diversion or . . .

"Would you do me a favor, 'Wayne?" Charlotte's gaze dances down to the printed-out form in my hand. I fold it over my thumb.

"Bryce has to leave school early today. He might not be back this week. I'm running a little behind. Would you mind taking something to the office for me? Unless you're . . ." Her gaze flickers to my form, then jumps back to my eyes. ". . . busy?"

I swallow.

With the hand that isn't terraforming Bryce's arm, Charlotte produces an envelope from a pocket. The school's fluorescent lights flicker over the now-familiar raised and shiny university hologram in the upper right corner.

I take the envelope and she turns around, dragging Bryce with her, her blue heels clacking against the tile.

"Who was that?" Kermit walks toward me.

"Charlotte," says Jane from behind me, slightly out of breath. "I decided I wanted to ride with you, and . . ."

"*The* Charlotte? From the truth encourager?"

I hold up the envelope. The hologram sparkles in its typical way. "She asked me to take this to the office. Apparently, Bryce is going to be missing a week or two of school." Chills run down my arms, even though she only asked me for a small favor. An easy favor.

"Let's open it." Kermit snatches at the envelope.

"Are you serious?" I hold the envelope out of his reach. "You really want me to look at what's in here? Open this envelope that isn't addressed to me? After everything you told me in the library?"

"She handed you—actually *handed* you—information! On a piece of paper! That's right there, in your hand!"

"Maybe when it's your life on the line, you can go about opening random stuff that isn't addressed to you."

"You've been opening stuff that isn't addressed to you for years, unless your name is actually Peter Le."

The bell rings, ending third period. We're about to be surrounded by students. Kermit waves us over to one of the wood benches along the edge. "Talk while it's crowded."

The hallway fills with voices and laughing and the sound of shoes on tile.

Jane positions herself against the wall, wedges herself in the corner made by a bench. "Did you two notice that Charlotte was holding Bryce's arm?"

I nod.

"Did you notice anything about that arm?"

"It was like a hot dog getting mashed back into dog meat."

"Gross, Kermit. But correct. Did either of you notice anything else?"

"It's starting to feel like you have a point."

"Get out of the middle of the hallway. Close your eyes if you need to. Visualize the arm, her fingers around his wrist, just so. Can you see his wrist? Can you see the skin puckered up around Charlotte's fingertips?"

"Does this count as gloating, Jane?"

"Will you please close your eyes!"

My eyes are already closed. The noise of feet and laughing and talking form a meditative barrier around my thoughts. At first I keep seeing Bryce's face—his eyes flickering, his nostrils occasionally flaring like a spooked horse's. I move my memory to his arm in Dr. Charlotte's grip, the wrist skin puckered under her fingers, white and pink and . . . bare.

"His wristband was gone."

"Ding ding ding. Maybe you would have gotten there first, Kermit, if you had closed your eyes."

Kermit glares at her.

"All I'm saying," she says, "is that it was worth noticing."

Someone sprints down the hallway, laughing. Their arm catches the edge of the papers in my hand.

"Sorry!" they yell over their shoulder.

"No running, Lewis!" Mr. Houston's voice, from somewhere.

"Actually," Kermit says, "it's great news that his wristband was gone."

"Why?"

Kermit swings his backpack off his shoulder and pulls out the purple Xbox controller from the front pocket.

"While D here was talking to Charlotte, I gave this a test. But when I clicked it to register Bryce, nothing happened. I thought it was broken. He'd been *selected*, if you recall. But if he wasn't wearing a wristband . . . that means Captain Kermit did not in fact make an error in the software! Which, of course he didn't."

"I'm not going to mention the gloating, Kermit, I'm not."

"Just like I didn't mention your 'you'd have won if you'd closed your eyes'?"

"That was a blunt fact."

"You were saying that your eye-closing idea was the right one."

"Excuse me!" I flap the papers at them. "Does the fact that he lost the wristband mean anything?"

"Here's what I'm thinking," Jane says. "And hear me out. What if Bryce didn't lose it. What if he didn't have his wristband because he quit, and Charlotte is taking him away *because* he quit? Like, punishment. Like, he was secretly not allowed to quit."

Kermit is shaking his head. "I understand that you want my super-awesome friend D to stay in the study with you. And your reasoning certainly sounds very exciting, and Kermit does love himself some excitement. But the rule is to always go with the simplest possible explanation. And the simplest explanation is that Bryce forgot to put the wristband on.

"Plus, if they took Bryce away for two weeks, what are they going to do with him? Interrogate him for a day or two, subject him to a touch of light torture, and then release him into his fifth period geometry quiz?"

"I know," Jane says, waving her hand. "I'm just saying it's a *possibility*, and a good reason to open the envelope—Kermit, why are you arguing with me? Don't you want to open the envelope?"

Kermit zips the controller back into his bag. "D, listen to Jane."

The crowd around us starts to thin. The warning bell sounds, two minutes left to get to class. I picture Charlotte's fragmented gaze when she saw the form in my hand.

"What if her giving me the envelope was like how she tried to tell me not to take my last pill? What if she *wanted* me to read what was in it before I quit, to stop me from quitting?"

Jane snatches the envelope from me. "Actually, this brings me to my final reason that we should look at what's in the envelope." She turns it over and runs a finger under the flap, which pops up with a light snap. "It's already open."

APOLOGY:REGRET :: WARNING: _____

Jane tilts the open envelope toward us, revealing the edge of folded paper inside.

"So you really think it's possible that Charlotte *wanted* me to open it?"

"I remain anti the whole sending-me-a-message thing." Kermit jumps his bag onto his back. "But it's hard to argue that she would hand you an unsealed envelope if she *minded* you looking at what was inside."

Jane hands the envelope back to me. "Right. If she really didn't want you to see it, she wouldn't have entrusted you with an unsealed envelope."

"Unless it's a test. To see if I can be trusted." I slide the folded paper out anyway.

Dear Glenville High Administration:

Due to unforeseen complications with our health study, Bryce Orr will be withdrawn for the remainder of the school year.

We will contact you before the start of next year to inform you of next year's status, and whether Bryce will be returning for his senior year.

Thank you for your cooperation. Bryce's continued participation and your assistance are greatly appreciated.

Best,
M. Mikulski, MD
Research Director

I hold the paper out so Jane and Kermit can read it.

"Mmm." Jane's face has gone blank.

"The rest of the year is not a week or two." Kermit takes the paper from me and turns it over to check the back. "I hate to admit it, but it does sort of seem like a warning now. Unless she didn't know what the paper said."

I consider the way she held on to that paper, the way she held on to my gaze. Her eyes flickering to the form in my hand. And Bryce's face, his limp, un-gelled hair. "She knew."

Kermit shakes his head. "We shouldn't get carried away here. And you know if Captain Kermit is saying we shouldn't get carried away, it must be true. There are so many other possible explanations. Maybe Bryce had some bad side effects and he's going to get treated—better to prepare the school for a long absence even if he ends up fine and comes back next week." He shakes his head again. "Look—D. I don't want you to quit. We still have no data that anything about this study is dangerous, and I think being part of something run by the C—" He glances around the emptying hallway. "—part of a heart study is a great opportunity. But—and I say this in a rare moment of non-manipulative honesty—if you really want to quit, this letter shouldn't stop you. I truly don't think they are punishing him in any way."

"But you think it's a warning, right, Jane?"

Jane fusses with her sweater sleeve. "It kills me to say this but—Kermit might be right. I'm changing my mind. There are so many other explanations. I'm too paranoid."

"Oh, Janey, such modesty . . ."

"Stop."

"Admitting inferiority . . ."

"Kermit."

"You were on a nice little roll there of being more correct about things than me. It was refreshing. Humbling. Made one's mind aware of the potential for expansion— Actually. Wait! I will practice humility and modesty. I will give Jane's idea one last benefit of the doubt, because, well, I have a brilliant idea. We'll go right to the source." He hands the envelope back to me and takes out his phone. "Let's call him. Ask Bryce himself."

Jane shakes her head. "He was clearly busy . . ."

"He can call us back later today, after Charlotte's done with him."

Kermit holds his phone between us and turns it on speaker. It rings.

Jane looks at me. "Does Kermit have the number of everyone in the school?"

"Phone number, phone passcode, ability to post to all socials, full medical records . . ."[23]

---

[23]. Once, he asked me which I thought was better: having someone's credit card numbers or having access to their private health records.

"Better?" I said. "Like morally better? Neither."

Turns out, he meant *financially* better, and the correct answer was *not* the one that obviously benefited finances.

"You can tell a lot about someone by their health. It's foundational. So much of what people do, the choices they make, are built on top of what their bodies and minds allow. Know their health, know their actions, know their lives. So yeah. *Value* is spelled I-N-F-O-R-M-A-T-I-O-N.*"

Then I asked him what my health records said about me and he said he didn't have my health records, that the whole conversation was hypothetical, of course.

---

* This was the original coining of his favorite phrase.

But Kermit doesn't gloat. He's frowning. Over the speaker, we hear a robotic voice. It's apologizing that the number we've dialed is no longer in service.

Jane's lips twitch. "Are you sure the number is correct?"

"Of course I'm sure." Kermit hangs up, clicks around on the screen, and holds his phone up to his ear. His frown deepens. "Bryce's mom's number is disconnected, too."

The panic that I've been struggling to dampen surges right back into my throat.

Kermit types. "Social media accounts active. Posted something this morning. But email password doesn't work. Password changed or account deactivated." Kermit tucks his phone back into his jeans. "Bizarre. Concerningly bizarre. Especially concerning considering Bryce owes me three hundred dollars. I'll swing by his house later to see if I can get more information, but . . ."

The final bell rings. The hallway is empty. We will get yelled at soon, even though we all have lunch period next.

Jane crosses her arms. Her fingers entwine themselves into her sweater threads. She doesn't look particularly pleased at maybe being right.

I look at the letter one more time before folding it back into the envelope. The first thing I feel is a glimmer of relief that I still have no choice about what I should do next. But the glimmer of relief alights on a Weirdness Log, and then my whole emotional forest is in flames.

Kermit's brow furrows. "For the record, I maintain that *I* was right: It wasn't a warning. But maybe a threat?"

Jane lets out a short laugh, as if this is a joke.

The sun shifts and blares through the window at the end of the hall. It blazes directly onto Kermit's cheeks. I can see the pores of his skin. I can see where wrinkles will form around his mouth in ten years. I can see how human he is and feel my own skin breathing and muscles contracting and I understand how the ability to die is both universal and entirely singular.

TEXTS

DAD
Remember I would like to schedule a time to talk with you about Mr. Houston's email.

ME
Not today.

Tomorrow? 6pm?

Not tomorrow.

HOPKINS STUDY APP

A quick 'n' easy one today!

In this game, you are drowning.

Tap the screen as fast as you can to flail your arms and legs until you either break the surface or your time has run out.

Unable to tap the screen? <u>Click here</u> to access alternative methods of playing. We try to make our study accessible for all! Everyone is welcome! All levels of physical and mental ability are fully valued!

Have Fun!

THAT NIGHT

I dream about white lab rats. Their organs have been removed and are stored in a separate bottle. The organs pulse. A scientist in a white coat says, "Even without vocal cords, the rats are still able to scream."

BINARY REALITY:

How Small-Town Communities Think & Feel About Digital Technology

An Oral History, by Naomi Le

We're mostly caught up now, with the urban centers. At least in access. Most of us have high-speed internet at home, at least one computer. Phones.

What's different is our history with it. It's not woven into the fabric of our lives, like it is for you city people. We didn't grow up along with it. We didn't watch the evolution of MySpace into Facebook into TikTok. We didn't have it slowly shorten our attention spans, train us to scroll and skim. It was just *bam* TikTok. *Bam* Snaps. So we have a different viewpoint. We're outsiders.

Think of it like dropping a guy from the early 1900s, who's only ever ridden in Model T Fords, into a modern-day Porsche. Everything is new. Everything is shiny. There are so many buttons.

That's the guy who's going to be like, "This is sick. Holy mother." But it's also going to be the guy that asks, "Do we really need so many buttons? Do we need it to move so damn fast?"

Timuel Black: Grape Creek, Texas

IN WHICH I'VE WON

Kermit has dropped by Bryce's house every day since the envelope incident four days ago. The family cars are still parked in the driveway, the house is still full of furniture, but the lights are off and no one answers the door. Apparently Bryce had a dog, Oscar, a yappy terrier. And yet—silence.

And so, the plan we came up with is not a plan: Keep going with the study. Even Jane has nothing to add.

This afternoon, Olive is sprawled on my floor, sketching. Her moose slippers stare up at me from the floor. A marathon of *Blue Planet* is playing on my laptop. She's sketching the sea life. I'm trying to spend quality time with Olive. In case, you know.

My phone keeps lighting up with texts from Kermit. He wants me to come over to discuss the "clues." To "make progress."

I ignore him. There are no new clues. The only chance we have to get information is Jane's next appointment, which is Tuesday. Three days from now.

Instead of answering Kermit's texts, I watch Olive draw and weigh again whether I should tell my father about what is going on.

Olive's pretty good. Her pencil makes soft shushing noises as it flies across the page. Her calm is almost origami-Jane-like.

She catches me watching. "You're being creepy."

I can't help smiling. "Not as creepy as that guy." I point at the television, where an anglerfish, maybe the exact one on my phone case, is opening its giant, tooth-filled jaws.

"I hope you mean 'guy' gender-neutrally," Olive says, "because that gorgeous specimen is a female. Aren't you watching? David Attenborough just explained how the male anglerfish is small, helpless, and eventually loses his own self-identity as he is literally absorbed—"

The doorbell rings. Olive's calm is transformed faster than the *Blue Planet* sandworms[24] can snap up a fish. She drops her pencil and rushes downstairs.

I heave myself off of the bed and trail after her. The front door slams in a distinctively un-Olive-like way.

"'Wayne!" Her footsteps start coming back up—slower now.

She is holding a cardboard box that is more than half her size. Her face, or what I can see of her face, is pink. "You've won something."

"I've . . . won?"

She tips the box forward onto the top step, where I'm standing, and spins it so I can see the side of the box that says in giant blue letters, "Congratulations! You are our winner! Your prize inside!"

"Huh."

"Aren't you going to open it?"

I cross my arms and nudge the box with my knee. It scoots three inches—it's very light. "No."

"Why not?"

This is obviously a Kermit prank. In fact, it's *so* obvious in a way that Kermit is usually not obvious, which makes me think he *wants*

---

24. Technically they are called *bobbit worms*, but I refuse to call them that because that makes them sound cute. They are the stuff of science fiction nightmares. Not the stuff of science fiction. Of science fiction *nightmares*.

me to know it's him, which makes me even grumpier about it. "I don't want to open it because . . . I don't know what's in it?"

Olive puffs her cheeks at me.

I nudge the box with my knee again. It slides another two inches across the stair landing. "I didn't enter any contests. It could be dangerous."

Olive picks up the box and thrusts it into my chest. Something thunks against the box side. "People win random stuff all the time. What's the worst it could be? Better question: What's the *best* thing it could be? What if it's something better than a prize for a contest? Like, I don't know, a love letter and gift from someone too shy to tell you directly?"

This gives me pause. I could see Jane sending me something by mail to make me feel better. She'd do it under the guise of a contest so I don't know it's her, so it's not personal. I give the box one more little shake. The thunk is soft.

"No way. There's someone you *want* a love letter from? Who is it? *Who is it?!*"

"No one!" I turn and head for my room. "Let's go get some scissors, then."

PODIATRY

I shake the box one more time before setting it on my bed. It's about as heavy as a bread loaf.

Olive hops up onto the bed next to it. "It's weird, right? Surprisingly light for such a large box."

"The most weird thing is, as already mentioned, I don't remember entering any contests."

"Maybe it's an automatic entry thing? Like if you used your froyo reward card enough times."

"You know I don't like frozen yogurt."

"It was an example. And yes, I *do* know you don't like frozen yogurt. Which is unfortunate. And wrong."

I pick up the box again. Shake it. It makes the same soft thunking sound. I put it back down. "Any guesses?"

"A trophy?" Olive slides the box onto her lap, tests its weight. "Mmm. It would have to be, like, an inflatable one. Or an ecologically minded trophy that has been made of compressed, recycled wood chips, previously referred to as particle board."

I shake my head. "Somehow I missed your fiftieth birthday."

She grins.

I find a pair of scissors in my desk drawer. "You sound pretty sure it's a trophy."

"Well, technic-ah-lly"—she adjusts invisible glasses on her nose—"*technically*, it's a prize. So, anything inside this box is a trophy."

"All right, Ms. Technically, you can open it." I hold out the scissors. "If you're careful."

She rolls her eyes and snatches the scissors from me.

The tape zips as she slices through it, then pops as she pulls open the flaps. On the bottom of the mostly empty box is a single pair of—

"Slippers?"

They are magenta, the color of the neon subtitle on Mirona's Miracles. They look way too small for me. There is also an envelope with my name printed on the front.

I brace myself for Olive's disappointment, but she is grinning into the box as if the fluffy slippers are fluffy kittens instead. "Oh my gosh! Slippers!" She plunges both of her hands into the box and pulls the slippers out. "Oh, they are so soft, 'Wayne, oh, you are so lucky! Touch them!"

I do touch them. They are quite soft. This is bizarre, even for Kermit.

"Look!" She points her finger at the plush heel of one of the slippers.

Embroidered in blue cursive script is "The Swedish Council of Podiatry: We know health & luxury."

Olive leans back into the box and pulls out the envelope. At the top left is a very sparkly hologram.

I take it from her carefully. The paper feels expensive—thick and slightly textured. My name has been written by hand with a fancy pen. The hologram, I see now, is of a foot. It flexes and contracts its toes when you tilt the envelope in the light.

There's a note inside printed on a single sheet of paper.

I turn it so Olive and I can read it together:

The Swedish Academy of Medicine
Podiatry Department
4413 Swedesiford
Stockholm, SDE 997822

Dear Wayne Le:

Greetings! And congratulations. You entered our Podiatry Award Contest, and your name was drawn as one of only two hundred winners!

Due to some unforeseen delays on our side (changes in administration, mostly), it has taken us an extra year to draw and announce the winners of this contest. Thus, it would not be surprising if you do not remember entering this contest. But enter you did! And now, you have won.

In this box, you will find a pair of slippers. You will find that these slippers are not only extraordinarily soft, but also extremely comfortable. They were, of course, designed by some of the greatest podiatrists in the world. We hope you enjoy them.

It would be totally understandable if you felt a smidge of disappointment, after waiting a long year, for a pair of branded slippers as your prize. Nice slippers, yes, but what in your language would be called "swag." Do not worry!

These slippers are not your real prize! We would like to present you with your grand prize in person. So, at a time that is convenient for you within the next twenty minutes, please scan the code below. This will initiate directions from your current location to our closest representative. Due to some Swedish laws regarding international awards (too complicated to explain in this letter) you will need to attend this meeting alone.

Thank you again for your participation, and again, congratulations!

The Swedish Council of Podiatry

"Oh, scan it now! Scan it now!"

"Mmm, no." *Seriously? Kermit will say. You really thought international laws could require you to receive an award alone? Did you like my hologram, though?* "What if I told you—with ninety-nine-point-nine-nine percent certainty—this is all Kermit going to elaborate lengths to get me over to his house? To bug me about the same stuff he's sent me"—I pick up my phone—"fourteen texts about in the last hour?"

Olive grins at me in a way that can only be described as Kermit-like. "Then I would say he must very much want to see you, and you not going would be very rude." Olive shifts her weight to her other foot. "There's also a zero-point-zero-one percent chance it might not be Kermit. In which case . . ." She wiggles her fingers in a way that once again reminds me of Kermit. ". . . excitement."

"At my expense."

"We fifty-year-olds have to live vicariously through the young'uns."

I sigh. I lost this battle the moment Olive decided she wanted me to go. "Fine, hand me the code."

"Yes!" she squeals, and a smile takes over her face, which makes it worth it already.

My phone scans the code and beeps. A spinning circle appears with the words "Contacting our nearest representative."

My phone beeps again, then dings. A pop-up says, "A representative, Timrek Karlsson, is able to meet with you. You may proceed on foot." The app displays the first direction: North on Maple Street for 0.4 miles, then turn left. It estimates my arrival time in forty minutes.

A large green button reads, "Click to Accept and Begin Journey."

I tilt the screen toward her. "You press the button."

NUTS

The directions lead me straight to the Experience Center.

I consider, one more time, turning around and walking back home, but the air outside is sharp, metallic, and very cold, and my cheeks are starting to burn. So I steel myself for Kermit's over-exuberance and step inside.

The app refocuses to give me directions within the Experience Center space, which lead me toward the Welcome Center–slash–Tiki Bar.

The Tiki Bar's fence and trash-can coconuts are decked out for Thanksgiving. A stuffed turkey hanging from one of the fabric flame torches squeals "Espresso your gratitude!" as I step to the counter.

The barista rests her arms on the glass display. Glittered cat ears poke up from her headband and twinkle in the track lighting. "Can I help you?"

"A peanut butter cookie, please." Now that I'm here, I'm looking forward to watching Kermit experience the Tiki Bar for the first time, listening to him petulantly list all the things he finds wrong with it. Maybe, I think, I'll even show him the basement.

The barista—her name tag says "Chelsea"—adjusts her cat ears, softens her forehead, and smiles. "We don't sell peanut butter cookies anymore."

"What?"

"Yeah."

"Since when?"

Chelsea tilts her head. The glitter on her cat ears twinkles. "Thursday. In fact, we don't sell anything with peanuts. Too risky." She lowers her voice, leans forward across the case of baked goods. "A guy *died* because his blueberry scone touched a peanut."

"In here?"

"No. But somewhere." Her glitter nails tap the glass countertop, and I stare at all the nut-free baked goods languishing underneath. All the optimism I'd managed to dredge up rushes right back out of me.

She points at a brown lump inside the case. "We do have nutless nut muffins. Got those in yesterday. They're made with some sort of tree bark? It sort of tastes like a nut . . ."

I pay her seven dollars and sixty cents. Then I take the white bag with my nutless nut muffin and scan the café again, looking for Kermit's annoyingly smug grin. A man, sitting at my regular table, catches my eye. He seems to be waving at me. Smiling. Beckoning.

He's mistaken me for someone else. Except—now he's mouthing my name.

STASH OF WHIPS

The man waving at me is small and quite old.

The closer I get, the more frantic his wave becomes.[25] He starts waving with two hands, like windshield wipers in pouring rain, and when I'm within reach, he pulls me into a fierce hug. For his being about five foot three and maybe eighty years old, his hug is unnervingly tight. My nutless nut muffin is crushed between us.

"Hello, Wayne. Is good to see you again." His accent is vaguely European. Strong. Possibly to blame for the missed *D* on my name. "It is *so* good to see you again."

"Yes, it is good to see you . . . again . . . It has been . . . so long?"

He pulls back. "Let me look at you." He does exactly that, over the top of his copper eyeglass frames. For a moment, I think he does in fact look familiar. Then he squeezes me again. My muffin squishes like a foam mattress. "Too long, too long." He lets go. "You will sit with me, of course? We catch up?"

"Uh . . . yes." I take the seat across from him. "Only for a minute, though. I'm meeting a friend."

He looks at me expectantly.

I put my crushed bag on the table. "So," I say. "What have you been doing, then, since we last . . . um . . . saw each other?"

---

25. I've learned that the best thing to do in situations like this is to pretend to know the other person until they say something helpful. For example, "Can't believe it's been seven years and three months since I saw you at your father's Labor Day BBQ, you've gotten so big, my nephew," and then you can say, "Good to see you, Uncle, for the first time in the seven years three months since my father's Labor Day BBQ."
Not that my father would ever host a Labor Day BBQ.

"Same old, same old." He takes a sip from his cup. The scent of coffee and chocolate bursts over our table. "I do love a good mocha, especially in weather like this. Just starting to get too much cold."

I nod.

From a leather satchel, he pulls out a notepad and a pen. He slides the notepad toward me across the table. With his finger, he taps the paper twice. "How is your school year going?" Then taps the paper twice again.

In precise capital letters, it says:

THANK YOU FOR ACCEPTING THE INVITATION SENT VIA SLIPPERS. I KNOW YOU DO NOT KNOW WHO I AM. PLEASE CONTINUE THE SPOKEN CONVERSATION AS NORMAL. IF YOU DO SO, YOU WILL BE SAFE.

He slides the paper back toward himself and begins writing more. "How–is–your–school–year–going?" he repeats as he writes.

YOU WILL BE SAFE?!

"Espresso your gratitude!" says the turkey.

I read the words on the paper again.

"Wayne? How. Is. The. School?"

"Uh. Fine. And . . ."

He looks up long enough to glare at me over his glasses. "And?"

"And . . . there are classes . . . which I go to . . . at . . . the school . . . where there are classes . . . that I take . . ."

He's scribbling away on the paper. The hair on the top of his head is white and thin. It looks soft, like the ears of a small dog. Brown dots speckle his skin. He looks so old. Frail. Yet I know from his hug that he is not.

Behind his head, the fabric flames that line the café's perimeter dance wildly.

My mind lands on Charlotte, the wires clamped onto my fingertips, the urgency with which she asked whether any strangers had sought out any information about the study.

I gauge my chances of getting to the door before he has a chance to, say, shoot me. Or nail me with a flying dagger. Or swipe at me with a samurai sword.

Something vibrates in his shirt pocket, and he pulls out a beat-up vintage flip phone.

He glances at the caller ID. "Excuse me, I have to take this." He flips it open. "Hi, Spooky." On the paper, he purposefully adds a period to the end of whatever sentence he's written and pushes the paper toward me. "Yes, Papa misses you too."

The paper says:

I AM HERE TO OFFER YOU TWO THINGS:

1) INFORMATION

2) AN OPPORTUNITY

IN EXCHANGE, I AM ASKING FOR YOUR COOPERATION FOR ABOUT TEN MINUTES. THIS MEANS

1) CONTINUE A REGULAR SPOKEN CONVERSATION— DO NOT AUDIBLY REACT TO ANYTHING I AM ABOUT TO SHARE WITH YOU. THIS IS FOR YOUR OWN SAFETY AS MUCH AS MINE.

2) KEEP YOUR WRISTBAND AS OUT OF THE WAY AS YOU CAN. UNDER THE TABLE, UNDER A SLEEVE OR COAT, IF POSSIBLE.

IS THIS SOMETHING YOU CAN AGREE TO DO? PLEASE RESPOND BELOW.

"How's your puppy?" he's saying. "Yes, they do have very soft feet. Mmm. Yes, they smell exactly like corn chips." Then he says something in another language. "Mmm."

The pen is waiting there on top of the paper.

"Papa's gotta go now. I miss you too, darling. Hopefully I find a way to see you soon." He flips the phone shut, takes a sip of his mocha. It leaves a mustache of white foam on his upper lip. It makes him look older and younger simultaneously.

Voices explode into the café. A group of pre-teens crowds in to buy their own whipped-cream-topped beverages.

"Espresso your grati—grat—gratitu—gratitude." The turkey's tone changes every time she gets cut off. Like her desperation is mounting.

The man wipes his whipped cream mustache off with a single finger. He sucks the finger clean before delicately wiping it on the corner of one of the brown paper napkins. The fabric flames dance behind his head. *Is this something you can agree to do?*[26]

The pen is cold and heavy. "Yes," I write.

---

26. In *Drone Wars II: Precision Strike*, there's a famous moment in the ninety-fourth level, what DroneWarsians call the Catch-94, where you're in the middle of what is essentially an unwinnable boss fight. When you've only got 21 percent of life left, an ally unit contacts you requesting your support.
 You are given the choice: Tell the other unit you can't help because your resources are already maxed out, or tell the unit to lead their enemies to you. The correct response is the latter, because *doomed* is binary.

THE MUFFIN

The man smiles at me. A big smile that takes up half his face.

"Please, relax. Eat your pastry. It has been so long, lots to talk about."

He scribbles, "YOU MAY CALL ME HANS."

I write back, "Does that mean your name isn't actually Hans?"

He smiles again. He puts his pen into his shirt pocket. He gestures at my paper bag. "Eat, eat, please. I have my drink. Let us enjoy our snacks over good catch-up conversation."

He takes a long, slow sip of his mocha, then squeegees the whipped cream off his lip. "Eat."

I pull out my poor, flattened non-nut muffin. I pick off a tiny piece and roll it between my fingers.

"What do you have this year for science? Biology? Chemistry?"

"Biology."

"Probably a little bit of both, yes? You have both biology and chemistry?"

"No. We only have one science at a time."

"Technically, maybe one at a time. But, in *reality*, it is hard to separate the two."

"No . . ." He's looking at me in a way that reminds me of Charlotte handing me the envelope. "I mean, may-y-be . . . ?"

He pushes his notepad to one side.

"When you put chemicals inside the body, then the chemicals

affect the biology. And then chemicals *are* biology, yes?" He sips his mocha and raises his caterpillar eyebrows.

"Ah. You mean the pil—"

He slaps the table and shakes his head vigorously. Clears his throat. "Mocha. Burned my tongue. Sorry to cut you off. You were saying? You are taking both biology and chemistry at the same time this semester?"

I shift my hips so my right hand, with the wristband, slides under my thigh. "Right. Yes, I am."

There's a flash of something in his expression. Sadness, almost, but it's gone before I can parse it. "I thought you might be. Now, let me ask you . . ." He rubs a finger, his ring finger this time, back and forth above his top lip, before tapping it on the table between us. ". . . how is your pancake?"

"What?"

He taps his finger on the table again, closer to my paper bag. "Your pastry. Your pancake."

"Oh, my muffin. I haven't tasted it yet."

He nods sympathetically. "Sometimes it can be scary to eat things you haven't had before. Especially when they come from outside of your own kitchen, because how do you know what is in them? Where did they get that pancake-muffin? you might wonder." He widens his eyes, seemingly only so he can narrow them right after. His caterpillar eyebrows go down. He wipes his top lip, even though there isn't anything on it. "Do you wonder?"

"No? I've never wondered about where they get the pastries."

His nostrils twitch. His finger travels in one slow circle across his bottom lip, his top lip, and back. "Maybe. You. Should."

I squirm. My chair squeaks.

"What if your muffin wasn't baked here, in this small, somewhat dirty but fairly friendly local café? How would you feel about that?"

"Okay? It would be another bakery, right?"

"It might have been baked somewhere . . . larger." He picks up his spoon and stirs the foamy top of his drink. The spoon tinks against the cup rhythmically. Then he sips it. He does not wipe away the foam.

"You mean like a factory? What's wrong with a factory?" A headache is blossoming.

"Larger than a factory. Think, organization that has all the resources. A larger, more powerful bakery. The *most* powerful bakery. With access to strange ingredients. Non-FDA-approved ingredients. Who knows what they might be putting in their muffins? It might be a bakery that uses"—he lowers his voice to a whisper—"cornstarch." He sips from his cup again.

"Ahhhh. You're talking about the C-I . . . ?"

Hans bursts out coughing. "Oh my. Excuse me. The cinnamon, sometimes it really gets you, a surprising kick. Yes, I am surprised."

He takes yet another sip. The liquid in his cup has not decreased. The layer of foam on his top lip is growing thicker and thicker. "Muffins have been made in these big outside factories for many years. That same factory you were mentioning? The C one? International bakery, very famous. They keep making these muffins, even though— No, better to show you. Eat." And when I hesitate, "Please. Is important."

I break off a piece of muffin and bring it toward my mouth.

Before it touches my lips, Hans slaps the table. "Wait! Are you sure you want that chemistry-biology inside of you?"

I lower my hand. The bit of muffin crumbles between my fingers as Kermit's chart of government studies flashes into my mind. "The muffin is . . . bad for me?"

Hans nods. His lip foam drips toward his mouth.

"Definitely bad?"

"'Bad' . . . This is subjective term. For some people, one muffin could make them very sick. Maybe they have gluten intolerance. Their body thinks gluten is poison. For other people, they can eat twenty muffins before they get sick. Some people will be fine with many types of muffins, but not the muffins that have the nuts." He pauses. He sips. His mustache is restored. "I like chocolate coffee drink. My dog? Poison. Subjective. Relative. Conditional. You see?"

I swallow. "If it was bad for me, how bad would it be?"

"Quite bad." He moves his left forefinger to tap the top of his right wrist. I shove my hand as far under my thigh as it can go without me toppling over. "I see them in my practice, sometimes. Since I am a doctor. Which you already know, of course, my . . . old family friend.

"Speaking of my practice, would you like to see a video? About my new doctor's office. Wait until you see the artwork we got for the waiting room. And very nice couches. Ergonomic. State of the art." From a bag below the table, he takes out a rectangular clamshell device, about the size of one of Olive's novels. There's a photo taped to the top of a round-faced girl riding a pony. "My granddaughter," he says, and then opens the device, revealing a blank, dirty screen on top, and a circular depression on the bottom. He touches the circle, popping it open, into which he encloses a shiny, unmarked CD. He closes it, presses a button, and puts the device in front of me.

It whirs and grinds, like it's chewing the disc inside of it. The screen remains completely blank.

He hands me a pair of sunglasses.

I put them on, cautiously, and through them see an image on the screen.

It does look like a photo of a medical office. But not a fancy, state-of-the-art office at all.

There's a row of beds in a makeshift hospital in some sort of tent. There are at least five people in white jackets attending to the beds, which are all full. I can't see the patients clearly, but they all look young. My age.

Hans reaches toward me and touches a button. The photo flickers to life.

The white jackets of the doctors whip into motion, zooming up and down the aisles between the beds. Across the bottom of the screen, text appears:

"SUPPLEMENTAL EMERGENCY HOSPITAL WARD, exact location confidential."

The footage cuts to a close-up of a bed. In it, there's a person—young, I think, though the camera can't focus on him well. His entire body convulses. His feet and hands have been bound, his chest is strapped to the bed. The sides of the bed are padded.

The footage cuts to another patient, also convulsing uncontrollably. A nurse stands by their side, trying to keep their head still enough to hold a light up to their eyes. Another nurse adjusts the wires sticking out of their arms and legs. The camera finally manages to focus on the person's face, and I instinctively pull back. It's as though someone took white paint and brushed a thin layer of it over their pupils.

The screen fades to black. Hans holds out his hand for the device and glasses. "Very nice, yes?"

"Excuse me?"

"My ergonomic couches."

I fold the glasses, lay them on top of the photo of the round-faced, pony-riding girl. "State of the art."

Hans runs his finger over his lip. He sucks off the foam. He wipes the fingertip on a new corner of the same brown napkin.

GORGEOUS GRATITUDE

Hans stirs his drink. The clinking fills the space between us. It's almost in time with the beat of the song playing. Almost, but not quite.

"Espresso your gratitude!"

Hans' caterpillar eyebrows are knitted together, forming two deep ridges on his forehead, like he's trying very hard to see something. Or very hard to un-see it. He sips.

"Why?" I ask. "Why would anyone make muffins?"

"This." Hans leans forward, so close to me I can see the milk bubbles clinging to the hairs above his lip. "*This* is exactly the right question." He pulls the notepad back toward himself and taps where he's written

1) INFORMATION

2) AN OPPORTUNITY

His finger lingers over *AN OPPORTUNITY*.

"But! We are limited in time. It is good question, but I do not want to be talking about theoretical, hypothetical, figurative baked goods. I want to talk about *you*. We were talking about your school schedule. Chemistry and biology, together. Wow."

I squirm.

"Rigorous. You must be very smart boy. Your father must be very proud."

I squirm again. The chair groans.

"Do you think you will stay in the program?"

"I—"

"Despite it being so rigorous? Despite it being potentially too much to handle, especially for a young brain, a brain not yet fully formed, one that may not ever fully recover from the effects of so much strain, one that may never recover from the effects of such rigorous biology and chemistry, in the body, in the brain, together? When taking so much might be an insurmountable mistake?"

Another crowd of people comes in. The turkey screams. The cat ears barista changes the music to an old Kanye West song. Kid Cudi whines about living something down.

"Do I have a choice?"

"You mean because it is part of the state's academic requirements? You are required to take a certain number hours of science. This is true. But there are choices still. You could go to class, and not ingest . . . the information. Give your mind a rest." His finger taps the paper again, right by the word *Opportunity*. "Or, you can go to class, ingest *all* of the information. Tax your brain to the max. And even, maybe, sign up for extracurricular science activities."

The Tiki Bar noises are pressing on my eardrums. "Are you saying I should . . . eat extra muffins?"

He squints at me. "You have muffins served during your science classes?"

I rub a hand across the back of my neck. "No, but I thought—"

He slaps a hand onto the table. "Please! You must pay close attention. Why would you eat extra muffins? I have just told you that they are made in a factory that uses cornstarch! Pay attention!"

My little piece of actual muffin squishes between my thumb and forefinger until it's a flatter-than-pancake penny of dough.

Hans brings his cup to his mouth. It wobbles against his lip and rattles against the saucer when he sets it back down. He draws his shaking index fingertip across his lip, then holds it, momentarily, between his teeth. "I am sorry. I did not mean to yell. It is all the excitement about seeing my old friend so unexpectedly. And the caffeine and sugar. I cannot handle it at my age. I am sorry. I understand that your brain may already be taxed. Maybe you do not want to talk about school anymore? Stressful subject. Let's talk about your muffin again. More relaxing, simple topic. How is your muffin?"

I nod.

"You have choices with muffins too. Blueberry. Lemon poppy. Some you might like more than others. Some might make you feel differently. So if you are eating muffins, you can observe, which muffin do I like? Does this blueberry muffin make my tummy hurt? Does this corn muffin make my vision blurry or cause seizures? Does lemon poppy give me heart attack, brain tumor, or stroke? You see now?"

I nod again, slowly.

"And this information can help you, and others, learn about the muffin ingredients. This is what I am saying, with the science classes. Except one step further. Maybe sign up for *extra* extracurricular activities and then, if you decide they are too much for you to handle, give your registration to someone else who doesn't know as much. A good idea would be maybe you call me, let me know. I have connections with many young people interested in the sciences, given that I am, as you know, a doctor. I can do a lot if you give me your even more extra extracurricular science classes."

"To get this—to get this straight. By telling you about extra—no, giving you extra-extra science classes, class registrations, you mean I should . . . send you any extra muffins?"

"Espresso your gratitude!"

He slaps the table again. "No! Pay attention, boy! Why would I say science when I mean muffins! I would say muffins if I mean muffins! You give me your extra-extracurricular science class registrations, then with this we learn about the muffin factory and then we will shut down the muffin plant! This is the only way we can keep you safe from muffins! Pay attention! Be logical!"

The barista looks over at us, eyebrows up.

I force my cheeks to lift. "Yes, okay. Ha-ha. Yes, I will enjoy my science classes, and sign up for more and give them to you. Yes. Ha. So fun. I love science. And sharing."

"Mm." Hans scrubs his finger around his lips, in two full circles this time. He looks at the foam he's collected on the fingertip, carefully picks up his napkin, and jams his finger into the very center of it. "Anyway. Serious conversation over. In the circumstances of *this* particular muffin, there is a sign on the wall of the café-bar. See it? There? It says, 'We Bake Everything In-House!' Behind the boy holding the orange drink with too much whipped milk?"

The sign is brown with hand-painted white letters. A stylized palm tree bends over the words. The *o* in *house* is a fallen coconut.

"Made in-house," I repeat, blankly. "That's a relief."

"Yes, well. Words are only as good as the person who speaks them." He sighs and stands up from the table. His cup is still full. "On that, I must be off. Must get rest for my, uh, medical conference tomorrow. Thank you for indulging an old man. I know a young lad like you must have many better options than hanging out with family friends. Hopefully you do not think it a waste. A mistake. Why not do you get a fresh paper bag from the counter, take the muffin to go? You can decide whether or not to eat it later."

He takes a card from his pocket and slides it across the table, wedges it into my bag with my muffin. "You have my number if you want to get in touch. You would get in touch if you have very solid, very certain things to say. Only then. Solid. Solid knowledge of extra-extra science class openings. You understand? It is dangerous for everyone to get in touch. So you do not let anyone see this card. And you do not use it unless you are sure whatever you have to say is worth the risk.

"But. If you do lose it, your father has my number, of course, because we are very old friends. Very, very old good friends. Tell him I say hello, yes? One last hug goodbye, yes?"

I stand up, and he hugs me again. Like the first time, it is extremely tight.

He waves to the cat ears girl on the way out. She waves back.

"Espresso your gratitude!" the turkey sings.

PRIZES FOR EVERYONE!

On the way home, I stop by a pet store and buy a turtle[27] for Olive. I plan to tell her it was the prize presented to me, at my very boring but also very exciting meeting with Timrek Not-Kermit Karlsson. I will make her happy if it's the last thing I do.

I try to imagine the sort of operation the CIA might be running, picture a building—a factory, even—full of suited agents or grunt civilians, monitoring all the feeds transmitted from all of our wristbands. The scale seems impossibly large. The likelihood that they will catch my muffin conversation seems fairly low.

But.

The headache that started up during my conversation with Hans is continuing to stab itself into my eyes.

I'm also freezing cold, but that might be because it's actually cold. It's starting to snow.

My heart is also showing symptoms.

For example, every time I pass a blue Subaru, it skips.

---

27. We have an old tank in the basement; my mom used to have fish. Colorful fish.

GUIDANCE

Setting: Front vestibule.

Me: *(Opens door.)*

Dad: *(Sitting on second-to-bottom step, zipping up his boots.)* Oh! I thought you were in your room.

Me: Nope. *(Kicks feet against doorframe to loosen snow.)*

Dad: Where were you?

Me: Tiki Bar.

Dad: Far to walk in this weather.

Me: It wasn't snowing when I left.

Dad: They forecast it.

Me: Right.

Dad: I'm about to go shovel the sidewalk.

Me: It's still snowing.

Dad: I don't want it to accumulate.

Me: Ah.

Dad: Did you buy something?

Me: A turtle.

Dad: *(Is focused on something distant, over my shoulder.)*

Me: Did you hear me?

Dad: *(Clears throat.)*

Dad: Remember I wanted to talk to you? About what Mr. Houston said.

Me: Right.

Dad: Are you going to schedule a time to talk to me?

Dad: It is important.

Me: Right, okay. I will.

Dad: How about now?

Me: I'm busy . . . Actually, you know what? Okay. Now is fine. Sure.

Dad: Now is okay?

Me: Can't be worse than the rest of my week.

Dad: Great!

Dad: Sit down, here on the stairs, have my seat. Take off your coat, it's dripping. I'll be back. Sit.

(Jangling of blinds on office door. A pause. Jangling of blinds on office door again. In his hands, a few sheets of paper and a small cardboard box.)

Dad: Two days ago, that was Friday, I got an email from Mr. Houston. *(Waves sheets of paper.)*

Me:

Dad: Mr. Houston, that's your guidance counselor.

Me: I know.

Dad:	He cares a lot about you, it seems like. Wants you to do well.
Me:	
Dad:	Take your coat off. Making a puddle.
Me:	*(Takes off coat.)*
Dad:	*(Holds out hand for coat. Hangs coat on rack.)*
Coat:	*(Makes a puddle in a different place.)*
Dad:	*(Looks down at papers in hand.)* Yes, he wants you to do well. Mr. Houston.
Dad:	So he said he wanted to keep me updated. Give me a chance to respond as soon as possible. Take action.
Me:	
Dad:	On the good news.
Me:	What?
Dad:	Do you remember writing an essay? For English class?
Me:	That has happened.
Dad:	He said your English teacher just submitted a grade for you, on an essay for a book. *Flowers for Algernon*. Your English teacher included a note with it for your record. Let me read it.
Dad:	"'Wayne has been showing remarkable improvement over the second half of this trimester. His comments in class, though rare, have been astute. This essay corroborates that, and 'Wayne demonstrates his increasing penchant for analysis,

	observation, and thoughtfulness. This was, by far, the best essay in any of my classes."
Me:	
Dad:	That is a very nice note. I think Mr. Houston is right. I should take action in response to this as soon as possible.
Dad:	To reward you.
Me:	
Dad:	*(Glances down at papers.)* I should ask how you are feeling now. How are you feeling?
Me:	
Me:	What?
Dad:	How does this news make you feel?
Me:	. . . What?
Dad:	You don't have to tell me if you don't want to. Just know that I am interested in knowing about your feelings. Whenever you have them, whatever they are.
Me:	
Dad:	So I want to move on to the next part of our conversation. *(Shifts papers around so the small cardboard box is in one hand and the papers are in the other.)*
Me:	
Dad:	I want to tell you that I am proud of you. You are doing a good job with English class, and a good job with the Hopkins project. You have been very responsible.
Dad:	This is your senior year, you know.

Me:	I know.
Dad:	And after senior year comes college. If you want to go.
Me:	I know.
Dad:	There is still time to apply. Your options may be better now. Or getting a job. You can go to college later.
Me:	I know.
Dad:	*(Finally looks all the way up from his papers.)* So I want to say to you, though you do not have to do it. I want to say to you, you could, if you wanted to, take an internship this summer.
Me:	. . . I know.
Dad:	Might be good for you. Look good on the résumé. Get some experience.
Me:	Right.
Dad:	*(Hands me the cardboard box.)* This is for you. I got the good quality paper.
Dad:	I would like to know how this makes you feel.
Dad:	*(Glances down at papers.)* But also take your time to think about it, if you don't know how you feel yet.
Dad:	
Me:	
Dad:	I'm going to shovel snow now. It's accumulating.

THINGS INSIDE THE BOX

The box contains business cards. In the center is my name, and under that "Intern, Assistant to CEO."

At the top of the card: a hound dog silhouette, my father's company logo.

HOW I'VE CHANGED:

1. Stood up for Charlotte.
2. Wrote a good essay.

THE RED SNOW SHOVEL

I stay on the steps for at least a half hour, as the swooshing and scraping of my father's shoveling slowly gets farther away from the door. From upstairs, the sounds of Olive still watching *Blue Planet* in my room.

The business cards, *my* business cards, are simple. Still, I can't stop looking at them. Can't stop tracing my name. The card is black and white. The world is gray outside. But everything around me feels bright, colorful. I feel full, full of colors and capability and certainty.

The turtle scrabbles against the pebbles in its temporary home—*I got this turtle for Olive. I did something to make someone happy.*

I did this. *I* did this.

I,

'Wayne Le. I took some of the potential that I was forever throwing away and used it.

Look at what I have done:

something.

Something that mattered to someone.

There's a contrast, a juxtaposition, that nudges at the edge of my mind. The way being alive,

loving being alive,

wanting to be alive,

stands out starkly, as starkly as my father's red shovel in the snow, against the certainty that you will die.

It twangs against the pavement.

I pick up a second shovel and go outside.

HOPKINS STUDY APP

Please make sure your wristband is in place. Find a place to be alone. Into your phone's microphone, tell a secret that you've never told anyone else.

This secret may be big or small.

Don't worry, this information won't be shared with anyone!

Don't like speaking? No worries! We want this to be as fun for you as possible! If you prefer, you may type your secret into the box below.

My Darling Secret,

Hello from Louisiana! You would like Louisiana, I think, because it's like a science fiction movie. An alien planet, with the bulbous tree trunks and the moss draping off the branches—if you squint, the trees melt into the water. It's a painting that was hung up before it was dry.

Wait! Don't delete this email! I actually have a purpose in writing you this time.

It occurred to me that there's some chance, especially being as young as you were, that you thought that me leaving, my unhappiness, was your fault in some way. That I didn't want to be near you. That you made me *want* to leave. So, let me say this:

It was not your fault. I did not want to leave you.

"If you didn't want to leave me, why *did* you?" you might, reasonably, ask. So, let me try to answer that.

I left because I didn't feel like myself anymore.

My mind was out of my control. After I'd have a breakdown, I wouldn't even feel responsible for any terrible things I'd done because it felt like it wasn't my own mind, like some other person had taken control of my brain and made me do those things. Or maybe like I was trapped in someone else, someone who was crazy, and I had to scramble, find a rope to climb back up to my own reasonable brain.

So in a way, it wasn't even *me* that left. That's what it feels like. I'm not responsible for leaving you.

Of course, it *was* me, and I *am* responsible. I'm not trying to dismiss that. In fact, I'm trying, here, to show you that if anyone was responsible, it was only me and my misbehaving brain. Not you at all. *I* made a mistake.

Now I'm finally on this medication that balances my brain chemistry more. You can't force yourself to be natural, no, but I see now that there's a difference between forcing and paving the way. It's like my self has finally grabbed the end of a rope. It's not a *map*, but it's something to hold on to, a tether to what feels like the real me.

Who is now leading me back to you.

I love you,

Mama

BEERNOG

"The smell of beernog is not as bad as I expected. But why would you *want* beer-infused lotion?" Jane presses her face to the scent crafter outside the body products store.

When I got to the Experience Center, I expected Jane to launch right into describing her own meeting with Hans, but she didn't. Which means, like with Charlotte, that he didn't contact her. Or she was smart enough to ignore the slippers.

I haven't been able to bring myself to tell her about him. In fact, I asked her if we could walk around the mall before talking in the basement. Surprisingly, she agreed.

Jane moves to the next store. I follow.

As I walk, the items in my jeans pocket rub against my butt: the business card from Hans, printed with only a PO box address, and one of the business cards from my father.

I touch each of the cards once, making sure they are both still there.

Jane watches a train display in a shop window. She's wearing her sweater today, of course, as well as a puffy vest and one of those hats with fuzzy earflaps with matching mittens. She notices me looking and tugs one of the strings hanging from her hat. "Can I ask you something?"

"Sure."

"What did you mean? When you said your mom had problems with pills?"

"That's personal, isn't it?"

Jane's lips twitch. "Right. Okay." She tugs her hat string. Her lips twitch again. "So. Tell me what you think of this. Given everything that's happening, given that everything is so much more complicated than we expected with this study, maybe it would actually be *more* productive if we let conversation go where it wants to go? And have that be our new rule?"

A tiny bubble of happiness bursts into my chest. "Are you saying . . . you want to get rid of our old rules?"

She sighs. "You don't agree. I know, I know—changing rules is very disconcerting. But hear me out! I was thinking, because of the new information we have, our conversations need to be more analytical, more trying to figure things out and not just expressing feelings. And because of that we should purposely not restrict our conversational flow. I see your mouth is scrunched up still, presumably with doubt and concern. So let me explain it just a little longer. I promise my reasoning is sound. Okay? So tell me this. What quality makes both poets and detectives successful?"

"I . . . I'm sorry. What?" The train in the window lets out a low-pitched *woooo*.

"I'll tell you. Connections. Ability to make connections. That's what poets and detectives share. Their minds draw connections that others wouldn't make. It's exactly like what happened with origami, you know?

"Actually, I know you don't know. I won't talk about origami too long, I promise. But it's relevant here!

"For thousands of years, origami was just this thing that people did for fun. They made paper toys, or decorations to tie onto gifts, or to, like, hang on special swords. Origami was play or decoration. Aesthetics and fun. And over time, especially recently, it got more and more complex, but was still like a weird-person 'hobby.' " Her nose wrinkles as she makes air quotes.

"Meanwhile over here"—she waves one of her hands off to the side—"you've got physicists and rocket scientists and whatever super-serious people trying to send satellites into space and alter DNA and expand blood vessels.

"So you have these two communities existing at the same time"—her hands bounce at either end of her spread-wide arms—"never realizing the connections they have to each other. Until people like Robert Lang came along and were, like, 'Hey, fancy physicists, I bet the paper folders could figure out how to make a satellite small enough to get into space. And the weird paper folders could figure out how to make tiny unfolding forceps that can be used inside blood vessels.'

"So you see, when you are solving problems, or trying to figure out mysteries, it's the connections between seemingly unrelated topics that often end up being the breakthroughs."

"To get this straight . . ." I touch the cards in my back pocket for good luck. ". . . you are saying we are not going to have any rules at all?"

"No! 'Wayne, absolutely not!"

"But . . ."

"The new conversation rule would be an anti-rule rule."

"But doesn't that mean . . ."

"Not only should we talk about other topics, we should go out of our way to talk about other topics. We should pay extra attention to when our conversation wants to wander, because that's probably our subconscious leading us to remotely connected topics. The new rule is, we should make extra effort to follow those off-topic conversations. Okay?"

I wrinkle my forehead to make it look like I'm considering very deeply. "Okay. I am convinced."

"Great. Great!" Jane pats down her hat's earflaps. "Though outside of our planned conversations, of course, we still don't know each other."

"Naturally."

"And you'll want a written addendum to our contract, correct?"

"Definitely the first thing I thought of."

She nods. "Good. Good. I'll get that to you this evening."

In the window display, a blue train zips into a tunnel and re-emerges.

"So, with that business taken care of, I'd like to talk about your mom. And what you meant about her pill problems. If you're willing."

"Ah. Right." We start walking again, moving up the escalator to the second floor. "Well—she was always trying different kinds of medication. She was sad. Or anxious? Or confused. I don't know exactly what was wrong. I was really young. And my father isn't exactly the most communicative person."

In my peripheral vision, the red blur of Jane's hat is nodding.

I shrug. "They never worked for her. She had all kinds of terrible side effects. She said they took her further away from herself. 'You can't force yourself to be natural.'"

Jane nods a couple more times. She fusses with her mitten flap.

We're passing a plant store, which is hosting classes on tree decorating. The sign out front says, "It's not just pines, and it's not just for Christmas." I adjust the business cards in my pocket.

"And then she left. In a screaming bloody meat cyclone." I think about the email my mom sent me yesterday and feel guilty for describing her this way. "Anyway. She says she's doing better now. That her new medication feels like it's handed her a rope. Like breadcrumbs toward the direction she needs to go. Or something."

"Ah, that's good for her. Thanks for telling me."

We take a couple more steps. We approach a palm tree that has an angel somehow affixed to its top.

Jane stops, studies the angel-affixation mechanism. "I'm the one that found my mom."

"Oh." I shake my head. "That's . . ."

"Yeah." She continues walking.

I touch the edge of my dad's business card—or the one I think is my dad's business card.

Jane steps to the railing and looks down at the bottom floor. "She was a musician. A composer. She was pretty good, I think. Though I'm biased." Her words are short, clipped. Her sentences fall apart in the middle like underbaked cake.

Jane shifts her weight. Her down vest sighs. From up here, the rows of leaf garlands and string lights are forcefully bright.

"I told you before that she had OCD, and how even after they figured that out, she refused to try the medications the doctors kept prescribing, refused to try therapy, refused to *try*. She said she'd rather have a sad soul than no soul at all, because her sad soul saw the truth in things. And her art was about truth. And, well. I wonder a lot what would have happened if she'd tried sooner, tried before Dad lost his job, before her brain was in an even worse place. The meds, therapy, anything. I wonder if the side effects would've been less. Or at least manageable. So yeah. Then, I found her. So much for keeping her soul."

I risk a look at Jane's face, the soft edge of her cheek and her delicate eyelashes.

"That was three years ago. Well, a little more than three." Jane taps her fingertips along the wooden railing.

"That's when you started origami."

She doesn't respond.

To our right, a family, their arms filled with bags, hustles off the escalator and past us in the other direction. Below us, someone is stringing lights around the fake palm fronds at the Tiki Bar.

Jane droops over the banister. The strings from her mittens dangle. "How are you feeling about your mom coming?"

I lean on the banister, too. "Weird."

Jane smiles. "Understandable."

Jane's half-mittened hand is resting there on the railing between us. I know what it would be like, to put my own bare hand on top of it. There would be the soft pillow of her folded-back mitten tops, the cold plastic of the button, and the warm satisfaction of her fingers fitting perfectly into the palm of my hand.

I move my hand toward hers.

A voice behind us makes us both jump. "Hey you two, come to our class!"

MARRIAGE PROPOSALS 101: A WORKSHOP

Someone claps us both on the shoulders at the same time.

It's a large man in a stiff beige suit with a stretched disposition. "Please come to my class. You're a cute couple. You'll have fun!" His fingers tighten around my shoulder bones. "Please."

His name tag says "Arb" and associates him with the jewelry store behind us: The Band Stand.

"Please." Arb's hand is still on my shoulder. Its desperate heat seeps through my jacket. "This experience was my idea, and we haven't met the minimum quota all week. I need two more people to come."

Jane looks up at me. Her lips are pursed together. They twitch left twice. "What do you think?"

"Don't we have to? Our new anti-rule rule, right?"

Jane nods at Arb. "Sure."

Relief spreads over his whole body. Even his suit looks less stiff. "You have no idea. I can't lose this job right now. And you won't regret it. It's a good class. We just didn't get it advertised right on the events calendar."

He leads the way into the jewelry store. We pass the sign out front advertising the event we've committed to.

"Oh no."

"Oh boy." Jane's shoulders wiggle.

"Thank you so much again. I'll just have you sign in." Arb hands us a tablet open to a form, which we sign under the other eight names. Then Jane leads us to a pair of empty seats near the center of a semicircle of chairs.

Six out of eight people here are wearing plaid-patterned, fur-lined boots, including the person to my right. They give me a huge smile. "Hey. I'm Zeke."

"I'm Charles," says the person next to Zeke, before reaching over Zeke to shake my hand. Charles also has plaid-patterned, fur-lined boots.

Jane leans close to me. Her earflap brushes my shoulder. "Smell that? Someone's using beernog." She taps my knee with hers, once, and leans away.

Arb walks around the circle, handing out pieces of oversize, laminated cardstock—like a menu in a diner, but printed with short scripts under titles like "How to Say I Love You" and "The Moment I Knew." Then he takes a seat facing the semicircle. "A sincere thank-you to all for coming to this workshop. A congratulations, too, on finding someone you care about so much that you're not only ready to take the next step, you're committing to taking that next step seriously, consciously, by doing a workshop like this. So, let's all take sixty seconds of silence to appreciate that commitment to yourselves, to each other, and to your reciprocal love."

The couples around us nod and touch the tops of their heads together and reach for each other's hands and—despite it being sixty seconds of silence—murmur things like, "I love you, honey," and "You're the best thing that's ever happened to me."

I look at Jane, in case she wants to tell me that I'm the best thing that ever happened to her.

"How is this real?" She's holding both her earflaps like her hat might blow off her head. "This is amazing."

"It's something."

"Oh, come on. Aren't you going to tell me how much I mean to you?" Her eyes are glittering. Not because of the special jewelry store lights either.

I swallow. "You mean a lot to me."

"Oh, honey," she says, and giggles.

HOW TO SAY I LOVE YOU

Welcome to The Band Stand's Proposals 101!

Congratulations on finding True Love. We are here to help you transition to The Next Step.

Practicing both this script as well as the corresponding expression of surprise and delight will certify that every singular moment of your **eventious** occasion will be photo ready—worth both remembering and sharing.

1: I have something important to ask you, {insert name}.

2: What's that, {insert name}?

1: You might want to sit down.

2: Is everything okay?

1: Yes. I am sorry to have worried you. There is something on my mind.

2: I hope you know I am always here to listen.

1: I do. And that's just one of the things I love about you, {insert name}. Which brings me to my next thought.

2: What's that, {insert name}?

1: I . . . (Pause! Count to three!) I am hoping to spend my life with you, {insert name}. Would you like to spend your life with me? (Present ring, purchased from TheBandStand.com.) I hope we will never be apart. (Repeat, softer) I hope we will never be apart.

2: (Face of surprise and delight.)

THE MOST VALUABLE GEMSTONE

After we've had time to practice the scripts, which Jane and I mostly spend trying not to laugh, Arb tells us each couple must act out a script in front of the class. "If you can do it as a performance here, you'll know you're ready for the *real* performance."

We can choose from an array of ten environments to display on the wall behind us, including a beach, a mountaintop, and a crowded restaurant.

Arb reveals a velvet-lined tray from behind one of the counters.

"Oh, aren't those pretty," someone says.

Rings sparkle against the deep-colored fabric. "Go ahead and select the one you'd like to use." Arb moves around the room.

"This one is gorgeous." Zeke slides a ring onto their finger.

"Mmm, yes," Arb says, "the princess cut surrounded by emeralds, that's a wonderful choice. And it looks fantastic with your skin tone." He raises his voice to address the room. "Just a reminder that these are all *exact* plastic replicas of ring styles we have available. All these ring styles, and more, are available on our website, in all sizes, and you get a twenty percent in-experience discount after finishing this workshop. TheBandStand.com."

He's in front of us now. The plastic jewels twinkle. "You kids enjoying yourself all right?"

"Oh, yes." Jane nods seriously.

"It is something," I say. Jane taps my knee with hers. "A fantastic something."

Jane smiles. "Just like you."

"Aww." Arb switches the tray to his other arm. "How long have you two been together?"

"Six months." Jane hits my knee with hers, harder this time.

"Best six months of my life."

Arb adjusts one of the rings on his tray so it's more in line with the others. "I know some would say you're a little young to be thinking about weddings, but take it from me, it's never too early to start getting ready. The skills you learn today will be relevant no matter when you embark on your True Love Journey. Go ahead and pick your ring. Or rings."

The plastic gems flash in the light. They all look the same to me. Shiny.

For some reason, I think about my father. It's hard to imagine him standing over a counter of rings, picking one. It's hard, even, to imagine him looking at them online, going right for the "Best Sellers" tab in the name of efficiency. But my mother did have one. It would catch on my hair when she stroked my head, tucked me in at night.[28]

Zeke reaches over me and touches a ring. "If I may, I think that rose gold solitaire is going to be your bag."

I refocus on Jane. "What do you think . . . sweetheart? The rose gold . . . solitaire . . . ? Is it your bag?"

"You know what? I was hoping we'd do something more original than a ring."

---

28. She read me the same picture book every night, until I was much too old for that and it started to annoy me. When she got sicker, though, she started forgetting to come read, and I would miss it. My mind would play it for itself. And then, of course, she was gone, and her voice in my head was no longer soothing. Even now, sometimes I have to play Clarissa to drown out her voice repeating words about llamas and pajamas.

"You were?"

"Rings are so old-fashioned and . . . Is that okay?" Jane looks up at Arb. "Can we skip the rings?"

"You kids and your fads. You'll come around once you mature. As long as you promise to buy your rings from The Band Stand when the time comes."

"We promise."

"Sorry," Jane says, after Arb moves on to the next couple. "I figured we'd do something else, something clearly not real. The ring feels so serious, I can't trust myself not to laugh. And that would make Arb feel bad. What else you got?"

I shake my head.

"Use what you've got in your pocket."

All I have in my pockets are the business cards. I don't need to look above me to confirm that a jewelry store, even one that has mostly plastic replicas, is filled with high-definition security cameras.

I do look up anyway. There they are.

"I don't have anything in my pockets."

"You had something in your back pocket before. Maybe a receipt or something? You kept fussing with it."

"Did I?" I stick my hand into my pockets as if I'm investigating. The edges of the cards stab me. I have no idea which is which. "A big bunch of dryer lint."

"That's perfect."

"Oh."

I search in my other pockets, but for once my pockets feel perfectly lint-free.

Arb asks for volunteers to go first. Jane throws her hand in the air.

"Our young, anti-ring lovers," Arb says. "Come on down."

"If we wait, I'm going to get gigglier and gigglier," Jane whispers. "Especially after watching everyone else do those scripts." She raises her voice. "We'd like the beach scene, please."

An ocean appears on the wall in front of us. The sound of waves comes from a speaker somewhere in the ceiling.

"The stage is yours." Arb waves an arm magnanimously at the wall.

"Well, Jane." I clear my throat. I can't remember any words.

"I love the ocean." Jane clasps her hands together and inhales deeply. "Aren't you glad to be here, enjoying this fresh, salty air, to celebrate our second anniversary? It's so beautiful."

I stare at the blue and green pixels rearranging themselves on the wall. The room is too light-filled, and we're too close to the wall for them to be anything but grainy dots.

"Oh, look!" Jane points somewhere at the wall. "Dolphins!"

I squint at the wall, the green-blue dots, and behind that, white paint. White like Hans' business card.

Jane slaps my shoulder.

"Ow. I mean, wow! Look at the dolphins!"

"They're so elegant, so full of joy. Living life to their fullest. Speaking of which . . . We've been together for so long now. Sometimes I get to thinking about our future together." She raises her eyebrows at me pointedly. "Do *you* ever think about our future together?"

"Oh. Oh yes, I do. In fact, uh, there is, something on my mind? Or, I have something to tell you? Uh, you might want to get down. Sit. Or . . . wait, I will get down?" I clear my throat. "Our love is so large that it cannot be bound or represented by material things . . ."

Jane drops to her knees and grabs my hand. Between her thumb and forefinger twinkles the rose gold solitaire.

"Invisible-D 'Wayne," she says, "let's do this."

The tips of her fingers touch my palm, skin to skin.

The audience applauds.

LAUGH & SHOUT WITH GLEE

"That was fun, wasn't it?" Jane prances next to me as I walk. "That was fun. This really was, as you said, *something*. A fantastic something."

Every three steps, she does a tiny leap, like she's barely holding back from full-out skipping.

Being next to her feels so comfortable now, like surviving that experience has fitted us to each other like worn-in mittens. Jane's own mittened hands are down at her sides, the finger flaps folded back. One of those hands dangles close to my own. I would like to take it. I would like to hold it. I keep feeling the ghost of her fingertips on my palm.

"To be honest, I don't believe in marriage." Jane's hat flaps bounce as she takes an extra-jaunty step. "Not other than for tax reasons, anyway. The whole thing—the rings, the clothes, the hundreds of people, the making a spectacle of yourself—eh. And I *definitely* do not believe in proposals, not any of that nonsense back there. Can you imagine? Probably you *can* imagine because we just saw it happening but . . . spending a month's salary on some rock? Probably an unethically sourced rock, I might add.

"And all these people getting these rings, they think it's this beautiful, rare thing just for them, when in actuality it's common enough to be worth building plastic replicas. In fact, thousands of people have that ring. It comes in a bunch of sizes and will fit many types of fingers."

We've automatically walked to our table at the Tiki Bar rather than the basement. Which means maybe I can wait until another day to tell her about Hans.

Jane scoots into her wicker chair. She waves both her hands like shooing flies from a salad. "Now that we don't have those rules in place, I am blabbering on about everything. Maybe we need some rules after all."

"I like you blabbering. It's *not* blabbering."

She doesn't respond. She's staring at the coconut-shaped trash can and shaking her head, as if she's replying to something the trash can said. "Did you notice how all the other couples cried? What were they crying about? That experience wasn't real. No one was getting engaged. And yet. *Yet.* I also find it beautiful in some way, like how, I don't know, the inside of a seashell is beautiful—how something is a bit gaudy, too much, too extra, too . . ." She places her two mittened hands flat on the table. "Sorry. I'm back now. I'm here. Thank you so much for doing that with me. Tell me, what did *you* think of it?"

"It was okay. Interesting."

"That's *it*? That's all you have to say about that whole experience?"

"No . . ."

"Take your time." She pulls a leg up and reties her boot.

Behind her, someone on a ladder hangs up a snowflake, and the whole aisle lights up with glowing winter shapes.

"When you say you don't believe in marriage—Do you not believe in . . ." I bring my hands together in front of my chest.

"Love?"

"I guess." My cheeks burn. "Or dating. Or like-liking or . . . even hugging . . . occasionally . . ."

"Of course I do."

"Oh. Okay."

She takes off her hat and brushes down the fuzz that lines the inside of her earflaps. "I think maybe that's it, actually. I think, maybe, I believe in it too much. Going through something like a wedding makes 'love'—which should be huge and important—feel petty and material and mundane. Weddings try to be on the same scale of love, and they . . . well, they're not. They only make it even more obvious how small we are."

Her lips go right. Her lips go left. Then they frown. "Probably I'm just young and naive and thus pretentious about the whole thing. Like Arb says, kids and their fads. What do *I* know about love, right? I'm not even eighteen and . . ." She snuggles her head back into her hat.

"Do you want to hang out sometime?" The words fall out of my mouth.

"We *are* hanging out."

"No. I mean. I mean, this was really fun today, and I mean, more like this. I mean for real. I mean, I like being with you." Words keep flopping out of my mouth. They lie unmoving on the table between us.

"Oh. Oh, I see."

"Like tomorrow? We could do it tomorrow. Or any day that works for you. Tuesdays, even. Though I don't mean one day per week, I mean ongoing days. Not necessarily in a row. And we can do whatever. I mean, hang out." The words stack on top of each other like wet, dead fish.

" 'Wayne."

"By hang out, I mean, we could sit together. But not in a boring way. I'll come up with better ideas later! Unless you like that idea, or . . ."

" 'Wayne."

"I mean, be together more, now that we don't have the study-only rule."

She bites her lip.

All my dead word fish stare at me. "I guess I will stop talking now."

Jane sighs and rubs the side of her nose. She sighs again. Her lips go back and forth more times than I can count. My neck is getting increasingly warm.

She sighs one more time. "We still have rules. Every interaction has rules."

". . . Oh."

She shakes her head. "Why did I say that? That's not what I meant. It's true, but it's not what I wanted to say."

Her hands have disappeared from the tabletop. She's sitting on them. She's curled into a sweater ball. She looks like she would rather be anywhere else.

"Rudolph" starts playing on the Tiki Bar speakers. We make it through the entire list of reindeer before Jane talks again. "I have a boyfriend."

I blink. I swallow.

"I'm sorry, 'Wayne."

Now I'm the one shaking my head at the coconut-shaped trash can. There's nothing about Jane's boyfriend in my AP Chemistry folder. I've never seen her with someone in the halls, and I have known her school schedule for the last two years. And surely, Kermit, who knows her favorite coffee drink and likely has her full medical records and text message history, would have mentioned this to me at some point.

"I thought the rules said we had to be totally honest."

"I *am* being honest. I really do have a boyfriend." Her voice is gentle. "We've been together over three years." She's watching me, careful. "It's, um, Dave. Dave Appleright?"

It takes me a second to place the name. "The basketball player."

"Yeah."

"Our school's MVP player, who graduated two years ago and is now in the army?"

"Yes."

"The shirtless Dave on the school's home page? The one on posters encouraging us to care about stuff that are stuck all over the library walls? The Dave Mr. Houston references as the most inspiring student to ever sit in his seats?"

"That Dave Appleright."

"Oh."

I reflect on what I remember about Dave Appleright. Not much. He was a senior when I was a freshman. He's essentially the school's mascot. I've never formed an opinion of him.

Until now. I seem to remember that he is *definitely* a jerk. How dare he wear jeans. How dare he play basketball. How dare he be so tall!

Another Dave factoid trickles back into my memory. "Wait a second. Wasn't not dating anyone part of Dave's whole 'thing'? Wasn't his nickname Dateless Dave?"

Jane has taken one of her hands out from underneath her. She's tapping her bottom lip. "Undateable Dave. He got so much attention in school. He wanted to avoid the dating drama on top of it. So he wanted to take himself out of the public pool and keep our relationship a secret."

"Okay."

"Anyway. Thank you. For wanting to . . . spend more time with me. I'm flattered. And honored. Any person should be honored if *you* wanted to spend time with them. For what it's worth, you're great. Really different from how I thought you would be. You're fun. You actually listen."

"Okay."

"I do think you're really nice."

"Nice."

"I'm glad you were the person I least knew, so that I could not not-know you." She sits back on both of her hands.

In the aisle in front of me, a mother is trying to get her child to walk. The child keeps going limp and the mother has to drag him along behind her.

I cross my arms a little tighter. My stomach is the snow after eight reindeer have pranced and danced over it. More word fish leap out of my mouth. "Isn't he a little tall for you?"

"What?"

"Isn't he— I mean, you're not— Isn't he—too tall for you?"

Jane sighs. She takes a hand out to rub her nose, then sits on it again. "I should probably go now."

"I'm sorry. I'm sorry!"

"This is my fault. We should have stuck to the original rules. That would have been better. It's ruined now, isn't it? It's ruined. We aren't going to be able to talk to each other now. Not about anything. Not openly."

"It's not your fault. It's my fault. I shouldn't have asked to hang out more. I shouldn't have said what I said, about him being tall."

She shakes her head. "Listen. Let me tell you this, in case we don't talk again. My appointment was nothing like yours—no dropped papers, no turning away."

"In case we don't talk again?"

"Which means what happened to you, maybe it wasn't a test. Maybe everything you saw was real."

My neck is getting hotter and hotter. "What do you mean, in case we don't talk again? We aren't going to talk at all? We can go back to the rules, the strict rules! Anything you want." I put my hand in my back pocket, but the cards don't reassure me this time. "I don't want to be doing the study alone."

"You're not alone." She stands up. Her lips have curled in on themselves. "Well, this was fun. Actually, no, it wasn't. Sorry—habitual leaving phrase. It was at least a little bit fun, though. Earlier. I'll see you around, yeah?"

I push my thumb down onto a business card corner in the sorry hope the tiny, sharp pain of it will distract me from everything else I feel.

THE BOTTOM OF A PRETZEL BAG IS DUST

I sit on a mall bench for a while, replaying the nightmare of the last half hour.

Next to me, an old woman is munching her way through a bag of cinnamon pretzel bites, oblivious to my pain.

Six weeks ago, I couldn't even look at Jane at the screening. I was planning to slowly edge my way into her life over the course of the next ten to fifty years, preferably without ever talking to her, probably through my mastery of origami kangaroos.

To actually ask her out? Where did that even come from?

What could have possibly caused my behavior to change? What could have *possibly* . . .

"Oh, fuck."

The woman next to me offers me a pretzel nugget. "I don't like early Christmas shoppers either, honey."

HOW I'VE CHANGED:

1. Stood up for Charlotte.
2. Wrote a good essay. Maybe?
3. Jane

NOT SMARTER

"You're not smarter."

Kermit has made himself a throne out of the largest of the pillows in the meditation room and makes a king-like wave of his hand to dismiss my idea that the pills have made me smarter.

I'm sitting in a significantly smaller pile of rejected pillows.

"I guess being smarter wouldn't make me ask Jane out."

Kermit snorts. "No. The opposite. Considering she was already dating Dave Appleright. What a moron. You, not Dave."

"I didn't *know* about Dave Appleright."

"That's my point. Had you been smarter, you would have researched it."

"I did . . ."

"And not research like your little 'Chemistry' folder on your desktop."

"How did you . . ."

"*Real* research, like Captain Kermit does. In fact, if you were *truly* smarter, you would have delegated your research to an expert. Me."

I throw my hands up in the air. "Why did *you* not know about it? You know the passwords of everyone in the school but you didn't know *this*?"

"Who says I didn't?" He grins.

"I hate you."

"No, I didn't know. I wouldn't do that to you. At least, not without some noticeable gain for myself." Kermit licks a glob of peanut butter off the side of his hand—residual from his afternoon PB&J, which I interrupted with my arrival. "Anyway. The pills, the study—it does seem to be making you . . . *better*, somehow."

I cross my arms.

"All your changes so far, they've been good."

"Five minutes ago, you said asking Jane out was moronic."

"It was. Definitely. But it was *less* moronic than never talking to her. So. Better."

"*Better* is scientifically meaningless," I say.

"Whoa-a. I'm still processing. It's not like we have a ton of data here. I don't know. More outgoing? More reckless? Somehow better with words? We need you to go out and do more weird shiba-inus. Unfortunately, though . . ." He yanks one of the pillows out from under my ankles and sticks it behind his neck. ". . . yeah, unfortunately you're now going to be self-conscious about everything you do. It's going to be near impossible to get more good data."

"Are you saying we're stuck?"

"Yeah, a little bit stuck."

I snatch one of Kermit's armrest pillows, stick it on my knees, and bury my face in it.

"But . . ." Kermit says, "we're not *totally* stuck. Good thing your best friend is a genius. Even without taking pills."

MY SOUND MIND

"I got you something," Kermit says. "A present."

I lift my face from the pillow just enough to peer at him—Kermit has never gotten me a real gift[29] in the entirety of our friendship.

From his shirt pocket he pulls out a folded piece of paper. He tosses it to me. He steals his pillow back while my hands are busy unfolding it.

"You printed me a news article?"

"You're welcome." He waves one of his hands, indicating I should proceed.

I read some of the words on the page. "An obituary. From thirty years ago."

He nods.

". . . Thank you?"

His neck pillow comes flying at my head. "Oh, come *on*, D! If you're going to talk about being smarter, at least *act* it. Read the damn thing."

I try. I can't focus, though, because my mind keeps trying to figure out what the pills are doing to it.

---

29. Non-Gift "Gifts" Kermit Has Given Me:
    - Answers to take-home math tests (Not a gift: I paid him. But he said my discounted price was a gift.)
    - A mechanical keyboard (Not a gift: He gave it to me because he was tired of using my "civilian, flat, non-clicky" keyboard every time he came over/hacked into my computer; also, he bugged it.)
    - A baby houseplant to "brighten up my room" (Not a gift: My dad grounded me for a month for having a cannabis seedling, which Kermit found hilarious because "how did you not recognize it?!"—which, I would have! I just never bothered to look at the thing very closely because it had a label on it that said it was a money tree.)

Kermit sighs. "Would it help if I promised that it's another part of the puzzle?" He has his serious voice on. Though he also sounds annoyed about having to wear his serious voice.

I force my eyes back to the words. Obituary. Someone died. Justin Mikulski. I read the name again.

That name.

"Mikulski?"

"Yep. I went back to your original letter for the study. The research director was listed at the bottom as Dr. M. Mikulski. And then I thought about the guy you met, the asshat that seemed like he had written the protocols."

"M. Mikulski. *M* like, like . . ."

"Michael. Exactly. A stretch, perhaps, but it was a place to start, if nothing else. And I think I was right. There are a couple Michael Mikulskis, but one caught my eye. He graduated from St. Mary's with a degree in chemistry, and then University of Maryland for medical school. After that, though, he's impossible to find. Except here, in this obituary."

The obituary is from the *Baltimore Sun*. There's a photograph next to the text—a young man in an army uniform with a one-sided, toothy grin, under which it says "Justin James Mikulski, 25 years old."

I skim, looking for any mention of Michael. There's nothing until the end:

> Justin died while doing what he was happiest doing, what he wanted to do his whole childhood—serving his country by flying. He was one of the seven soldiers who lost his life when their Black Hawk helicopter, which Justin was piloting, was shot down during what should have been a routine scouting

mission. Remaining family—his father, George; mother, Joan; younger sister, Amy; and older brother, Michael—will miss him dearly, but they could not be more proud of him.

I read it again, looking for whatever it is I'm supposed to see and understand.

"I don't get it."

"That's because I haven't given you the second part of your present yet." He tosses another folded-up paper at my feet.

It's a news article, this one from the *Avenue News*. The headline is "Local Boy Leads Support Group for Teens with Anxiety." There's Justin Mikulski again, younger this time, my age, at the center of a group of about ten high schoolers sitting on school steps. This time, Kermit's done me a favor and highlighted a paragraph of text farther down.

Justin, who has battled anxiety his whole life and been institutionalized twice—one time spending three months in a group home—explains his impetus for starting the school club. "What has made my own anxiety feel twenty times harder is believing I'm alone. I couldn't get anything done—I was literally fainting from the stress. When I got to the group home, I realized my belief wasn't true. I *wasn't* alone. Not at all. In fact, a lot of teens have anxiety. After I realized that, my fainting stopped. I could do things again. So when I got back to school, I wanted to tap into that and give us all a sense of belonging. Show other anxious teens that there are a lot of us. That's why I created this group."

I read the paragraph twice.

"I got nothing."

"Justin had clinical anxiety."

"I got *that*."

"*And* he was in the army."

"I got that, too."

"So you don't got 'nothing.' You got it all."

"Kermit . . ."

"Remember at the start of every *Drone Wars* edition, in the intro, there's that montage of being selected to pilot the drones?"

"Not on *Double Tap* . . ."

". . . and there's that line about how"—he puts on a deep voice—"'the finest physicians in the country have ensured that you're sound of body and mind'?"

My heart stops. I do got it all. "Justin shouldn't have been able to pass the medical screenings."

Kermit pokes me in a shoulder. "He shouldn't have passed. He definitely shouldn't have been able to be a pilot. Not with that history of fainting. And remember what Mikulski said to you at your last appointment? Something about how helping out someone he loved was his greatest mistake? *And* he's a doctor?"

I lean against the wall and slide down into the pile of pillows, remember Mikulski's hand edging forward, his nail-bitten fingertips resting on my desk. "You think Mikulski lied to get Justin past the screenings?"

Kermit nods.

"Then Justin crashed. And died."

Kermit keeps nodding. "There's extra evidence that supports this, too. I did more research about exactly how he died. There was one survivor from the flight, a door gunner. He reported that even though the copilot got shot early, Justin had ample time to fire at the attacking aircraft, but instead he just *sat there*. He froze. Couldn't pull the trigger. So his death, the deaths of all those people, would kind of have been—at least I could see Michael feeling this way—it would have been Michael's fault."

"Transitively."

"Transitively."

Across from me, there's a closet with mirrored doors. I can see myself, surrounded by pink and purple pillows. My lips are pinched and my forehead has one thick line running through the middle. There are dark circles under my eyes. I look five years older than I looked this morning.

I think about Michael, tracing his finger around and around that heart on the desk. Talking about goats.

Helping someone do something that ended up being their death—that could feel like your own death, too.

I reread the obituary. "His name is Justin James."

"Mikulski."

"Right. But Justin James is the name of the building my appointments are in. At Hopkins."

"I didn't know that. That makes all of this"—Kermit whacks the papers in my hands—"feel even more important. You have to mean a lot to someone for them to pay to have a building named after you."

I crumple the papers into my fists, make them as small as they can go. "So what does it mean? What does this say about what the study's about? What do the pills do? What does the CIA want from me?"

"That," Kermit says, "is where I'm stuck again. But it feels, well, important."

I flop the remaining two inches down, so my head is all the way on the floor. It does feel important. The importance sits heavy in my bones.

Above me, the sunlight dances playfully across the ceiling. It dances across the printed papers in my hands, the carefully highlighted words and passages.

"Why are you doing this?" I say.

"Hm?"

"Helping me figure this out?"

"You really need to ask me that?"

A bird's shadow flitters through the sunlight.

The familiar swishing sound of Kermit dusting something off his sneaker sole. "The information could be *very* valuable."

"It's dangerous."

"Plus, you're my friend. You think I'm going to let you do this alone?"

There's a long, long pause.

"It's interesting."

The sun goes behind a cloud. In the mirror, I see that he's closed his eyes.

SAME-SAME

When I get home, Olive is standing on one of the roll-y kitchen chairs in her hot-pink "prize" slippers, washing the rocks from her turtle's tank in a bowl on the counter. A nature podcast is playing softly from Dad's tablet.

I hover in the doorway watching her for a few minutes, until the podcast launches into listing its sponsors. "Do I seem better to you?"

She turns the podcast off. "I didn't know you were sick."

I put my bag down by the fridge. In front of it, the turtle is investigating shredded lettuce that Olive has piled onto her special blue plate.

"No, I mean, like, *better*. Like a better person."

"Are we back to talking about if you're 'changing'?"

"Maybe."

"Is there something you aren't telling me?" She uses her hands to pull herself along the counter and roll her chair toward the sink. The water hisses over the pebbles.

"Maybe."

I can't see her face, but she's probably puffing her cheeks.

"Do I seem smarter to you? More focused? More outgoing? Better in any way at all?"

"No. You seem the same." She pulls herself back toward the fridge, opens it, and pours herself a glass of juice. "Isn't he so cute? He was the best prize you could have ever gotten." She gestures at the turtle with her juice glass before spinning back to her rocks. The chair squeaks and wobbles.

I grab the stepladder from behind the door to the laundry room and place it next to her chair. "Can you please use this?"

"This chair is fine."

"It's dangerous."

"I like it!"

"Fine," I say, but I station myself behind her in case. "You're sure?"

"I do this all the time."

"You're sure I'm not better?"

She spins the chair around to look at me. She wobbles again and I grab the chair's arms. She uses one of her Council of Podiatry toes to push my hands off. "You're not better. You can't be better. You're already the best."

"You're only saying that because you love me."

"Exactly." She pushes herself off my shoulders so she chair-surfs back toward the sink and simultaneously sends me out of the room.

HOPKINS STUDY APP

This assignment tests your reflexes.

You're on a hill. A ball, containing a single fortune cookie, is rolling away from you. Oh no!

Inside the ball, inside the fortune cookie, there is a small piece of paper. A fortune, if you will. That fortune is an answer that you need to survive. And yet, there it goes! Spiraling away from you down the hill! "Oh no!" is right!

Please guide your character down the hill, jumping over rocks and ducking under tree branches, to catch the ball before it reaches the river at the bottom and gets swept away forever!

You will have three tries. You may view the keyboard controls here. As always, if you have different accessibility needs, please reach out! We aim to include all! Have Fun!

BINARY REALITY:

How Small-Town Communities Think & Feel About Digital Technology

An Oral History, by Naomi Le

If I'm being honest, I'm not one hundred percent sure the internet is a good thing. Of course, I like a lot of it. The movies, staying in touch with old friends, the recipes. And the ingredient shopping. I like food. *(Laughs.)* I made something called doubles last week, from a Caribbean travel blog. Delicious. That wouldn't have been possible without my computer.

And of course, I don't want our kids to be behind, I want them to have opportunities in the world, outside of Independence. So they have to learn how to use technology.

But I have to say, it used to be, we knew what was real. I knew what to believe, or at least, I trusted in truth, that truth was a real thing that you could quest after and maybe one day find.

Reality was real. Or we *thought* it was, and that was enough.

Computers have filled our lives with information and noise. Everything feels uncertain, like the platform of facts we've built our lives on could disintegrate at any second, every single truth must be questioned. Do people in Trinidad really eat doubles? Am I actually eating them, right now? Are we really alive?

Claire Hellstern: Independence, Louisiana

REFRESHING CHANGE

Twinkling multicolored lights dance around Mr. Houston's two doorways. Mr. Houston's tie is equipped with a matching miniature set of flashing lights. Upon my entry into his office, he throws a handful of powdery white glitter at my head. It drifts down to join the not-insignificant pile of matching white powder near the edge of his welcome mat, evidence that Mr. Houston's annual winter celebration is well underway.

"Merry Kwanristmukah!" he yodels as I sit.

As always, it's a little painful to listen to Mr. Houston's overexuberance. But unlike always, I am really glad to be here for my end-of-trimester review. It's awkward, yes, but it's a typical awkward. It's a reminder of my underachievements, sure, but it's a comfortable, normal, predictable reminder of my underachievements.

It's a relief to know that about fifteen minutes into our conversation, Mr. Houston's computer will "magically" start to play Vivaldi's *Four Seasons* "Winter," and Mr. Houston will say, "Vivaldi's *Four Seasons* 'Winter'? Well, this calls for a celebration!" And he will offer me my choice from a basket of colorful, bizarre stickers.

It's a relief to know exactly where I belong, to know exactly where this conversation will go, to know precisely my role, which is to sit in this itchy chair and feel appropriately disappointed in myself.

Mr. Houston takes his own seat. " 'Wayne, before we get started,

I have to apologize. I'm running a bit behind. My daughter had an emergency this morning, nothing to worry about, just her typical thing with the school lunch tacos, yada yada, but I had to drive over there to talk to her teacher. So, I am uncharacteristically unprepared for our meeting. I hope you'll sit tight while I pull up your file and give it a quicky-quicky look-see."

He wiggles his mouse. Types in his password.

I scratch my wrist where a bit of the chair touches my skin.

His computer makes beeping and swooshing sounds as notifications fly in.

"How's that study been going?" He pulls up the school's admin website and logs in. "Probably getting close to done, right? I'm proud of you for sticking with it. Some of my other students have been complaining about the workload."

"Workload?"

"The assignments that they get from the app. They say they are time-consuming and kind of disruptive. You haven't felt that way?"

"I don't think so."

"Good, good. That's great. Has it been interesting?"

"Definitely."

"Excellent. Glad you're learning something. Let's see here. Pulling up your file."

A loader spins in the middle of his screen.

I notice that Mr. Houston has decorated the framed photo on his desk—of himself, his husband, and his daughter—with stickers to give them all festive hats and mittens, even though they are all wearing shorts on a sunny beach.

"I apologize again . . ." Finally, it loads. Mr. Houston leans toward the screen, highlights some of the text with his cursor as he reads it. "Yes, yes, oh, that's right! I talked to your father, excellent job on that English essay, really exciting news, that. Great work, and let's click over to your final exam scores, and..."

He gasps.

"Mr. Houston?" Mr. Houston has a hand pressed to his chest. I start to stand up. "Mr. Houston, are you—"

"'Wayne! What a surprise! Is this really... Let me just check... Yes, that is your name up there..." He clicks to refresh the page. "It must be correct. I think it's correct! 'Wayne!"

He pumps his fists at the ceiling. "This was a fantastic trimester for you. Your final exam scores are in and high, high, all high. It is remarkable. I am, in fact, remarking upon it!" He pumps his fists at the ceiling again. "It is almost unbelievable!"

Mr. Houston clicks to refresh the page again. Four more times.

This chair feels like someone had their hair cut in it, and all the little hair pieces are edging through gaps in my clothing. They stab me in a million separate places, through my sleeves, through my pants, into my thighs.

The corners of my business card, the one from my father, which since last week I moved to a separate pocket, add their own, more vigorous skewerings of my skin.

He refreshes the page one more time.

I can't bear to stay in this chair any longer.

"I need to pee." I nearly knock over the chair as I throw myself out of it and backward toward the entrance door, where there is now a large wall that I run straight into. The wall is warm and deep-chested.

"Whoops!" the wall booms. Then, "Mr. Houston! Hope I'm not intruding. I had to come to your office first!"

The wall has a face that looks somewhat familiar. It makes my skin even pricklier.

Mr. Houston joins me by the entrance door, pats the wall on the shoulder, gives it a hug. "Do my eyes deceive me? My favorite, most inspiring student of all time? Never an intrusion, never! 'Wayne Le, meet one of our school's greatest icons, one of our city's greatest role models, an every-day do-gooder and basketball champion—"

"—Dave Appleright."

"Correct!" Mr. Houston pumps his arms toward the sky.

BLUNDERPUSSYFOOTING AROUND

"Merry Kwanristmukah, Mr. Houston!" Dave Appleright slaps Mr. Houston on his back.

"Yes! Yes! Merry, merry!" Mr. Houston practically dances in place. "We weren't expecting you until next week!"

"Got leave early." Dave unzips his winter jacket. He's wearing an army uniform underneath.

"Nice to meet you." I edge around to Dave's left and make a clear signal that I am trying to move past him and through the door. "I'll get out of your way so you two can catch up. We can talk later, Mr. Houston, this seems like a real special occasion . . ."

"*Nonsense!*" Mr. Houston pulls the entrance door shut behind Dave so the three of us are trapped inside. "The more the merrier."

"The merriest Kwanristmukah!" Dave's voice is a perfect thunderstorm, deep and rumbling and full of dimension. Somehow my hand has ended up in his and is being shaken cheerfully, like we're about to play a round of mini golf.[30]

"Exactly. And 'Wayne, you being here is not a coincidence. It is fate! Dave is someone perfect for you to meet. A real inspiration. Only a couple years older than you and he's accomplished so much."

---

30. Unless you're playing mini golf against Olive, who acts like her entire future is staked on getting her ball into the hole first, and anyone who might interfere with that future is an unforgivable cabbage hat.*

> * Olive went through a phase—that she convinced me to participate in—of collecting outdated slang to use as insults.

Any remaining vigor gets sucked out—*fwoomp*—through my shoelaces.

"Any of my accomplishments are thanks to you, Mr. Houston." Dave turns to me. The ceiling lights catch on the sharp shelf of his cheekbones. His eyes are blue—something I wouldn't normally notice—but they are *so* blue, and I picture Jane gazing into them, falling into them, paddling around in them like they're a forest lake in springtime. They blink at me before crinkling in a smile.

"Not true, not true. 'Wayne, did you see the article a few months ago about the cat Dave rescued? The cat wandered onto their base, and it was Dave, here, who befriended it, made it a cozy bed in the weapons room, made sure it had a home when the army moved out." Mr. Houston clutches his chest. "Inspiring. What was the kitty's name again?"

"Blunderpuss. Blundy. Sweetest little fellow."

Mr. Houston re-clutches the chest that he's already clutching. "Blundy."

"That's very nice," I say. "I do feel inspired. I do. But I need to get going . . ."

"'Wayne here is having the moment of epiphany that you once had, Dave. His achievements this trimester have surpassed any of his others, by far. That's why I felt it was serendipitous that you could talk to each other. Tell 'Wayne a little about how you got where you are now, would you?"

"Oh, I don't want to . . ."

"Don't be modest. I want him to hear it from you. Encourage him along this upward path he's found for himself. Think of it as practice for the upcoming fundraiser speech."

"Oh, all right."

Dave claps me on the shoulder. "'Wayne, is it? What is it you're interested in doing in the world?"

His voice is not merely a thunderstorm. It's a perfect, evening summer thunderstorm swelling clear and deep and musical. There's lightning over a distant mountain. A purple sky. There's a cat, on a lilac cushion, purring its echoed response. People are mailing postcards of Dave's thunderstorm to each other; they are sharing the photographs of Dave's thunderstorm on social media and getting a million hearts. And Jane, Jane is outside, a burgundy raincoat over her burgundy sweater, her Doc Martens glistening, twirling as the rain begins to fall.

I scratch my neck and gauge how much I would break if I climbed over Mr. Houston's desk to get to the other door.

Dave smiles again. "That's okay, don't mean to put you on the spot. Let me tell you about me, instead. Listen to this: I was required to meet with Mr. Houston twice a week for my first two years here. Twice a week! No one meets with Mr. Houston twice a week, right, Mr. H?"

"It's true. You were a nightmare! He was a nightmare!" He gives me a thumbs-up.

"It was dark times. I was constantly in trouble, grades that could barely be called grades. They benched me on the team. I was considering dropping out completely."

"It was you who replaced the water fountain with a urinal, wasn't it?"

Dave laughs. "I'm still not telling."

"I know it was you!"

"Do you? Do you, though?"

"Yes! No. Yes! Oh, this guy." Mr. Houston gives Dave a side hug.

"So yeah, Mr. H believed in me every step of the way. Gave me an actionable plan. 'SMART goals for smart souls.'"

"I forgot about that! I *knew* this was serendipitous! 'Wayne, we will start that program after Thanksgiving break."

Apparently there is still vigor in me because it continues leaking out of me, slowly, dripping like dirty, melting snow, contaminating the pile of snow glitter I'm standing in.

"You need to! That phrase plays in my head at least once a day. I don't know if it was Mr. Houston's goal-setting tools, or learning more about how the world works, or just getting older, or what, but one day things clicked. I realized, I don't have to sit back and let things be awful. I am an agent of change.

"What I'm saying is, I didn't always *care* like I do now. So there's hope for you, too. You just have to figure out, you just have to answer, What is it you want to do in the world? What is it you want to change? What do you want to fix? And that answer can be different every day. But the key is to have a clear vision, a defined answer. Just—caring—that's what leads to action on shit."

Mr. Houston claps a slow, firm clap. "And now, here you are. With all of Glenville High 'striving to care about stuff like Dave cares about stuff.' "

"Aww," Dave says, "it's really nothing impressive." He puts a hand in a pocket and pulls his jacket to one side, revealing his breast pocket covered in stripey ribbon things.

Mr. Houston's hands are fists. He's struggling to keep them down by his sides and not continuously pumping at the sky. "Dave—thank you for your service. Thank you for being *you*." He turns to me, fists still jittering.

I am a fish. I am a fish that is somehow still capable of drowning, despite being a fish. "Um. Yes. Thank you, Dave."

Dave winks at me. "You're welcome."

Mr. Houston's fists win the struggle. They waggle at the ceiling. "Do you see this, 'Wayne? This is who you could be, this is who you could be!"

I am a popped balloon in the hand of a toddler. I am a dropped ice cream cone. I am that fish that never learned how to breathe underwater and drowned and then floated on the top of the water for a week and then started to decay and sank back to the bottom.

Mr. Houston's computer dings then. The ding is followed by swelling violins.

"What magic is this? Do I hear Vivaldi's 'Winter'? Why, what a day! This calls for a celebration!"

Dave claps and bounces on his polished boot toes. "Stickers!"

Mr. Houston falls under his desk to retrieve his prize basket.

The pathway to the exit door is clear.

L-I-ABILITIES

Outside the school, there's a dead tree. It hangs over the field. Its trunk is thin, too thin for its height. When the wind blows, it bends and creaks.

At any school event—games, fundraisers, a drive-in screening of *Brave New World*—there are always parents complaining about it.

"I hope the school is ready to get sued," says every Glenville parent, ever.

Now, I stand beneath it, my back pressed against its trunk. I try to breathe.

"*I.*"

Its trunk is thin, spindly, waiting for the right breeze to snap it in two.

RORSCHACH

The cold weather and snow have not kept people away from Selfation, Selfie Theme Park.

In fact, the park has seized upon the opportunity. Banners at the entrance boast about holiday and winter photo opportunities, and inside, lines crisscross the event spaces. People are photographing themselves as if they are having a snowball fight with 3D-printed snowballs, or sipping from a steaming cup of water while wearing a "perfectly wintry" hat selected from an array of options, or laughing in a sled at the top of a fake hill, with a fan blowing back their hair.

There's also a "Limited-Time-Only Cancún Tent," inside of which are photo opportunities to portray a beach vacation.

Jane would love this place. It's like Proposals 101, except rather than having experiences, you merely *look* like you're having experiences.

When the last bell rang and people started flooding out of the school, I fled my post by the tree. I came here trying to make myself feel a little better.[31] I thought being around people, happy people, in a strange new place would distract me.

It's not working. Everyone is taking photographs to portray lives

---

[31] Olive says that my wallowing is like an energetic black hole, where it sucks all the positive energy out of anyone around me until they have no choice but to wallow, too. "You could also say it's parasitic," she says, "but that's a little too *active*. It's more like it destroys things without you trying, which is even *more* depressing."

that aren't quite real. Exactly like how my new self, whoever I am, is not quite real either.

Toward the back of the park are Selfation's permanent, non-winter-themed exhibits. On the side of one of the buildings, a pair of elaborate twenty-foot painted wings reach up toward the top floor. There's a phone-holder so you can take a selfie of yourself from a distance, and employees hold up big foil rectangles to help direct the sun for "Your choice: dramatic or elegant lighting!" The line to use the wings loops back and forth through the velvet ropes.

The building hosting the wings is brick and stout. From the side of the building, hanging over the large doors, a painted sign announces "The Farm Zone." A stylized silhouette of a goat accentuates the lettering and I recall Dr. Michael Mikulski holding up his fingers to make goat horns on his head.

When I pull open the barn doors, the smell of hay and animal seeps out, along with a blast of warm air. The orange of heaters glows down from the beamed ceiling. The bells on the collars of two large goats make soft tinkling sounds as the goats turn their heads to stare at me. A sign near the door lists all the photo opportunities available to me: brushing a pony, having a clothing item chewed on by a goat, being chased by chickens, falling into a pig's mud puddle, getting face-licked by a fuzzy baby cow.

As my eyes adjust, I make out a figure perched on a stool in one of the distant corners. They've got a small brush in one hand, with which they are applying paint to their fingernails. The flowing volcano of hair looks very familiar.

Miranda Hawthorn, of Mirona's Five Dollar Miracles, painter of our lobby mural, with the leggings that should not be ogled. Jane's ex–best friend.

"Welcome." They're wearing cowboy boots. Their legs are leggings-free.

I move my gaze hurriedly away from Miranda's legs and attach it firmly to the nearest goat. "Hello."

"The dee is in the eff zee."

"I'm sorry?"

"That's you. D, here in the F Z. The Farm Zone."

I risk a glance toward them. They've capped the nail polish and set it on one of the fence posts. Their hands grip the edge of the stool. A dragon ring, with bejeweled green eyes, winds itself over and under their fingers. Their nails are shiny, reflecting the light of the heaters. The shiny nails, gripping that stool, are right by the edge of their skirt.

Which are right next to their thighs.

I look away.

"Mr. 'Wayne Le, are you just going to waltz into my sad, unpopular Farm Zone, where I spend most of my working hours completely alone, and not even come over to say hi?"

I tuck my hands into my armpits. "Probably. Yes."

"That's not very nice."

Then they extend their hand toward me, like they want me to . . . Actually, I'm not sure what they want me to do with it. It is dangling at the end of their arm, their pink nails like bait on a line.

Food pellets crunch under my soles as I move toward them. I focus on the pig in the next stall.

"Isn't the nail paint still . . ."

"Quick dry." They shimmy their fingers. I take them. They are cold. I squeeze them once and glue my eyes to the pig. It's sleeping on its side, its bristly stomach rising and falling.

Miranda touches my sleeve. "So really, what brings you in here?"

"Farm animals. Specifically, goats."

"Mm. Right." They flick a fleck of hay off my coat. "Alone."

"I'm sorry?"

"You came here, to Selfation, alone."

I nod.

They tilt their head to the side and squint at me.

"Don't most people?"

They tilt their head the other way.

"It's a theme park for selfies, isn't it? Don't you take those . . . alone?"

They laugh. "You are funny."

"Oh."

They tilt their head back to the original side.

A sheep baas.

"Well, I've seen the goats now. I'll take my selfie and then I'll be out of here."

"No one ever comes in here just because. Farm animals aren't seasonal, and they don't make for glamorous photographs. Not compared to ski slopes and trips to Cancun."

"Uh-huh."

"Where's Janey? I haven't seen you two together at school. Usually people-who-don't-know-each-other still find ways to *know* each other between classes." They wink. "It seems like you definitely wouldn't be here alone if you were *knowing* each other outside of school. Yeah? So, do you, or do you not?" An animal snuffles in the hay. "Know each other."

"Oh. No. I— We don't."

They shift their weight on the stool. "Would you mind coming closer? They make me wear this stupid outfit. Because miniskirts are practical for farming? Stupid, right? It gets very, very cold. I am cold. Come closer, please."

I'm already close. I step one step closer. Their legs are, in fact, covered in goose bumps. Their dragon ring undulates as their fingers move, latch onto the edge of my coat, and pull me in so Miranda's knees are against my stomach.

"There. Do you mind this? Is this okay?"

I don't mind it. It is warmer. Their perfume is floral and not barn-like at all.

"No one ever comes here. It's like a forgotten island. That's why it's so interesting that you're here. By yourself. You didn't happen to come here because I told you I worked here, did you?"

"What?" I step back. "No!"

They grab my jacket and pull me in so I'm touching their knees again. "And you wanted a chance to talk to me? Alone?"

I shake my head vigorously.

"If it was true, I wouldn't mind. I told you last time that I didn't mind sharing. Lydia doesn't mind sharing."

"I like goats."

"I've been asking around about you," they say. "Since seeing you at my aunt's non-experience store-store."

"Did I— Am I in trouble?"

They pull back to look at my face. "You are so *sweet*. Trouble? What? No."

Both of Miranda's hands are on my jacket now. Their fingers are running along my shoulder seams. I am definitely not cold.

"After our encounter at Mirona's, I naturally needed to know a little more about you."

"... Naturally?"

"So I sought out information from the greatest source of information at Glenville High. You know what that is?"

I blink.

"*Who* that is?"

"... Kermit?"

They boop my nose. "He let me in on your little secret. On how you're doing something great for our country."

"Me?"

They boop my nose again. "You. He said you were doing a special, very important research study."

Then Miranda brushes my hair off my forehead before returning their hands to my jacket. "You never know with Kermit, though, if you're paying for truth or buying into some elaborate scheme." They must be very, very cold indeed, because their cowboy-booted leg is now wrapped around me. "So it's true, then?"

"What's true?"

"You're doing a great, secret research study, yeah?"

Their hands are traveling lower and lower on my jacket.

I swallow.

"So modest." Their hands are at my waistband, on my belt. "Would you mind," they say, "if I touched it?"

"What?"

"Just a little."

Their hands drift over to my wrists. Their fingertips tickle the skin under my sleeves.

"Your secret wristband that is going to change the world. That's what Kermit said. Do you mind?"

"Oh," I think I say, "oh, that."

"Wow." Their hands drop from my wrists and to my hands. They interlace themselves with my fingers. "Wanting to change the world is a very attractive quality."

"I think you're going to be very disappointed if you think I am changing—"

"Modesty. Also a very attractive quality." They put my hands on their waist. "For the first time, I might be glad that no one ever comes in here. I did mention that no one ever comes in here?"

There are thoughts in my head, probably, but the ink of my thoughts is smearing, running, blurring together, I can't . . .

"I'm saying," Miranda says, with more edge in their voice, "that if you *did* come in here just to talk to me, and if you were hoping you might get to do more than talk, well, I am cold and bored and I find you attractive and I guess I wouldn't mind." They tilt their chin up, and whether they pull me with their leg or I simply tip forward, I don't know.

Their lips are there to catch me, and that is not a bad thing, so I stay there.

My weight is on my hands on the stool on either side of their hips, the edge of their skirt, their cold knees and smooth skin, and it is so nice to think about something else, to not think, to have my thoughts like smeared ink so I couldn't read them even if I tried, only dark, blurry, beautiful smudges, and doing something like this, kissing Miranda, the more I kiss them, the more they take my lip with their teeth, the more I feel the curve of their hip in my hand, the blurrier my thoughts get, and I love it.

So I kiss them about the study, and the pills, and the business cards that weren't for me, not really, and my mother coming home, and Jane's face when I asked her out, about how much I hate hate hate Dave Appleright and Miranda pulls away for a second to say, "Wow, quiet boys can kiss," and I take all the terrible things and put them into my tongue, my teeth and forgetting and smell the place behind their ear and touch the soft soft skin of their waist and let the thoughts bleed away.

But then I feel their hands on my hands, the dragon ring cold and hard and unforgivingly material, and their fingers are so much regular fingers, I touch them and I am not there, not like with Jane, Jane's warm mittened hands, where there was a whole universe in our touched-together fingertips.

And then all the running ink of my thoughts, all the ink from different thoughts is flowing into each other, there are different tones, shades, and it is forming shapes, like one of those blot tests, bleeding out toward the edges, and the shape has wings, the shape is a moth.

The moth flies off the page and into the future, and then all I can see is the whiteness of the page, white paint over eyes, the thrashing heads, the white of the pills, the pills that maybe are making me able to kiss Miranda back.

I pull away. "Sorry," I say. Miranda doesn't protest. Instead, they are looking past me, over my shoulder.

"Welcome to the Farm Zone!" they say brightly. Then, "Oh hey, hi!"

I turn around, and there is Jane in her burgundy sweater and her hat and her mittens and her plaid down vest, and one of her mittens tucked up so cozy in the hand of, oh yes, Dave Appleright, with his perfectly chiseled jaw and his shoulders so strong, they take up almost the whole doorway.

Jane is staring at me. Her lips are making and remaking a tiny O.

KNOWING WHO YOU KNOW

"Dave?" Miranda hops off their stool and pushes past me. "David Justin Appleright? Is that really you?"

"Hey, Miranda." Dave's voice thunderstorm reverberates across the ceiling beams before shooting down in lightning bolts aimed directly at my head.

Miranda throws themself around Dave's shoulders. "I thought you weren't getting back until next week! Oh my god, you're like a rock!" They squeeze Dave's upper arm. "I like it. Wow. But wait, when did you get back?"

"Today. A couple hours ago. Haven't even seen my mom yet."

"Then why are you *here*?"

Dave laughs. "To see you."

"That is *not* why we came." Jane's chin is lifted two inches too high, so she's talking to the wall above our heads. Now she turns it away from us, toward the nearest stall, where a blanketed pony is munching on something in a bucket. "We are here because this theme park is one of the most major developments since the last time Dave was home. And it seemed like it might be a great place to walk and talk to each other."

Miranda's face goes blank, and resets, like they're only now registering Jane's presence. Their gaze drifts down to where Jane's mitten is swallowed by Dave's gorilla-size glove.

Jane yanks her mitten out of it.

"Janey! Hi, you! You know Dave?"

"No."

Dave laughs again. "She does." He gently takes up her mitten and kisses it. "There's no need to keep the secret if people see us together, Kumquat." He kisses her mitten again. "Plus, Miranda's good with secrets. Right, Mir? You aren't going to say anything to anyone?"

Miranda's eyes go wide. "Oh my god. Oh my god! You're saying what I think you're saying, yeah? The undateable Dave has started dating?"

"Nope." Dave's smile is perfectly lopsided. "The undateable Dave has *been* dating. The undateable Dave was never undateable at all."

Miranda squeals; their hair poof wobbles. "Oh my god. This is some juice, yeah? This is some juice I'm going to put into my industrial-strength steel secrets safe. But not until I juice it a bit more. I need the details. Like—how? What? And Janey—like, *what*?"

Jane's cheeks have shaded a light pink. Her free mitten is tapping against her thigh.

Dave laughs yet again, and I'm wishing he would stop doing that because it's hard to properly hate someone who is so good-natured, when he turns toward me. He grabs my hand and moves it up and down like he's pumping air into the deflating bike wheel that is me. "'Wayne! 'Wayne Le! Long time no see, buddy. Happy Kwanristmukah. We can trust 'Wayne here, too. He's a real solid guy."

Jane's mitten stops tapping. "You two know each other?" Her voice is the blade, and the blade is directed toward my skull.

"No!" I say.

"We sure do. 'Wayne here is a fellow Mr. Houston fan. Soon to be another happy and productive follower of the SMART goal protocol!" He slaps me on the shoulder. "Wait, do *you* two know each other?"

"No!" Jane shouts.

I shake my head.

Miranda's eyes go from me to Jane, and then they widen again, then narrow, then widen, like the door on her industrial-strength safe is shaking as the secret inside pounds to get out.

Dave thrusts Jane's mittened hand in my general direction for me to take. "Y'all are in the same grade, you need to hang out! 'Wayne Le, this is Jane. Jane also follows the SMART goal protocol, but not because of Mr. Houston. Jane already knew about SMART goals when I met her, because she's naturally smart. Smart about SMART. Actually, that's how we first connected. Right, 'Quat? Go ahead, make friends."

Jane's hand, inside her mitten, grips my hand too hard. "Hello. It's very nice to meet you, Damien."

"Uh. Hi. It's 'Wayne."

"Right! Sorry. Nice to meet you. I think I've seen you around the halls."

"You two should hang out! Janey gets lonely when I'm overseas. Would be good for her to have another goal-oriented friend."

"Definitely," I say. "I'll, uh, try and find you around, Jane."

Jane takes her mitten back. "I actually keep myself pretty busy. I don't need more friends."

Dave laughs. "Sorry. She's pretty blunt. One of the many things I love about her." He pats the top of her head.

Miranda looks at me pointedly, their gaze almost as sharp as Jane's voice. "Wow, Janey. I have to say, I wouldn't have seen this coming. I am rather impressed."

Dave hugs Jane to his side. "I wanted to keep it a secret, to protect my little kumquat from the social spotlight. She doesn't deal well with attention."

Jane strokes the neck of the nearby pony, looking like she's both too hot and too cold, and I wonder why she's letting Dave and Miranda talk about her like this.

Miranda is still staring at me, a laugh playing at the corners of their eyes. "Janey certainly doesn't want attention from too many people. And you, Invisible-D 'Wayne, you impress me more every time we meet. All of the people you seem to not knowingly know, yeah?"

"He does seem to not know a lot of people," Jane says, glaring at me.

Miranda's almost-laugh turns into a full-on smile. Then they pat at their hair poof, like they are calming the secrets inside. "Right. Anyway. Why'd you all come to the Farm Zone, anyway? You want to take selfies with our baby cow or something? He's outside."

"No. We're just here to observe." Jane is still glaring at me. "And I think I've observed enough. I think we should leave."

Dave laughs one more time. "Right. We were intruding! We'll be gone soon and you can get back to your . . . salvation of self." He winks.

"Or now," Jane says, with one resounding pat on the pony's shoulder. "We could leave *now* and let them get back to their salvation *now*."

"Guess we're leaving. Chat me up, 'Wayne. You too, Miranda. I'm home for three months, we gotta hang." He gives Miranda a hug. "And don't forget to grab tickets for my fundraiser, if you haven't already. We're almost sold out!"

MY GOODLY FAMILY OF LIES

"Interesting, interesting, interesting." Miranda perches back on their stool, facing me. "Who knew you were living such a very interesting life, you quiet, nearly invisible, Invisible D. But Janey, that's even more surprising—what she's been up to with you. You *and* Dave."

"We're really not—"

"*Especially* Dave. Dave Appleright and *Jane*? Did you know that I've known Janey for a long time? Like a really long time, yeah?"

"Yeah." I am trying to figure out how long I need to wait before leaving. "Since first grade."

"Aha! You *do* know each other."

"I—"

"Stop. I'm not going to say anything. No judgment. I don't know the arrangements y'all have and it's none of my business, yeah? Unless, of course, you want it to be my business. Or unless you're feeling like sharing details just for funsies?" Miranda pauses, watching me. They rub the goose bumps on their shins. "No? Maybe later. So yeah. Janey. I've known her since first grade. She was my first friend in Glenville. And I think I was *her* first, and only, friend in Glenville. So I know her really well."

The pig rolls over to his other side, crunching the hay beneath his shoulder.

"It's hard for her to do anything that surprises me. The Dave thing does, though."

"I only found out the other day."

"What! I can't believe she didn't tell you. The whole time you were hanging out together?"

"We really weren't—"

"It doesn't make sense. It doesn't make sense!" They adjust the dragon ring, move its head so it sits on their knuckle. "Does it make sense to you?"

"No."

"Thank you! I'm glad it's not just me. It's truly *bizarre*."

They slide off their stool and pull a tackle box out from behind some hay bales. "I assume we aren't going to resume our previous activity, yeah? Mood is kind of shot. Feel free to hang out and chat, though. I like the company. It really does get boring as balls in here." They kick one of the hay bales toward me. "Grab a seat. Goss with me." They pull out a large canvas from behind a stack of decorative barrels. It's blocked in with shapes, and even though it's unfinished, the colors and lines already showcase Miranda's particular style, remind me of their school lobby PacSun-horse-shop mural.

The hay crunches as I sit.

"'Wayne. I know you're quiet. But sweetie, I cannot gossip on my own. Entertain me. Either give me some details about your sneaky linking or speculate with me. Make some unfounded assumptions! Ask me questions that force me to make uninformed conclusions! The Jane-Dave thing is bizarre to you—why? Go!"

One of the chickens approaches me, pecks at my shoelace. "It's bizarre because—they don't match each other at all. What could Jane possibly see in Dave?"

"*That's* what you think is bizarre?" Miranda flicks open the plastic tabs on their box, pulls out brushes and tubes of paint. "Honey, that's like the only part of this that makes sense. First of all, have you *seen* Dave? Or touched him? God. Especially now. I did *not* expect that much of a change when I hugged him. I totally would pay to do that again. *Mmm-mmm-mmm.*"

They squeeze some of the paint onto a dinner plate. The chemical smell crawls over the dusty scent of the animals.

"I didn't think Jane—"

"—would care about stuff like that? Yeah. She'd want you to think that she's above it. But everyone cares about stuff like that, whether they admit it or not."

"But—"

"But, okay. Sure. Let's pretend she doesn't. She does, but we'll say she doesn't. Even without that, there are a million reasons that Jane would want to be with Dave."

The chicken continues to peck at my shoe. Little stabbing, poking nudges that don't exactly hurt, but could start to at any time.

"Dave is— He takes action on shit. Everything he does, it's around a goal, a cause, a purpose."

"Are you saying she likes him because they're similar? Because Jane also likes to take action on stuff?"

Miranda swoops their brush into several colors, splotches it a few times on the plate before spreading the color onto the canvas. "Ah, you're still at that phase with Jane. You think she's an activist. What is she on about now? Saving the red wolves? A food drive for tsunami survivors? Oh, that look on your face. You liked that about her, huh? Me too.

"But no, she's no activist. It's always something new. We were going to sell cookies to raise money for a children's hospital. Did that happen? No. For a while, she was passionate about organizing a pet-fur drive for oil spills, to protect coral reefs, and that never happened either.

"So, no. Jane isn't going to lead an initiative on the rights of humans or women or panda bears or whatever, no matter how much she talks about it. But Dave is. He does. He takes action on shit. He and I—we worked together on a bunch of projects. We designed T-shirts to raise money for Hurricane Ariel disaster relief, designed the graphics for the Rare Disease conference. So, of course Jane would want to be with someone like that. He's who she wants to be."

Their brush makes long, scratching sounds.

As much as I don't want to believe it, part of what Miranda says echoes exactly what Jane described about Miranda, why despite all of their differences and their past, Jane wishes they could be friends. And I wonder if it's true. And I wonder if my experience with Jane is not true, or it's not *yet* true, or despite being truer than how I knew her two months ago it's still only part of the ever-evolving truth of knowing her, or knowing anyone, or if we all have different truths of each other, or if we never have truths, and the best we can do is accumulate a community of well-formed relationship lies.

I pull out a piece of hay that somehow got lodged in my shoelaces. "She looked so uncomfortable, though. Like she didn't want to be with him."

Miranda looks up from their painting. "Oh, honey. You really like her, don't you? It wasn't just a fling of the schling for you, yeah?"

I tug at my jacket cuffs.

"Oh, sweetie." They shrug. "The fact that you like her—you, who are doing some secret world-changing thing"—they gesture toward my wrist—"makes me think, maybe I'm wrong? Maybe their relationship isn't bizarre at all. Maybe she's changed. Maybe Dave sees in her what you see in her, and it's true—she's grown up. Or maybe being around Dave turns Jane into the person she wants to be. And maybe Dave likes being that person who does that for her, someone she looks up to. I could totally see that. He loves being the helper, the protector, the person responsible for making other people care."

They swish a few more strokes onto their canvas before looking at me again. "This is not what you wanted to hear. I'm sorry. But as long as Dave is interested, you don't stand a chance. You already knew that, yeah? You poor soul." They put their brush down. "You want to make out again? It's distracting, at least."

That makes me laugh, pulls me back into myself. "Thanks. No. Thank you. I think I should go." I stand up, gently nudge the chickens away from my ankles.

"Come back and visit me sometime? Or we could do a project together, next time you embark on a world-saving mission?"

"Sure."

On the way out, I turn back. Miranda's painting is still unfinished, but it's already beautiful.

It makes me understand why Jane was friends with Miranda: how they are someone who paints a PacSun into their mural of ideal society because they truly believe that the new world we're heading into is somewhere we might actually want to be.

Plot Point

Hey. Hi! Hi. Sorry to barge in like this. Sort of. I'm not that sorry. Some things needed to be said. I thought maybe, probably, you'd have some questions or grievances. And if you don't, you should. So, I'm going to assume the best of you, and answer them.

You should be thinking: *Hey, Jane, do you like being a character that primarily serves as a way to demonstrate the complexities of "selfness"? Do you like existing in a role that helps our male hero learn that self is ever-changing, ever-evolving, and fluid and refracted and nebulous and uncatchable, undefinable?*

No. Let's be real—no one likes being a plot point in someone else's story. Though it's true, what Dave said: I don't like being the center of attention.

Still. It's not so bad. If I wanted to leave, I could. Now, for example. Now's an easy out, I could make a clean break that no one would wonder about too much.

But I'm going to stay. It could be worse. I could just be here to tell 'Wayne he's a good guy.

Instead, I get to show him that "I" is not fragile. Just because something can change doesn't mean it breaks. Think of a piece of paper, folding and unfolding, into a car, a bear, a universe of planets, a million possible forms.

And also, it doesn't really matter what I think of myself, does it? I mean, do you know who you are? All of the yous from yesterday and all of the yous from tomorrow? Do you understand all of the decisions you make? Do you?

Do you really?

WELL-STRUCTURED VALUES

Kermit is laughing, even though there is absolutely nothing funny going on.

"Dave Appleright, your new best friend."

"We are *not* friends."

"You are. You will be. I am not allowing you to waste the opportunity to gain such valuable social collateral. It will transitively trickle down to me. And how can you say no to spending time with those quad muscles?"

"Can we stay focused?"

"I am very focused. Do you think you could arrange a meetup? With the three of us? Me and Dave's two thighs."

Kermit pulls his sweatshirt over his head and makes a cushion out of it to sit on. The scent of The Domestic Hunter breaks free and fills the meditation room. I faceplant into a lavender pillow.

He let me have the majority of pillows this time, which means that despite how he's talking to me, he feels really sorry for me. He pats my knee. "Don't you see that it's *good* that Jane probably hates you? *Great*, even."

I stare at him over my pillow's edge.

"Her *hating* you means that she *likes* you."

I remove the cushion from my face. "Someday I want to record you talking and make you hear the words that come out of your mouth."

"Greatest idea you've ever had. I'd love to have something intelligent to listen to while I'm working."

I pull the hood of my sweatshirt over my head.

"Look," Kermit says. "I don't want to sit around debating about the pointless quest of your heart. If she hates you, if she likes you, the result is the same: She's never going to like you more than she likes Dave, so you're sad. You ruminate. You wallow. Wanh-wanh, the end. What's clear is she isn't totally, one-hundred-percent indifferent to you."

"Awesome."

"And. We also know that she *did* used to be completely indifferent. You were, in fact, the person she found most uninteresting out of all the people in our class."

"Do you need to frame it like that?"

"So her liking you—finding you somewhat interesting now— could be related to your personality change."

"You don't think it could be because it's easier to be interested in people you know something about? And now she knows something about me, which is actually interesting?"

"No."

"You always raise my self-confidence."

Kermit side-eyes me. "Can you at least pretend you think I'm right for five minutes so I can get to my point?"

I bite my lip.

"If the pills have made you more of a personality Jane likes, let's look at the data points we have in what Jane likes in a personality: Miranda. Dave. And that means, maybe, that your personality has become more like theirs."

I cross my arms. "I don't want to be more like them."

"Your petty petulance is limiting your already limited capabilities for critical thinking."

I very non-pettily make a mature hand gesture in his direction.

He sighs. "So, the question to ask is, What are the ways in which Dave is superior to you?"

"You do realize why I might not want to talk about that, right? Why this very topic might be specifically painful to me, on this day, after what I experienced literally five minutes ago?"

"It was not *literally* five minutes ago."

I put the pillow back on my face. He snatches it away from me. I moan. "Miranda said that Jane likes Dave because he takes action on stuff."

"That doesn't really help. We already concluded that you were taking more action on stuff. So what is it about Dave's character that helps him take action?"

Kermit leans against the wall. I put my head on my knees.

I picture Jane and Dave in the Farm Zone, her mitten tucked into his giant, well-structured hand, connected to his well-structured arms, the ones I can too easily picture in perfect detail because of the photograph I have to see every time I pull up the Glenville High website, Dave in the basketball jersey, his bare, muscled arms lifted up toward the basketball net, the school's ridiculous motto in big letters running over his hips . . . I look up. "Kermit. 'Glenville High Strives to—'"

"'Care About Stuff Like Dave Does.'"

BABY TERRORIST

"Is that scientifically possible?" I sit up. "To make someone 'care' more? And why would they want to?"

Kermit doesn't say anything. He's rubbing his temples with two fingers from each hand, like he's mixing his brain into a perfect stew.

The sounds of Mrs. Shah preparing dinner filter in from down the hallway. A knife against a cutting board. The murmur of a television. Pounding, stone on stone, and the smell of coriander and cloves.

That's how my thoughts feel in my brain. Like they're being pounded, ground together.

I think back over the last month and try to discern if *I* care more.

Kermit pulls his fingers away from his head. "Let's start with your second question: Why would the government be interested in the science of . . . we'll keep calling it *caring*, but I think this is oversimplified. Why would they want to make someone care? The answer is, terrorists."

"Terrorists?"

"People perceived as a constant threat to national security. People who have been radicalized, so to speak. People who are willing to commit violence, and even die, for their causes. To fly airplanes into buildings. To drive vans with bombs into parking lots and blow themselves—"

"I know what a terrorist is."

"You never know, with you."

I glare at him.

He hands me back my pillow as he stands and begins pacing. "My point is, terrorism is a certain kind of caring. Caring to the maximum degree about a cause. Caring so much that you disregard consequences."

I twist my fingers into the pillow tassels. "Wouldn't the government want to make people care *less*, though? Wouldn't they want to make people *not* terrorists? If they make people care more, how does that help?"

Kermit resumes stirring his forehead as he paces.

"Well," he says, after he's made four loops around the space, "drugging your own people would be easier. You have access to them always. So if the CIA made a very controlled dose, and administered it to the American soldiers who already care at least a little bit about the 'right' causes, then we'd have a set of our own radicals who are willing to kill and be killed? I don't know. I don't know."

But I'm on my feet. "This is right. You're right."

"I am?" Kermit clears his throat. "I mean, of course I am." He rubs one temple. "Why am I right?"

I toss the pillow onto the floor.

"Remember Justin Mikulski? Why he died? He sat there. He wasn't able to kill. He didn't care enough. He couldn't pull the trigger."

LEVELS OF CONCRETE

Now we're both circling the meditation room floor.

I kick a round pillow out of my path. "It matches up with the assignments in the app. Kind of. Now that I think about it, the assignments are kind of provocative? Like, 'try and survive.' Maybe they're trying to get me worked up as a way to measure how much I care?"

Kermit passes the doorway, spins on his heel, then walks in the other direction. "Wanting to survive enough that you pull the trigger. How willing you are to take action on shit. How much risk you're willing to take for the sake of what you believe in."

"Like asking Jane out. Like telling Charlotte that Michael was an asshole. Like meeting with Hans even though I knew it was wrong. And it matches with the name, maybe? Mothlight. Because if a moth is drawn to a flame—"

"The moth will kill itself." Kermit high-fives me as we pass each other. "Apprentice, I'm seriously considering giving you a promotion. Look at you! Participating in this conversation! Adding real observations!"

I'm walking toward my mirrored reflection now. When I reach the mirrors, I turn around. "Something else Miranda mentioned was Jane. How Jane isn't good at taking action on things."

"The same Jane we met in the library?"

"I know."

"The one who brought her own tiny spoon just to shove it, figuratively, in my face?"

"Maybe the Jane we've been talking to is . . . already different?"

Kermit stops to check his sneakers' toe boxes.[32] Then he resumes his pacing with a stiffer, more penguin-like gait. "She came in third in the national origami championships. Do you know how hard that is? To come in third, nationally, at *anything*? You have to care. Like, a lot." He checks his toe creases again. "But yeah, I guess if what Miranda says is true, then our disbelief is proving the point. Jane's so successfully changed that we can't see her any other way."

"Right. So how do we figure out if it's true? Get to where we're sure enough that it's worth telling Hans?"

"I don't know. But talking to Jane might be a good place to start?"

My socked feet stop moving. I run a toe along one of the grooves in the wooden floor. "But she basically said she didn't plan to speak to me again. And that was *before* the Farm Zone."

Kermit turns and walks back toward me. He pats me on a shoulder, which makes me feel sorry for myself.

I run my toe along the wood plank again. The sock catches on a splinter. "I never thought I'd say this, but I wish Bryce was around. To ask about his experiences with the study."

"Mm."

"He would be willing to share information. He was really easy to talk to."

---

32. Kermit hand cuts toe guards from sheets of thin plastic that are supposed to keep his sneakers from creasing. He tried to get me to use them, once, since being around me and my shoes is "embarrassing." I refused. In fact, whenever I get new sneakers, I get a tiny bit of pleasure out of taking the paper out of the toe and purposely bending them back, preferably while Kermit is watching.

"Or really easy to get talked at by."

"And his hair gel wasn't *that* bad." The splinter relinquishes my sock. "Not bad enough that I would have wished him— You know."

"How about you talk to someone else? I have a list." Kermit pats my shoulder again, harder this time, and I move away from him.

From the kitchen, a microwave beeps. My ribs feel like they are crawling together, fingers entwining, afraid to let go.

"I'll talk to Jane."

Kermit nods. "Good."

An oven door slams. "Five minutes to dinner," Mrs. Shah calls.

"Got it!" Kermit yells back.

"Tell 'Wayne he can stay for dinner."

"He can hear you himself!"

An extra-loud slam of an oven door. "Keshav! You tell him!"

"Fine!" Kermit turns to me. "You are invited for dinner."

I hesitate.

"Unfortunately, even if you do stay, we can't keep talking about this. My parents will expect me to eat out there, at the table, like a *family*." Kermit glowers.

"I would *love* to stay for dinner," I say.

HOPKINS STUDY APP

Please find a quiet area for the next exercise.

Check that your wristband is correctly positioned with the black circle on the inside of your wrist.

We will be playing a variety of audio clips. All you need to do is stay calm! That's all! Simple, right?

Try to keep your breathing as steady as you can. Try to keep your heart rate from increasing. Yes, really try to control your heart rate!

Because of the wristband, which monitors your pulse, we will know if you didn't give it your full effort, and there shall be consequences. ;)

Don't let your likely failure stop you from Having Fun!

My Darling Secret,

Hello from Asheville, North Carolina! Something about the mountains, the blue hazy range of them, makes me nostalgic for what this country must have looked like before humans settled here. There's a yearning in these mountains for the infinite.

Or maybe I'm the one with the yearning, because there are only two months until I see you again. Until I'm *home*—that's still how I think of it, after all this time.

I'll be there for your birthday. Did you realize that? 18. Wow.

I regret not being there for your . . . well, all the years, but your teen years, especially. They're the hardest years, what you're living through now.

I remember mine. I remember my best friends at the time—Reggie and Sofia—the taste of the cheap, awful danishes I'd buy from the school vending machine, the cut grass smell of the field by the track where I'd spend my lunch period, and . . .

the exhausted helplessness I'd feel in the afternoons when I'd get home. The weight of getting up in the morning. The feeling like nothing I did mattered or would ever matter.

I didn't know it at the time, but that's when my depression started developing. That's kind of typical—for it to start around this age. Your age. It's partially genetic, you know. I hope you are doing okay. I hope, if you are not okay, you are talking to someone about not being okay.

I didn't mean to fall into this topic every single time I write you. I guess it feels important for me to explain myself to you. Not to make excuses, not exactly, though part of me feels like if I explain this, you'll be more likely to forgive me.

Which I suppose is what this letter is about, like every one before it: I want you to know I'm sorry.

Two months. Two months!

Every time I get a break—from work, from life, even when I'm standing at an Airbnb mirror, brushing my teeth—my mind counts the hours until I see you again. Hold you again.

You smell a little bit like limes, did you know that? You probably don't know that. It's the kind of thing you only get to learn from a mother. Because it's the kind of thing only a mother would notice.

Love always,

Mama

BOMB-PROOF AGENDA

When I walk into the Tiki Bar, Jane stands up without acknowledging me. She zips up the puffy plaid vest over her sweater, dumps her empty Cubano mug in a bus bin, and hurries toward the basement door, which she flings open, barely missing my nose. She takes the stairs two at a time.

At the bottom, instead of walking toward the green haze of Mirona's Five Dollar Miracles, Jane makes a sharp right into one of the room-shaped shells. There, a small circle of space has been cleared of mannequin parts. Two folding chairs face each other in the middle of the circle.

Jane sits in one. I sit in the other. She watches me. Her face is stiff. Her expression is blank. Kind of. It's blank like a wall that's been painted white over a meat stain.

I swallow. "Thanks for meeting with me."

"You said it was important. Or rather, Kermit did. 'Critical urgency,' he said." She makes her air quotes.

I swallow. Kermit ended up having to message her, because she didn't respond to any of my pleas to meet her here or in the library.

The glow from Mirona's filters through the windowless storefront. It outlines Jane's nose, her crossed arms, the snake of her leg that's wrapped all the way around the other, the salt stains on her boot tip. The glow lands on a metal nuclear fallout shelter signs that's screwed into a nearby concrete column.

I pull out the notes I prepared, a bulleted list of everything to tell her about the study. I scan for an easy one to start with. One that won't vaporize what's left of our not-a-relationship. My conversation options: Hans. The sick girl from his video. Justin Mikulski's helicopter. The pills making us care more. And the one that scares me most: asking Jane about what Miranda said about her—whether it's true that she's as bad at getting things done as, say, me.

"Well? It looks like you want to say something that you don't want to say." Jane points at my papers with her chin.

I flip the papers over. I restrain the urge to crumple them into a ball. "I'm sorry about Miranda."

Jane blinks. "You needed a bulleted agenda to tell me that?"

"No. I, uh. No."

She blinks again.

"It's not an agenda."

"That's disappointing."

"Oh."

"I thought I might be having a good influence on you."

"You are! You are . . ."

She uncrosses her legs and arms. "I'm kidding. But more seriously, you and Kermit didn't make me come out here, where I spent thirty minutes setting up this awkward interrogation-chamber-like meeting space in this cold—though nuclearly safe—basement, a space that is weirdly, I might add, close to where Miranda sometimes works, to apologize about Miranda, right? That hardly counts as 'critical urgency.'" Her air quotes have taken on a violent edge, even through the cushion of her mittens.

"That's not why I asked you to meet me here."

"Okay. Good. Especially because you don't need to apologize, because you didn't do anything wrong."

"I didn't?"

"Of course not."

"But I hooked up with your ex–best friend right after asking you out!"

"So?"

"It made you feel—"

"Oh, it did?"

"..."

She leans forward. "Did you ask me?"

"I— What?"

"Did you ask me how it made me feel?"

I bite my lip.

"Because I don't care."

The room feels, suddenly, even more dark and creepy than when I thought Jane was unforgivingly mad. I realize, resentfully, Kermit was right—Jane being upset with me was way better than her not caring at all.

"You really don't care at all?"

"No."

"Then why did you block my number?"

"I didn't." Her boot begins jiggling. "For long." She's seemingly transfixed by a stray mannequin torso sitting near the doorway where we came in, and the room's darkness eases itself a little bit off my shoulders.

"Oh. Well, great, then."

"Yes. Great. We're on the same page." She scratches her knee.

"Well...?"

"...Yes?"

"Aren't you going to apologize?"

"But you told me *not* to apologize."

"For assuming I would want an apology in the first place!"

"Oh."

Her foot jiggles faster.

"I'm sorry."

"Thank you. I forgive you." Her lips twitch left, then broaden into a full smile, and the prickled bush that has been stabbing my stomach since this morning withers slightly.

She sticks her mittened hands underneath her thighs. "So, then. What's on the 'critically urgent' paper that isn't an agenda?"

UNSUNG ENEMIES

The paper is sharp and unnaturally loud as I turn it back over.

"It looks like a list," Jane prompts.

"It is." I scuff my heel against the floor.

"A list of . . . ?"

"Discussion topics."

"That sounds a lot like an agenda."

My smile is forced.

"Would it be better if I just read it to myself?"

The sound of footsteps makes us both look up. A round silhouette hustles its way down the hall. The battery-operated parrot outside of Mirona's squawks its welcome. Then silence again.

I shake my head. "There's kind of a lot on the list."

She puts her hands on her knees.

I clear my throat. "Well. To start with. Have you gotten any packages with slippers?"

"No?"

"I guess I'll start there."

So, I tell her about my visit with Hans, about the video he showed me, about his plea for information, and how this directly correlates to what Charlotte had said about people out there looking for ways to disrupt the study.

Jane listens with her eyes closed, her arms crossed. Her lips turn down at the edges.

Maybe it would have been better to let her read it. The spoken words dangle shapelessly in this dark, concrete space—like poorly made lies, like something out of a bad conspiracy movie, a plot that your little sister made up.

Except Olive's stories make more sense, have happy endings, and involve at least one cat.

I look away from Jane's furrowed forehead and force out words about the articles about the Mikulskis, Justin and Michael. When I get to the end of the story about Justin, about how he shouldn't have been allowed to enlist, which means that perhaps Michael lied for him, I pause.

Even though in Kermit's room, in real time, it all made so much sense, now all I see are the gaps, the convoluted logic, the impossibility. The tense pull of Jane's forehead makes me question sharing it even more—why worry her over clearly inconsequential events?

Jane opens her eyes. She crosses her arms even tighter. She frowns. "This is helpful."

"It is?"

"All of this data keeps piling up. It validates my thoughts, like I'm not making it all up."

"You believe me?"

She squints. "Why wouldn't I?"

"Well." I rub a hand over my face. "I don't know."

"It *is* borderline unbelievable that you fell for the slippers."

I can't help smiling, a real smile now. "Don't start."

"Start? Start what? Pointing out the obvious ploy that you walked yourself right into?"

"I knew it was a ploy! Except I thought it was a Kermit ploy."

"Despite you being absolutely unbelievable, I do believe you." Then she breathes out a heavy sigh and makes a wrapped rope of her legs again, folds forward. "But of course, the problem is I *want* to believe you. Like I told you in the library, part of me wants this to be the real thing."

"Why is that a problem?"

She shrugs. "It makes me dangerous. Untrustworthy."

Mirona's electronic parrot squawks. The round silhouette makes its way past our dark room, its shopping bags rustling. An elevator dings, and then it's quiet again.

PLUGGING THE PLUGS

I unfold my paper again and review the next item on my list, even though I already know what it says: "Ask if what Miranda said is true."

To my right, the green light catches the outline of a mannequin head at the exact angle to make its eyes glow.

"Your face is telling me that we haven't gotten to the end of your agenda."

I nod.

"And that you want to talk about the remaining items even less than the first ones."

I shrug.

Jane folds her mitten flaps back, buttons them. Then she reaches into her vest pocket and pulls out a small notebook with a pen slipped through the spiral. She flips it open to the first page and clicks the pen.

"'Awkward Miranda encounter at Selfation,' check." She draws a line through something on the page. "'Resuming conversations between J & D.'" She draws another line. "'Extra information about the study.'" Another line.

"Is that a list of . . ."

"All the things you might want to talk about, yes. I like to be prepared." She taps her pen against the page. "I did *not* expect you to talk about muffins or slippers, though." She writes something at the bottom of her page, then draws a line through that, too. "Okay. So. I have two items left here. The first is that you want to go over the lists we were supposed to make. But would you avoid that? Unlikely. So how about option two: 'Something Miranda told him about me.'"

I fold my own paper and put it in my coat pocket.

Jane meets my eyes, then quickly looks away. "Ah." Her voice goes quiet. "Miranda's unfortunately predictable. Go on then. It's nothing I haven't heard."

"After you left, we talked about you. Um. Why you're with someone like Dave, and, uh, Miranda said that you probably like Dave because . . ."

Jane closes her eyes.

". . . because he cares about things."

"Like, 'let's all care about stuff like Dave does'? That's why I like him?"

I nod, then realize she can't see me. "Right. Well, actually, Miranda said you like him because he takes action on things that make a difference."

Jane inhales, then exhales slowly. "How worried should I be that none of this sounds bad so far? I'll answer that for myself. I should be worried. Check. I am worried. Go on."

"Miranda said you'd be attracted to his consistent action-taking because you, um, have no ability to take action on stuff yourself. Because you don't really care enough about anything."

Jane nods. She nods again. The fingers of her right hand twist at the sweater threads on her left arm. One breaks. "Damn it." She squeezes both of her hands between her knees.

I scoot my folding chair closer, then spin it around so that I'm sitting next to her instead of across from her. It feels better. Less like an interrogation in a room that was bombed fifty years ago. More like we are two weird friends hanging out, for some probably excellent reason, in a cold, dark, and creepy nuclear bomb shelter.

Jane's shoulders rise and fall at uneven intervals.

"I'm not telling you about it because I believe them. I wanted to talk about it because it *doesn't* seem like anything I know about you. So I thought maybe, you know . . . the lists we were making, about how we had changed? That maybe the you I was getting to know was, I don't know, hugely different from the you that Miranda knew."

Another shadow hunches down the hall, bags rustling. They're using their cell-phone flashlight, and it creates dramatic, sharp shadows, draws lines around all the scattered mannequin bodies and heads. Jane and I instinctively shrink down, turn our faces away, until we hear the squawk of Mirona's welcome parrot.

Jane rubs her nose. "Thanks for saying that. Thanks for thinking Miranda was wrong. The thing that makes it hurt like it does, though, is that they might be right." She sniffs.

I stuff my folded paper even farther into my pocket. My chest feels tight, like it does after I say something snappy to Olive or don't like a gift from my father even if I say I do. "They're not right. I'm sorry I mentioned it. I only did because of how it related to this idea Kermit and I had—that the pills are making us care more about stuff. Clearly you take action on stuff. Clearly you care about things very much. Kermit said it too—you're in all advanced classes. You've been doing origami competitions for only three years and still made it all the way to the national championships."

She looks up. "Where I came in *third* place. I didn't win." Her expression is grim.

"Jane—"

"The awards and medals Dave has gotten? Not third place. Miranda didn't get to redo our lobby mural because they came in third place."

"I don't think—"

"Remember how I told you I had a more personal reason to stay in the study? Well, this was it. Proving that I care enough to stick with something."

"I don't understand."

Jane picks at one of the newly broken sweater threads. "Okay." She sniffs again. "I guess I'll just tell you everything. That was our new rule, right? Follow where conversation leads us?" She rubs both her hands over her lips, up to her eyes, and stays like that for a long time. I become aware of a low-key humming, a generator or heater or fridge, and the faint trickle of water in a pipe.

Jane's vest crinkles as she moves her hands away from her mouth. "Here's the thing. I want to go away to college. To CalTech. I *need* to go there. That's where Robert Lang went, the person who changed the landscape of origami, and he still lives right nearby. I want to follow in his footsteps, maybe even convince him to let me intern for him and help astronauts and doctors with better understanding of the math behind complex folding.

"But my father won't support me going away for college. 'I'm not going to waste money on what's bound to be a failure.'" She makes air quotes from her knees. "He's not wrong to worry. I've never been on my own. I'm really bad at the seemingly mundane things. Like eating. Remembering to brush my hair. Checking administrative boxes if they seem pointless or illogical. Saying hello to people."

"Can't you get better at those things?"

Her shoulders go up and down. "That's my argument. And I've made progress. But it's so hard. Like— What's something you really hate doing? Like, you hate doing it with all of your might?"

"Uh . . ."

She leans forward. "Writing essays? Public presentations?"

I shake my head. "Telling Olive—that's my younger kind-of sister—bad news."

Jane looks at me. "That's really nice, actually." She smiles gently. "So when you do that, do you know that feeling where it's like your whole body turns into, I don't know, one of these concrete pillars here"—she waves at the dark shadows around us—"and every action feels conscious and heavy?"

I nod.

"For me it's like that with a lot of regular life things. Like plugging in my phone. 'I must plug in this plug. Okay. I am moving my arm, I am still moving my arm, keep going, arm! One more inch! There you go! Oh wait, time to breathe! Now, fingers, you must close, first the index finger, now the next one.'

"My mom seemed to understand. Or at least, she tried. She used to tell me it was because of how my brain is set up—being autistic and having uneven capabilities and such—how I'm really great at things most people might find really hard. Like, if someone asked me to write a novel, I could do it. Or program a JavaScript database search tool. Or transcribe a violin concerto by ear, writing with my nondominant hand. Or memorize two hundred types of moss. I'd be ready to jump right in this very second! My brain is great at that stuff.

"But as a trade-off, my brain is super bad at the things a lot of people have no trouble with. Saying hello to people takes as much effort as what outlining an essay might take for someone else. The world isn't set up for brains like that.

"What this means is, I'm great at taking action until a computer needs to be plugged in. And there's always, eventually, a computer that needs to be plugged in. Both literally and figuratively.

"Would I have won the origami championships if I'd been able to figure out something to eat that day?

"From Dad's point of view, it's like—how am I going to get through school after months of also having to plug plugs and choose my meals? Without a private room to hide in after being around people all day?" She pulls the zipper on her vest up and down a few times. "Do you see what I'm saying?"

"I guess. But I don't see what that has to do with whether you care enough."

She nods. The green glow dances across her lashes as she blinks, her lips as they twitch to the left several times.

"Mm. That comes from the message the world gives me, I guess. Most people don't believe how hard those things are for me. Very specifically, my dad.

"He always was annoyed at my mom for 'coddling' me, letting me get away with my 'laziness.' 'Jane, *everyone* has to do things they don't like. That's called *life*. If you can solve calculus problems, surely you can spread some mayonnaise on toast. The problem is you don't *care* enough.' " She inserts a flurry of air quotes into the air in front of us. "Which doesn't make sense, especially when I don't even like mayonnaise *or* toast."

She takes off her hat and holds it on her lap, runs her fingers through the fuzz inside.

"I sound totally resentful here, and I'm not. I love my dad. We're just so different. And especially since Mom died, he hasn't been the same. Grief, it does weird things. Takes what is logical to a whole other plane of existence. A non-reality plane of existence.

"It's the same for me, I guess. I'm aware of the logical contradictions. But it's one of those situations where you think someone is wrong, but you've heard it so often, you start to believe it. I do believe it. And not believe it, at the same time. Am I just making excuses for myself? Do I simply not care enough to get through the things that need to get done?

"And then having Miranda saying the same thing as my dad—Miranda, who has spent more time with me than almost anyone—and you start to think—I start to think—it doesn't matter what is true. What other people see, what the world chooses to think of you, *that's* what ends up mattering.

"Not in an existential way, because sure, the truth still matters, obviously, but in a *practical* way, as in it's what other people think of you that counts toward what the world lets you do. You aren't good at fractions? No problem—you can be a fancy business consultant or the secretary of defense. You aren't good at making eye contact? Welp, you're worth more dead than alive! Off you go to Spiegelgrund, where your brain can lounge in a jar for a decade or five." She puts her hat back on and yanks down on the two dangling tassels.

"You know how people are always telling kids to not care what others think? 'Just focus on being true to yourself.' I hate that. I all-the-way hate that. You *have* to care about what others think or you're totally fucking yourself over."

The parrot squawks, and the white light of a phone flashlight flickers against the columns.

Jane sits on her hands, drops her chin to her chest. Her eyes are closed. She's less than two inches away from me, yet she looks entirely alone. I fold my own hands between my legs to counter my impulse to hold her.

The metal door at the top of the stairwell bangs, and Jane lifts her chin. When she speaks again, her voice is calmer, but sharp, hardened into her blade.

"I've just given you a lot of information and I am rambling and

I'm running out of talking juice, so I'll stop soon, but I want to get to my point. Which is that Dad refused to help out with paying for college if I go away from home.

"So when the letter for the study came, I had this idea. That if I could do this study, this mundane, uninteresting thing that disrupts my schedule and requires me to interact with people and goes on for a while, and also the whole time remember to eat meals and do laundry and, yes, keep my laptop charged, then Dad would agree to let me apply to CalTech, and go if I got in.

"I didn't think he'd agree. Because clearly doing a three-month health study is not the same thing as living across the country. But he did. I don't know why.

"Of course, the study has turned out to be anything but mundane. And yeah, I was interested in the study from the beginning, so I was cheating. I am cheating. Maybe I'm an awful, useless person after all. Who knows?" She crosses her arms.

"You're not . . ."

"I'm done talking now. I think I'm panicking. Yes. I'm panicking. Could you please hold me? Please. As tight as you can. Please." She doesn't move toward me. Instead, she's gone entirely still.

So I move my chair closer and wedge my arm behind her back and hold her to my chest.

"Tighter. Please." Her voice is even and calm.

I hold her as tight as I can. She's smaller than I expected, and full of sharp corners, and it's a little like holding a metal statue of a log. But even through her vest, her sweater, I can feel the pulse of her heart against mine, and the longer I hold her, the softer her muscles go, the more regularly and frequently her breath moves in and out.

We sit like that for a long time. Two groups of people go past us into Mirona's and out again.

No one would say this is romantic. It's not. And no, this is not what I had in mind when I imagined one day holding Jane. But if I can be the concrete pillar that makes her, well, less of one, I'm more than okay with that.

A FEW POUNDS OF FUR

Eventually, Jane squeezes my arm once and pulls it away from her shoulders. "I'm okay now. Thanks. Thank you."

I let her go. She takes off her hat and tucks her hair behind her ears, then pulls the hat back on.

"So yeah. Sorry about that. A triggering topic, apparently." She pulls her legs up onto the chair with her, hugs her knees. "To answer your question, I'm not sure if what Miranda says is true. Do I not care enough about things to take action on them? Maybe. But I haven't noticed any change in myself at all."

She reaches into her vest for her little notebook and flips to the last page. She passes it to me. At the top of the page, it says, in tidy capital letters, HOW I'VE CHANGED.

Underneath that, the page is blank.

"What about your assignments? Do they have anything to do with caring about stuff? Or seem designed to get you worked up?"

She flips to a folded back divider in the middle of her notebook. There it's headed ASSIGNMENTS in the same tidy letters, followed by a full page of writing. She hands me the book, and I realize it's not just one page of handwriting, it's about twenty, front and back.

"You've had this many assignments?"

"You haven't?"

I scan her descriptions, and they don't look anything like mine. Her assignments are all much more standard, things like "Today's calories from protein vs. fat," and "Five-paragraph essay on what you believe about fitness," and "Without researching, describe associations with 'Pilates.'"

I hand the notebook back to her. "Yeah, these don't seem related to 'caring' at all."

"Yours do?"

I describe several of my recent assignments—steadying my pulse, telling secrets—and though we both find it notable that we have had totally different experiences with the assignments, we can't come up with any new ideas for what those differences might mean, or how they might relate to the ability to "care." I tell Jane about how I feel like I'm different—how I've become better, more prone to taking action on stuff.

She taps her knee to mine. "I wish I could support your hypothesis. It's an interesting one. Being able to make people care more could have some dramatic and useful effects. And it's still possible, I mean, the differences in our assignments might mean we're in different groups or something."

"But yeah. I'm not out there leading any raids. I'm still having trouble remembering to eat. The main change in my life is that I've convinced my dad he doesn't need to worry about me." Her fingers tap along her arm.

"Sorry to go back to this, but it's going to bother me. Did Miranda say why they think I don't take action on things?"

"I don't think it's true . . ."

She flaps her mittens at me. "Just tell me."

I sigh. "They mentioned something about a children's hospital? And something about pet fur and oil spills?"

Jane stares up at the ceiling. I worry she's going to panic again. Her shoulders start moving irregularly. Then she opens her mouth, and laughs. "The hospital was from third grade. *Third grade!* The coral reef drive was fifth. What eight-year-old do you know that's going to successfully start and run a business on their own?

"I did successfully make and sell cookies, by the way. I sent fifty-four dollars to the children's hospital. And two pounds of pet fur to make oil spill mats. Which is a lot of fur!" She shakes her head. "Okay. I feel better now. God. Miranda is so cool and yet also so annoying. Why do I want to be their friend? Why *am* I dating Dave?"

Before she answers herself, before I have a chance to ask her to answer herself, one of the mannequin heads in the corner of the room falls off the table. It rolls across the ground, and then there's the squeaking and knocking of other plastic parts sliding across each other.

We both spring out of our chairs, adding more crashing to the chaos.

"Hello?" My eyes are glued to the darkness. Now it's my muscles that have become metal logs. "Who's there?"

I take one step forward, and Jane grabs the back of my jacket.

"Hello?" It's quiet now, except for my breathing, Jane's breathing. Then, a tiny, tiny sound, closer to us, not far from our feet.

"Oh my gosh." Jane drops to her knees. "Come here, baby. Come here, little sweetness."

A very dirty, very skinny, very nervous cat crawls onto her lap.

BEYOND

The cat is shivering, cautious, but pushes his tiny face into Jane's hand.

She holds still and lets the cat take the lead, nudging his nose into her thumb pad, his chin onto her fingertips.

I crouch down on the floor next to her and hold my fingers out for the cat to sniff.

Jane's eyes are large, focused entirely on the cat, and somehow shining even in the dim light. "Why is he down here? He's so thin." Her fingers find a clump of dirty fur on his neck and rub through it. "Do you think he's stuck down here? Do you think he's lost? You don't think someone *left* him down here on purpose?" She strokes down the cat's dusty tail.

The cat lets me touch his head, his ears. They are crusty and stiff, like he's gotten hurt recently, though I can't imagine by what. "He seems like he's been down here awhile."

Jane sits lower to the ground, crosses her legs, and the cat curls up on them. Her fingers go back and forth across his fur, untangling clumps of dirt. She's pulled back into herself, and it's the same feeling as before, like she's totally alone, but not in the same lonely way.

Everything about Jane is present and soft.

Beyond.

"I love him," she whispers.

And I think about what she was talking about before, about how the kids who can't make eye contact were sent away to be killed. How could any person ever send Jane away to be tortured and killed? How could anyone meet Jane and think she's not worthy of life?

A flush of heat flashes through my whole body. "Jane. You know what you were saying before, about them using autistic kids as targets?"

She does look up at me then, her hands gently resting on the cat's back.

I continue. "Do you think this study is like that? Do you think we've been targeted?"

"You're autistic, too?"

My hands are suddenly sweating. "No. I don't know. It's . . . My mom keeps sending me these emails. About her health. Like, her depression and anxiety. And last night, she sent me one asking me whether I'm depressed or anxious. She said it's genetic. And then your mom . . ."

Jane is nodding. "How did I not see the potential there? I was too focused on figuring out what the pills were about, and not looking at *who* the study was focused on. Which is pretty ridiculous, considering, but also goes to show that even if you have a ton of knowledge about the history it's still hard to see when it's happening right in front of you. If there's anything to see, that is. But yeah, it wasn't just autistic kids who were targeted. Other studies targeted different unworthy groups, including people who were depressed."

"And the original letter said we were chosen at random. The same letter that called it 'consensual.' Which is almost like backward extra proof that it might be right."

Jane runs her hands along the cat, who has started purring. Her hands slide under the cat, and she lifts him to her chest, stands up.

"Let's go. This is something we need to start thinking about right away. You talk to Kermit, see if he can get information from the other participants' health records. I'm going to do some reading. And all three of us should come up with ideas about what we should do next and meet in two days. That should be enough time, I think." She unzips her vest and lifts up the bottom of her sweater to put the cat underneath. "Yes, you don't need to say it. I am indeed suggesting that we plan to make a plan." The cat's head appears out of the neck hole. He's not shivering anymore.

LAST APPOINTMENT NOTICE

Dear Dwayne Le: #33923810,

 Thank you for your continued participation in our study. Your attendance is required at an in-person appointment on December 6 at 1:30 p.m. This will be your final appointment.

 Your school has been notified of your absence. It is your responsibility to make arrangements for missed schoolwork ahead of time. We look forward to seeing you then. Thank you again for your contributions to our project. We hope you've been having fun.

POP QUIZ

Why, historically, has the United States favored performing experiments on minorities, immigrants, and people with mental health diagnoses?

a) If you end up hurting them in the process, there will be more jobs for the *real* Americans.

b) If you end up killing them, there will be fewer sad people in the world. In fact, more people may be happy.

c) It's less amoral because they don't count as whole people anyway.

d) If you are able to change their personalities/habits/character, that's called "effective assimilation."

e) All of the above.

HOPKINS STUDY APP

Another writing assignment today, sorry!

In the box below, please share one example of a time something of yours disappeared. Then write about how you managed to find that item again. If you never found it again, please hypothesize about where it might be now. Feel free to be creative in the second part of your answer.

Sorry again for the writing prompt! We do try to keep the writing assignments to a minimum, but developing the mini games is expensive. If only we had the Pentagon's budget for game development. Alas we are but a small, humble study with limited funding.

Hopefully you find the writing exercises at least a little bit FUN!

BINARY REALITY:

MENTIONS AND REVIEWS

"THE BEST JOURNALISM YOU PROBABLY AREN'T READING: Naomi Le's Oral History of Technology . . ."

"Who would have thought that through the lens of an affiliate marketing website, we would receive one of the most comprehensive portraits of democracy, the floundering state of it." —*The Washington Post*

"The irony is not lost on us. These interviews are published on the internet, and the internet is itself a map of oral histories, a sample of truths and untruths. But Naomi manages to get people to speak in such a way that you know at once they have finally said *their* truth, and in that truth is reflected our country's conflict over what we can still believe." —*Vanity Fair*

"Naomi Le has proved herself to be the Studs Terkel of our time. In a world that's overstuffed with voices trying to be heard, finally, again, we have someone willing to listen." —*The Los Angeles Times*

GOLDEN HOUR PERSPECTIVES

"I've called you here today to discuss the beginning of the end." My voice echoes in my mostly empty bedroom.

Kermit squints at me, into the sunlight streaming through my blinds-less bedroom window. "You're dying?"

Jane shakes her head. She's sitting on the floor in the carpet depression left by my bedside table.

Olive looks up from my bed, the only furniture left in my room other than the swivel chair, which Kermit immediately claimed, and the computer desk, devoid of my computer, obviously. I'm sitting on the empty desk now.

I spent the last two days packing up almost everything in my room and shuffling it into the basement so I could have one place where I felt relatively safe.

Which made it the perfect location for Kermit and Jane to come meet and talk through our ideas for potential plans, given what Kermit texted to us this morning: "Statistically significant." Meaning that he found a relationship between study participants and their parents having a diagnosed mental illness.

They left their phones—and, in Kermit's case, multitude of other electronic devices—in the designated laundry basket I labeled and positioned in the upstairs hallway.

Olive was already in here, sketching the tree branches now much too visible through my windows. When she saw Jane with the cat (now named Yoyo) tucked under her sweater, she disappeared downstairs and returned five minutes later with a toasted bagel—the cube of cream cheese not touching—and watercolors.

"I think 'Wayne is being dramatic," she now says.

"Only a little," I say.

"But what is he being dramatic about? *This* is the question." She points a bagel piece at me, swipes it through the cream cheese, and crunches into it.

"The only thing I have to be dramatic about."

Kermit squints harder. "You didn't decide to quit the study. Need I remind you of Bryce?"

"I haven't forgotten Bryce. I'm not quitting. The opposite, actually."

"You're . . . signing up for another study?"

Jane shakes her head again. "Kermit, you seem off your game."

"It's the unfiltered sunlight. It clogs my gears."

I lean to the left so I'm blocking even less of the sun. Kermit holds a hand in front of his face. "Dude. System error."

I smile and sit straight again. Clearing out my room gave me a lot of time to think. And whether it's because of the pills I've been taking or not, the thinking I did feels better than my usual thinking. Worth sharing. "I've thought through what I'm pretty sure are all our remaining options. And I've come up with what I think is a really solid plan. Even Jane is going to be impressed with my ability to plan. Listen. The thing we need to focus on is the drugs."

"Drugs?" Olive drops her bagel piece. Yoyo stretches out from his place on the bed and bats at it with a paw. "You're on drugs?"

"Of course not! I'm talking about—"

"Should she be in here?" Jane tilts her head toward Olive. "Does she know about . . . you know . . . ?"

Olive narrows her eyes. "Do I know about *what*?"

I scratch my knee. "She doesn't know."

"Well, I'm definitely not leaving *now*."

"Olive's not a threat," Kermit says.

"Make me leave and we'll see about that."

"Oh yeah, definitely nonthreatening," Jane says. But she smiles at Olive. Olive smiles back. They each pet one of Yoyo's ears.

I run a hand across the back of my neck. I'm starting to overheat. "It's fine. We can trust her. Right, Olive?"

Olive eats the last bite of her bagel and picks up her paintbrush. "I'm just in here for the golden hour tree branches. I'm not interested at all in what drugs you're talking about or this top-secret plan that I maybe shouldn't know about and this soft cat and this new Jane friend D has invited even though he hasn't finished redecorating."

"Redecorating?" Jane raises an eyebrow.

The confidence I had at the start of the meeting is quickly disintegrating. "Olive, fine. We're talking about the Hopkins health study."

Kermit makes air quotes that rival Jane's in vigor. "The 'health study,' aka a major CIA undercover project. Wherein 'the presumed vitamins' are actually personality-altering drugs."

The wind blows. The branches tap on my window. Two crows start cawing back and forth.

Olive looks at me, then back at Kermit, then at Jane, then back at me. "You have convinced yourselves that the CIA is running your health study? And that some vitamins are changing 'Wayne's personality?"

"Cor-rect," Kermit says, giving her a thumbs-up with each syllable. "And Jane's personality, too."

"Maybe," Jane says.

"They have changed him," Kermit says. "Look at him. He's barely recognizable."

Olive squints. "He looks the same to me."

"Not like that."

"I *know*, Kermit, I was kidding. I don't think he's any different."

"He made a list," Jane says.

"One whole list?"

Jane smiles.

"It's a list of how I've changed."

Olive nods, but she's somehow also shaking her head at the same time. "*This* is why you keep asking me if I think you're any different?" A snort escapes at the end of her sentence.

"It's real, Olive. Remember the prize box? When the slippers came?"

Olive kicks out a leg so I can see her slipper-clad foot.

"The meeting I went to was actually an old guy warning me about the study."

"An old guy."

"The turtle I brought you—"

"Bob."

"—it wasn't a prize. I bought that at the pet store on the way home."

Olive tucks her pink-slippered foot back underneath her and points her brush at me. "So you lied."

"No. Well. There wasn't a good way to tell you. They're spying on me at all times."

"Except now?"

"It's complicated."

"The redecorating."

I run a hand over my chin.

"You think they are spying on you through your *things?*" Her cheeks puff.

"They *are*," says Kermit. "I proved it."

"Kermit, your definition of *proof* is highly dependent on what will make you correct."[33]

"I like her," says Jane.

I sigh. "Speaking of spying through my things, Kermit, when I was clearing out my room, I found four. *Four.* Four different sensor thingies."

"You only found four?"

"I am going to ban you from my room again."

"They weren't recording anything private! Just passwords! Nothing *personal*. No video."

"Can we please focus?" Olive says.

"I really like her," says Jane.

"D, can I at least have them back? They're expensive."

"Focus!" Olive is running her hand over and over Yoyo's back. Her lips are scrunched like she's physically restraining the judgments from gushing out.

The crows are getting louder.

I take a deep breath. "Right. So. I made a list of how I've changed, and I'm pretty sure I do more stuff. I take action on things I wouldn't have before. For example, I actually made a plan. The plan I'm trying to talk about now, if you all would let me. I came up with a really great plan."

Olive snorts again. "Uh-huh. Go on, then, tell us your really great plan. I promise not to turn you over to the CIA next time they stop by."

---

33. Olive's never had a lot of patience for Kermit. When she was eight, she offered to bring me a new best friend back with her from her summer trip to Vietnam. She even had her mom text me photos of her top two candidates—another eight-year-old girl "who both acts smart and is actually smart" and a colobine monkey.

Jane takes her little notebook out of her vest pocket. She clicks her pen. "I'm ready to hear this amazing plan you've come up with."

Three pairs of eyes watch me expectantly. My conviction that my plan is anything worthwhile has managed to completely disintegrate somewhere between Olive's skeptically askew paintbrush, Kermit's persistent smirk, and the laughing of the crows.

IDEA VACUUM

I blow out a long stream of air. The crows stop cawing.

"So. My last appointment was scheduled. And that got me thinking about how this is our last chance to get information. We need to go all in on what's at the center of the study. The pills. What the drugs are.

"And what I came to is, what we need to plan to do is, I mean what the plan should be is—we need to steal a pill."

Jane and Kermit are leaning forward, Kermit's pink high-tops tapping away on my carpet.

"Yes?" Jane says. "What's next? How are we going to steal said pill? And what do you propose we do with it after we steal it?"

"I was thinking we would come up with that part together. Here. Now." I bite my lip.

The crows start up their laughing again. Yoyo squeaks out a yawn.

"Well? What do you think?"

A look passes between Jane and Kermit. Jane clicks her pen closed and sticks the notebook back into her vest, which feels a lot like having a door slammed in your face.

Suddenly, Kermit gives me two thumbs-up. "I wouldn't have expected it from you, Apprentice. But I think you've done a great job here. See, Olive? See how motivated and plan-ny he is? Have you ever seen him like this before? Moving forward with stuff on his own? Pills. It's the pills."

Olive shakes her head and resumes her painting.

I sigh. "You both already thought of this, didn't you?"

"No. No way. This is all totally new to me. Let's keep on going. Right, Jane? Let's come up with some potential next steps for 'Wayne's brilliant plan. Stealing the pill, definitely the right next move. Great thinking, D. How are we going to steal the pill?" Kermit is about to explode out of his sneakers.

Jane taps her chin. "What if . . . hmm . . . I'm thinking some sort of contraption, something non-suspicious, that we could carry into the room and use to hold the pill."

Kermit does explode out of his chair then. The chair goes spinning into my wall. "Excellent idea! Fantastic idea! Exactly this idea! And look at this, look at *this*!"

From his pocket he removes a striped green cylinder. He thrusts it into the middle of the room. "What do you think *this* is?" The cylinder has a cap and a gold clip and very clearly looks like a fancy pen.

"I'm guessing it's not a pen."

"Wrong! It *is* a pen." Kermit unscrews a piece off the back of the pen. "That is *also, secretly*, a pill container!"

Olive lets out the loudest sigh in the history of sighs. "Why would you make a pen-slash–pill container if you hadn't thought of the idea until ten seconds ago?"

Kermit's pen-holding hand sinks two inches.

"Kermit," I say, "did you actually pass up an opportunity to gloat?"

Olive frowns. "He didn't exactly pass it up."

"You were so excitedly proud of yourself, D. It was cute. Actually, now that I'm thinking about it, how lucky you are to have a best friend that is modest and kind . . ."

"Kermit!" Jane kicks his shoe.

"Do NOT get dirt on Paulina! She's an LE collab with Travis Scott!"

I grab his arm and force him back into the office chair. "Go on then. Show us your masterpiece."

He turns his foot to check his sole and, apparently satisfied, holds the pen into the middle of the room, slightly too close to Jane's face. "I was doing some reading about the CIA and various devices they've used for poisoning people over time. And something they used pretty regularly was pens. They're small, something that someone would have in their pocket, and an object you'd expect someone to take out to use during a meeting. And then buttons or levers could, like, release aerosol poison into the air, or drop it into coffee, or shoot darts, or, you know, whatever was most likely to be deadly.

"So I picked this gal up at that antiques store next to the pet emporium. She was a real mess, but I gave her a little love. Isn't she beautiful? And, thanks to me, now she features a very convenient pill-size container. *And* she writes."

He uncaps the pen and tilts it back and forth in the sunlight, his expression reminding me of the day he discovered the world of collectible sneakers.[34] "She's from the 1940s. Fourteen-karat-gold nib. Celluloid."

---

34. A summer afternoon. Kermit's parents had invited me with them on a family trip to visit DC museums, something they did at least once a year. That year, one of the museums was the Octagon House.

Kermit took a photo of the winding three-story main staircase. "Can you imagine having such a successful business that you'd have something like this as your *winter* home? That's my new goal."

"*That's* what you got out of the tour?" Mrs. Shah said.*

Later, when we had an hour of free time to walk around on our own, we passed some shops. A long line snaked out of one of them. "What's going on here?" Kermit asked someone. "Is there something free?"

"Nah," the man said. "The opposite. We're investing in shoes."

* The Octagon was built as a winter home for one of the wealthiest plantation owners in Virginia. The museum promised to transport visitors to the early days of the United States, when Washington, DC, was a small, rural community with great** expectations.

** Air quotes optional.

The sun catches iridescent parts of the green stripes. The gold feather clip creates dancing circles of light on my ceiling. It looks very expensive.

Jane clears her throat and gently pushes the pen away from her nose. "So. I need to ask. You think it's going to be entirely expected that a seventeen-year-old is carrying around a super-fancy fountain pen?"

"Well . . ."

"From the 1940s?"

"Charlotte is probably not going to know it's from the 1940s, specifically."

"Like, let me empty my pockets, here's my cell phone and my key and my Pizza Joe's loyalty card, three balls of dryer lint, and, oh yeah, my golden pen? For all the writing I do by hand?"

Olive snickers.

"You wouldn't be carrying it in the same pocket as your key! Not after all the polishing I've done. The microscratches!"

"And how are you going to get the pill into the pen? 'Hold on one moment, Charlotte, I need to unscrew my pen-shaped pill container here . . .'"

"I was thinking you'd do a carefully practiced drop action thing? Or maybe, like, sleight of hand, redirect Charlotte's attention while you're tossing it into the minuscule container? You have time to practice—"

Olive laughs again. "So . . . literally magic?"

"It's not *literally* magic, because magic inherently *can't* be literal, because magic doesn't exist."

Olive flips her sketchbook closed. "Unfortunately, or fortunately, it's time for my piano lesson. I will have to miss the remainder of this ridiculous conversation. You all, enjoy your . . ." She moves her hand in circles. ". . . game." Then she heaves herself off of my bed, kisses Yoyo on the head, opens the door—barely—and slips out.

"Too young to know the evil ways of the world," Kermit says, staring at the closed door. "She will learn, she will learn. Alas."

Jane clears her throat. "This is really all you've got to show?"

Kermit twists the pen back together and clips it carefully in his shirt pocket. He folds his hands in his lap. "For someone who is so keen to schnoodle all over my idea, I don't hear you offering anything better."

Jane looks at me. "Wasn't he so proud of himself? Wasn't it so cute? How could I crush such earnest excitement?" She reaches into her vest pocket. "And now, presenting, the finest piece of paper engineering I have yet accomplished." She pulls out a small, white, crumpled paper ball.

MODEST SOLUTION

Jane tosses the ball into the center of the room. It falls flatly with a soft *poof*.

I crawl off the desk and crouch down so my face is near the floor. My breath rocks the ball. It looks like any other piece of crumpled paper. It's about the size of the yarn pom-pom on Olive's winter hat.

Jane's lips twitch to the left twice.

From his office chair, Kermit begins a slow clap. "Fine. I'll hand it to you. It's brilliant. It's so good. This is your life's work, right here. You win."

"I didn't know we were competing." A small squeak escapes Jane, something akin to a giggle.

"Do you hear something?" Kermit asks me. "Does it sound remarkably like gloating?"

Jane giggles some more.

"Does one of you want to explain?"

"Come on, D."

"It's an origami box that looks like a crumpled piece of trash?"

Kermit points at me. "Yup. It really tickles my fancy. You know, I've always wanted to get a vanity license plate that looks like it isn't a vanity license plate."

"You want to pay to have a license plate that looks like you didn't pay for it?"

"That's the mark of true wealth."

"How is it a *mark* if no one can see it?"

"What I'm saying is that this is in the same vein. An intricately folded, yes, 'engineered' masterpiece that looks like total randomness. An absolutely *non*-engineered piece of trash."

Jane is jiggling and bouncing from her place on the floor. "That's not all, that's not all! Watch, watch, watch this!" From her vest she reveals an aspirin. She puts it on the floor, right next to the paper ball. Then, she sticks out one finger from one of her folded-back mittens and gives the top of the paper ball a light tap. The pill disappears. "Did you see it! Did you see that? Are you amazed!"

"Again." Kermit joins us on the floor now.

Jane picks up the crumpled ball, lifts a couple flaps, and the pill falls out onto the rug. She refolds the ball, places it next to the pill. "Are you watching? Make sure you watch. Pay attention!" She taps one of the top creases.

This time I see it, but only barely. The bottom of the paper splits and walks forward, consuming the pill in its wake like a tiny, crumpuldy monster.

"Did you see it? Did you see it?" Jane's shoulders are wiggling like a bowl of rice pudding left on top of a dryer.[35] "I based it off the design for the origami forceps now used in surgeries, but I altered it since it needed to have a trigger that was super sensitive, so that you could activate it without it being noticeable. And of course, it had to look like something totally inconspicuous. It still folds decently flat, too, watch." She picks up the ball and pushes in two locations. The ball collapses into a tidy rectangle, thick enough to hold the pill but not much else. "This'll make it easy to fit anywhere you need it to

---

35. The first time was an accident. A snack forgotten in light of a *Drone Wars III: Reaper Reconnaissance* mission drop.

fit." She lets go, and the paper springs back into its trash ball form. The wiggling from her shoulders travels down to her toes.

I pick up the ball and sit so my back is against my desk drawers. Up close, the perfection is more apparent. The creases, the ones you can see, anyway, are not crisp. They're rounded, precisely imprecise, and clustered more on one side like the ball was made in someone's fist, their fingers clawing the paper inward.

"It's amazing."

Jane wiggles a little more. "Thanks. The outside is mostly wet folding, to get that more rounded, natural look. I have time to make us both one, so we'll have two chances. And I can make them from paper that makes sense for us to have. Or that appears that way, at least—I do have to use a specific paper to get it to work. This is more than you probably wanted to know. I'm excited to get to use it! Minus the obvious reasons for *not* being excited."

I tip the ball over into my other hand. "Wow. It's really, you're really..."

Kermit stretches his arms above his head. "Hate to interrupt this celebration of Jane's brilliance, but should we discuss what we're going to do with the pill after we steal it? Either of you come up with ideas for *that*?" He leans back and sticks his legs out straight in front of him. Then he opens his fingers out wide and completes his stretch, like we recently finished watching a movie he's seen four times.

Jane's wiggling stops. "Go on."

"Go on, what?"

"Whatever it is you're going to say."

He smiles at the ceiling. He wiggles his stretched-out fingers. He looks at us to make sure we're watching, then smiles up at the ceiling some more.

"This is that gloating nonsense that takes up valuable time."

"Hypocritical much?"

"Oh my gosh."

I try the obvious. "Do we send the pill to Hans?"

Kermit crosses his ankles. "*Nyehhh*. Do we trust Hans? What if the CIA is *actually* doing something good and Hans is trying to stop them? You're a better version of yourself, let's not forget. That's a good thing, maybe.

"Or, alternatively, say the study *should* be stopped. It's still not safe to send the pill to Hans, because what if Hans was a plant to see if you'll do something in an act of caring, essentially proving that the pills were working. No. No, this won't do.

"And, most importantly, does sending it to Hans get *us* any answers? Hmm? Hmm? I for one am not willing to put myself at risk—"

"You aren't at any—"

"—if I'm not going to get some answers. No. Take your time, give it a think."

Yoyo jumps down from the bed and bats gently at the paper ball. Jane tucks it away into a pocket. "You are seriously infuriating."

"*Fine.*" Kermit leans forward so his elbows are on his knees and cracks his knuckles. "I have a connection with a guy down at the forensics lab."

"The . . . forensics lab?"

"Mmm. Brian. He owes me some favors. I helped modify their security system with this advanced—"

Jane groans.

"And I won't share that right now despite it being *very impressive*. The plan is, one of you will give me a shaving off your stolen pill and I'll have Brian run it."

"Run?"

Jane has started bouncing again. "Spectrometry!"

"Does the fact that I came up with ideas for *both* steps of this plan, even though one was not the winning idea, mean that I win overall?"

Jane slaps his knee. Then she claps her mittened palms together. "It's a *literal* solution!"

Kermit starts to protest. Then he smiles. "It is. Touché. It is literally a solution!"

Their fists bump and explode.

"Excuse me," I say. "Hi."

Kermit raises his eyebrows at me. I raise my eyebrows back. The crows caw.

Kermit says, "Organic chemistry is an evening hobby of mine. It's like crossword puzzles but useful."

I lean to the side so the sunlight hits Kermit directly in the face.

"Okay, okay! Spectrometry essentially separates the components of a solution by weight. I'm saying that I'll figure out what's in the pill."

"Whoa."

"Don't get too excited. I won't be able to get the specifics. I might not be able to tell you what the pill *does*. Or why they are giving it to you. Or whether you're a totally different person. It's a literal and figurative solution, but it's not a perfect solution." He taps his fingers on his chair arm, then looks at Jane askance. "Let's take a moment here to admire my modesty, eh?"

She threatens his shoe with her own.

WARMER, WARMER

Setting: Cleaning up the kitchen, after dinner. Evening before the last appointment. An Olive-shaped blur is on the other side of the glass tile wall, at the unused table in the dining/guest room, writing letters to legislators about the effects of global warming on coral reefs.

Dad: Big day tomorrow.
Me: You have no idea.
Dad: After your appointment, will you get your letter?
Me: I don't know.
Dad: Or do they mail it?
Me: I don't know.
Dad:
Me:
Dad's Face:
Dad: Almost there. I am excited for you.
Me:
Dad:
Dad's Face: EoFF.
Dad: You'll text me right after your appointment?

Me: Sure.
Dad: Right after, okay? Before you drive home.
Me: Right after. Sure. Okay.

HOPKINS STUDY APP

You will see a ball bouncing around the screen.

Use your finger to slide the paddle back and forth to keep the ball bouncing for as long as you can.

Before you start, please close your eyes and visualize the following: The ball is the truth. The ball represents what is right in the world. The ball represents what is just.

Did you do it? Did you visualize? Was it fun?

The stakes are high! Don't drop the ball!

BINARY REALITY:

How Small-Town Communities Think & Feel About Digital Technology

An Oral History, by Naomi Le

I grew up here. My father worked in the mines. Didn't get my first smartphone until about five years ago. Does that count as a computer? It does, right? A pocket computer.

At that time, I'd just gone through a breakup, and my little sister had died—car accident—so it was a bad time. I was in a bad mental place. And the phone, the internet, well, it got me in pretty deep—all the information, the conspiracies, the answers to everything in the world that didn't make sense. I needed that, those answers. Any answers. So I fell into it, held on to it. Those theories got me up in the morning, gave me a reason to live, this feeling like I understood these secrets.

I don't mess with the conspiracy theories now. What finally got me out of it? Every time I saw someone happy, I would start to cry, feeling so bad for them because they didn't know what was coming. And I thought, *This is no way to live, where you can't see other people happy.*

The core of it is this: You can't separate computers from what it means for access to information, to *mis*information. And you can't dismiss people as crazy or stupid for believing what they've come to believe.

I think you become an adult when you stop needing to

understand everything. You can look at yourself and say, *I'm okay with the fact that the world is larger than I am. I don't need to have all the answers.*

Alex Chin: Hazard, Kentucky

THE AVERAGE OF AVERAGE IS NOT EVERYDAY

Inside my non-Jordans sneakers, my pink stealth socks are panther-pad soft as they move me along the dirty, broken tiles, past the taped-up clip-art signs.

They move me past the three other teens waiting in folding chairs, heads bent over text messages, farming sims, *Drone Wars: Double Tap*, to the sign-in sheet on the metal desk, where Jane's name is listed and already crossed out.

My matching pink T-shirt conceals—silently, stealthily—the folded flat paper ball box that sticks out slightly from my back pants pocket.

Jane's muffled voice hums through the door's glass window.

The paper scratches against my hip skin, and I remember that wolf-shirt kid, his gun handle, the easy crescent of Abrams' smile.

A PLAN THAT IS A PLAN

Option 1: Jane nods at me upon leaving. This means she successfully stole a pill and I should not risk stealing mine.

Option 2: Jane does not nod. She failed to steal the pill. I attempt pill take-age.

OR MAYBE ONLY PLAN-SHAPED

The window rattles. Dr. Charlotte steps into the hallway.

"Hello, 'Wayne." The *D* its own syllable, still. "You're up next, I think." She crosses my name off the paper on the metal desk.

Behind her, Jane walks out. Her vest is zipped all the way up. Her mitten flaps are down, covering her fingers. Her face is blank, the blank that's a painted white wall with meat stains underneath, her mouth is perfectly centered and frozen and small, and she looks at me, her eyes a deer's, and

Option 3: she shakes her head, twice.

LIST: THINGS THE SAME

- Two desks,
- Charlotte in her
- White coat with
- Perfectly dirty cuffs and her
- Pill-shaped shoes on the
- Dirty, cracked floor,
- Ghost equations on
- The dusty chalkboard by the
- Unbroken flask and its
- Perfect layer of chalky, dirty dust.

LIST: THINGS DIFFERENT

- On Charlotte's desk,
- Wires, red and black, with
- Silver clips winking in
- Sunshine.
- A third desk in the corner with
- Abrams
- Waving two fingers,
- Weapons dangling over the chair lip,
- Swaying, so gently,
- Laundry hung out to dry.

SNAKES 'N SHAKES

Charlotte waves her arm toward my chair before taking her own seat. She rests her hands on either side of the pile of polygraph wires.

One of the silver clips has spilled off Charlotte's desk and onto mine, and it reminds me of Hans pushing his paper toward me, Michael Mikulski creeping his fingers over the lips of our desks. I remember the teeth of those clips on my fingers.

Two head shakes means: Jane got caught in a lie. I shouldn't take the pill.

Two head shakes means: Or I should?

The origami paper ball is making my lower back irresistibly itchy, and I remember, too late, that I was supposed to empty my pockets when I sat down like it's what I always do—take out my phone, my keys, a wallet, and this crumpled ball of trash.

Abrams is watching something on a tablet. He's tilting his head back and forth like he's got cheerful music playing through his earpiece.

Charlotte picks up her clipboard from the floor next to her chair. "Since this is our last time meeting in person, I need to read you some final notes and next steps." The paper crackles as she flips it up.

As Charlotte reads to me—something about how the first phase isn't over until I complete another month of assignments, how to return my wristband, when I'll get my letter and stipend, something about how I will default to continued participation for the rest of my life—I replay and replay Jane leaving the room.

A head shake is the opposite of a nod. Two is more than one.

Charlotte places the clipboard back on the floor. "Any questions about that?"

I shake my own head. The silver snake clips on my desk dance.

Her unblinking gaze hovers. One of her thumbs plays with the wires. She leans forward. She picks up the silver clips. "Let's get started, then."

I nod.

Two head shakes means: Jane already shared everything. Charlotte already knows everything.

Two head shakes means:

I hold my breath, hoping it will slow my heart rate down before the metal clips clamp on.

Charlotte drops the clips. She pulls out the medicine bottle. "Got them to change this to a pop-off lid." She gives me the tiniest flicker of a smile as she balances the pill in front of me, her gaze unmoving.

RIPPLE EFFECTS

The pill rocks gently. The reflection of the pill in a metal clip rocks gently, too.

Abrams chuckles at something on his screen.

Charlotte picks up one of the wires between her fingers and toys with it.

My mouth is so dry. "Could I . . . Could I have a cup of water?"

Charlotte gestures at Abrams with her chin. He stands up, retrieves a tiny paper cup from under the lab bench. The pitch rises as he fills the cup. He puts the cup on my desk, next to the pill.

Charlotte hasn't moved. "You've never asked for one before."

I nod. I rub my lower back where the folded ball's corner is poking my skin.

I pick up the cup of water. Waves ripple across its surface, its own lie detector.

FOR A TIN STAR

High Noon, my father's number one favorite movie, is about a town marshal, which I think is basically a sheriff, who has spent his life protecting his town.

On the day the marshal retires, he needs his townspeople to step up and help him defeat a gang that's coming to kill him. The whole movie is this guy going around asking people, people he's spent his life protecting, to stand with him and help him this single time, and one by one each person refusing.

In summary, it's about this dude, this one good guy, fighting on his own for what's honest, what's right, trying to make up for every other person's complete lack of honor, every person's lack of ability to take action on shit.

He takes action on shit even though he knows he probably has no chance of surviving, no chance of making any difference at all.

Individual Interjection

Hi. Hi! Me again. Sorry. I know. Annoying place to interject. I'll be quick.

Me being me, I had to look up this movie after reading D's reference to it. It's interesting! Not the movie itself. Or I don't know if the movie is interesting, I didn't watch it. I'm not going to. But reading *about* the movie is interesting.

What's interesting is that people can't seem to decide if the plot, and the marshal guy, are quintessentially American or quintessentially *un*-American:

Isn't—some people say—having a chosen hero-like maverick, glorifying the individual, the definition of being American? But at the same time, isn't criticizing our people's lack of "integrity" and lack of "caring" and lack of "taking action on shit" completely *un*-American?

It's like—for an individual to be glorified, the general public must be scorned.

And then get this: It's been the favorite movie of a lot of American presidents. Yet, the guy who wrote the script got kicked out of the country. He didn't even get credit for writing it until the day before he died. He was literally not accepted as American.

Oh! One last thing. Just FYI. Not to correct 'Wayne, it's his book and all, but it's actually the marshal's wife who saves the day at the end.

THREE ACTIONS (ON STUFF)

I bring the pill to my mouth. I swallow the water. I drop the pill into my sleeve.

FREE

The desk wobbles as I scramble out of it. "Thank you!" I take three giant steps toward the door, my arm bent, the tickle of the pill bouncing against my elbow.

"'Wayne." Charlotte's voice is hard.

Abrams stands. He rests a hand on his belt.

Charlotte nods at him and he moves, his belt jangling with every fall of a boot.

For once, he's not smiling.

I cross my arms to secure my sleeves.

He moves to the second lab bench, the one with the unbroken flask. He opens a cabinet at the bottom and takes out a cardboard box about the size of a coffee tumbler. He stands in front of me. "We're sending you home today with two free bottles of multivitamins, as encouragement for you to continue caring for your health." He slips the box into my arms. "They're good. Gummy. I particularly like the grape." He smiles then. Opens the door for me.

As I leave, I look back. Charlotte is hunched over, writing frantically on her yellow legal pad.

EMPTY QUIVER

The scent of The Domestic Hunter has filled all the space my furniture once occupied, and is coupled, as it often is, by the citrus of Kermit's leather cleaning fluid. Kermit lounges in my desk chair, one floral camo Uptown propped up on my desk next to his fully spread-out cleaning kit.

Jane, on the floor, seems to be making the final folds on a unicorn.

"The deed is done." I let the pill fall out of my sleeve, where it has been rolling around the whole ride home, and onto the desk by Kermit's foot.

Kermit's bristle brush continues to make *whfft whfft* noises against his outsole.

"I did it," I add. "I didn't even need to use the special box. It went okay. I'm okay."

Jane creases three tiny folds to make the shape of a hoof. Her hands are slow, measured, like they were in the library as we discussed the history of government experiments. In the thrill of taking the pill, of escaping the lie detector, I'd forgotten about Jane's double head shake. It comes back to me now. My pride dissolves back into anxiety.

"I guess you're okay, too."

She finishes folding another hoof. "Don't sound so pleased about it."

"I was worried about you. A head shake was not in the plan."

"I thought it would be clear."

"I thought it meant something went terribly wrong."

"It did." Jane mists her unicorn with her water bottle, then carefully tilts up its head.

Kermit scrubs at something invisible on his shoe's outsole. "Pass."

Jane hands him the water mister. Kermit sprays his sole three times.

I turn to him. "You've been awfully quiet." I touch the pill. "Doesn't this make anything better? I did it. I stole a pill. We can move forward. Figure things out."

Kermit doesn't even look at it. He sets the mister on my desk and resumes scrubbing his shoe.

"Charlotte turned away for her. Exactly like she did for you last time."

NO POINT COMPLETE

It's not worth talking about. We do, anyway, of course.

How if Charlotte turned away, then the whole thing was an act, and if it was an act, then it was planned, and if it was planned, then anything Jane stole was meant to be taken.

Meant to be analyzed.

Meant for us to see.

How if we were meant to steal pills, then swallowing pills, what chemicals the pills contained, probably wasn't ever the point.

Whatever is in the pill I stole, too, wasn't ever the point.

We go in circles over Hans, Bryce, the unbroken flask.

"What I don't get, though," I say for the third or fifteenth time, "is how my personality changed if the pills didn't contain anything of consequence."

And Kermit, surprisingly calm, responds for the third or ninety-sixth time, "There are other ways to medicate people. Aerosols. Topicals."

I fiddle with my unused paper ball. Pressing it flat. Letting it pop back again.[36]

---

[36]. In origami, the question of whether any shape can be folded flat is an NP-complete problem. This is a scary math term, but all it means, really, is that it's a type of question that has an answer that you *know* is correct when you find it (e.g., you look at it, and yes, it does fold flat) but it is very hard to figure out that correct answer. It is even hard for computers to figure out the answer.

The idea is that if someone could figure out a way to solve one NP-complete problem (e.g., figure out the pattern for making a flat-folding origami dragon) quickly, then that same method for figuring it out could be used to solve all NP-complete problems quickly (e.g., we

And Jane, shaking her head quietly from the floor, her herd of paper unicorns growing, each one's head a little lower, horn pointed forward, progressively inclined to attack.

---

could effortlessly figure out how to flat-fold spaceships, and make optimal decisions about who should get kidneys next, and fill out all the Sudokus).

In summary: Should answers that are clear also be obvious?

Should all problems that have clear answers also be easy to solve, if only we . . .

. . . well, if only we knew how to solve them?

Lifelike Is Not Alive

Hi. I know, I know. I don't think this is my book now, I promise. This is 'Wayne's book. I know!

But I have to say something. I can't help it. I think it's relevant here.

I mean—clearly. If I didn't think it was relevant *here*, I would have said it somewhere else.

Anyway.

In origami, there are things called judgment folds, which are the folds that don't have exact rules for placement.

These are the folds that give the piece personality. The seemingly insignificant choices about how high your deer's neck should be raised. The position of your scarab's legs.

Your decisions about these folds can change whether your paper cicada is listening to the wind, or resting after a meal, or perched on the edge of a leaf about to take flight.

People think origami is about being exact. And it is. You have to be exact. That's part of why I like it. I love being exact.

But those instances where you must decide, those minute adjustments in angle and placement, those are the instances that make the difference between a rabbit that's ready to run and a rabbit that will probably get eaten.

Between a rabbit that is lifelike and a rabbit that is *living*.

That has aliveness.

Am I making any sense at all? I'm sorry for talking so much about origami. I know you probably aren't interested. But I'm also trying to say something that isn't really about origami.

What am I trying to say?

I guess it's that if you could change those big rules, you'd, I don't know, make a rhino instead of a rabbit. And that's a powerful position to be in, choosing rhino or rabbit.

But I guess what it is, what I'm trying to say, to ask, is this: What's *more* powerful? Choosing *what* something is or choosing *who* it is, and whether it's alive?

HOPKINS STUDY APP

Writing exercise time!

Sorry, as always, for the writing exercise. However, great news! You have unlimited time for this prompt as long as it's submitted before midnight:

Please elaborate on a time that you purposely did not follow a rule. A time you purposely made a mistake.

Please share with us how you broke the rule, how you felt about breaking it at the time, and how you feel about it now. Was it *fun*?

The mistake may be a big mistake or a small mistake. Don't worry, your information is secure and anonymous! Feel free to share even your greatest misdemeanors.

Hey. Hi. This is me. Not Jane. Me, the author.

I'm not sure if this ending is necessary. My editor thinks probably not.[37]

You may want to skip it. That will depend, probably, on whose ending you think is most important. On whose story you think this is, and what you think this book is about. On what you've decided you'd like to believe. And whether you like answers or questions.

Or maybe you don't care either way. In which case, neither do I.

---

37. In a future edition of this book, after this author has died, forgotten by everyone except their cats, this manuscript will be rediscovered and reprinted, but without this optional section. You will have to purchase it separately, as a digital download or in a little bound pamphlet. Controversy will ensue as to the secret meanings embedded in the book ("What does it *mean* that Dave's middle name is 'Justin,' like Justin Mikulski?" and "What's with the *Drone* game?"), and whether those meanings change whether the ending is included or skipped. Readers will scrounge for proof about whether all the dangling threads are intended to make a point or are in fact a lucky consequence of the author's true ambivalence.

The controversy will drive the book to number two in sales (number one being, of course, *Megortherox: Conquered, Conquering, Con King*).

SCIENTIFIC STUDY IN MINIATURE

I wait for my father on the couch outside of his office door for his 5:00 p.m. return home. I show him the box of vitamins. I elaborate on what I already texted him, what I can remember about what Charlotte said about how the study phase one isn't over yet.

He nods, his face showing only a hint of EoFF, and says, "I think you will make it to the end." Then he heads into the kitchen.

The Magnificent Seven plays from his tablet. He's restarted it from somewhere in the middle of the movie. The curry pot bangs onto the stove.

I feel achingly unsettled, weird, about the conclusion Kermit and Jane came to: that there was nothing meaningful in the pills at all. The fact that my father thinks I can make it to the end, that he has any faith in me at all, that he now wants me to work with him—that's more proof than anything else that something in those pills fundamentally changed who I am.

The light from my father's microwave clock glows through the doorway of his office.

Used to be, as a kid, I'd go in there every day. Do my homework while Dad worked at his desk. His office was my favorite, safest place in the world.

From the kitchen, the sound of a knife on a cutting board.

I creep toward the office and go inside.

The smell, the dusty cedar weight of it, squeezes me back through time.

The barrel chair I used to curl up in is piled with papers and books. The chair itself is torn, ugly.

And small. Everything is so small.

I pull out my father's desk chair. Sit.

His desk. I'd loved this desk. The magnifying paperweight. The collection of expensive pens tucked into the upper hutch. The particular squeak of his chair wheels.

There are so many things in this room that I'd forgotten.

The tea set on his bookshelf, which he uses—or used—every afternoon to do a short tea ritual. The collection of miniature airplanes, which, if I'd finished my homework, I'd been allowed to carefully touch. His once-precious cowboy hat, from our family trip to Dallas, draped over a lamp on the top shelf. He used to wear that hat when we went out for dinner.

We used to, I remember, go out to dinner.

It's unsettling, this thought that my old habits slipped away when I wasn't watching. I see myself now, and I see myself then, and I can't see the connection between the two.

It's like walking in the snow and looking back to find you have no footprints. You wonder whether you made the trek at all.

There are other things in here, too, things I don't remember. A half-painted wooden duck next to a collection of tiny potted paints. A single purple flower, a real one, in a coffee mug next to his monitor.

He paints? Where did he get that flower?

It's a struggle to figure out how this room once fit into part of myself, how to navigate that gap between my prior self and whoever it is I am now.

From the kitchen, the ticking sound as he lights the stove.

I used to sit in his lap, typing on his keyboard. He still has the same keyboard. The letters are worn off and dirty.

I touch a key.

The screen lights up.

THE SINGLE DAD'S GUIDE TO PARENTING

The e-book is open to page 126. Some lines are highlighted yellow.
At the bottom of page 126 is the start of a sample script:

```
YOU:    I need to speak with you. Could we
        schedule a time to speak?
THEM:   How about tomorrow at eight p.m.?

        Allowing your child to choose the time
        that you speak gives them an element of
        control. This will help keep them in a
        mindset that is more open, less defensive.
        This is the mindset that is needed for a
        real, honest conversation.

        TIP: Remember! A real, honest conversation
        is your ultimate goal. You should not
        enter into the interaction attempting to
        convince your child of anything, because
        this . . .
```

The page cuts off there.
Over the sound of him chopping, I hear part of his movie:

". . . this responsibility is like a big rock that weighs a ton. It bends and it twists them until finally it buries them under the ground."

I need to get out of here.

As I push back from the desk, my foot hits Dad's cardboard trash box. Something from one of the papers jumps out at me.

My name. My name written multiple times.

THINGS INSIDE ANOTHER BOX

The notes are written in my father's tidy handwriting.
They are formatted like the sample script in the e-book.

```
'WAYNE:   I'm actually really busy right now.
ME:       It's okay if you're busy right now.
ME:       Please text me a time that would be good
          for you to talk.
```

And

```
ME:       How are you feeling?
'WAYNE:   I don't understand.
ME:       How does this news make you feel?
'WAYNE:   I don't want to talk about it.
ME:       You don't have to tell me if you don't
          want to. Just know that I am interested
          to know about your feelings. Whenever you
          have them, whatever they are.
```

I keep pulling out papers. Almost every one is like this. Drafts of scripts. With me. Drafts full of words that sound very familiar, conversations I've lived through, and some that I haven't. The box is full of these papers. Sometimes in his handwriting, sometimes printed out from the e-book and edited. All the way to the bottom of the box.

KNOWING

Once, my mother took me to a farm. The farmer let me meet the pigs. He let me touch their bristly heads, their wet and grainy snouts. He let me talk to them. Let me look into their eyes, their almost-person-like eyes, as they registered my face, my voice.

Then he showed me the devices they used to kill them.

"If you are going to eat meat," my mother said, "you need to know. *Really* know."

There is something different about knowing something with your mind and *really* knowing it. It's the difference between *thinking* Mr. Houston exists outside school, and then actually seeing him buy celery at the Giant.

The difference between *thinking* your mother is gone and running your finger inside her left-behind shoes, feeling the strands of cobwebs breaking.

The difference between thinking your father must have his own thoughts and feelings and wants and desires and seeing a purple flower in a vase that he got from somewhere, or someone.

The *thinking* that your father is trying, and *knowing* he really is, his printed scripts cold and sharp in front of you, the serifs like tiny thorns in your eyes.

DATES

I start putting papers back into the box, trying not to read any more.

One paper stops me.

There's a tiny picture on it. The photo is a preview of my business cards. The receipt.

There's a date on the receipt.

The date is last January.

Almost a year ago.

He bought these cards, he wanted me to work with him, ten months before I'd even heard about this study.

A cabinet door. The jangle as he takes down dinner plates.

"Oh," he says simply, and then a sharp crash.

Inside me, something also is breaking.

HOW TO FOLD AN ORIGAMI DRAGON, ACTUALLY

The blinds rattle. I drop my half-folded origami dragon into the trash box.

"Thought I heard something in here," Olive says. She opens the door barely enough to slip inside. "Are you stealing Dad's mail again?"

"No."

"You're going through his trash."

"No."

"Are you . . ." She narrows her eyes. ". . . wallowing?"

"No! Why would you even ask that?"

She puffs out her cheeks. "Well, you're doing origami with trash, for one thing. And secondly, you're making your wallowing face."

"My wallowing face?"

"Yeah, like all . . ." She squinches up her eyes and lips into what looks like a constipated pony.

I wave a hand at her.

She smiles. "So?"

I say, "You were right."

"You *were* wallowing?"

"No. Well, yes. But I meant that you were right about the study."

"No way," she says, with so many buckets of sarcasm, you could paint a whole house. "You mean—let me get this straight—it *wasn't* the CIA?"

"It *was* the CIA."

She rolls her eyes. "If you say so."

I throw one of Dad's pencils at her. "Do you want to hear how you're right or not?"

"Go on."

"You were right that the study wasn't changing me. The pills weren't changing me."

"So you aren't magically a better version of yourself?"

I shake my head. "Apparently not."

I brace myself for another sarcastic comment, but instead, she steps forward. She wraps her arms around my waist. She squeezes me hard.

My Darling Secret,

Hello from Hughesville, Maryland! It's starting to feel familiar. I am so close to home.

I need to be here a week for my assignment. And then, then, I will be there, in Baltimore, sitting in my old kitchen, making hot chocolate—with peanut butter on a spoon!—for you, just like I used to.

If you want, that is.

Anyway: This email is only to say, one more time, that I love you. I can't wait for next week.

I lied. One extra time: I love you.

Mama

THE RIPENESS IS RIPE

Setting: Kitchen, after Dad finishes reading the completion letter from Hopkins.

Dad:
Dad's Face:
Dad: It's not a bad letter.
Me:
Dad: They could have used better paper, though. This one, you can see the printing on both sides.
Me:
Me:
Dad: But it's still very good. Good job.
Dad's Face:
Me: Thanks.
Dad: Just because you have this, doesn't mean you don't need to focus on your schoolwork.
Me: I know.
Dad: This letter is not going to be enough on its own.
Me: I know.

Dad: Any moment, something could happen, put
         you back at square one.
Me: I know.

Dad stands up and squeezes three mangoes along his lineup on the counter. He picks up the one in the middle, sniffs it, then gets a paper plate and a knife. "You want some?"

"Sure."

The wheels on his chair click as he settles back down, scoots back to the table.

Dad: Have you thought about it any?
Me:
Dad: Whether you are going to work with me this
         summer?
Me: I'd like to.
Dad's Face:
Dad: That's great news.
Me:

"It will be great experience for you, for your résumé." He puts the fruit down, the knife down. He wipes his fingertips on a piece of paper towel before picking both up again. "Your mother comes next week." He's looking at the knife blade, aligning it with the mango skin, cutting the skin in a long, thin strip.

"How do you . . ." I clear my throat. "How do you feel about that? Her coming home?"

The whole peel falls away in one large octopus of mango skin.

One of his eyebrows triangles upward. The very corners of his lips creep down. In his eyes, there's a haunting of something.

His face smudges back to neutral. "We need to make sure the sheets are clean in time."

He pushes a plate with half the mango on it toward me. Takes a forkful off his own plate. Chews it while staring at the table. "Eat some. The ripeness is just right. Not too sweet."

I do. It is still sour, still crunchy, and a little bit green.

I say, "The ripeness is just right."

Dad's Face: Smiles.

MAIL

Dear Mr. Dwayne Le,

    Congratulations. This letter marks your successful completion of the initial phase of the Hopkins health study.

    Enclosed find a signed letter of commendation that elaborates on your dedication, perseverance, reliability, and hard work, not to mention your generous devotion to taking action on causes larger than yourself.

    We hope that you will find this useful for whatever you choose to pursue: college applications, job interviews, and so forth. Based on your performance in our study, we feel strongly that no matter what you do next, you will succeed. We very much hope that you will continue to work with us in the future.

    Enclosed also find a check for $200. Your insurance plans will be adjusted automatically—new cards will be mailed separately.

    We know that a study such as this one can feel faceless and, perhaps, unimportant. We want to assure you that your participation was both absolutely essential and absolutely appreciated.

    In fact, thanks to you, and the results you helped us confirm, our study will be moving to a larger-scale phase of testing at the national level. This will begin within the next few months.

This is exciting news for us, and dare we say it, exciting news for the world.

Congratulations, again.

Sincerely,

M. Mikulski

M. Mikulski, MD
Research Director

Acknowledgments

Thank you to:

The people who take words and make books: Julie Strauss-Gabel, Ilana Jacobs, and my editor, Andrew Karre, who believed I could do better, so I believed it too. Anna Booth for making the pages beautiful, and also more readable, for wrangling cacophony into visual sense. Kristin Boyle for a not-too-tidy cover design that fulfills my Cold War propaganda dreams. Rob Farren for insights on listservs and froyo; Natalie Vielkind, Rye White, Madison Penico; production manager Vanessa Robles.

The people who connect the book with people who might read it: Karter Powell; Felicity Vallence, Shannon Spann, and the rest of the marketing team at Penguin Teen; the people who help get books to schools and libraries and to the students and kids who need them: Carmela Iaria, Venessa Carson, Trevor Ingerson, Summer Ogata, Judith Huerta, Danielle Presley, and Gaby Paez. Thanks to Jenn Hanson-dePaula, as well as the Haywood County Arts Council, for your support in developing my own comfort with talking about this book.[38]

Huntz Liu, for the actual-paper (!) sculpture that makes the cover dramatic, geometric, textured, and unlike any other.

Advisors: Cynthia Leitich Smith, for reminding me to have grace;

---

38. Developing comfort is not the same as being comfortable, but even a half-sewn quilt with prickly pins improves a concrete floor in winter.

Louise Hawes for teaching me to trust characters; An Na for insisting that stories need some sort of plot; and William Alexander, for fishing me out of the despair pit and convincing me to write this manuscript instead of all the manuscripts I didn't actually want to write.

The VCFA community, through which I eventually met my agent, Kelly Dyksterhouse. Kelly, thank you for believing this novel had a chance, even if it was going to be a cold, hard pea of a chance.

People who gave writing encouragement: The Highlights Foundation, and the workshop leaders N. Griffin and M.T. Anderson; the team at Tin House, especially Ashley Woodfolk, who convinced me once and for all that 'Wayne was worth fighting for. Tawes for spontaneously driving with me to Vermont in January. Dr. Chet Mikulski, who let me quit a forensics master's program on the condition that I write a novel where the villain was named after him.

Those who gave places to sleep and chairs to write in: Mamta Jhaveri for a futon in Baltimore and peeling me off the floor all the times I forgot to eat; Rachel Dull for a cozy yellow chair to battle the Michigan gloom; Lauren Harr and Arrowmont for giving me space to draft a new ending; Citizen Vinyl for making me pour-overs even after they were (wrongfully) removed from the menu.

My feedback folk: Melissa Cole, who I promised I would thank two times for helping me figure out an ending[39]; the most acquaintance-y of colleagues, Miriam Chernick, for being so maximally collegially collegial. Teehee.

The Buncombe County Public Library System, especially Raj and the children's department at Pack, who tolerated my mile-long request lists.

(This is me thanking you a second time, Melissa Cole.)

My family: my sister, for reading this novel as your one book

---

39. Not the ending, but *an* ending.

every twenty years; my mother and father for encouraging my ever-changing interests and passions; my brother for saying "taste buds of your heart" so many times I needed to write a chapter about it; my nephew Alex for telling me that if anyone could write a book he would actually read, it would be me.[40]

Miyamu for being the best friend I've ever had. And Zachary for all the things, but especially keeping the plugs plugged.

Lastly, thank you to all the people who are making the tiny folds. Choosing the ones that make the world more alive.

---

40. I considered saying the book was *for* you, Alex, but I still don't think you'll ever actually read it.